HOUR OF NEED

ALSO BY MELINDA LEIGH

Midnight Exposure

Midnight Sacrifice

Midnight Betrayal

SHE CAN SERIES

She Can Run

She Can Tell

She Can Scream

She Can Hide

He Can Fall (A Short Story)

ROGUE RIVER NOVELLAS

Gone to Her Grave

Walking on Her Grave

HOUR OF NEED

A SCARLET FALLS NOVEL

MELINDA LEIGH

This is a work of fiction. Names, characters, organizations, places, events, and incidents are either products of the author's imagination or are used fictitiously.

Published by Montlake Romance, Seattle

www.apub.com

ISBN-13: 9781477827079
ISBN-10: 1477827072

Cover design by Marc J. Cohen

Library of Congress Control Number: 2014912700

Printed in the United States of America

To Charlie

My best friend and so much more for the last twenty years

Chapter One

Friday 9:00 p.m.

Tonight's celebration felt as hollow as Lee's confidence. Anniversaries were a big deal, especially this one. A little more than a year ago, Lee hadn't thought he and Kate would make it to their ten-year milestone. He should be happier, but he couldn't shake the nag of betrayal.

He should have told her.

Actually, he should have discussed the situation with her before committing. Her stake in the outcome was as large as his, but this wasn't the first decision he'd made solo.

The raw March wind whipped across the stucco facade of La Cusina. Stepping down from the brick stoop of the Italian restaurant to the sidewalk, Lee steered his wife around a patch of ice on the asphalt. Her high heels were sexy but precarious on the slippery spots. Although he probably shouldn't worry. As a former nationally ranked figure skater turned coach, Kate spent as much time on ice as on solid ground. They walked past the bank and the bakery, both closed.

"Maybe next year we can do more than dinner for our anniversary. Wouldn't a cruise be perfect? Aruba, Jamaica . . ." He hummed the first line of the Beach Boys' "Kokomo."

"I'm happy to get out to dinner." Kate leaned closer, using his larger body to block the wind. Spring didn't come early in upstate New York. "How many times have we had dinner out since Faith was born? Oh, yeah. None. If Carson had been this difficult, he'd be an only child."

Their six-year-old had been born easygoing.

"It's her elaborate plan to weaken us into submission so we'll give her anything she wants." Their sweet four-month-old turned into a wailing banshee when the sun set. But they both knew the baby wasn't the only reason they hadn't had a date night lately.

"Sleep deprivation *is* an established form of psychological torture." Despite her banter, Kate's laugh sounded forced, as if she was just going through the motions of tonight's celebration.

Lee's chicken marsala took a quick spin in his gut. Kate had been quiet all night. Was she simply worried about the baby or was she unhappy for some other reason? He'd logged too many billable hours these last few weeks. They'd barely seen each other. Paranoia dug its fingernails into his heart. He didn't want to lose his wife. Those nights he'd slept in the guest room eighteen months ago were the loneliest of his life. He'd been isolated. Kate wasn't just his wife. She was his best friend.

They turned the corner and set off down the side street where he'd parked the car. Mature trees lined the quiet lane, their branches hanging over the sidewalk. On a bright summer day, the shady canopy was quaint, but on a frigid and dark night, the added shadows shifting with the wind were unwelcome. Lee tripped over a slab of concrete pushed above the sidewalk by shallow tree roots. Kate caught his arm and held on until he sorted his feet under his body. Typical. Even handicapped by three-inch heels, his athletic wife was his supporter.

"Thank God for Julia." Kate reached into her pocket, pulled out her cell phone, and glanced at the display. In her other gloved hand, the Styrofoam takeout box of lasagna crackled as she shifted her grip.

"Any calls?"

"No, but we'd better get home. The poor girl is probably ready to scream after a couple of hours of Faith's howling." Kate pocketed her phone.

Their teenage neighbor had been a savior as the last few months had passed in a sleep-deprived blur.

"I know." Lee sighed. Their big night out was over. Back to the ear-splitting reality of a colicky infant, but he'd take it. Their marriage had gone through a rocky patch. They'd come through it, and if he made partner, everything would be all right. *If* being the key word. Their entire future rested on him being chosen for partnership, and the weight of the decision he'd made this week sat on his shoulders like an anvil. Had he let ambition ruin his marriage?

He needed to tell Kate soon about the case he'd taken. Refusing the Hamiltons hadn't been an option. He couldn't look those parents in the eye and say no, especially with his gut telling him the situation was more complicated than it appeared. After two days of inquiries into the case, he was even more disturbed. But controversy didn't necessarily translate into popularity. In a small town, there *was* such a thing as bad press. The lawsuit could affect his chance for partnership, and he wouldn't be the only one in the line of fire. Everyone in Scarlet Falls had a heated opinion. With the investigation centered on the rink where Kate coached, she was sure to be embroiled in the fallout.

He glanced sideways at her profile, her expression unreadable in the darkness. Would she stand by him? Without Kate's steadying presence, Lee feared he couldn't succeed.

On the bright side, a win would all but guarantee him the partnership. Frank Menendez, the new associate, wasn't shy about lobbying for the promotion. Lee needed an edge over his ruthless competition. The case was a gamble, but given what he'd discovered, the odds of winning were in his favor. He just had to have faith and work hard. Then everything would be all right.

He wasn't going to tell Kate tonight. She was already stressed. He hoped her tension was all about the baby and not a replay of their marital strife. Whatever it was, he wasn't going to ruin their anniversary. He was going to let his wife enjoy as much time as possible before he brought more worries crashing down on their family.

Kate patted his arm. "They'll be grown and gone before we can blink. I can't believe Carson is six already."

"If we can just get past the colic." Among other things.

"Amen. God, it's cold." Kate zipped her coat higher under her chin. "We should move somewhere warm. It's March. I'm totally over this thing called winter." A scraping sound diverted Lee's attention.

"Me too," he said absently. His ears strained for another odd noise. The wind blew. Clattering, winter-bare tree branches waved overhead.

Head bowed against a sharp gust, Kate quickened her steps. Lee grabbed her arm and pulled her to a halt.

"What's wrong?" She turned to him, the question furrowing her brow.

"I don't know." He scanned the dark street. A dozen vehicles were strung out along the snow-edged curb. The restaurant rode the edge of the commercial section of their quiet, boring town. The other businesses along this side street had closed hours ago. A block ahead, the neighborhood turned residential. The thin air smelled faintly of garlic, wood smoke, and snow.

There was absolutely no reason for the unease brewing in his gut. "Something's wrong."

Kate lifted her head. "The streetlight is out."

"I guess that's it."

They started forward again. Kate slipped, and Lee wrapped a steadying arm around her.

A man stepped out from behind a truck and headed up the sidewalk in their direction. Work boots, jeans, and a black leather jacket were normal attire. Even the baseball cap that shadowed his face was ordinary. But something about the man's posture put Lee on edge. There was readiness in the set of his shoulders, unnatural purpose in the cadence of his stride, and though the man wasn't staring at them, Lee could feel the energy of his focus.

He pushed Kate behind him and veered into the street. They'd cross and continue on the opposite sidewalk. Their car was barely twenty feet away. Lee pulled out his keys, planning to get Kate locked into the vehicle and then deal with the man if necessary.

But the man stepped into the street and cut off their path. He raised his hand. Lee's attention locked on a semiautomatic handgun, the barrel elongated by a silencer. Pointed at Lee and Kate, the muzzle yawned as large as a manhole cover.

"Wallet, keys, purse." Gloved fingers curled in a *gimme* gesture.

Lee dug his wallet and keys out of his pockets. He reached back, took Kate's handbag, and handed the items over. The man lowered the gun to tuck the purse under his arm and pocket the small items. Lee breathed. Being robbed sucked, but it was the best possible outcome of this scenario.

The gun came up again. Shocked, Lee froze. Moonlight glinted on metal as the muzzle flashed. The bullet tore through his skull with a searing blast of agony. Then his brain disconnected from his body. His knees buckled, and he did a slow-motion face-plant on the frozen blacktop. Liquid dripped into his eyes, obscuring his vision. But he felt nothing. Absolutely nothing. Not the pain from the wound. Not the warmth of the blood flowing into his eyes. The patch of ice beneath his cheek should have been cold. Kate's screams sounded far away, though he knew she stood just two feet behind him.

The gunman said something to Kate, but the ringing in Lee's ears drowned out the words. He strained to hear.

"Stop screaming and answer me," the man said.

But Kate couldn't stop. If anything, her shrieks grew louder, the pitch rising with hysteria, and then faltering with sobs. Lee tried to lift his head to see what was happening, but his muscles wouldn't respond to his commands.

His gaze fixed on a pair of tan work boots. Blood speckled the toe. He moved his eyes. Kate dropped to her knees beside him. The takeout box hit the street. Lasagna spilled out, tomato sauce staining the roadside slush red. *No, Kate. Run*, was what he wanted to say, but nothing came out of his mouth. Paralyzed, he was unable to react, unable to protect his wife.

Clack psst. The second shot sounded like a pneumatic nail gun firing. Only Lee's eyelids could flinch. In his peripheral vision he saw his wife collapse across his legs like a marionette with snipped strings. Grief crushed his heart.

Kate. I love you.

What had he done?

Ellie smoothed joint compound over the patch in the drywall. Her living room was shaping up. The upstairs renovations were finished. Soon it would be time to tackle the ugliest kitchen ever designed. She could hardly wait. Except then she'd sell the house and move again. That was the whole point, but this was the first neighborhood she'd be sad to leave.

"Do you want some tea?" her grandmother called.

"No, thanks." Ellie stretched a kink in her neck. "What time is it?"

"Almost eleven."

Alarm slipped through Ellie. "Julia isn't back." Her fifteen-year-old daughter was babysitting for the next-door neighbors, the Barretts. Lee Barrett was also an attorney in the firm where Ellie worked as an administrative assistant.

Nan appeared in the doorway. "What time did they say they'd be home?"

"By ten."

"They're only an hour late. Maybe the restaurant was slow or they got a flat," Nan reasoned, but her voice was tinged with concern. "They could be enjoying themselves. It is their anniversary."

Ellie tossed her trowel on the drop cloth and picked up her cell phone from the top rung of the stepladder. "If they were running late, they would have called." She texted her daughter and waited three minutes. No answer. "I'm going over there."

She washed her hands and snagged her neighbor's key from the drawer. Grabbing her jacket, she went out the front door. Cold, wet wind slapped her face as she hurried across the front lawns. Hoping the dog wouldn't bark, she used the key to let herself in. The Barretts' golden retriever, AnnaBelle, raced down the hall to greet her. Footsteps approached.

In yoga pants and a sweatshirt, Julia carried the four-month-old infant into the foyer on her shoulder. Her hair was pulled into a high ponytail, well away from grabby baby fists. "I thought you were Mr. and Mrs. Barrett."

"They said they'd be home around ten, right?" Patting the dog, Ellie hung her jacket on the newel post.

"Right." Her daughter bounced lightly on her toes and patted the baby's back. "I was just going to call you, but Faith is getting loud. I was afraid she'd wake Carson."

"I should have come over sooner. I didn't realize how late it was." Ellie lowered her voice, not wanting to disturb the six-year-old boy sleeping upstairs. "Has Mrs. Barrett called?"

"No. I texted her twice. Mr. Barrett, too." The baby fussed and Julia walked back to the kitchen. "I'm getting worried."

Ellie called Kate and then Lee. Both lines went to voice mail. "Here, let me take her for a while."

"Thanks. There's no making her happy once night comes." Julia passed the baby over.

"I'm sure they'll be home soon." Taking Faith, Ellie took a turn around the downstairs. She continued to walk, her anxiety growing. Lee and Kate were never late. This was the first time they'd left the baby for a night out. Ellie had expected them to come home early.

At midnight, Julia fell asleep on the sofa, and Ellie reached for the phone. Two hours was long enough. It was time to call the police. Lee and Kate could have been in an accident.

AnnaBelle's ears pricked forward and the dog headed for the front of the house. Ellie followed, catching the retriever by the collar to stem any barking. She looked out the front window. A police car was parked in the driveway. An officer approached the door.

Ellie's stomach cringed as she held the dog back with her foot and opened the door. *Please let them be all right.*

"Is this the Barrett residence?"

Ellie swallowed, her throat dry. "Yes."

"May I come inside?"

She stepped back to give him room. The dog broke free and shoved her nose into his hand. He scratched her head absently. "Who are you, ma'am?"

"I'm Ellie Ross. I live next door." Ellie glanced up the stairs. Putting a finger to her lips, she waved the officer toward the kitchen. Behind her, his footsteps were heavy on the hardwood. Facing him in the bright light, she eyed his grim face. The worst of news was coming. Sympathy radiated from the young cop. She braced herself. "Just tell me."

He breathed it out in a quiet voice. "I'm sorry. Lee and Kate Barrett were killed a few hours ago."

"How? Car accident?"

"No, ma'am. They were shot in what appears to be a robbery."

Stunned, Ellie reached for a chair, the news weakening her knees. As soon as she sat, Faith began to cry.

Julia sat up. Her sleepy eyes misted as she met Ellie's gaze. "Mom?"

Ellie got up, wrapped her free arm around her daughter and told her what had happened.

A tearful Julia took the baby. "Should I call Nan?"

Ellie nodded. Shock blanketed her. They couldn't be dead. Not mild-mannered, dependable Lee, whose idea of risky behavior was eating runny egg yolks. And Kate. She could make Ellie laugh without saying a word. Just the other night, Kate had showed up at Ellie's front door with a bottle of wine and the need for adult conversation. She'd helped Ellie patch wallboard—patches Ellie had needed to redo the next night because they'd finished that bottle, but it had been worth it. She called very few people friend. Kate was special.

Ellie closed her eyes and rested her cheek on the baby's head. Her mind swam with all the events Kate and Lee would never experience with their children: first dates, first dances, graduations, weddings, grandchildren. The images overwhelmed her. She opened her eyes, just as Nan let herself into the house. Ellie couldn't fall apart. The children needed her to function.

She passed the baby to her grandmother, then did her best to answer the officer's questions about the family. "Kate has no family close by. Lee has a brother who lives locally, plus a sister who is usually traveling and a brother deployed to Afghanistan." Ellie gave the policeman their names. "I'm sorry. I don't know their numbers. I could look in Lee's office. I haven't seen any of them in a while."

"We'll take care of it, ma'am," he said. "Child services will try to locate the local relative."

More cops showed up at the house. The noise woke Carson, who came downstairs crying. Ellie rocked him on her lap. She didn't want to tell him what happened. That kind of news was best left to family.

An hour later, a middle-aged woman bustled through the door. She took the kitchen chair opposite Ellie. "Miss Ross? I'm Dee Willis from child services. I haven't been able to reach anyone on the list you gave us. We need to talk about the children."

Ellie wrapped her arms around Carson tighter. "They can stay with me."

"I'm sorry, that's against policy," the social worker said. "You can complete a form to become an emergency foster. It'll only take a few days."

But to Carson, a few days would be forever. The little boy's silent tears soaked Ellie's shirt. Helplessness flooded her.

"Julia, please take Carson." Ellie shifted the little boy to her daughter's lap and went into the living room for privacy. Whipping out her phone, she dialed her boss. Working for an attorney had a few benefits. But Roger didn't answer his phone. Damn it. She left a message and returned to the kitchen. She gave Julia a pointed look and nodded toward the doorway. Julia carried Carson out of the room.

Ellie waited until she heard the stair treads creak before addressing the social worker. "The children know us. Can't you make an exception?"

"No, I'm sorry." Mrs. Willis's calm and businesslike voice grated on Ellie's raw nerves. "As soon as the background checks go through, you can ask the judge, but tonight, I have to take them with me."

Ellie knew the woman must see situations like this all the time, but how could she be so matter-of-fact about taking two small children from their home? Anger rolled over Ellie's grief. Pain and helplessness compounded in her chest until her ribs ached.

My God, it was Friday. She doubted anything would be done over the weekend.

The social worker started collecting the baby's gear. "It might make things easier on Carson if you help him pack a bag."

Ellie didn't want to make things easier. She wanted to snatch the children and hide them at her house. She glanced around and counted three uniformed policemen and another in a suit who seemed to be in charge. He'd introduced himself, but she'd already forgotten his name. Detective McSomething.

There was nothing she could do.

She went upstairs to Carson's room. He sat on the bed with Julia and cried while Ellie packed enough clothes for a week into his backpack. She knelt on the floor in front of him and took his little hands in hers. "Just hang on, OK? I'm going to do everything I can to bring you to my house."

He sniffed, wiping the back of his hand under his nose. "The lady said Mommy and Daddy died."

Ellie's heart broke. Did he even know what that meant? She sat next to him and hugged him tight. "I know. I'm sorry."

She was even sorrier to carry him out to the social worker's car and put him inside. Sadness choked her as she watched them drive away.

Chapter Two

Afghanistan, Saturday 5:30 a.m.

March dawned cold in the Hindu Kush. Just before daybreak, cool gray light peered over the mountains on the horizon. In the back of a mine-resistant all-terrain vehicle, or M-ATV, Grant tucked his hands in his armpits and scanned the ridge that ran parallel to the road. The supply convoy was giving him a lift back to the forward operating base near the Pakistani border where he was stationed. Grant's vehicle was at the middle of the column. A platoon of infantrymen escorted the column of supply trucks. For additional support, a unit of the ANA, Afghan National Army, brought up the rear.

The steady rock and rumble of the vehicle could have lulled him to sleep if he'd let it, but the Taliban liked to attack in the gray hours. A soldier couldn't relax in Afghanistan. An attack could come from anywhere: a civilian with a backpack, an IED detonated by the roadside, or a traitor in their midst. The options were endless. Grant's gaze swept along the ridge as the convoy entered yet another wadi. The valley was the twentieth prime ambush spot of their journey.

He'd been in zero direct engagements since his promotion to major just before this last deployment. On his last two tours, he'd been out on frequent patrols and skirmishes. In an odd way, he missed the intimacy of being part of every mission, the daily grind of patrolling the hills and wadis, the brotherhood instilled by combat. The diplomacy and paperwork required by his new position as operations officer isolated him from the men. He worked hard to establish a relationship with them, but sometimes he felt like all he did was go to meetings, like the one he'd attended yesterday at battalion command. Discussing the political ramifications of military policy gave him a headache.

The low ridge to the east shadowed the valley. A hint of pale yellow edged over the jagged horizon, silhouetting the skyline. A half klick ahead, the passage narrowed. In minutes, the convoy rumbled into a dry streambed barely twenty meters wide. On the right, a steep slope led to a ridge thirty feet above the road. A sheer cliff face comprised the left wall. Conversation halted as all eyes searched the rocks on either side for any sign of enemy activity.

The road exploded in front of the supply convoy, shaking the ground under the trucks. Grant's heart kicked into gear. Men jolted into action. The heavy vehicle rocked again as another explosive hit the dirt. More rockets whistled and boomed ahead. The passageway was too narrow to turn around, and since the enemy had planned this ambush, no doubt they were waiting in case the convoy found a way to double back.

They were trapped in a kill zone.

Grant scanned the surroundings. They needed men on high ground, and there was only one way to get the advantage. They would have to take it from the enemy.

He dismounted and ran two vehicles ahead to join the lieutenant in charge of the platoon. They ducked behind Lieutenant Wise's armored door. The perpetually sunburned redhead wiped a coating of Afghan dust from his freckled brow. Though his actual age was likely around twenty-four, the blue eyes studying the ridge were battle-aged.

Another rocket sailed over the ridgeline and exploded in the rocks on their flank. The ground rocked and dirt burst through the air. A shard pinged past Grant's head and stung his face. Machine-gun fire laced the vehicle. Bullets strafed the ground at his feet. A tug on his pant leg signaled a close call. He squinted at the ridge to the east. Muzzle flashes flared in the dim. In unison with the soldiers around him, Grant lifted his M-4 and returned fire.

The ground trembled under his boots as more rockets exploded. Warm liquid dribbled into his eye, obscuring his vision. He swiped at the cut on his forehead, took aim, and fired again.

He might miss the camaraderie of being part of a combat platoon, but he did not miss having rockets fired at his ass.

Ambushes like these were more common than they should be, so First Platoon was ready for this one. Lieutenant Wise was on the radio, calling the base for air support. An Apache was being dispatched, ETA fifteen minutes. The platoon sergeant shouted orders to the men.

"Lieutenant, we need to take that ridge." Grant pointed above them. A bullet ripped through his sleeve.

"Yes, sir. I'm already on it." Wise and his sergeant had the situation in hand. Grant stood down. He would not be that dickhead officer who interrupted the smooth flow of platoon operations. He was just a passenger on this convoy.

The soldiers returned fire on the rockets with heavy machine guns and lobbed grenades over the crest. Wise ordered a squad through a gap in the rocks. ANA forces guarded the convoy's back.

Using the vehicle as a shield, Grant hunkered down with the remaining men and provided cover fire for the soldiers heading up the hill.

The Taliban had known they were coming. The insurgents had eyes everywhere. US forces were fighting in a land where they couldn't trust anyone. Not the local interpreters who worked for them. Not the villagers they supplied with food and medicine. Not even the Afghan soldiers they fought with side by side. No one.

Two dozen Taliban soldiers in man jams and AK-47s poured over the ridge. The eight-inch knives dangling from their waists reminded Grant that beheading some Americans on Al Jazeera would cap off the Taliban's evening like a party. The enemy had the high ground advantage, but Grant's heart sang as his men surged up the incline in the direct line of fire. The enemy fell back, scrambling up the ridge with Grant's men in pursuit.

The ambush *should* have been over, averted without a single American casualty.

Gunfire sounded at his back. Grant whirled. Next to him, Wise went down, blood pouring from a wound in his thigh. Shots whizzed past his head. Where the fuck were those bullets coming from? Behind them?

He scanned the area for the shooters. Five Afghan soldiers had broken rank, turning and firing on the US forces they were supposed to be supporting. Wise was on the ground, shouting into the radio. The traitors' muzzles flared. Two Afghan soldiers dropped. Most of the platoon was ahead of Grant, and the lieutenant was focused on not bleeding out.

Grant lifted his M-4. Chaos erupted in the ANA. Who was on which side?

An Afghan soldier took aim at Wise, no doubt trying to cut off his communication. Shouting to the soldiers on the other side of the vehicle, Grant leveled his weapon and shot the obvious traitor. His face exploded in a red mist. There was no point in aiming at a body's center mass when Grant knew the enemy was wearing body armor supplied by the US government. Four men broke out from the Afghan ranks and took aim at the vehicle in front of Grant, where the gunner in the turret was firing heavy machine gun rounds onto the ridge.

The sergeant was shouting orders. Grant dropped to a knee and fired on the turncoats. The soldiers in the vehicle ahead turned and finished the job. The traitors went down under a massive wave of machine-gun fire.

Was that all of them? Could there be more Taliban spies among their ranks? How the hell would they ever know?

Explosions and artillery fire slowed. The unit medic stopped the bleeding in Wise's leg and turned to Grant.

"Major?" The young corporal pointed at Grant's face. "Let me get that, sir."

Vaguely aware of blood dripping in his eye, Grant let the medic swipe some antiseptic and slap a butterfly bandage over the cut on his temple. Wise was loaded into the vehicle. He was still working the radio.

The squad that had gone over the ridge was called back. Steady whumping signaled the arrival of air support. The Apache swept over the ridge, blowing the shit out of anything on the other side.

Grant scanned the platoon. It appeared Lieutenant Wise had the most serious injury. But despite the win, damage was done. The Taliban had infiltrated the ANA. How could these American soldiers ever trust them as allies again?

When the bombs ceased, Wise sent a squad over the ridge to check for survivors, but they found none. The convoy moved on and reached the base a few hours later. Grant didn't breathe easy until the trucks rolled through the gates and were behind the concertina wire. But lately, even being in the compound wasn't a guarantee of safety, not with the Taliban determined to infiltrate the ANA at every opportunity.

His army combat uniform was shredded from bullets and stained with blood and Afghan dust, but Grant headed directly to the command center and reported to Lieutenant Colonel Tucker.

Tucker was in his office. Under a thick head of salt-and-pepper hair, he turned a piercing green gaze on Grant. "Have a seat, Major."

But Grant was too keyed up to sit. Exhaustion and tension competed for control. He closed the door, paced the dusty room, and relayed the details of the ambush.

"Major," Tucker interrupted with a raised palm, "I'll get a report from Lieutenant Wise."

Grant stopped. Something was up. He'd been Tucker's second-in-command for ten months. The colonel squinted at him, his weathered skin creasing around his eyes. "Sit down, Grant."

Wary, Grant eased into a chair. When Tucker used his first name, the news was personal.

The colonel eyed Grant's forehead. "Is that serious?"

"No, sir. Just a scratch." His adrenaline flow ebbed. Deep in his limbs, Grant felt every ounce of fatigue from two nights with no sleep.

Tucker opened his desk drawer. He poured two tumblers of scotch from his stash. He handed one across the desk to Grant and waited until Grant had tossed his back before speaking. "I got a call from the States."

Grant stiffened, bracing himself. Had his father finally succumbed to his physical and mental afflictions? The retired army colonel had held out far longer than anyone would have predicted. Grant had been expecting a call about his death since he'd been deployed ten months ago. "What happened? Is it my father?"

"No. I'm sorry, Grant. It isn't your father." Tucker's eyes went hard, and his words were the last thing Grant expected to hear. "Your brother and his wife were killed."

Grant's ears were still ringing from the battle. He couldn't have heard that right. He only had one married brother. Grant usually spent part of his leave with Lee's family. Lee was the family touchstone. There was nothing remotely dangerous about his life. "Excuse me, sir?"

"Your brother Lee and his wife, Kate, were killed last night."

Liquor and grief numbed a path through Grant's gut. This was impossible. "How? Car accident?"

Tucker shook his head. Sympathy softened his voice. "It seems as if they were robbed."

Once Grant digested the initial shock, his next thought was of the children. Carson and Faith were alone. Orphans.

He stared at the floor. "I have to go home."

"Pack your bag. Emergency leave paperwork is already being processed. Sergeant Stevens is arranging transport." Tucker returned to his desk. "I'm sorry for your loss."

"Thank you, sir." Grant stood, willing the wobble from his legs. He faced loss of life on a daily basis. But the death of his quiet suburban lawyer brother was different. Grant wasn't prepared for the emotional hit to his flank. He'd been ambushed all over again.

He checked in with Sergeant Stevens. He'd gotten Grant a spot on an outbound troop transport helicopter. Grant had a few hours to prepare. He packed, showered, and donned fresh ACUs on automatic pilot. It wasn't until he was seated in the Chinook, watching the dirt cloud churned up by the tandem rotors, that it sank all the way in. Pain bored through Grant's soul like a bullet.

Lee and Kate were dead.

Chapter Three

Monday night

Grant wiped a layer of mist from his face. The temperature in his hometown of Scarlet Falls, New York, was similar to the aching cold he'd left behind, but he appreciated both the moisture in the air and the absence of moon dust, the dirt powder that coated everything, including lungs, in Afghanistan.

Taking a deep, pine-scented breath, he followed Detective Brody McNamara up the concrete steps and into the side door of the municipal building. From the outside, the Colonial-style structure blended into the quaint small-town image, with blue clapboards and barn-red shutters. Inside, it was all tired office building. But since the detective had agreed to meet Grant at twenty-two hundred hours, he wasn't complaining about the lack of interior design.

The police station shared the two-story structure with township administration. Just inside the doorway, a freestanding sign directed visitors upstairs to the tax collector, zoning office, and township clerk on the second floor. The cops had the ground level all to themselves.

He followed the cop through a gray tiled lobby. They passed the elevator and a reception counter, then walked down a short hall into a dark, open room. Detective McNamara flipped a switch on the wall. Overhead fluorescents illuminated a cluster of cubicles and a row of metal filing cabinets. A few closed doors banked the far wall.

"Sorry, we're a small force. Night staff is skeletal, just patrol and dispatch." The detective skirted the cubicles and unlocked the center door. McNamara was a year or two older than Grant's thirty-five, with the ruddy, windburned complexion of a skier. Jeans and a navy-blue jacket with an SFPD patch on the sleeve hung on a rangy body. He led the way into a cramped but neat office. Two plastic guest chairs fronted an old metal desk. McNamara rounded the desk and dropped into his chair.

Restless, Grant stood. "I appreciate you meeting me here this late." He'd called the cop from I-87 an hour before he hit town.

"Glad to help, Major. I'm sorry for your loss."

Grant's throat constricted. He'd been shot once and nearly blown up twice by IEDs. He had enough shrapnel buried under the skin of his leg to set off a metal detector. Keeping people like Lee and Kate safe was the reason he fought. How could his little brother, secure back here in the States, be dead?

Suddenly exhausted, Grant eased into a hard-backed chair. "Where are the children?"

The cop reached behind him. A mini fridge sat on top of a credenza. He pulled out a bottle of water and offered it to Grant. "As I said on the phone, we were unable to reach any family members the night your brother and his wife were killed. Child services placed them in a foster home."

Grant's sister, Hannah, was in Jakarta on business, but the youngest of the four Barrett siblings, Mac, was local. Given Mac's troubled past, the lack of response to Grant's messages was concerning.

Grant accepted the bottle. His eyes burned. He squeezed them shut and rubbed his forehead. "Can I get you some coffee, Major?" the cop asked.

"No, thanks." Grant twisted off the cap and drank, forcing icy water down his tight throat. He'd spent the last seventy-two hours in transport from Afghanistan to New York State. Layovers in Kabul, Kuwait City, and Germany had dragged out his return trip. His life had been normal, at least as normal as life on a forward operating base in Afghanistan could be. Now everything was different. His priorities—his entire life—had exploded like a roadside bomb. "I just want to find my niece and nephew."

"I understand, but I'm afraid there's nothing I can do until morning." The cop brushed a hand over his buzzed head. "Look, I know you want to see them, but the kids are probably asleep by now. You don't want to drag them out of bed in the dark. They'd be frightened."

Which is exactly what had happened on Friday night when their parents had been murdered. The cop was right. Replaying that scenario wasn't in their best interest, but Grant didn't want to think of Carson or Faith spending another night in a strange house, with strange people, after losing their entire world. Of course, since he'd been deployed before Faith was born, Grant was a stranger to her too, and he hadn't seen Carson in ten months. Would the boy even recognize him? "Are you sure?"

"I'm sorry." The cop laid a pair of reading glasses on the desk. "There are a lot of rules and red tape involved. Middle-of-the-night calls are for crises only. Where can I reach you?"

The last thing he wanted to do was be alone in his brother's house, surrounded by happy memories that would be no more, the house where he'd spent two weeks with Lee, a pregnant Kate, and Carson the previous May. He wanted to get a hotel room, with impersonal surroundings that wouldn't remind him his brother was dead, but the children would no doubt feel more comfortable in their own home. Grant had better make sure the house was ready for them.

"I'll be staying at my brother's house." Grant gave the cop the phone number for the house. "You have my cell number."

The cop picked up a pen and wrote the information down.

"My father doesn't know?" Grant asked.

"No." McNamara shook his head. "As you requested, I'll leave that to you."

Grant's breath hitched, the thought of telling the Colonel about Lee's death driving the finality of the situation home. "Thank you. My father's health is shaky. I'll go out to the nursing home tomorrow."

Lee had been just two years younger than Grant. Growing up, they'd been as close as two kids with polar opposite personalities could be. Grant saw everything in black and white, while his brother noticed every shade of gray. Had their dad known how different the brothers would be when he'd named them after opposing Civil War generals? The plastic water bottle crunched under his too-tight grip. Grant loosened his fingers.

"I'll contact child services first thing tomorrow," McNamara said. "I'll call you as soon as I hear from them."

Grant didn't like the situation, but after thirteen years in the army, he knew all about rules and procedures and when to pick his battles. The next question hurt to ask. "Do the bodies need to be identified?"

"No. That won't be necessary. The medical examiner used dental records." The cop shook his head, his eyes going flat. "I know you want to see them, but ask yourself if you want that image in your head forever or if you want to remember your brother and sister-in-law as you saw them last."

The statement was a solid kick to the chest. Were Lee and Kate even identifiable? Grant pictured the insurgent he'd shot in the ambush, layering the traitor's ruined face over his brother's. His fingertips trembled. He'd had no time to decompress after the ambush before being slammed with Lee's death. Every time he closed his eyes, he saw his M-4 fire and that insurgent's face blow apart. He *knew* he hadn't had a choice. Either he pulled that trigger or the lieutenant died. This wasn't his first combat kill. Taking a life, even in war, left an imprint, but he could hardly compare this situation to anything he'd ever experienced before. Everything was backward. If one of the Barretts were to die, it was supposed to be Grant.

Anger flared in his belly, and he welcomed its steadying heat. Better pissed off than pissed on, as his first sergeant used to say. "What can you tell me about their murders?"

McNamara leaned back in his chair and studied Grant's face for a minute. "Are you sure you want to do this now?"

"Yes. I only have thirty days." Time was ticking away. His leave had started the moment he'd stepped off the military transport in Texas that morning. Besides, he was never going to *want* to do it anyway. "When we spoke on the phone, you said they'd been robbed."

"Robbery is one of our working theories." McNamara shifted forward and planted his forearms on the edge of his desk. "A resident called the police to report a woman screaming. A patrol unit was dispatched. Lee and Kate were found on a side street around the corner from an Italian restaurant in town. The restaurant staff said your brother and his wife had finished dinner roughly ten minutes before the call came in. It appears they were walking from the restaurant to their car when someone intercepted them. The cause of death for both was a single shot to the head. Your brother's wallet and keys were missing, and so was Kate's purse. Their car was stolen." The cop hesitated.

"But that's not all?" Grant asked. McNamara's body language projected dissatisfaction. "What else?"

McNamara tossed the pen onto the blotter. His mouth thinned. "Your sister-in-law was still wearing her engagement ring."

Grant followed the cop's logic. "An experienced robber would have looked for obvious jewelry."

"Maybe. Kate was wearing gloves, so I'm not going to make any assumptions at this time. We're still investigating." The cop rubbed his chin. "Who benefits from their deaths? I didn't see a will in the house. Do you know if they had one?"

"I would imagine he did. He was a lawyer. Dotting *i*'s and crossing *t*'s was his profession." Grant should have expected the police to search the house for clues. His brother had been murdered. Dead people didn't have expectations of privacy, but the thought of McNamara or anyone else rifling through Lee and Kate's personal belongings, discovering intimate secrets about the couple, sparked Grant's fury. This should not have happened.

"The house is big and old. We could have missed something. If you find a safe deposit box key or a will, we'd like to know." McNamara interlaced his fingers. "Both of their phones were stolen, but we recovered their call, contact, and calendar data from the cell phone company. We're still reviewing the information, but we might have some questions regarding abbreviations and notations. Your brother's firm has been less than cooperative about giving us access to his work computer and office. I've asked for a warrant, but they're fighting it, citing client confidentiality."

"Of course." Grant drank more water, the cold liquid settling in his belly and chilling him from the inside out. "I'll call you if I find anything."

"Can you think of another motive for the attack?" McNamara asked. "Did your brother have any enemies?"

Grant shook his head. "My brother was a suburban lawyer and a family man. I can't think of anyone who would want to hurt him."

"But you've been overseas for ten months." McNamara met his gaze.

"Right." Grant shoved his guilt away. Combat had taught him to compartmentalize, to put grief in the backseat until the mission was complete, but that was easier said than done when it was his brother who was dead. "I can't believe someone killed Lee and Kate for their car or wallet. It doesn't make sense. Why kill them? Why risk a murder charge?"

McNamara sighed. "I have no idea. Maybe he resisted." But the cop's eyes weren't satisfied with his own argument. Grant could feel discontent rolling off the detective in waves.

"That doesn't sound like Lee. He wouldn't have taken any chances with Kate's life." Grant screwed the bottle cap on too tightly, cracking it.

"Criminals are scumbags. Some of them get their rocks off killing people. Drugs make people do crazy things, and addicts will do anything to get money to buy more drugs."

Grant leaned forward, resting his elbows on his thighs and holding the water bottle between his hands. He met McNamara's level brown gaze head-on. "Drug addicts are sloppy. Lee's murder sounds . . . efficient."

"Maybe."

"Do you have any evidence at all?" Grant asked. It had been three days since Lee and Kate were killed. "Murder weapon? Fingerprints? Surveillance video? Anything? Did anyone hear the shots?"

"Unfortunately, there aren't any surveillance cameras in that area. It's a quiet side street." McNamara shook his head. "Their credit cards haven't been used, and we can't pick up a signal on their cell phones, which means the batteries were removed or destroyed. The car's GPS isn't transmitting, so it was likely disabled. I'll try to keep you as informed as possible." The cop stood, signaling their conversation was at an end. "When you decide on a funeral home, you can call the medical examiner's office. They'll call you when your brother and sister-in-law are ready to be released."

Which meant the medical examiner wasn't finished with the autopsies, something else Grant didn't want to think about right now. He was going to have to plan his brother's funeral, and that was bad enough without constantly visualizing the insult to Lee's and Kate's bodies. But how many mental pictures could he suppress? His brain was under a barrage of violent images. He pressed his sweating palms against his jeans. His lungs felt inelastic, each breath painful to draw.

McNamara squinted at him, obviously concerned. "Is there anyone else to help you with all this, Major?"

"My sister should be in town in the next day or so." But until then, Grant was on his own. Kate never spoke about her family, and Lee had mentioned more than once that she and her parents were estranged. How could Grant contact them? Should he even try?

"You should also be aware that the perpetrators likely have a key to your brother's house and the address."

"Right. Changing the locks goes on the top of my list." Grant shook the cop's hand. He needed to get out of there. His body's thermostat was off, and feverish heat was building under his jacket.

McNamara ushered him out to the parking lot. The damp night air coated his skin with moisture.

Grant slid into the driver's seat of the rental car. He started the engine and checked his phone. No return calls from Hannah or Mac. Grant had been playing phone tag with his sister, who was en route to New York from Jakarta. But where the hell was Mac?

He drove down the main street and headed toward Lee's house. His hometown of Scarlet Falls was a small suburban community in upstate New York, about an hour north of the state capitol in Albany. With the Appalachian Mountains to the west and Hudson Valley to the east, the town was picturesque, but the economy had been limping along since Grant was a kid. The region wasn't thriving but it wasn't going bankrupt either.

It was, in a word: average.

But in this ordinary slice of American suburbia, Lee and Kate had been brutally murdered. Had it been robbery? Or something even more sinister?

Ten minutes outside of town, Grant entered Lee's neighborhood. For the most part, the residences were large, old homes on oversize lots. No cookie-cutter tract house for Lee. No, a year and a half before, he'd sold the small starter home and moved up to a more prestigious address. Lee must have been doing well at the firm. He'd leased a BMW at about the same time.

Grant turned onto the right street. In the sparse light of the occasional streetlamp, the neighborhood looked barren. When he'd been here last May, the valley had been gleaming green. Shrubs had been trimmed and fronted with flowers. Kids rode bikes and played hockey in the street. Moms pushed strollers to the playground on the corner. Now, warming temps had muddied the landscape, thawing in the daytime and refreezing at night. Moonlight gleamed on the layer of frozen muck. Grant hadn't spent much time here since high school. The dreary vista was more depressing than the images in his memory. As a teen, he couldn't wait to get out of town, as if staying here would make him stagnate.

Lee and Kate's old Victorian sat behind a long, narrow front lawn. The Cape Cod–style house on the right was dark, but lights still burned in the two-story Colonial on the left. Streetlights were few and far between out here. Grant turned at the mailbox and parked at the head of the driveway. The big house was dark, almost forbidding. Trees loomed over the roof and cut off any light from the moon. Grant's headlights cut a swath of clarity through the gloom and illuminated the front porch.

He got out of the car and stared up at the house, suddenly realizing he didn't have a key. How was he going to get in? With a sigh, Grant trudged around the property, checking first-floor doors and windows in case one was left unlocked. No luck. He might need to go to a hotel after all, which meant a drive back out to the interstate, but at this point, sleeping in the car was looking good, despite the damp cold. The front seat of a sedan certainly wouldn't be the worst place he'd spent the night. At least Scarlet Falls didn't have enemy forces trying to kill him. He went back to the rental car. His truck, parked in a base storage facility in Texas, had a toolbox and flashlight in the back. Not this vehicle.

He opened the trunk and pulled the tire iron from the spare tire well. He could break a window, but then he'd have to fix the window. Probably not his best option. His gaze strayed to the house next door, and he remembered Lee's pretty brunette neighbor. They'd met a couple of times during his last visit. Even after ten months overseas, a man didn't forget a woman like Ellie Ross.

"Can I help you?"

Reaching for his sidearm, Grant whirled at the feminine voice. His hand hit empty jacket.

A small, older woman stood in the driveway. Darkness obscured her features, but he had no trouble seeing the shotgun in her arms. He froze, the sight of the gun sending his adrenals back into overdrive. He flashed back to the ambush and a figure in digital desert camo pointing a weapon in his direction.

How did she sneak up behind him? Was he *that* distracted?

"Drop the tire iron," she said. "And don't move."

"Don't worry." He let the tool fall into the trunk and raised his hands as she pointed the twelve-gauge at the dead center of his chest.

Chapter Four

"Nan!" Ellie squinted into the darkness. Beyond her shotgun-wielding grandmother, the man standing in her neighbor's driveway looked familiar. But her eyes hadn't adjusted to the lack of light, and he was standing in the shadow of his open trunk. "You cannot point a gun at someone."

"Well, he was skulking around the house in the dark. He looked like he was going to break in." Nan tapped a white athletic shoe on the pavement. Frenzied barking emanated from their house. "A girl can't be too careful. Lots of crime around here lately."

"He parked in the driveway, Nan. That's hardly criminal behavior." Ellie gently liberated the gun from her grandmother and let the muzzle tip toward the ground. "That barking is going to wake Julia. Would you please go inside and make the dog stop?" Then Ellie would try to convince the man not to call the police—or a psychiatric ward—on her grandmother.

Nan gave her a pointed look, but she complied, walking toward their house.

The stranger closed the trunk and faced her, and she recognized Lee's brother. "Grant?"

At six foot four, his broad shoulders and wide chest filled out his brown leather jacket.

"Hello, Ellie."

Sadness crept up the back of her throat. "I'm sorry for your loss."

"Thank you." He cleared his throat.

"I apologize for my grandmother," she said. "She's tired of reporters and photographers. Plus, there have been other people who actually were skulking around the place in the dark looking for a way to break in. We called the police a few times. They said once the media releases the victims' names, it isn't uncommon for criminals to target the house. Is there anything I can do for you?"

"I don't have a key. I was hoping there was an unlocked window or door. No such luck."

"I have one. Let's go inside, and I'll get it for you."

"I was just thinking about knocking on your door." He sounded grateful. "Don't know why I didn't do it right away."

"I imagine you have a lot on your mind." Now that the crisis had passed, she shivered hard. She hadn't taken time to put on a jacket when she saw her grandmother—with her gun—stalking the man out front. But now Ellie's Spackle-smeared T-shirt and jeans were no match for the night air.

They crossed the wide, snow-crusted front yards and stomped up her steps. The porch light shone across his face. He had the same blond hair and blue eyes as Lee, but the resemblance stopped there. Tall and thin, Lee had had a Gregory-Peck-as-Atticus-Finch way about him. He'd been unassuming and scholarly. Larger and more muscular, Grant was a dominant physical presence, one that she felt along every square inch of her exposed skin. Even if she hadn't known he was a soldier, she would have guessed it from the hardness of his body, readiness in his stance, and wariness in his eye. Despite the grief etched on his face, she was transfixed for a moment. Ten months in the desert had sharpened his Scandinavian features and given him a harder look. Handsome before, his masculinity had amplified tenfold. His posture and body were leaner, edgier, poised to react.

He caught her staring. The slightest smile turned up the corner of his mouth, and a blush heated her face.

She turned away from the light and opened her front door. AnnaBelle pranced out onto the porch. Despite the fierce barks, the golden retriever was all feathery wags and whines for the newcomer.

"Nice dog." He leaned down to stroke her head.

"She belongs to Carson," she said.

Grant stopped midpet. Devastation crossed his face, sadness aging him years in the span of a moment. "I didn't know they had a dog."

"They haven't had her long. Lee picked her up at the animal shelter over the summer. AnnaBelle and Carson are best friends." She stepped into the house and toed off her boots. Turning, she patted her thigh. "Come on, AnnaBelle."

"Are the children coming home?" Ellie asked, tears filling her eyes. "Social services wouldn't let me keep them, and my application as an emergency foster spent the weekend in bureaucratic limbo. Background checks take time, they said." The dog circled her legs, tripping her. Catching her balance, she nudged the overly affectionate retriever out of the way. "They let me have the dog."

"The kids will be home early tomorrow." He wiped his feet on the mat. "They wouldn't call for them tonight. Policy."

"Yes. I learned all about social services *policy* over the weekend." Ellie swallowed her bitterness.

The dog and man followed her into the house. As she moved through the hall, she broke open the shotgun action, plucked out the shells, and locked the rifle in a gun case in the hall closet. "You're still in Afghanistan?"

"Yes. I'm on emergency leave."

She led him past her gutted living room.

"How's the remodel going?" he asked, gesturing through the archway, where supplies and tools occupied the space that should have held a dining room table.

"Slowly." She walked into the kitchen. The cabinets shone with a painful shade of Day-Glo yellow, and the peeling wallpaper featured sunflowers the size of a human head. The faded vinyl tiles underfoot used to be black. The overall effect was nauseating. "I can't wait to do this room. It feels like you're being attacked by bumblebees. The kitchen will be gutted next. Walls have to come down. It's going to get ugly."

"When we talked last, you were working on the master bath."

He remembered. Warmth filled Ellie. They'd met a few, memorable times. Kate had been obvious in her attempts to push them together. She'd invited Ellie to more barbecues during Grant's two-week visit last May than in the whole summer that followed.

Ellie gestured toward the table. "Do you want to sit down? Can I get you some coffee?"

"No," Grant said. The confines of the small room amplified his size. The man was solid. He must spend considerable time training in the Middle East. He had muscles on top of muscles. Not that she was staring. Much. "I'd just like to get settled for the night. It's been a long trip."

"I'll bet. Let me find that key." She opened the drawer and rummaged through bottle openers, pens, and other assorted junk. "I know it's here. I just used it the other day."

Slippers scuffed in the hall, and Nan walked in, her insatiable curiosity drawing her to their guest like a bee buzzing around a can of Orange Crush. She sized up Grant in the bright kitchen light in one head-to-toe visual sweep. Under her fluffy helmet of dyed brown hair, Nan's gaze changed from suspicious to interested in one blink.

Uh-oh.

Ellie gestured. "Nan, this is Major Grant Barrett. Lee's brother. You were in Florida last spring when he visited."

Nan's gaze softened. She walked closer and took both his hands, her eyes shining with tears. "Oh, I'm so sorry, Major. Your brother was a nice man."

His mouth tightened, and his Adam's apple bobbed as he swallowed. "Thank you. Please call me Grant."

"Grant needs the house key." Ellie spied it on a wall hook. AnnaBelle followed her to the key rack and back. "Is there anything else we can do for you?"

"Not tonight," he said, taking the key from her hand. "I might have some questions for you tomorrow, especially when the kids come home. Thank you for taking the dog and for watching the house."

"It was the least I could do." Ellie went to the pantry and hoisted a fifty-pound bag of dog food up onto her hip.

Grant rushed over. "Let me get that." He tucked it under one arm as if it didn't weigh more than a bag of flour. She kept her eyes off the bulges under his sweater. Mostly. This was hardly the appropriate time to appreciate the major's attributes. But she knew they were all sorts of fine. An image popped into her head of Grant playing outside with Carson last May. Carson had turned the hose on his uncle. The vision of Grant stripping off his wet T-shirt, wringing it out, and chasing his giggling nephew across the yard had been imprinted in Ellie's brain for the last ten months. And replayed itself a thousand times like a video on YouTube, usually at very inappropriate and inopportune times. Like now.

She set a coiled leash on top of the bag. "She doesn't wear the leash much. If you call her, she'll come."

"Mom?"

All heads turned toward the doorway. Her daughter, Julia, stood under the arch.

"Do you remember Major Barrett?"

Julia nodded. "I'm real sorry." She sniffed. A tear leaked out of a swollen eye, and she heaved a long, shaky breath. She'd taken the Barretts' deaths hard. In addition to babysitting Carson and Faith, Kate was Julia's figure skating coach. Ellie went to her daughter and wrapped an arm around her shoulders. Her sexy thoughts of the hot major faded, adding another layer to her sadness. If things were different, if he wasn't an ambitious military officer constantly moving all over the world, if she wasn't so bound by the betrayal of her past, if their current meeting wasn't mired in grief, then maybe something could happen between them.

But that was way too many *ifs*, all impossible to change.

Grant shifted his weight toward the front door as if he couldn't escape fast enough. "It's late. I'd better go. Thank you again."

He called the dog, who went willingly, always thrilled to meet a new human. Ellie escorted them outside to the front porch. AnnaBelle followed Grant across the grass and up onto the stoop of the house next door. Ellie shut the door and locked the deadbolt.

"Night." Rubbing her biceps, Julia went upstairs.

Nan stood in the kitchen, one fist propped on a hip, brows pinched in deep thought. "That man's going to need help."

Ellie crossed her arms over her chest. "If Grant needs help, he'll ask for it. Until he does, we are going to mind our own business."

Nan ignored her, bustling around the kitchen. "Nice-looking man. Fit. Clean-cut. Always did love a man in uniform."

"He wasn't in uniform."

"I have a good imagination." Thank God Nan had been away last year. If she'd seen Grant without a shirt . . .

"Oh, no." Ellie wagged a finger at her grandmother. "Don't even start."

"Start what?" Nan lifted an overly innocent shoulder. "I was simply making an observation."

"Well, don't," Ellie said. "He's on leave. He's not staying."

"Uh-huh." Nan pulled a loaf pan from the cabinet.

"I don't do casual."

Nan snorted. "You don't do anyone."

"Nan!" Ellie protested.

Her grandmother held up a forefinger. "Look, you made a mistake when you were young. The only one still making you pay for it is you. I can count the number of dates you've had in the last few years on one of these veiny old hands. You need to let it go and move on with your life."

"I've been involved with a man who wasn't around. I'm not doing that again." Ellie would rather renovate than date. "You're exaggerating. I've dated more than that. It's just been a while. I've been busy."

"Not much more." Nan pulled her recipe box from the back of the counter. She flipped through rows of handwritten, butter-splotched index cards.

"What are you doing?"

"I'm wide awake." Nan took the flour out of the pantry. "I'm going to bake."

"It's after eleven."

"When Carson comes home, he'll want something familiar to eat." How like her grandmother to turn her insomnia into a comforting meal for a sad child. "And men the size of Grant need sustenance."

When Ellie had turned up on her grandmother's doorstep pregnant at seventeen, with the baby's father absconding for the West Coast and Ellie's parents issuing a their-way-or-the-highway ultimatum, Nan had taken her in without a single reproach. *What's done is done*, she'd said. *Let's focus on the future.* The next day, they'd picked a theme for the nursery and started painting the spare room.

Nan paused, baking pan in hand, staring at their reflection in the dark glass of the kitchen window. "I can't sleep. I keep thinking about Lee and Kate and those poor children."

Her grandmother didn't have to finish. Ellie couldn't get their friends out of her mind either. Her throat filled and her eyes burned with unshed tears.

"Grant will get the kids back tomorrow." She gave her grandmother a one-armed, sideways hug.

"Thank God."

"Yes."

They stood in silence for a minute, each thinking her private thoughts.

Nan's were probably about Grant.

But Ellie was not setting herself up to be left again. She was just fine on her own. Lonely, but fine.

"I'm going to bed." Ellie returned to the living room to make sure her tub of Spackle was tightly closed. In her bedroom, she looked out the window. Lights glowed in the windows next door. How would Grant fare with the children? Carson was an easygoing kid, but grief would make even him challenging. Then there was Faith. How would a military bachelor handle the hours upon hours of screaming? Kate used to say that the baby had the lungs of an Olympic athlete.

Poor Kate.

Ellie might have known Lee longer, and he was the one who'd talked her into buying this house as her next project, but she'd formed a friendship with Kate since becoming their neighbor. They had a lot in common. Both of them were estranged from their parents. Kate knew what it was like not to be able to call her mom on holidays. Now Faith and Carson wouldn't have a mother to call either.

Breath hitching, Ellie went into the master bath, the first room she'd remodeled when she bought the property. Creamy porcelain tiles replaced the 1950s pink-and-black motif. She turned on the rain shower, stripped, and stepped in. The water was still cold. She slid down onto the tile and let the tears come, picturing Carson crying in the backseat of the social worker's car, the baby wailing, the dog whining and pulling against her collar. Ellie could still feel the bite of night air on her tear-dampened face, as cold and real as the shower water running over her skin now.

How long was Grant's leave and what was he going to do with the children when he returned to the military? Even more important, what would the children do without *him*? Lee had two additional siblings, but where were they? Kate hadn't seen her parents in ten years, and from the stories she'd told, the kids were better off without them. Ellie's chest ached with grief for those orphans.

The water warmed, smoothing her goose bumps. Ellie climbed to her feet and washed her face. Lee and Kate's children weren't Ellie's responsibility. Neither was the dog she missed already. The woman from social services had made that clear. Like Ellie had told Nan, she intended to mind her own business unless Grant asked her for help. He had his own family. He didn't need nosy neighbors butting into an already difficult situation. But with the hot major and two children she cared about living just next door, keeping her distance wasn't going to be easy.

Grant unlocked the front door of his brother's house. He whistled for the dog, who was sniffing a circle on the snow-covered lawn. "Here, girl."

Three females and their tears were more than he could handle. Their collective sympathy threatened to challenge his tenuous hold on control. But Ellie Ross's long dark hair, scattering of freckles, and big brown eyes could tempt a man to accept some comfort.

He jerked his attention away from the pretty neighbor. In less than a month he'd be back in Afghanistan. Ellie, with her baseball-and-apple-pie wholesomeness, wasn't a casual fling type of girl.

Grant was too focused on his military career to squeeze a relationship into his life. Making general required 100 percent dedication. He'd seen too many of his comrades miss their families, and he'd shipped too many parents home in flag-draped coffins. In his own youth, he'd witnessed firsthand the sacrifices made by an army family. Grant only dated female army officers who weren't interested in the whole domestic deal. But somehow Ellie had already encroached on his imagination on more than a few cold, lonely desert nights.

AnnaBelle sniffed a shrub in the flower bed that fronted the porch, then trotted through the open door. In the entryway, Grant tossed the keys on the hall table and sat in the adjacent chair to remove his wet boots. More than a hundred years old, the Victorian had a classic center stairway design, with an abundance of small rooms and narrow halls. Everything was dark, from the scarred pine floors to the heavy case molding around the windows and doors. The house wasn't appealing. Why had Lee wanted it so badly? He'd talked of renovations, knocking down walls and adding windows to bring some light into the gloomy house, but it didn't appear as if any improvements had been made since Grant had visited last year except for boarding up the nonfunctioning dumbwaiter in the butler's pantry. Grant smiled, remembering Lee's rare childish excitement when they'd first moved into the house. He'd wanted to fix the old pulley and lever system. But Kate had been terrified Carson would fall down the hole. As usual, the practical Kate had won.

The dog followed him into the kitchen. Grant filled a bowl of water and set it on the floor. A bay window behind the table looked out onto the snowy woods behind the house. Last spring, Lee and Kate had hosted numerous barbecues, all not-so-subtly designed to bring Grant and Ellie together, in that backyard. He could picture her now, standing on the grass, her sundress showing off smooth shoulders and a length of bare, tan leg, a wide smile tempting him to get to know her better. Much better. It had taken all of Grant's determination to keep his distance. Just a few weeks away from deployment hadn't been the best time to start a relationship. As if he had ever had time for a personal life.

He dropped onto the sofa in the adjoining small family room. Picking up the remote, he turned on the TV. He flipped through channels until he came to a hockey game but barely saw the screen. Lee and Kate's deaths seemed so senseless and surreal. Tomorrow the kids would be home. How was he going to manage a baby he'd never met and a grieving six-year-old he hadn't seen in ten months?

Chapter Five

Donnie crouched behind the driver's seat of his van and watched the big man and dog go into the Barrett house down the street. He lowered his binoculars. Who was that?

Fuck.

He did not need this shit. Yanking off his knit cap, he rubbed the stubble on his scalp with a brisk scrubbing motion. He couldn't get lucky with this job. Three nights he'd attempted to get into the house, and all three times he'd been spotted. That bitch next door kept calling the cops. She seriously needed to be taught a lesson. With some hard-core punishment, he could teach her how to be submissive. There were so many different ways he could violate her body.

A memory intruded in his fantasy as he remembered his own lessons. He could still feel the concrete under his palms and knees and the blows to his face and body as he was beaten until he'd begged for it to be over. The humiliation of not only being forced to submit to the ultimate physical violation, but to have pleaded for it just to end the torture, had crushed his soul. Blood had dripped into his eyes and mouth. He was so fucked up now that the metallic taste or smell of it still gave him an instant hard-on.

When this job was over, he'd release his frustrations. He turned his attention back to the house he was watching. This whole job was backward. The killing was supposed to be the hard part, and the recovery easy. Instead, the murder had been almost effortless—beyond effortless—euphoric.

There had been so much blood spreading out across the icy street he'd needed to exorcise a few demons with his new girlfriend. Good thing she dug pain as much as he enjoyed inflicting it.

He chewed on a ragged cuticle that tasted like hamburger grease. The longer he sat here, the greater his chances of getting caught. Although, according to the news, the cops had nothing. Sure, they pretended they were embroiled in an "ongoing investigation," but he knew that meant they didn't have squat. His fingerprints and DNA were in the system. If he'd left any personal trace evidence at the crime scene, his mug shot would have been on the news. He didn't shave from head to foot as a fashion statement.

He was clean on the murders, but his client was holding back the balance of payment until the whole job was complete. He couldn't sit out here forever. The neighbor was bound to notice him. He copied the license plate number of the sedan in the driveway. Probably a rental, but he'd check. Then he could try to hack into the rental company's website and get a name on the big bastard that was holding up his job.

He should have stuck with cyber crime. It didn't require him sitting out in a cold van, freezing his nuts off. But after eighteen months in prison, violence called to him. Rage built up inside him, the internal pressure growing until his very skin grew itchy and tight. Killing the Barretts had released the tension. Hurting people was a need. He might as well get paid to do it.

Tugging the hat back on his head, he blew into his cupped fists. His breath fogged in front of him. Fucking March was still ball-shrinking cold. But running the van's engine wasn't an option.

Nothing sucked worse than surveillance in the winter. But he didn't have many options. He *had* to get into that house. And soon. He'd already blown through his retainer, and the client was freaking out.

At some point the Barrett place had to be empty.

If not, he was going to have to come up with another way to get what he needed. His gaze drifted to the bitch's house next door, and he wondered how much she knew.

What would it take to make her tell him everything?

Chapter Six

Ellie's second cup of coffee cooled on her desk as Detective McNamara exited her boss's office. The detective had been at Lee and Kate's house on Friday night. After the children had left, he'd asked her questions about Lee and Kate. The cop gave her a polite nod as he went out the frosted glass front door. Ellie swallowed the grief rising in her throat. On her lunch hour, she'd call Nan to find out if the children were home. She wondered how Grant was holding up. Even grief-stricken, the major seemed . . . solid, and she wasn't referring to his impressive physique.

The cop hadn't been out the door for more than two minutes when shouts blasted through her boss's closed door.

"What the hell are you doing? You're running my firm into the ground," Roger Peyton Sr. yelled. "None of this ever happened when I sat at that desk. Do I need to take over?"

Murmurs followed as Roger Peyton Jr. tried to placate his father, who held on to the bulk of the partnership equity with greedy, Scrooge-like fists. Five more minutes of alternating yelling and mumbling followed before the door opened again and a remarkably spry eighty-year-old bustled out. The cane in his grip looked more like a potential weapon than a necessity. Ellie fixed her gaze firmly on her computer screen. Peyton associated her with his son. When he was angry at Roger, his irritation bubbled over to include her.

He turned a bony, hawkish face toward Ellie. "Good morning, Miss Ross."

The deep gray of his eyes always surprised her. She half expected them to glow red.

"Good morning, Mr. Peyton." Ellie returned to her typing. Looking busy was the best way to avoid any further discussion with the old crank. Nothing on this earth except hustling employees and tidy profits pleased the man. When he exited, the building exhaled in relief.

Her intercom buzzed. "I need to see you in my office, Ellie."

Ellie picked up her steno pad and walked across the dark blue carpet into her boss's expansive suite.

Roger was at the wet bar, pouring himself a generous shot of Glenfiddich.

Smoothing her skirt under her, she perched on a red leather wing chair facing his antique mahogany desk. She poised her pen over the notebook and waited. To her right, a bay window looked out onto First Street. Blue velvet curtains framed the view and puddled luxuriously on the floor. "If you keep drinking at nine a.m., he's going to outlive you."

Roger snorted. "He's going to outlive me no matter what I do. I suspect he negotiated an airtight contract at the crossroads."

At fifty-seven, Roger Peyton Jr., one of the three partners of Peyton, Peyton, and Griffin, was waiting for his father to die. Until Peyton Senior passed on, Roger had to run all major decisions past the old man, who mired the business in the traditions of the 1950s. There were no female attorneys and no male paralegals. The firm was small enough to slide eel-like under equal opportunity legislation. Men dressed in suits and ties. Women wore skirts, pantyhose, and pumps. Casual day was for the riffraff not lucky enough to be employed by this prestigious firm. Peyton Senior liked to drop by for surprise visits. Now that arthritis kept him from playing golf, fault-finding and yelling seemed to be his hobbies.

Half the office employees would pop a bottle of champagne when the old guy finally kicked.

Ellie had worked enough crappy jobs that she was willing to deal. If stodgy earned her a decent paycheck and medical benefits, then she could be as old-fashioned as the next girl, even if the job occasionally required sacrificing a tiny portion of her soul.

"Did you finish packing Lee's personal items?" Easing back into his seat behind the desk, Roger adjusted his double-breasted suit and tugged his French cuffs into place. He took a long pull of scotch and stared at her for a minute, as if trying to make a decision.

"Yes," she answered. "His things are ready for his family to pick up. I've started sorting his clients as well. This afternoon I'll distribute his physical files to the other attorneys according to the list you supplied."

"What would I do without you?" Roger studied the amber liquid in his tumbler. "We're in big trouble, Ellie. Not just my dad ranting and raving at imaginary problems because he enjoys it kind of trouble."

She straightened.

"Have you seen the case file?"

"No."

Last month, the town had been rocked by a vicious case of bullying and the associated suicide of seventeen-year-old Lindsay Hamilton. The two alleged ringleaders of the campaign to torment Lindsay were members of the elite Valley Figure Skating Club, a competitive skating team Lindsay had joined upon her move from California to New York. The bullies were also in the top of the junior class, student council officers, and two of the brightest stars in the community. Their families had deep roots in Scarlet Falls. Lindsay's parents claimed the bullying had driven their daughter to take her own life. The allegations were denied by the accused and their parents. No witnesses came forward. Threatening texts were sent from untraceable burner phones, and Lindsay's phone had been wiped clean by a cell phone virus. The police had dropped the case due to lack of evidence, but Mr. and Mrs. Hamilton were determined to pursue their case in civil court. Last week, Lee had agreed to represent them.

The Hamilton case was the only case not reassigned. At some point, one of the senior partners would have to call Mr. and Mrs. Hamilton, but so far, Roger was playing the out-of-sight-out-of-mind card. Ignoring things and hoping they'd go away was his favorite business tactic.

"I think Lee took that file home with him. I need it, Ellie. Really need it. I need you to get into his house and look for it." Roger tossed back the rest of his drink. He got up and poured himself another, then brought the bottle back to his desk. "Did Lee tell you he'd agreed to take the Hamilton case?"

"Yes, I knew. Lee met with the Hamiltons the day he . . . died." She couldn't say the word *murdered*. The thought of Lee and Kate being killed was still foreign and unreal. Speaking the words aloud hurt. She looked up at her boss and decided not to mention Lee's previous meeting with the Hamiltons a few days before his death.

"Did you mention the case to anyone?" Cold anger congealed in Roger's gray eyes—and Ellie knew why her boss was so upset. Lee hadn't gotten Roger's approval before taking the case. Associates were encouraged to bring in clients, but there was an understanding that sensitive issues would be cleared with the partners first. Lee, clearly unsure of his chances, had opted for forgiveness instead of permission. He'd met the Hamiltons at their home instead of bringing them into the office—in hindsight, another sign he didn't want Roger's input on his decision. Now Roger was taking the heat for Lee's decision. The Hamilton case was controversial. The buttoned-down senior Peyton didn't approve of controversy. *Peyton, Peyton, and Griffin was built on a foundation of solid law practice, not media circuses.*

"No," she said. "You should know I would never be indiscreet." Even though it had felt wrong, she'd kept her mouth closed when Roger had been cheating on his wife.

He scrubbed a hand down his face. "But someone here knew and leaked the information to the police."

That explained the detective's visit.

He waved his glass, his mind still whirling behind his gray eyes. "Now that Lee's gone, you're probably the only person I trust around here." With the senior Peyton still controlling the business, employee loyalties were divided.

"Perhaps the Hamiltons?" she suggested.

"It's a possibility. They have been outspoken." He pursed his lips. "We'll have to go into damage control mode. I'll draft a statement for the media. Let me know the instant the first reporter calls."

"All right." Ellie stood.

"Unfortunately, there's more."

She froze.

"We're missing money." Roger tipped the bottle over his glass.

"You have a client meeting at eleven." Ellie reached across the desk and took the bottle from him. Crossing to the wet bar, she returned the scotch and poured him a cup of coffee from the carafe.

Accepting the coffee, he sighed. "Our accountant called my father. A series of fraudulent checks were cashed over the past few weeks."

"How much?" Ellie dropped back into the chair.

"I don't know yet. Not enough to ruin us. Don't worry."

But Ellie couldn't help it.

"You're with me on this, right, Ellie?" Roger toyed with the cup's handle.

"Of course." What else was she going to say? It wasn't like she could refuse. *Damn it.* She didn't want to be put in the middle of the Peyton family feud. Jobs weren't that plentiful in Scarlet Falls.

Between Nan's pension and Ellie's salary, the bills were covered. Rehabbing and selling a house every few years had netted them some savings. When she flipped her current home, there should be enough money to put her daughter through college provided Julia stayed in state. Life might not be exciting, but Ellie would take steady and solid over a thrill. The last time she'd been impulsive, she'd ended up pregnant—and alone.

"The accountant is trying to trace the money trail, but I need to find it first." Roger turned desperate eyes on her. "I need to protect the firm."

Ellie tried to summon some pity, but Roger made it difficult. He was nice enough, but weak, and he'd demonstrated his lack of loyalty by dumping his sweet wife of thirty years for a high-maintenance trophy edition. It was his lifestyle he wanted to protect, not his employees.

"I need you to help me, Ellie."

Exactly what she didn't want to do. But realistically, the old man had already put Ellie solidly on Roger's team. If Roger was out, so was she.

"I'll see what I can find out."

His eyes brightened.

Ellie returned to her desk. Her eyes went to the expense report she'd been preparing, but her mind was stuck on the firm's problems. Lee had taken the case even though he knew it wouldn't be a popular decision with the senior lawyer in the firm. If the police wouldn't prosecute, what made him think he could win? And did either the Hamilton case or the missing money have anything to do with his death?

A rough sound startled Grant awake, the vision still clear in his mind: Lee's face exploding in a red mist. Panting, he swept his gaze around the room. A muffled bark made him look over the edge of the mattress. AnnaBelle wagged at him. The mattress shifted as the agile dog jumped up to stand over him in the queen-size bed. "I wish you'd have woken me a couple of minutes earlier."

She stretched out and rested her head on his chest.

His hand swept through the silky, golden fur. "I suppose you need to go out."

AnnaBelle wagged harder, jumped down, and danced on the hardwood. Grant swung his legs over the side. Six a.m. He had hours before the cop was supposed to call. Sleep had been elusive, his mind replaying his kill shot in the ambush over and over every time he dozed off. He had to get his act together before the kids got home.

He stepped into a pair of shorts and tugged a sweatshirt over his head, then dug his running shoes from his bag. A run would clear his mind and take the edge off the young dog's energy. "Let's go."

He snapped AnnaBelle's leash on her collar. Outside, the dog peed on the lawn before they set off down the street. Grant kept the pace slow, unsure of the dog's fitness, but the retriever had no trouble keeping up. Forty minutes later, they returned to the house. Grant showered, dressed, and called a locksmith.

His phone vibrated and displayed a message from his sister. Be home tomorrow afternoon. The second buzz was Detective McNamara letting him know the kids would be home in two hours. Still nothing from Mac. Grant paced. Five miles wasn't enough to burn off his tension.

He had two hours, more than enough time to go see his father. No excuses.

"Be good," he said to the dog, flat out and sound asleep on the wood floor.

Five miles of rural highway took Grant to the nursing home parking lot. Walking through the sliding glass doors, he unzipped his jacket and stopped at the reception desk in the lobby.

A gray-haired woman in bright pink scrubs looked up from a laptop. "Can I help you?"

"I'm here to see Alexander Barrett," he said.

"The Colonel is in room fifty-two." Smiling, she wrote a number on a cardboard pass and handed it to him. She pointed over his shoulder. "Make a left at the end of the hallway."

Grant followed her directions. He passed a small cafeteria where ambulatory residents were eating breakfast. Wheelchairs were tucked under tables, walkers parked next to chairs. The scents of syrup and bacon mingled with disinfectant. Despite the attempt to make the atmosphere cheerful, there was no disguising the nature of the institution. Considering the state of most of the residents, it had broken Grant's heart when they'd moved Dad here two years ago.

He turned into his father's room. His dad had deteriorated since spring. His arms had withered, and his skin had taken on a yellowish hue. The Colonel's eyes were closed and his chest labored with heavy breaths. Oxygen tubes snaked from his nostrils around his ears. An IV line trailed from his wrist to a trio of bags hanging from a stand. In 1991, a convoy bombing during Operation Desert Storm had paralyzed the Colonel from the waist down, but the determined soldier hadn't allowed his injury to hold him back. He'd done as many normal things as possible, including custom-rigging an ATV so he could take his boys out in the woods. He'd lived in his modified home until dementia robbed him of his remaining strength and dignity, the ultimate insult for a brave man who'd fought as hard as the Colonel.

Grant paused to read the medicine labels: the usual concoction of fluids, antibiotics, and steroids. The Colonel's white hair was clean and combed, and the bed linens appeared fresh. A biography of General Braxton Bragg lay open on the bed tray. Someone had been reading to him. Grant and Hannah spent a hefty sum of money each month to supplement the Colonel's benefits and ensure he received excellent medical care. It was all he could do from the other side of the globe, but with Lee handling the day-to-day details, Grant and Hannah shouldered the financial burden.

"Hi, Dad." He pulled a chair up to the bed and touched his father's forearm.

The Colonel's clouded eyes, once a bright and piercing blue, blinked vaguely on Grant. "Who are you?"

"It's Grant. Your son. I'm home on leave."

"Grant. General Grant?" Confusion creased his features.

Only the Colonel would remember the historical figure he'd named his firstborn after and not his actual firstborn.

"Not yet, Dad, but I'll get there," Grant promised.

"I don't have a son." Agitation sharpened his father's tone. "Who are you? Are you trying to rob me?"

"No, sir." Grant stood. The ache in his chest expanded. "I was just leaving."

Once Dad's paranoia got rolling, it would take the nurses hours to calm him. Better to leave and try again another day. Besides, there was no point telling him about Lee when he didn't recall Lee existed. Maybe the Colonel's memory loss was a blessing today. His son's death would have broken him if he were whole.

Grant found his dad's nurse at the station around the corner and let her know what happened. She promised to check on him. Grant got back into the rental car and glanced at the dashboard clock. Thanks to his abbreviated visit, he had time for one more stop, the law offices of Peyton, Peyton, and Griffin. Anything to avoid going back to Lee's empty house.

His brother had worked in an established law firm that occupied a converted stately three-story home on First Street. Miles of white trim set off pale yellow clapboards. Grant parked in the rear lot and followed the paver path alongside the building to the front door. He stepped into a polished foyer turned into a lobby. In the center, behind an antique desk, sat Lee's pretty neighbor, Ellie.

Gone were the ripped jeans and stained T-shirt, the wallboard dust and paint smears. Not that construction-worker Ellie wasn't hot, but this . . . this feminine version reminded him too much of the Ellie from last spring—the Ellie in that sundress.

"Grant." She rose, rounded the desk, and held out her hand. A pale blue blouse and slim gray skirt hugged her curvy body to just above her knees. Below the hem, her shapely legs ended in low-heeled pumps. Her hair was coiled in a neat bun at her nape. She wore minimal makeup. The effect was wholesome, natural, and demure.

Grant ignored the pleasure that lightened his chest. But damn, that smile. It brightened everything that had gone bleak inside of him at the nursing home.

"Hi, Ellie." He took her hand. Her skin was soft and smooth in his rough palm.

"What can I do for you?"

The erotic image that popped into Grant's head was both unexpected and inappropriate. He should be ashamed, but my God—

Damn sundress.

He released her hand. "Actually, I was hoping I could talk to Lee's boss. We've been playing phone tag."

"Let me see if he's free to speak with you." She went back to her desk and picked up the phone.

Grant gave her space. He strolled to the other side of the lobby and checked out the portraits of the senior partners hanging on the wall. Was being old and unhappy required of a senior law partner? Who wanted to look at a bunch of crabby old men when he could stare at Ellie?

"He'll see you now." She crossed the lobby, her heels silent on the blue carpet. She opened a door and stood aside.

"Major Barrett, come in." Roger Peyton Jr. emerged from behind his desk to shake Grant's hand.

"Mr. Peyton." Scotch fumes hit Grant's nostrils.

"Call me Roger, please. Mr. Peyton is my father. Would you like coffee?"

"No, but thank you. I just came to collect Lee's things. I have to get back. There are so many details to address. I'm sure you understand."

"Of course," Roger said. "Please accept my condolences. Such a tragic event. We'll certainly miss your brother here at the firm."

Grant breathed through the stab of pain. No matter how many people offered their sympathy, he couldn't wrap his mind around Lee's death.

Roger appeared to sense his discomfort. "If I can be of any assistance, legal or otherwise, please don't hesitate to call."

"Thank you."

Grant sidestepped toward the exit. "I don't mean to rush, but I have to be back at the house soon."

Roger ushered him to the door. He pasted a trying-too-hard-to-be-casual smile on his face. "I believe your brother had taken some client information home. If you find any of the firm's property, would you please return it? Confidentiality is a very serious issue." The man's thin lips flattened and his eyes darkened.

"I'll be going through my brother's office over the next few days. If I find anything that belongs to the firm, you'll be the first to hear."

"Thank you." The anxiety that simmered under the alcohol-induced glaze in Roger's eyes seemed like more than confidentiality.

As he exited Roger's office, Grant made a mental note to check out Lee's boss. Did whatever was wrong with the firm have anything to do with his brother's death?

Chapter Seven

Ellie felt Grant's gaze hot on her back as she led him to Lee's medium-size office down the hall.

She flipped the light switch on the wall. Fluorescent lights overhead flickered, then illuminated. Two copier paper boxes sat on top of an empty desk.

Grant scanned the space. His gaze settled on the boxes. "He was here for seven years. That's all that was his?"

"He didn't keep many personal items here. Mostly photos." Ellie stood aside. Grant always seemed too close. Or maybe she was just too aware of him.

He lifted one of the lids, pulled out his brother's nameplate, and ran his forefinger over the name LEE BARRETT engraved into the brass.

"Were you and your brother named after Generals Lee and Grant?" she asked.

"We were." He sighed, his chest deflating. "It wasn't so bad for us. My youngest brother, McClellan, got the worst of it. We nicknamed him Mac out of pity. My father is a Civil War buff."

His gaze lifted from the nameplate to study her face. Heat rose into her cheeks at the scrutiny, but she didn't look away. Grant's directness was both refreshing and disconcerting.

"Oh, excuse me." A masculine voice startled Ellie.

She whirled. The other associate, Frank Menendez, stood in the doorway. The box in his arms made it painfully clear he was moving into Lee's office.

Ellie recovered her composure. Damn Frank. The seat of Lee's chair had barely cooled.

Lured from a law partnership in Albany, Frank had been with the firm for less than a year. He had been Lee's competition for the partnership. Hired by Roger Peyton Sr., Frank played for the opposing team. Ellie tried not to hold it against him. The family rift affected most of the firm's employees. It was nearly impossible to avoid being claimed by one side or the other.

She motioned between them. "Major Grant Barrett. Frank Menendez."

Frank set his box down on the credenza behind the desk. "Sorry for your loss."

"Thank you." Grant shook his hand. From the sad drift of his gaze, he was aware that Frank was moving into his brother's office.

Frank shifted his weight in the awkward moment of silence that followed. He nodded to the stack of files on the credenza. "I'll bring these out to you, Ellie."

"All right." Suspicion bloomed in Ellie's mind. Frank wasn't ordinarily helpful. What was he up to?

"I need to get going." Grant picked up the boxes.

"I'll show you out." She escorted him to the lobby without any more conversation. She pushed the front door and went onto the porch to hold it open for him. "I'm sorry about Frank."

"Nothing to be sorry about." The stoic gaze he turned on her made her eyes tear. "Thank you for everything."

Damn.

"Good-bye." She shivered, the cold blowing right through her thin silk blouse.

"I didn't mean to make you cry," he said.

"It's just the wind." She blinked the mistiness from her eyes.

He leaned closer. Ellie caught a whiff of a mild aftershave, a woodsy scent that reminded her of warm spring days. His leather jacket was open. The V neck exposed the masculine column of his throat. What would that solid body feel like under her palms?

"I'd like to talk to you later. I have a few questions." His gaze darted back through the doorway to the law firm lobby, and Ellie knew that his questions would be about the missing case files and Frank Menendez, and that she wouldn't be able to answer them.

Grant Barrett, and his soldiering-on-through-his-grief fortitude, awakened emotions inside her: respect, empathy, and an inexplicable desire to rest her head on his chest while he wrapped those strong arms around her. What would it feel like to have someone to share life's burdens? None of which would excuse talking about the firm's private business. She was contractually bound to maintain client confidentiality. She needed this job, and he was only here temporarily. She had no future with a man who would leave her. Been there, done that.

But none of those reasons stopped her lips from blabbing, "All right."

It was a good opportunity to see if the Hamilton file was in Lee's home office, as Roger had requested. *Ha.* Like that was why she'd agreed. Mentally, she rolled her eyes at her own ridiculousness. But while she was in Lee's house, lusting over his brother, she would keep her eyes open for the Hamilton file. The children would be home then, and Ellie needed to see how they were faring, especially Carson. She could still picture the utter despair in his eyes. Regardless of her determination to keep her relationship with Grant neighborly and platonic, she would do whatever was necessary to help the kids adjust.

Through the glass front door of the law firm, Grant watched Ellie walk away. Why had he asked to see her again? Was it just to talk about the firm and his brother? Or was this a desire of a more personal nature? If it was, he'd have to cool his libido. He didn't have the time or energy for unwanted desires, personal or otherwise.

What was wrong with him? He was thinking about a pretty woman while carrying his brother's effects? But he couldn't seem to help himself. When was the last time he'd had a date? In the army, fraternization was limited to other officers, and the number of female officers was limited on the remote base, unlike if he'd been stationed in Kabul or even Kandahar, where US military facilities were larger. At the moment, his career was a lonely one, but it wouldn't always be this way. He'd date again when he was transferred back to Texas.

As he drove out of town, he occupied his rambling mind with Roger's request. The law partner was understandably concerned about confidential client information going missing, but Grant's instincts told him Roger was hiding something. Of course, Grant would much rather dive into a mystery than simply accept that Lee and Kate were dead.

He drove back to the house with sorrow clamping around his chest. AnnaBelle greeted him in the foyer, pressing her head against his legs. Grant knelt down and rubbed her neck. No doubt the dog was missing her family, too. "The kids'll be here soon."

He'd barely hung up his jacket before a bark from the dog alerted him to an approaching car. Grant let the locksmith in, and while the man rekeyed tumblers, Grant went into Lee's office and boxed up all the case files he could find. He had enough on his plate. He didn't need an imaginary conspiracy.

He'd just seen the locksmith drive off when tires grated on gravel outside. The dog leaped from her bed and bolted into the hall. Nerves humming, Grant went out onto the front porch. He pushed the whining dog back in the house with his knee and closed the screen door. A middle-aged woman in slacks and a coat exited a tan sedan. She opened the rear door. Carson slipped out, his skinny body dwarfed by a thick ski jacket. He didn't look much bigger than he had been last spring.

Grant approached the car. "Hey, Carson. Do you remember me?"

Crack! Slam.

On instinct, Grant nearly dove on top of his nephew. He stopped his forward motion just in time as the dog bolted past, reminding him he was in Scarlet Falls, not Afghanistan. The social worker's eyes bugged. Grant's pulse hammered.

"It's OK," Grant said, not sure who he was trying to reassure, the social worker, Carson, or himself.

The boy dropped to both knees and flung his arms around AnnaBelle's neck. Grant glanced back at the house. The screen door flapped against the house on one hinge. *Note to self: the screen door will not hold the dog.*

Carson loosened his grip on the retriever's neck. The dog whined, and the boy returned to the car for a red backpack. AnnaBelle took the strap, turned, and raced for the front door, backpack dangling from her mouth.

"I'll be damned," Grant muttered. He turned back to his nephew and went down on one knee. "Do you remember me, Carson? I'm Uncle—"

The boy launched himself at Grant. He caught the tiny body. Carson's arms wrapped around his shoulders with more strength than Grant expected. The boy's entire frame shook. He buried his face in Grant's sweatshirt and held on, as if he could lose Grant at any second. Overwhelmed by the boy's desperate embrace, Grant wrapped his arms around the slight frame. His eyes burned, and he blinked back unshed tears. Anger rushed through him. This should not have happened. Carson shouldn't have lost his parents.

"I'm glad to see he remembers you, Major." The woman offered a hand. In her other, she held an infant car seat with a baby strapped inside. A tiny face peered out from under a thick pink blanket. "I'm Dee Willis from child services."

Balancing Carson in one arm, Grant shook her hand. Carson was clinging so tightly, Grant could have let go and the boy wouldn't have fallen. But he would never do that.

He took the car seat, the responsibility of two children loading him down far more than their combined weight.

"Let me get the rest of their things." The social worker returned to her car.

Grant led the way inside, Carson still wrapped tightly around him. AnnaBelle spit out the backpack, then pranced and whined around Grant's legs as he led the way back to the kitchen. He set the baby seat on the floor next to the kitchen table. AnnaBelle gave her a happy sniff and rose on her hind legs to paw at Carson. Crouching down, Grant let the dog give the kid a solid slurp. The boy's grip loosened, and he reached out one hand to stroke the golden head.

Mrs. Willis set a small suitcase on the floor and a tote bag on the kitchen table. She was frowning at the dog. "There's enough formula and diapers in the bag for a few days, but she's a bit colicky."

"Colicky?"

"She cries at night."

"Oh." Grant wrote all of the baby feeding information down on a notepad by the phone.

She fixed Grant with a doubtful look. "I wouldn't let the dog get too close to the baby. Have you ever cared for an infant, Major? Because the foster family informed me that this baby is a challenge, even for an experienced caregiver."

"Yes." Technically, he'd only babysat Carson a few times each year during his annual visit, but she didn't need to know that. He gave her a level stare.

"Can you change a diaper?"

"Yes."

Her brow wrinkled as if she didn't share his confidence.

"If it's too much for you, the children can always go back into foster care," she said, and he decided he didn't like her very much.

Carson's grip tensed, the bony arm around Grant's throat pressing against his windpipe and threatening to strangle him. This was not the time to have this discussion, not with a terrified kid within earshot. Carson needed the same confidence in Grant's abilities as the troops he'd led into enemy territory.

"Ma'am, I've cleared buildings in a-hundred-and-thirty-degree heat wearing seventy pounds of body armor. Faith is a baby, not an IED. I assure you. We will be fine." He wasn't worried about feeding the kids or changing diapers. Those were tasks. Tasks were learned, but the emotional and psychological aspects of caring for two orphans terrified him. How did he talk to Carson about his parents' deaths? "My sister will be here tomorrow, and I'm expecting to hear from my brother any time."

"All right, then." She placed a business card on the table. "Call me if you need anything. We'll need to have a discussion about permanent arrangements for the children."

"Thank you." He showed the insensitive bitch out, with Carson clinging to him as if they were neck-deep in floodwaters.

Returning to the kitchen, he sat down. Carson's legs were wrapped around his waist. They sat in the quiet kitchen for a few minutes. What should he say to the kid? Faith made a fussy sound, breaking the silence.

"You hungry?" Grant asked Carson. "Sounds like Faith might be."

Carson shook his head.

"I guess it's time I figured out how to feed your sister."

Carson gave him a squeeze, then climbed off his lap. God, he was small, all bony arms and legs. His sad blue eyes peered out from under a shock of straight blond hair and freckles.

"*Can* you feed her?" Carson's look was more hopeful than doubtful.

"I'll get the hang of it," Grant bluffed. How hard could it be?

With a serious nod, the boy went to the tote bag and pulled out a bottle. "You put the powder in here. Then you add water and shake it up."

"Good to know. I'm probably going to need your advice from time to time." Grant rooted through the bag and came up with a can of formula. "Is this it?"

Carson nodded. Grant read the back of the can and mixed up the formula. The baby's fussy sounds escalated into crying. A high-pitched shriek pierced the kitchen. Grant jumped and fumbled the bottle, catching it just before it hit the floor. Faith launched into a scream that sent a flood of apprehension through Grant. *Holy . . .*

"Hurry up!" Carson covered his ears with his hands.

"Hello, Faith." Grant crouched in front of the wailing baby and unsnapped the car seat's harness. He picked her up, his efforts to be gentle hampered by her stiff body and kicking legs. He hadn't held a baby since Carson was born. He'd forgotten how fragile they seemed. He settled in a kitchen chair and tucked her in the crook of one arm. She took the bottle with a greedy mouth, her big eyes staring up at him with rapt attention while she sucked away between hiccups. He snatched a tissue from the box on the table and wiped the tears from her face. A small current of relief eased through him as she calmed and drained the bottle.

"Now what about us, Carson?" he asked.

"I'm not hungry." Carson sat next to him, resting his head on a bent arm, watching. At least while he'd been helping, he'd been reactive. Purple smudges underscored his eyes. Freckles popped on fair skin. He looked like he hadn't slept in days.

"I am. Any suggestions for lunch?"

"Waffles." Carson slid out of the chair. On his way past, he gave his baby sister an affectionate pat on the head.

"I didn't get much sleep last night," Grant said. "I could sure use a nap."

Carson pulled a box of waffles from the freezer. He dragged a step stool to the counter, eyed his uncle, and then loaded the toaster. When the waffles popped out, he put them on a plate. "Daddy always eats four, and you're bigger than him."

Eats. Present tense.

The ache in Grant's heart swelled until he wasn't sure he could swallow food. He cleared his throat. "Thanks. I don't think I can eat so many, though. Are you sure you can't help me out?"

Carson plunked a bottle of syrup down on the table. He went back to the cabinet for another plate, forks, and knives. "Mommy likes me to set the table."

"You're doing a great job." Grant kept his voice clear. Obviously, Carson wanted to talk about his parents, so talk they would, even if Grant would prefer to bury his grief until it had formed a solid scab like the thickened skin over the bits of shrapnel in his leg. His to-do list rearranged itself. Lee's estate issues got bumped. *Call school about grief counseling* shot up to number one, and *buy books on children and grieving* took the number two spot. He'd need to read a baby book, too. Kate probably had one or ten around the house.

Carson moved a waffle onto the second plate. He poured syrup over it until it floated.

Faith's bottle was empty. Grant set it on the table and eased her over one shoulder. She let out a reverberating belch that would have impressed a mess tent full of recruits. He put her back in the car seat and helped Carson cut his waffle. They dug in together. Two kids, both eating. So far, so good.

Carson gave his baby sister a suspicious glance but finished his breakfast.

Grant loaded the dishwasher. Now what? He'd planned on getting the kids to take a nap so he could dig into Lee's paperwork and make a few calls. Grant needed to know more about his brother's life. Maybe he'd ask Ellie Ross next door. She seemed kind and intelligent. And pretty. Not that *that* mattered.

"What do you want to do?" he asked Carson.

The boy lifted a shoulder. Kids needed fresh air, right?

"Do you want to go outside and play with the dog?"

Carson shook his head. He looked like he would pass out where he sat. Grant spied crayons and paper tucked under the bowl in the center of the table. The fridge was covered with colorful, primitive drawings of stick people and grass and trees.

"Would you draw me a picture?"

"OK." Carson breathed out the answer as if the request was a huge imposition.

Great, he'd had the kids less than an hour and he was floundering already. Maybe that social worker was right to doubt him. A raw, wet sound jerked his attention back to the baby just as she spewed what appeared to be ten times more than she'd eaten all over herself, the car seat, and the floor.

Karma had a sick sense of humor. The baby *was* an explosive.

"I guess I have to get her cleaned up."

Carson huffed. "Better get used to it. She does that all the time."

Carson's head was bent over his drawing. Grant lifted the baby out of her carrier, holding her at arm's length. He found clean clothes in the laundry room. He wiped her off and changed her clothes and diaper, which took longer than field stripping and cleaning his rifle. But then his M-4 didn't try to wiggle away from him. A bath would have to wait until he reconnoitered the baby-bathing facilities and did some research. Faith babbled and grabbed at her toes while Grant stuffed her into a one-piece suit with a zipper up the front. He drew the zipper up her chest, and she let loose again. Regurgitated formula splashed over both of them.

Carson looked up from his drawing and heaved a long, disgusted sigh. The situation would have been funny if the prospect of Grant not being able to care for the baby wasn't so terrifying.

The social worker's statement rang in Grant's head. *This baby is a challenge.*

Words that had seemed bitchy at the time now felt prophetic.

With her pumps in her tote and snow boots on her feet, Ellie buttoned her wool coat, pulled on her gloves, and walked out the firm's back door. She'd worked an hour over her official five p.m. quitting time to finish a rush client report, throwing off her evening schedule.

She hurried around the building to the small parking lot. Still on her to-do list was a stop at the grocery store. The sun had fallen behind the buildings an hour before, and shadows stretched over the frozen ground. The wind whipped across the lot. Her boots crunched on the half-frozen snowpack. Ellie clutched her coat lapels together and dug her keys from her pocket. Her old minivan sat in the rear of the lot, where employees were required to park. Prime spots closer to the building were reserved for clients.

Shivering, she passed into the shadow of a giant oak tree. She pressed the fob button, and her car doors unlocked with a chirp. Sliding behind the wheel, she started the engine and turned the heater on full.

Something jabbed at her hip. Ellie jumped, her heart knocking against her rib cage.

"Don't turn around," a male voice whispered.

Without moving her chin, she rotated her eyeballs down and right. Just over the center console, a gloved hand pointed a gun at her lower back. As her eyes adjusted to the dark, she saw a shadow in her peripheral vision. A man lay on the dark floor behind the van's front seat. Fear solidified in her stomach like ice.

He motioned with the barrel. "Eyes front."

Her gaze snapped forward. Her panting breaths puffed out and fogged the windshield. There was no one in sight. The only other car in the lot was Roger's Mercedes, and his office was in the front of the building. He'd never see or hear her. A hedge separated the law firm's parking area from an oral surgeon's lot next door. Not that it mattered. Their office wasn't open on Tuesdays.

Options whirled in her head. She couldn't get out of the car faster than he could pull the trigger. The way the gun protruded from between the seats, there wasn't room for her to try and grab it. The close quarters also made getting out of the way of a bullet impossible.

He prodded her again. The muzzle poked her in the kidney. "Pull out of the lot and make a left on First Street. If you shout or draw attention in any way, I will shoot you."

Light-headed, she shifted into reverse and depressed the gas pedal. The vehicle jerked backward. She stomped on the brake, and the car lurched to a halt.

"You dumb bitch," he whispered.

Ellie breathed and willed her shaking limbs to obey. She could crash the van once she got out of the parking lot. That was her only chance.

"No speeding, and if you crash this ride, I'll be able to shoot you no problem. I'm wedged tight back here. I'll be fine."

Her hopes dimmed. The air bag would deploy in her face and immobilize her. She'd still be helpless.

What did he want? Was he going to kill her? She wanted to open the door and run, to take her chances in the parking lot, where she had at least a chance of getting away. Once he took her somewhere else, he could do anything he wanted to her. But there was no way she could get out of the van fast enough.

She turned left onto First Street. Under her coat, sweat soaked through her silk blouse, and her snow boots seemed bulky and awkward on the van's pedals. Cruising at twenty-five miles an hour, she stopped at an intersection.

"W-where do you want me to go?" she asked.

"Make a left." He ground the gun into her back as he answered in the same hoarse whisper.

She drove past the elementary school, now empty and dark. He levered his upper body higher to look out the window. "Pull into the parking lot of the thrift store."

Two blocks later, she turned at a lighted sign. St. Paul's Thrift Shop closed at four. Ellie had been there many times. She'd bought most of Julia's baby clothes secondhand. Gravel and ice crunched under her tires as she drove past the converted brick bungalow that housed the used clothing shop. Inside, the building was dark. A single light by the rear door cast a yellow glow across the pavement. He could kill her right here, and there was no one close enough to hear the shot. The lot was empty, except for one car parked in the very back. Light reflected off the windshield. Was there anyone inside?

Fresh terror sent sweat rivering down her back. She could smell her own fear, amplified under the heavy wool of her coat.

"Stop," he said.

She braked and waited, her hands clenching the steering wheel like a life buoy.

"Put the van in park and raise your hands."

Ellie followed the instructions. She was alone. He might have reinforcements. She fought to keep her breathing under control. Freaking out would not help. *Think!* She had to get away, but shock paralyzed her brain. Escape seemed impossible.

He tossed something over the seat into her lap. She flinched.

"Take a good look."

Ellie dropped her gaze. An eight-by-ten envelope. She opened it and slid out two photos. She picked one up, her pulse stammering as she recognized Julia walking up the driveway after school, her full backpack dangling from one shoulder. The second photo was her grandmother stooping to pick up the paper in the driveway in front of their house.

"I know where you live. I know who you love. You will do exactly as I say or your daughter and your grandmother will suffer. Do you understand?"

Ellie's head bobbed as if her neck had no muscles.

"You're going to find the Hamilton file and give it to me."

Shock swamped Ellie. This was about the Hamilton case? "I don't know where it is—"

"I don't give a fuck. Find it or I pick one of them to hurt." Reaching forward, he collected the pictures and envelope, tucking them inside his jacket. He pulled the gun away from her back, opened the sliding van door, and got out. Baggy black pants disguised his body, and a black hooded jacket shadowed his eyes. A scarf covered the lower portion of his face. Dressed differently, she could pass him on the street with no recognition. He'd whispered their entire conversation. She couldn't even identify his voice. In fact, since he'd taken his pictures with him, she had no proof the event even occurred.

Hoodie Man leaned back inside. "Tell no one about this meeting. If you call the police, I will kill your daughter. You can't hide from me. I'm watching."

"How do I contact you?"

"You don't. You'll hear from me. If you find the file, I'll know." He closed the car door and walked toward the headlights.

Ellie's reflexes short-circuited. She sat frozen for a few seconds before she startled into action. She needed to get the hell out of that parking lot. She jerked the gearshift into drive and pulled out onto the road. Keeping an eye on her rearview mirror, she made several turns until she was sure no one had followed her. Twenty minutes later she pulled into her driveway. The grocery store would have to wait. She had to see Julia and Nan. Now.

She got out of the car and scanned her street. Widely spaced streetlights gleamed on the snow. At least a dozen cars lined the curb on her block alone. How would she know if someone was sitting inside one of them, watching her? She squinted in each vehicle as she drove past, but black windshields gave nothing away. At the corner fifty yards away, Ellie could just make out the shape of someone walking two dogs. Nothing seemed out of the ordinary. The window of the house next door glowed, and Grant's rental car was parked in the driveway of the Barretts' house. Could Grant help? In a way, they were in this together. If her extortion was tied to one of Lee's cases, the murders could likely be linked as well. Grant would focus on finding the man who'd killed his family members. Ellie wanted to keep hers alive.

Did that make them allies or adversaries?

She resisted the pull. She couldn't trust a man she barely knew. Guilt burrowed in her belly as she started up the walk. Hoodie Man *must* be Kate and Lee's killer. Ellie shouldn't help him conceal his crime, but her family's safety had to come first. She would do anything to protect her grandmother and daughter.

Anything.

At the base of her porch steps, she paused, glancing over her shoulder. Wind gusted, sweeping snow from the roof and onto Ellie's head. She shivered, her body shifting from nervous heat to cold as her adrenaline ebbed. Her gaze lingered on each car parked along the curb. Could someone be sitting in one of those vehicles?

I'm watching . . .

Chapter Eight

Lindsay
November

I slam the car door. Mom waves and drives off. Standing on the concrete apron in front of the ice-skating arena, I stare at the front of the hulking building.

Why do they hate me?

I scrape the toe of my black Converse on the cement. I'm in no rush to go inside. Mom is headed to the grocery store. I could just slip around back and wait for the free skate hour to be over. Before we moved here, I couldn't wait to get to the rink. Now I really don't care. I'm tempted to quit the team. It's not like I'm going to be an Olympic star or anything. I only skate because I love it.

The rink is the one place I've always been able to forget my problems, and now they're trying to take it away from me. At school, the hallways are covered with cameras, and teachers lurk everywhere. It's hard for the Shrew Crew to do real damage to anything but my pride. The skating arena is where my tormentors choose to get creative.

I play with my lip ring. My mom will come into the rink when she's done shopping to ask Coach Victor about my practice. If I don't skate, she'll ask questions. She'll poke and pick at me until I bleed. Then she'll blame me for my complaints. She won't let anything ruin her new life. She loves New York State. Me and Dad, not so much.

Our new home sits on almost an acre of land in a small development. Big and yellow and white, the house has four bedrooms, two stories, and a porch that spans the whole front of the building. Behind the house is a meadow and woods. After living in a furnished shoebox in San Francisco for the last six years, my parents couldn't wait to move to this country suburban bliss. A trail through the woods leads to my school, though I'm not allowed to walk. My parents don't think it's safe.

"Upstate New York will be green. We're saving so much money, you can get a horse if you want. There'll be snow in the winter." They say all this as if it's supposed to make leaving my friends and the city I love sound attractive.

I still don't buy it.

What would I do with a horse? We've never even had a cat. The apartment was tight for the three of us. There was no room for a hamster or fishbowl, but to me, it was home.

We've been here three weeks. So far, the only thing that has been OK is the weather. To remind myself of this one and only high point, I close my eyes and turn my face to the afternoon sun. Its rays warm my cheeks and turn the inside of my eyelids blood red. So far, early winter has been mild. Unlike my parents, I'm not looking forward to ice and snow. I have no idea why my parents think this is such a BFD. It's not like I've never seen snow. In California, we drove up to Tahoe a couple of times to snowboard. It wasn't my thing. I spent more time flat on my face than standing on the board. On the bright side, if the lake down the road freezes, I'll be able to skate outside. No need to come to the rink.

I dig my phone out of my pocket. No messages from Jose back home. I miss California and my friends with an empty ache, something like hunger, but it can't be alleviated with food. No worries, though. Jose, best friend not boyfriend, isn't home from school yet. It's only lunchtime in Cali. He'll text me later, and then maybe I won't feel so alone. If the wireless signal holds, we can even Skype tonight.

I miss going to the Bay City Ice Rink with him every day after school to practice. Jose is a male figure skater. He knows what it's like to be bullied. I just want to go home and get away from this nightmare of suburbia. I miss walking down to the wharf and listening to the sea lions bark. I miss everything from the steep streets to the fresh seafood. The sushi here sucks and so do the kids.

And on that note, I'd better get inside. Someone is coming out. A member of the advanced team and her mom. Their practice must be over. Maybe Regan and Autumn, my nemeses, will already be gone.

Smiling, the mom holds the door open, a gaping mouth waiting to swallow my will to live. I'm being overly dramatic, but that's how it feels, this sense of impending misery that crushes my chest.

I pass through the lobby and walk down the hallway to the rink. Free skate has started. A dozen skaters are warming up. Watching them, Coach Victor leans on the rink half wall. He nods to me as I pass by. I scan the ice. No sign of Regan or Autumn. Oh, wait. Their dads approach Victor. The coach is trying to watch his skaters. I've only been here a few weeks, but I know the score. It's not that different than back home. Regan and Autumn are the stars of the team. Their dads pay the arena a lot of money each month. They've bought and paid for Victor's full attention. He gives it to them now. I catch a snatch of their conversation, something about Victor needing to step it up. If they don't make nationals next year, they'll be looking for a new coach.

I feel sorry for Victor. He's been nice to me, but let's face it. He's been with the club for seven years and not a single one of his skaters has won a major event yet. I know some of this is luck. He can't control who joins the club, but the parents will look for any excuse when their precious little darlings lose. Plus, there's a rumor going around about Victor and one of the married skating moms, and that this isn't his first indiscretion. Seems like Victor is a dog. Ew. I can't even think about a guy that old doing it. I don't know if it's true, but a scandal won't help him keep his job. He's already one losing season away from unemployment.

Another door leads to the locker room. Sweat gathers in my armpits as I traverse the narrow hall and push through the door marked Girls. If Regan and Autumn aren't on the ice, then they must be in here. What can I do? Victor saw me. I have to get my butt on the ice or he'll tell Mom I'm wasting my practice time—and her money. He seems to have taken an interest in me.

Not that this is a biggie. He's not the greatest coach in the world. But his praise feels good anyway.

Voices ricochet on cinder block walls and rows of metal lockers set up in four U-shaped sections. Six girls are changing in the first niche. No sign of Regan or Autumn yet, but I know they're here. My pulse skips, and my stomach turns queasy. I walk past the second alcove, and there they are, dressed and packing their equipment into duffels. Five more minutes and I would have missed them.

With their pretty highlights and trendy mall clothes, they look more like California natives than me. Like every other day, the aggression and hatred in their eyes makes me shudder inside. The metallic din fades into the background. Their hostility becomes palpable, an invisible force that presses against my body and squeezes the air from my lungs.

They hated me from the very first time they saw me skate. Why? Is it my Goth clothes? Compared to my friends back home, I'm pretty tame. I don't even have any tats. Black hair, combat boots, and a lip ring aren't exactly unusual. Plenty of kids dress like me at school. But at the rink, pretty is as pretty does. I stand out like Frankenstein on the ice. I only made the novice skate team, so why do they want to get rid of me so badly?

I lift my chin and turn my eyes toward the third section, where three younger girls are closing their lockers and gathering equipment bags to leave. As I pass Regan and Autumn, my foot catches and I hurtle forward. My chin hits the concrete. My teeth snap together, sending an ear-ringing shaft of pain through my face and head. My duffel slides across the floor and hits the feet of one of the girls walking toward me.

"Hey, watch where you're going, freak." She kicks it away.

I look down. The corner of Regan's bag sticks out into the aisle. She approaches me. "Oh my God. Are you all right?" Her voice is sickly sweet, and the evil slant to her lips sends her true message.

"I'm fine," I mumble as I get to my feet. My chin burns where it scraped on the floor.

"Too bad you're so clumsy." She returns to Autumn and whispers something in her ear. Autumn's shoulders shake as she laughs.

I give her a glare, then roll my eyes at her, but my attempt at pretending she doesn't bother me isn't fooling anyone. Humiliation heats my skin and stirs the orange juice in my stomach into a nasty, acidic combination. My face is hot. My skin is pale, so I know my cheeks are flaming red by the time I get to the empty alcove and claim a locker. The commotion draws girls out from their locker nooks. Half the kids are smirking. The other half look away and pretend not to notice. No one else wants to be Regan and Autumn's next target. I don't blame them. It sucks. Why should they stick up for me? They don't even know me.

My eyes burn, but I will not cry.

Instead, I try to shrink, to blend into the gray metal lockers around me as I change into the black tights I wear for practice.

Regan and Autumn leave, heads bent together. They are talking about me, maybe laughing, maybe planning something awful for my future. I can tell. I can feel their animosity wafting through the air even after they've left the locker room. The other kids won't even look at me. A girl walks by, listening to her iPod. The tinny sound of music leaks from her earbuds. I sit on the bench to lace my skates. Once I get out to the rink, I'll be fine. The locker room is their main torture chamber. On the ice, Coach Victor is strict.

I don't even want to skate anymore. I know that's their ultimate goal, so I guess they've already won. With a deep breath I launch to my feet and walk out to the rink. Regan and Autumn are standing with their dads and Victor. They watch me with way too much interest as I leave my skate guards on the wall and start to warm up. My muscles loosen. A sense of freedom flows through me, as it does every time I lace up my skates.

"Get warmed up. I want to see you working on that double axel," Victor shouts as I skate by.

I see Regan lean over and say something to Autumn. They laugh.

"If you want to make nationals next year, you don't have time to worry about anyone else. Focus on your own routine." Victor's admonishment echoes across the ice.

I appreciate his support, but the reprimand will give them one more reason to hate me.

Chapter Nine

The sunlight gleamed on a fresh layer of snow. Ellie turned into the narrow alley that ran alongside the firm. Her tires grated on the inch of snow the plow left on top of the gravel. She emerged in the rear parking lot. Fresh powder clung to the budding branches of the mature oak at the rear of the plowed square. From a brilliant blue sky, sunlight glittered blindingly bright on whatever it touched.

If she hadn't been worried about her family's safety, the scene would have been lovely.

Ellie parked in the rear of the lot. Her heart drummed as she unlocked her doors and got out of the vehicle. She crossed the lot. On the rear stoop, she knocked snow from her boots and gave her surroundings a final scan before inserting her key into the door. She disengaged the alarm. With hesitant steps, she glanced into the break room-kitchen combo. Empty. Her ears strained for sound but she heard nothing except the rumble of the furnace and whoosh of hot air from the radiators.

All seemed normal, except that last night a man had threatened to kill her daughter.

Ellie changed her shoes and got to work, starting in Frank's office.

With shaky fingers, Ellie slid the USB drive into the slot on his computer. The office was silent around her. At seven a.m., no one else had arrived yet. Roger would come in around eight, the rest of the employees shortly after. This might be her only chance to get a look at Frank's computer files. Many of the attorneys worked late, but early hours were less common. But if anyone did come in early, she would say she was doing software updates. Without an in-house IT specialist, Roger preferred Ellie take care of the simple, routine tasks rather than pay for a computer tech. She was already on the payroll. Employees were accustomed to seeing her on their computers. Hopefully, Roger would support her, since he asked her to snoop. Not that she cared much about fraud at the moment.

Frank was the only person at the firm she could imagine had any reason to snag the Hamilton file. He was also the newest hire and had been in competition with Lee for partnership. Frank directly benefitted from Lee's death. So she'd search his desk first.

On a tight timetable, she copied the hard drive of Frank's desktop to the memory stick. The orange light blinked as the machine worked. She spun the chair to open the drawer in the credenza behind the desk and skim through the files. The crunch of tires on gravel outside startled her. Someone was here. She glanced at the clock. It was barely seven twenty. No one else ever came in the office this early. The flash drive's blinking orange light taunted her.

Come on.

She closed the credenza. The orange light went dark. She shut down the computer and bolted for the kitchen. With shaking hands, she measured coffee into a filter. The noise outside must have been someone next door. It didn't matter. She'd accomplished what she'd come in early to do. All she could do now was pray Frank's computer skills weren't adequate for him to know she'd copied his documents. She should have Roger's support, but Frank would complain to the senior Peyton. In confrontations with his father, Roger got wishy-washy.

Was it possible that Frank had taken the file home? He'd moved into that office before she'd finished sorting Lee's files. She could be searching the law offices in vain because Frank was holding the very file she needed. The file that would keep her family alive. Even worse, the file could be in Lee's BMW. There'd been no report of the car turning up, but the thought that the information her extortionist wanted could be impossible to locate sent nausea roiling through her stomach.

What would she do if Hoodie Man came back and she didn't have the file? And who was he?

She could rule out two people immediately. There was no way Grant would fit behind the seat of her van. She also eliminated Roger. He'd been in his office last night while Hoodie Man waited in Ellie's vehicle. Hmm. On second thought, was it possible that her boss had gone out the front door and circled around to the parking lot? But why would her boss threaten her to get the file? He'd already asked her to find it for him.

Her head ached with too many unanswered questions. She filled the coffee pot and pressed On.

She glanced at the clock. She still had time to search the rest of the desks. Leaving the dripping coffee machine, she settled at one of the paralegals' desks. While the computer copied files onto her flash drive, she silently opened and searched desks. A half hour later, Ellie had found nothing even remotely related to the Hamilton file.

"Ellie?" Roger's voice snapped her out of her thoughts.

She snagged her memory stick and stuffed it into her jacket pocket. Smoothing her skirt, she emerged from the paralegal's cubicle. Roger stood in front of her desk.

Smiling, she walked toward her boss. "Good morning."

"You're in early. What were you doing?"

"Software updates."

"This early?" He raised a conspiratorial eyebrow. "Did you encounter anything interesting?"

"No, sorry."

"Well, shit." Frowning, he glanced at his watch. "I have a nine o'clock appointment. Have you made coffee?"

"Yes, I'll fill a carafe." Ellie hurried back to the kitchen and poured coffee into a thermal pot.

"Liar." Frank startled her.

She dropped the coffee pot. Hot liquid splashed up her legs.

Frank jumped backward. The sloshing coffee barely missed his pants. "Are you all right?"

"Yes." Miraculously, the pot hadn't broken when it hit the vinyl floor, but coffee splattered her pantyhose and shoes. Burning patches on her shins jolted her into action. She stepped away, wet a paper towel with cold water, and pressed it against her shin. She cleaned off her shoes then tossed paper towels on the floor.

"Let me help you." Frank squatted next to her and tossed napkins on the mess.

"It's all right. I've got it." Ellie dumped the soggy mess into the trash and started a fresh pot.

Frank sauntered out, glancing back to toss a caught-you grin over his shoulder. "I saw you searching Sue's desk. But don't worry. I won't tell. Your secret is safe with me."

Ugh. Frank was not the guy she'd choose to entrust with secrets. Watching the coffee drip, Ellie put a hand on her aching temple. She didn't have the energy to worry about Frank. His little games couldn't compete with extortion—unless he was Hoodie Man.

The dream made no sense. Grant hadn't witnessed his brother's murder, so why did he keep seeing it in his mind?

His eyelids were lined with sandpaper, or at least that's what it felt like when he opened his eyes. His view was dry and blurry. He was oddly weighed down, and a steady tapping noise sounded like a bomb ticking. He blinked. His vision cleared, and a tousled blond head came into focus.

Carson sprawled across his body. Grant's shoulders hung off the edge of the family room sofa. Next to them, the baby swing clicked each time it passed the center line of its arc.

Ah, yes. The Night From Hell replayed in his mind. He'd tucked Carson into bed and walked the baby up and down the halls until two a.m., when a nightmare brought the little boy back, tearful and hiccupping. The dog had picked bedlam hour for a barking fit, too. The swing had become his savior. The instructions stated that babies weren't supposed to sleep in the damned things, but these were desperate times.

Grant closed his eyes. Another hour of sleep might dull the ache in his head.

"Uncle Grant." A tiny finger pried open his eyelid. "Are you awake?"

Grant opened his other eye. "I am."

Carson dropped Grant's eyelid and propped his chin on his hands, bony elbows in the center of Grant's chest. His blue eyes were a scant three inches from Grant's face. Hearing the boy's voice, AnnaBelle jumped up from her bed in the corner, trotted to the sofa, and stuck her wet nose between their faces.

"She has to go outside." Carson squirmed off Grant's body.

A knee squashed his groin. "Oof."

Removing his nephew's knee from his crushed privates, Grant eased upright. Carson ran to the back door and opened it. AnnaBelle bolted out into the yard.

"She's OK out there by herself?" Grant squinted out the window. Last night's clouds were gone. In a brilliant, crystal-blue sky, sunshine slanted across four inches of fresh snow.

"She'll be right back." Carson went to the refrigerator and took out a juice box. He brought it back to Grant. "Can you open this?"

"Sure." Grant shoved the straw through the hole and offered it to his nephew.

"You hafta put the flaps up or else it'll squirt all over."

"Gotcha. Flaps up." Grant handed it back.

Carson took a long pull from the skinny straw. "Am I going to school today?"

Grant considered the exhausted eyes looking up at him. On his list of many phone calls was Carson's elementary school. "Do you want to go to school today?"

Carson shook his head.

"Then you'll stay home today." Grant checked the baby. Still sleeping. "We'll talk about that again in a few days, all right?"

Carson nodded.

"Waffles?" Grant heaved to his feet and stretched his back. He felt like he'd been on an all-night march. He needed coffee. Now. He shuffled into the kitchen and started the machine.

Sunlight spilled through the back window. What time was it? He blinked at a clock on the wall. Ten a.m.

Faith stirred, and Grant started a bottle. He'd already learned that a screaming fit before a feeding increased his chances of being firehosed with baby gak. In an exhausted blur, he fed the kids breakfast. No, wait. Brunch. Whatever.

He mainlined coffee and cleaned up the kitchen. Before he had time to think about a shower, it was noon. The doorbell rang. AnnaBelle sprinted for the front of the house.

"Maybe that's Aunt Hannah." Praying help had arrived, Grant rubbed his bleary eyes.

Carson didn't respond. Carrying the baby, Grant went to the front door. He peered through the sidelight. His sister stood on the porch. One hand rested on the handle of a spinner suitcase. A briefcase was slung from her shoulder. He opened the door wide. AnnaBelle surged forward.

Breezing through the doorway, Hannah halted the dog with one raised hand and a command. "Off."

The dog's tail stopped midwag, drooping to the floor.

"Since when don't you like dogs?" Grant leaned over to kiss Hannah on the cheek.

From her pointy heels to the short cap of polished blond hair, his sister looked every inch the corporate attorney. She stopped in the foyer to slide her long black coat down her arms.

"Since I traded your hand-me-down jeans for adult clothing." She went to the closet and hung her coat. Her tall, thin frame was draped in a white cashmere sweater and pale gray slacks. Against the peeling green wallpaper, her Saks attire looked elegant and out of place.

Hannah walked closer. Her heels clicked on the scratched parquet. A small, curious smile tilted the corner of her mouth. She reached out and gave the baby's foot a tentative squeeze. "You must be Faith."

"Haven't you seen her before?"

"No. Before Jakarta I was in Berlin. Before that, Prague." She lifted her gaze from the baby to Grant. Her eyes misted. "How are you, Grant?"

The air left his chest. "I don't know. A little overwhelmed by it all, I guess. I didn't expect to be the first one here."

Nodding, she sniffed. "I came as soon as I could get away from the negotiations."

"Wait. You didn't come right away?"

She backed up a quarter step. "You don't just step away from a billion-dollar deal."

"I stepped away from a war, for Christ's sake." Grant gritted his teeth and stopped. Arguing with Hannah for being Hannah was pointless. His sister had made partner in a high-powered firm by being single-minded and ruthless. She would never settle for less than complete world domination. Not for the first time, Grant wondered if their father had picked the wrong child to push into the military. The Colonel had wanted a general in the family. Hannah would make a great general. Or dictator.

"Never mind. You're here now and that's what matters." Grant let it go. As they'd learned this week, life was too short. "Why don't you say hi to Carson before you go change?"

The grief hit her eyes again, and she struggled to suppress it. She wasn't a cold person. She felt plenty, but like the Colonel, she'd never been comfortable with emotional expression, hers or anyone else's. "Where is he?"

"The kitchen." Grant led the way.

"Hey, Carson," Hannah said in a soft voice from the center of the room.

Grant elbowed her forward, prodding her toward their nephew. Hannah shot him a don't-rush-me glare before sitting next to the boy. Grant gave her credit for going to Carson's level.

"What are you drawing?" she asked, tilting her head to see the picture.

Carson shrugged. "A man."

"He's crying," she noted. "Is that a house?"

The little boy nodded. "It's our house."

"Why is the man crying?"

Bony shoulders lifted and fell. "I dunno."

"I like the shamrock." She rose. "I'm going upstairs to change."

She was going upstairs to cry, Grant thought. "I'm in the guest room at the end of the hall. Take the room next to it." Lee had wanted the big house for family get-togethers. The first time in years that Grant, Hannah, and Mac would all be under one roof, Lee was gone.

Hannah brushed past him, her mouth tight, her control slipping.

He handed her one of the new house keys. "Are you all right?"

Nodding, she closed her fist around the key and turned away. Hannah hadn't always been so distant. None of them had weathered Mom's death well. Grant and Hannah had run from Scarlet Falls and all its disappointments as soon as possible. Mac had a local address, but he spent half the year traveling all over the globe. Only Lee had stayed.

Grant gave her a half hour to get herself together. He inspected the contents of the baby's bag. Like his own pack, it focused on bottled water, dry clothing, and sanitation items. He restocked items that seemed to require restocking, then added a couple of kiddy granola bars he found in the pantry in case Carson got hungry while they were out.

"Hey, Carson, let's take a drive out to Uncle Mac's place." Grant was hoping there'd be some sign of his youngest brother at his cabin. It wouldn't hurt Carson to catch a combat nap in the car. The kid was exhausted.

At the foot of the steps, he called for his sister. She'd changed into jeans and boots but still wore the cashmere sweater. Her face was bare, the makeup washed away, her eyes puffy and red-rimmed. Casual and clean-faced, she looked ten years younger and more like the girl he'd grown up with than a corporate attorney.

"Let's take a ride out to Mac's place."

"You still haven't heard from him?" She frowned.

"No."

"I'm sure he's fine." But she didn't sound convinced. "You don't think he found out about Lee and Kate and—"

"I have no reason to think Mac is in trouble." Grant shook his head. "But I'll feel better if we find him."

"Me, too." Hannah nodded. "Let's go then."

Mac hadn't relapsed in the ten years since he'd gotten out of rehab, but if he'd found out about the murders . . .

"You want the baby or the box of files?" Grant nodded toward Lee's office.

"I'll get the box," Hannah said.

Not surprised, Grant took Carson out front and opened the back door of the rental car.

Carson shook his head. "I hafta be in a booster seat."

Shoot. Of course both kids needed safety seats. "Where's your booster seat?"

"In Mommy's van." Carson trotted back into the house and emerged with a set of keys. They trooped around the house to the detached garage. Kate's silver minivan was outfitted for kids. Toys, bottled water, snacks, and little nets to stow everything. Carson climbed into his booster seat and fastened his seat belt. Grant snapped Faith's seat into its base unit. He leaned on the carpet. Crumbs embedded his palm. His knee squashed an empty juice box.

Hannah came out of the house with AnnaBelle on her leash. "She was whining. I didn't see why she couldn't ride along."

Grant opened the rear door for the dog. Hannah put the box of files in the cargo area. AnnaBelle jumped in. The insides of the van windows were already smeared with dog slobber. Not the dog's first car ride. Hannah rode shotgun.

He started the engine. "When was the last time you talked to Mac?"

She lifted a shoulder. "I haven't talked to Mac or Lee in over a month."

"Me either," Grant said. "Were we always like this? I seemed to remember we were closer as kids."

Hannah sighed. "When Mom died, everything changed."

"True." Grant backed out of the driveway.

Mom had been the backbone of the family. She'd handled four young kids with a husband who was away most of the time, and when he finally came home, he was paralyzed.

"Lee used to call me every Sunday." Hannah shook a piece of hair out of her eyes. "But the last couple of years, I got the impression he was swamped and stressed at work. We talked less and less. I was all over the world. The time differences were a pain." She sighed. "None of my excuses will change the fact that he's gone. I should have called him more, and now I can't."

Nothing altered reality and instilled regret with the same permanence as death.

Julia stepped off the bus and shrugged into her backpack, the weight of the straps digging into her shoulders. She fished her phone out of her pocket. Three text messages displayed on the screen. All of her friends were already home. None of *them* took the bus. They all drove to and from school. She was going to be sixteen in a couple of months. She'd get her own driver's license. But she doubted it would matter. They couldn't afford another car, and none of her friends lived close enough to give her a ride.

She scrolled past the first two messages to the one from Taylor, another thing that didn't make her mom's short approved list. But at some point, a girl had do what a girl had to do, and Julia was sick of being left out of all the fun. She didn't drink or do drugs. Her grades were straight *A*s. Instead of being rewarded, her mom practically kept her prisoner with a bunch of ridiculous rules. She wasn't allowed to date older boys. Taylor was eighteen, and the only boy she was interested in. Julia's fun was limited to skating, and now even that would suck without Mrs. Barrett as her coach. She flicked a tear from her cheek.

A funny sensation tickled the back of her neck, like someone was watching her. She glanced around, but there was no one in sight. She looked ahead. Her house was two blocks from the bus stop. One block left.

She went back to her message from Taylor.

Can u get out tonight?

Omigod. He wanted to go out with her.

Don't act too excited. She texted back: maybe.

That prickly feeling itched her neck again. She glanced behind her. A white van with a ladder on the roof sat at the curb in the middle of the block. A man in green coveralls was leaning into the back. Just a workman. Her phone vibrated. She opened another text message.

Taylor: Maybe?

Julia: u kno, crazy mom

Taylor: I can come get u

Julia hesitated, thumbs hovering above her phone. Guilt passed over her, but excitement crowded it out of her mind. If her mom was reasonable, she wouldn't have to sneak around. She typed k and sent the message.

Taylor: What time?

Julia considered. Mom usually worked on the house renovations until around eleven o'clock. It would have to be late, after Mom settled into a deep sleep. At least AnnaBelle was back at the Barretts' house. There was no way she would have been able to sneak past the ever-alert golden retriever.

12, she texted.

Taylor: K.

Goose bumps raised on her arms. Suddenly anxious, Julia zipped her jacket higher and glanced around. The white van sat empty. The man was gone. Everything was normal. Her sudden attack of nerves must be from the decision she'd just made. She didn't care. She'd never disobeyed her mom before. OK, she had, but not like this. Sneaking out was a whole new level of deception. If she got caught, she'd be in big trouble. But she was going out tonight. Seeing Taylor would be worth the risk.

Chapter Ten

"The turnoff is coming up."

"I see it." Grant slowed and steered onto the dirt road that led up to Mac's cabin. The minivan bumped along the frozen ruts.

Hannah glanced in the back. "Hope this doesn't wake them."

Both kids slept, heads lolling against the sides of their car seats. Grant parked in a cleared area in front of the cabin. Mac's beat-up Jeep sat in front of the house. Mud splattered the fenders and windshield.

"Wait here with the kids," he said. "I'll see if he's inside."

He closed the door softly, went up onto the porch, and knocked. No answer. Cupping his hand over his eyes, he looked through the window but didn't see anyone. He tried another window. Mac's car keys were on the kitchen table next to a backpack. He must be inside. Why wasn't he answering? Anxiety welled in Grant's chest. He pounded on the front door with a fist.

"Hold on," someone shouted within. A minute later the door opened, and a rumpled Mac stood in the doorway. Sporting a scraggly two-week beard and bloodshot eyes, he was barefoot, dressed only in a pair of unbuttoned jeans. He dragged a hand through his bushy blond bedhead. "Grant?"

"Where the hell have you been?" Grant shouldered his way into the cabin. "I've been trying to reach you for days."

"I got home about four this morning."

Grant scanned his brother's bedraggled appearance. *Please. Please, let Mac not be using again.* He needed his brother's help. "Where were you?"

"Not doing anything bad. I swear." Mac held up a hand. "I was finishing up my study on a family of river otters on the Scarlet River. Been camping for almost a week. My phone battery died last Friday. Not that it matters. No cell reception out there anyway."

Grant exhaled the breath he'd been unconsciously holding. "You can't do that to me, Mac."

"You need to have a little faith, Grant," Mac shot back. "I know I fucked up big-time, but that was a long time ago." He blinked a couple of times, then his gaze sharpened. "Wait a minute. You're not due home from Afghanistan for two more months." Apprehension dawned in his bleary eyes. "Who died? Dad?"

Shaking his head, Grant guided his youngest brother into a chair. His relief that Mac was all right shifted to dread at having to break the news. Mac's butt went down hard, his eyes hardening, preparing for the worst.

"Lee and Kate," Grant said softly.

Mac's face went blank for a few seconds, as if he couldn't comprehend the words. He stared back at Grant, the shock and horror gradually sliding over his expression. "No."

Grant closed his eyes. Mac's disbelief brought back his own reaction to receiving the news a few days before. Pain burst fresh in his chest like a flashbang. He turned toward the kitchenette. Giving his brother a minute to absorb the news, he went through the motions of making coffee, though probably neither of them wanted it.

"Car accident?" Mac's train of thought echoed Grant's original assumption when he'd gotten the call in Afghanistan.

The coffee pot hissed as Grant dropped into the chair across from Mac. There was no way to smooth the news over. "No. They were murdered. Not sure why. Robbery maybe."

Mac's mouth opened, but no sound came out.

"I know." Grant rubbed his eyes with his fingertips. "I can't wrap my head around it either."

"That can't be right. Not Lee and Kate—" Mac's voice cracked. His Adam's apple bobbed as he swallowed hard.

Grant got up, filled a glass with water, and set it on the table in front of his brother. Mac stared at the water. His spine snapped rigid. "Where are the kids?"

"They fell asleep in the car. Hannah's outside with them." Grant summed up his last twenty-four hours. "Child services delivered them yesterday. Last night was rough. Faith screamed. Carson cried. No one slept."

"I can't believe they spent three days in foster care. How do they seem? Are they OK?"

"I don't know what's normal for them. The baby pukes a lot."

"I think that's pretty normal for her. How about Carson?"

"Quiet. Exhausted. Terrified," Grant said. "You'll probably be a better judge than me."

"Why would you say that?"

"You see him more than I do."

"Not really. I'm not here much. I was in South America most of the winter. I'm supposed to go back next month."

The coffee pot beeped. Grant got up and poured two cups of coffee. "South America?"

"Giant river otters."

"Do you have to go?"

"Only if I want to keep my job, my grant, and continue the research I've been working on for the past three years," Mac said. "Why?"

"The kids. Someone has to raise them." Grant set the mugs on the table and sat down.

Mac scrubbed his face with both hands, then flattened his hair. "Yeah, I guess it's you, me, or Hannah."

They exchanged a look.

"Right. You or me," Mac qualified. He lifted a fist over his shoulder. "You want to shoot for it?"

"Rock paper scissors isn't going to cut it." Grant snorted. "They aren't the last piece of pie."

"No, they're not." Mac sighed. "I'm sorry. You're going to have to give me a little time to take this all in. I still can't believe . . ."

"I know."

"The police are sure it's them?"

Grant wished with all his heart he could say no, that the police could be mistaken about Lee and Kate's identities, but he couldn't do that. "Yeah, they're sure."

Mac slammed a fist on the table. "How the hell does a suburban lawyer get killed in a robbery?"

Donnie scanned the residential street. Daylight wasn't the best time for a break-in, but the house was empty. The big guy staying at the Barretts' house had even taken the dog with him. Donnie got out of the white van. The rear windows were heavily tinted to block prying eyes. He'd put a few tools and a big metal box with a handle in the back in case anyone looked. The ladder he'd secured to the roof rack solidified his cover and had come in handy a few times.

He got out and grabbed a clipboard. His dark green coveralls, emblazoned with Robinson's Gutters & Siding on the back, gave him a great excuse to circle the yard and study the exterior of the house.

At the back door, he glanced around. No one in sight. He pulled the key ring from his pocket. None of the four keys fit. Damn. Either the Barretts hadn't carried a key to their own house or someone had changed the locks.

Donnie walked back to the van. Opening the rear door, he slid a glass cutter into his pocket and picked up a measuring wheel. Rolling the wheel in front of him, he measured his way around to the rear of the house. A large bush in the flower bed concealed the air conditioning unit. Allowed to grow untrimmed, the shrub also shielded the laundry room window. Behind the cover of the evergreen, he climbed onto the AC box and cut the window glass. A flip of the lock gave him access. He paused for a full minute. No beeping. No alarm. No security system. Sweet. He lifted the sash and pulled his body through the opening. Inside, a few tugs straightened his coveralls.

He started his search upstairs. An hour passed. Then two. Frustration built as he moved to the first floor. He'd had two objectives. Two. And he couldn't deliver. The killing had gone off without a hitch, but the recovery was fucked. If he were playing baseball, a batting average of five hundred would command respect. But in his world, anything less than a perfect score was failure. The agreement was all or nothing. He wouldn't get paid half for completing 50 percent of his objectives, and leaving a job unfinished wouldn't help his future employment opportunities.

Another hour later, he rifled through the last kitchen drawer. Damn it. Not here.

His gaze fell on a few kid's drawings on the fridge. He stiffened. Blue shamrocks. Wait. It was almost St. Patrick's day. Maybe the picture was just a coincidence. The kid could be color blind or plain weird. He walked closer and peered at another drawing of a man. Right under the crayon man's eye sat a hollow teardrop.

Mother. Fucker.

He pulled up his sleeve and inspected the ink blue shamrock on the inside of his wrist. A glance in the chrome toaster mirror showed him the empty teardrop tattooed below his right eye.

The teardrop had been the mark of humiliation, drawn on his face while he'd been pinned to the concrete by four prisoners. The Aryan shamrock represented his revenge. They'd helped him kill the BFG gang member who'd raped and marked him. Killing the rival gang member had gotten him into the AB. He hadn't had much choice, but "blood in, blood out" meant that the Brotherhood now owned him for life. He was not fucking going back to prison. He was done with that shit.

He must have fucked up during one of his visits to the house. That kid had gotten a good look at him. He now had a new objective.

The kid had to be eliminated.

The cabin door opened, and Hannah carried a squalling Faith inside. A bleary-eyed Carson trailed behind her, followed by the prancing dog.

"I think she's hungry." Hannah handed Faith to Grant as if the baby were a live grenade, but then considering the projectile vomiting, the analogy was fair.

Mac rubbed behind AnnaBelle's ears. "How's the happiest dog on earth?"

Grant mixed formula, and Faith sucked greedily.

"Maybe you should think about eating slower," he said to her.

She batted her eyes and ignored him.

Carson wandered aimlessly around Mac's cramped quarters. He stopped in front of a fishbowl on the sofa table. "Uncle Mac, your fish is dead. Again." He fixed Mac with an accusing stare.

"Oh, yeah." Mac walked over to stand beside Carson. "I meant to drop him off at my neighbor's house. I knew there was something I was supposed to do before I left." He gave Carson a hug. "How are you, buddy?"

"I'm OK," the boy said in a small voice. He looped an arm over AnnaBelle's neck.

Mac picked up the fishbowl and headed for the hallway that led to the back of the cabin. A toilet flushed. He came back out into the main room and washed his hands. "Are you hungry?"

Shaking his head, Carson crossed the room and climbed up onto the chair next to Grant. Carson knelt and peered over Grant's shoulder at the baby. "Is she done?"

"Almost. You want to go home?"

Carson nodded, then rested his forehead against Grant's shoulder.

"OK. We found Uncle Mac, who promised not to turn his phone off again. We can go as soon as your sister is done eating."

"Is she gonna puke?"

"Let's hope not."

Faith did *not* barf, which Grant considered progress. He loaded the kids into the van, then turned to Mac, who'd followed them outside. "We need to make some plans."

Mac nodded. "I need some time to get myself together."

Grant opened the car door. "OK. Don't take too long. And I meant what I said about your phone. Keep it on and charged. I really need your help, Mac."

"I got it." Hopefully, Mac would remember his phone better than his fish. For a smart guy, he could be spacey. "I'll be over first thing in the morning."

Grant got into the car.

"Any ideas for dinner?" he asked Hannah.

"It's not even close to dinnertime." She shook her head and turned her face to stare out the passenger window. Like him, she'd learned about the murders from half a world away, with no family member to soften the shocking blow, and she didn't look like she was handling Lee and Kate's deaths well.

At least she probably wasn't seeing a guy's face repeatedly blown to bits in her sleep.

"Our mealtimes are a little messed up today." Grant looked in the rearview mirror. The kid had refused to eat the peanut butter and jelly sandwich Grant had made him for lunch. "Carson? Any requests for dinner. How about chicken nuggets?" To get a meal into the kid, Grant would even resort to fast food.

Carson just shook his head. Grant drove the remaining twenty minutes in worried silence. At the house, he pulled around back and put the van into the garage. When he opened the rear door, he saw the box of files that he'd forgotten to drop off at the law firm.

Tomorrow. He was too damned tired to do it today.

Hannah unlocked the back door, and they all went into the kitchen. Grant flipped on the light. He set the car seat on the floor. Barking, AnnaBelle tore down the hall, her paws sending the carpet runner flying.

Grant scanned the room. The papers he'd left in neat stacks on the table were askew. The kitchen drawers hung open. Items on the counter had been shifted. Grabbing the baby and the dog's collar, he turned and herded them all back out the door. He could hear AnnaBelle lunging against the front door.

"What's wrong?" Hannah resisted.

He whispered in her ear. "Someone was in the house."

Chapter Eleven

Grant hustled them back to the van. He put the kids and dog inside and handed the keys to Hannah. "Lock the doors, drive down the street, and call the police."

"Where are you going?" Hannah protested.

"I'm going to check the house."

"But—"

"I'll be fine." He closed the van door.

As soon as the vehicle pulled away, Grant turned back toward the door. Anger and purpose sped his strides as he sprinted up the walkway. God help anyone he found in his brother's home.

He crept inside through the door he'd left open. He listened, but the house was silent. He stopped in the kitchen and selected the utility knife from the block on the counter. Rage boiled in his veins and blurred his thoughts as he stalked into the hallway. Reverse gripping the handle, he started searching rooms. The office and dining room were clear. If someone was in the house, he'd find him.

Grant walked up the stairs. He slid into the kids' rooms, checked their closets, and peered under beds, then crossed the hall to Lee and Kate's room.

Grant stood in the center of the master, listening for a creak of hardwood that would give away an intruder. In his peripheral vision, a curtain moved. He crept across the floor with silent feet and swept the fabric aside, the blade poised for attack. But the space was empty. Air from the floor radiator blew into his face and moved the drapes.

With his fingers clenched on the knife handle, he turned away. Clothes hung from half-open drawers as if they'd exploded. A pair of silk panties lay in the middle of the room. The intruder had gone through Kate's intimates. Grant's fury compounded as he eased back into the hallway and trod toward the guest rooms, then went up to the third floor and checked the attic.

A wide-open, dusty—and empty—space greeted him.

Disappointment flooded him. One minute with his brother's killer. That's all he wanted. That's all he needed.

Breathing hard, he stopped at the base of the attic steps. To do what? He hadn't had a choice in Iraq and Afghanistan. He'd killed to protect other soldiers. He'd killed for his country, but to kill for pure revenge would be different. He looked down at the knife in his hand. If Grant had found someone behind that curtain, would he have slit the intruder's throat? Without even making sure he was the same person who'd killed Lee and Kate? The answer was a disturbing maybe.

Frankly, he wasn't sure what he would have done.

He dragged the sleeve of his sweatshirt over his sweating forehead. His adrenaline rush ebbed, leaving his hands shaky. He flexed his fingers. The physical letdown would pass. His fury, however, remained at low simmer in his gut. He breathed in and out and willed his anger to cool. He needed to control his temper. Carson and Faith were reliant on him to take care of them. He couldn't lose it.

Grant jogged down the stairs and peered out the living room window. A marked police car pulled into the driveway and two uniformed cops got out. A dark blue sedan parked behind the black-and-white. Detective McNamara stepped out of the second vehicle and walked toward the house.

Grant greeted the cop on the porch. The flow of cold air chilled his clammy skin. "There's no one in there now, but there was."

"We'll just have a look inside." The uniforms disappeared into the house.

Eying the knife in Grant's hand, McNamara held out a hand. "You should have waited for us."

Yes. Grant handed him the knife, handle first. "I'm pretty much an expert at clearing buildings." His argument sounded weak because it was lame. He'd gone into the house hoping to find someone to take the brunt of his anger.

McNamara accepted the knife. "Yeah. I bet you are, but you don't do it alone, do you?"

"No," Grant admitted.

The minivan pulled into the driveway. The sliding door opened, and Carson jumped out. He bolted across the lawn and hit Grant in the legs with a full-body hug hard enough to knock him off balance. Grant pried his thin arms from around his thighs and picked the boy up. "What's wrong, buddy?"

AnnaBelle circled them, barking.

Carson buried his head in Grant's shoulder. "I was scared for you."

Oh, shit. He'd fucked up. The kid had lost his parents, and Grant had left him in a frightening situation and put himself at risk. Carson might not fully understand the circumstances, but he could probably pick up on Hannah's fear and Grant's aggression. Holding the trembling child, Grant realized things were never going to be the same again. It wasn't about him and what he wanted anymore. The kids had to be considered first in each and every decision.

The uniforms came out of the house. "House is clear. The laundry room window was opened. He used a glass cutter."

"Dust the doorknobs and window for prints and look for footprints under the window," McNamara said to the uniforms. He turned back to Grant. "You'll have to give us a list of what was taken."

"That's going to be hard. I don't exactly have an inventory." Grant carried Carson inside.

"Burglary is pretty common when—" McNamara stopped and glanced at Carson. "In a situation like this."

"I'll call an alarm system company today." Scanning the rooms as they walked back to the kitchen, Grant shifted Carson in his arms. Kid had a grip. "I don't see anything obvious missing."

"Maybe they heard you coming in, and you scared them off." McNamara returned the knife to its block on the counter.

"It's possible. We weren't exactly quiet," Grant agreed.

Carson lifted his head and sniffled. "My pictures are gone."

Grant stared at the refrigerator. "They were probably knocked to the floor. I'll move the fridge and check later, OK?"

Carson shrugged. "I can draw new ones." He squirmed, and Grant set him down. The boy knelt on a chair at the kitchen table and pulled out his paper and crayons.

"We'll find them," Grant said and then turned back to the cop.

"We'll have a patrol unit drive by tonight," McNamara said. "Hopefully, this was just someone who saw the news and was looking for some easy cash, but I'd push to get an alarm system installed ASAP."

"I'll call them as soon as we're through. Do you have any recommendations?"

"I can give you a few names," McNamara said, turning as noise came through the open door.

Hannah schlepped the baby and diaper bag into the kitchen. Faith was sleeping. Hannah set the car seat in the far corner. AnnaBelle brought McNamara a tennis ball.

The cop patted the dog's head. "I don't suppose she's much of a watchdog."

"AnnaBelle isn't much of a threat to anyone, but she barks," Grant said.

"Better than nothing I suppose. I'll go check out the damage." McNamara went into the laundry room.

AnnaBelle moved with the cop. Grant grabbed the dog's collar. "You better hang with us."

Holding on to the dog, he looked over Carson's shoulder. He was drawing another crying man. Was that supposed to be Grant? He hadn't cried in front of the boy. Maybe Carson was simply expressing that he knew Grant was sad. Should Grant have cried? He scrubbed a hand down the center of his face. He had no clue what he was doing. With a sense that he was missing something, he handed the dog off to his sister and started making a mental list of items that might be missing.

Something was wrong with the entire situation. Something that went beyond his brother and Kate being robbed or car-jacked. Grant scanned the adjoining family room. An e-book reader sat on a shelf, next to the TV and DVD player.

"I'll be right back." He tousled Carson's hair and went upstairs to his room. His bag was unzipped and obviously searched. He pulled out his electronic tablet. In the master bedroom, in addition to the open drawers, a few shirts and a pair of slacks had fallen off their hangers to puddle on the floor of the closet. Someone had swept the clothing from side to side. Grant crossed the wall-to-wall carpet to the dresser. He opened Kate's jewelry box. She wasn't much of a bling girl, but Grant recognized the pearl earrings that had belonged to his mother. Lee had given them to Kate the first Christmas after they were married.

Suspicions confirmed, Grant returned downstairs to talk to McNamara. This wasn't a robbery. The house had been thoroughly searched and valuables ignored. Faith was already crying in the kitchen, and Grant could hear Hannah's voice. He headed toward the laundry room, intent on talking to the cops, but Carson met him at the bottom of the stairs. How was he going to communicate his discovery with the cops and take care of Carson at the same time? Grant picked up the child.

AnnaBelle barked, drawing Grant's attention to the living room window. Ellie's daughter, Julia, was walking up her driveway.

He opened the door and called out, "Julia?"

She stopped and waved at him.

"Would you like to babysit for an hour?" *Please say yes.*

"Sure!" She smiled, and her step lightened. "Give me five minutes to dump my stuff."

In ten, the experienced teen was in the kitchen holding Faith in one arm and playing Candy Land with Carson with her free hand. All three seemed content.

The detective came back into the kitchen and Grant took them into the office, where Hannah joined them. Grant shut the door. The space was cramped, but at least Carson couldn't hear the discussion. The kid was scared enough.

Clearly still juiced from the incident, Hannah paced. Grant, who hadn't slept in days, took the desk chair. "I don't think this was a robbery. Too many things were disturbed and not stolen."

"There are other possibilities." McNamara looked at Hannah and gestured toward a Windsor chair that was old enough to be an antique. Once painted black, the finish had been worn down to shiny dark wood in the seat and arms. "We're taking a cast of a footprint in the flower bed. We're going to try and match it to one we took from the scene of your brother's murder."

"No, thank you." Hannah said, continuing to walk even though she only had room to take two steps in each direction. "You have a footprint?"

McNamara eased into the chair as if he wasn't certain it would support his weight. It creaked but the structure held. "We found a clear print in the snow where your brother and his wife were killed. That's a public street. It might not be the killer's print, but if it matches the one under the window, then I'll be convinced it's a solid lead."

Hannah stopped and faced the cop. "Do you have any evidence besides a footprint?"

"Unfortunately nothing concrete enough to share at this time." McNamara propped his elbows on the armrests and intertwined his fingers.

"Really?" Hannah's brow arched. "Are you any closer to finding out what happened to my brother and sister-in-law? It's been five days since they were killed."

"I really can't give you unsubstantiated details, ma'am. I'm sorry." McNamara didn't react to Hannah's sharp tone, which Grant knew would piss her off more than yelling.

"What *can* you tell me, Detective?" Hannah tapped a frustrated toe on the floorboards.

McNamara didn't blink. "We have a cast of the footprint in the snow at the murder scene. We'll try to match it to the one in the flower bed. If we're lucky, we might be able to tell what size and type of boot the culprit was wearing. We didn't find any usable fingerprints here or at the other scene. We have no witnesses, but we have recovered the bullets, so if we recover a weapon, ballistics will know if it's the gun used in the murder."

Hannah's body was immobile, but her eyes flinched. Grant tried to keep the image out of his head, but he knew what a bullet to the head looked like up close.

"Grant told me you had copies of their calendar and contact information from the phone company. Did those yield any clues?" Hannah leaned a shoulder on the wall, her casual posture a ruse.

McNamara rubbed an eye. "I've gone over every entry. They all seemed very straightforward and normal. I didn't see anything out of their ordinary daily patterns. But I'd like to give you a copy of that information to read over in case we missed something. You might have more intimate knowledge of your brother and sister-in-law's lives. One of the entries could have a special meaning."

"Have any of their credit cards been used?"

"No," McNamara said.

"And you still haven't located the car?" she asked.

"No." McNamara's voice tightened with each answer.

"Do you have a single suspect?" Hannah pierced the cop with an icy blue stare.

"The investigation is still in process, Ms. Barrett. I really can't speculate." The cop was doing his best to not react. At this point, it looked like work.

"I'll take that as a no," Hannah said. "How do a small-town lawyer and a skating coach get murdered without any suspects?"

McNamara's mouth tightened. "I never said we didn't have any suspects. I just can't tell you who they are. I wouldn't want to cast public suspicion on innocent people."

Grant watched Hannah digest his statement. His sister was struggling with Lee's death. Like Grant, she preferred to channel emotions into action. The inability to take the offensive bottled her nerves. At some point, she was bound to explode. Grant could empathize.

He interrupted the stare down between Hannah and the cop. "When can you bring the calendar and contact information, Detective?"

"I'll bring the papers by later today," McNamara said, rising. "You'll let me know if you see anything strange?"

"I will," Grant said.

Grant walked the cop to his car.

"I don't understand why someone would need to search my brother's house," Grant said.

McNamara shook his head. "I went through the whole house the day after the murders. I didn't find anything of interest."

"I've looked, too." But Grant was going to keep searching. The cop pulled away, and Grant went back to the house. Someone thought Lee had something to hide.

Chapter Twelve

Ellie hurried up the walk to her front porch. She stamped her feet on the cement and shook a few snowflakes from her head. Heavy gray clouds on the horizon appeared ready to burst, matching her mood. She breathed in and out. *Hold it together.* Nan's and Julia's lives depended on her keeping her cool and finding that file. The clock was ticking.

She unlocked the front door and went inside. "Julia? Nan?"

Silence greeted her. Oh, no.

Ellie rushed back to the kitchen. A piece of notepaper on the counter caught her attention. She snatched it.

Julia and I went next door.

Relief almost made her giddy. They were fine. Clammy and sweating, she opened her wool coat. After a long day at the law office, she preferred to take out her frustrations on her renovation project. But not tonight. She went upstairs and changed into jeans and a sweater. She grabbed a jacket on her way out the door. The note from Nan provided the perfect excuse to pay Grant a visit and start snooping. She hadn't been given a deadline, but if the man from last night contacted her again, she intended to have that file.

On the Barretts' front porch, she knocked, though AnnaBelle had already announced her presence with frenzied barking.

What if she didn't find the file? Her stomach churned with possibilities. Assuming he even kept his end of the bargain. With people who threatened to kill, there were no guarantees.

Grant opened the door. Faith was draped over one broad shoulder. Blocking the dog with a knee, he moved back. "Ellie, please come in. I'm glad you came over. I want to ask you some questions."

"Hi, Grant. Hello, Faith." Ellie patted the baby's shoulder. She walked into the warm foyer and greeted the whining dog.

"Let me see if I can pawn this baby off on someone so we can talk." He led the way back to the kitchen.

"Hi, Mom." Julia sat at the kitchen table with Carson. A Candy Land board lay open in front of them.

The little boy forked macaroni and cheese into his mouth. "Hi, Ms. Ross," he mumbled around the food. He picked a card and looked at it, then moved his piece.

"Hi, Carson." Ellie walked over and folded him into a long hug. Still eating, he returned the gesture with one arm.

Nan was at the kitchen counter slicing pound cake. Seeing her daughter and grandmother safe eased the panic scurrying inside Ellie's chest.

Grant leaned close to her ear. His breath drifted across her cheek. She stilled the urge to lean closer.

"Your grandmother brought us baked macaroni and cheese. It's the first thing Carson's eaten all day. I can't thank her enough."

"When Julia watched Carson in the afternoon, Nan liked to hang out with them, too. She gets bored when the house is empty."

"I haven't seen Carson since last May. I'm happy for all the guidance I can get. Are you hungry?" Grant shifted Faith to his other shoulder. "She made enough to feed a platoon."

His arm touched Ellie's, hard as iron. Tempted to press against his solid body and absorb some of his strength, she resisted. She needed to act normal.

"Tons is the only quantity she knows how to make." Ellie watched the little boy move his plastic game piece on the colorful board. He seemed quiet, but almost normal. Maybe he was going to be all right.

Her gaze snapped back to Grant. He was a take-charge sort of man, ready to tackle domestic problems with the same determination he likely put into his military career. He obviously cared about his brother's children. But what would happen when he went back to Afghanistan? A battle-hardened army officer could hardly be satisfied playing house for the next eighteen years.

What if she told him about the threat to her family? She remembered Kate telling her how worried Lee was about his brother, the conditions he'd fought under, his combat injuries. Lee had shown her Grant's Purple Heart. If anyone could handle the man who'd threatened her, it might be Grant. But would he help? Would he keep her secret or would he insist on calling the police? The man had been clear about not involving the law. Unfortunately, she didn't know Grant well enough to trust him, and she couldn't take the risk. With no clues as to the identity of Hoodie Man, she was on her own.

She forced a smile onto the stiff muscles of her face. "No worries, though. Carson would eat mac and cheese for every meal if you let him."

"I've been picking your grandmother and daughter's brains for the last hour and taking notes. Let me find my sister to take Faith. Do you have a few minutes now?" Grant watched her with intent eyes that narrowed in suspicion.

She needed to improve her game face. Grant would not be easy to fool.

"Sure." Ellie nodded, trying to appear casual when she wanted to race through the house searching for the file.

Grant turned to Nan and raised his voice. "Mrs. Ross? Have you seen my sister?"

"I told you to call me Nan like everyone else." Her grandmother slid the wide blade of the knife under a slice of cake and lifted it onto a plate. She pointed to the back door with the knife. "Hannah is outside on her phone."

Grant went to the window. Through the glass, Ellie could see a slim, blond woman pacing the back patio, coatless, arms curled around her middle as if she were freezing. Grant knocked on the glass and pointed to the baby. Hannah shook her head and pointed to her phone.

"I'll take little Faith." Nan held out her arms.

"Are you sure?" Grant hesitated. "If you stop moving, she starts screaming."

"She is not the first colicky baby I've walked." Nan tossed a clean dish towel over her shoulder.

Grant handed Faith over. Nan took her with expert arms. "You two go have a nice talk."

Ellie followed Grant to the home office. He closed the door. The small room was set up to make full use of little space. The desk and hutch were pushed against the far wall. To the right of the door, a credenza held a printer and a stack of law books and periodicals. Grant gestured toward a wooden schoolhouse chair next to the desk. Ellie perched on the edge of the seat, her gaze searching for files. It wasn't here. Or at least it wasn't in plain sight. She needed to get a look inside the credenza and desk.

Grant swiveled the office chair to face her and eased into it.

"If Nan is intruding, please let me know," she said.

"God, no." Grant shifted his weight. The chair creaked. "I'll take all the help I can get. I'm thrilled to see Carson eat. Between your grandmother and Julia, I now have a list of his favorite foods and the recipes to make them."

He leaned forward and rested his forearms on his thighs. The small space brought him close enough that she caught a whiff of that woodsy aftershave. The skin around his eyes crinkled into crow's feet, though she guessed he was only in his midthirties. War and responsibility aged a man, she supposed. She pictured the photo of him that graced the mantle in the living room. He was in uniform, rifle in hand, squinting through the Middle Eastern desert sun. A few wrinkles didn't make him any less attractive. In fact, the lines made his face more compelling in a masculine way that sent a tiny shiver through her belly like a warning shot.

Her attraction for him was natural and evolutionary. A man had threatened her family, and Grant looked like a strong, capable protector. Biology aside, she was not getting involved with him. She needed that file and that was the end of their relationship.

Ellie shifted back on the seat. Polite small talk eluded her. All she could think about was the Hamilton file and what would happen if she couldn't find it. She scrambled for conversation. "How are you?"

One side of his mouth lifted. "Terrified of screwing things up with the kids."

"You seem to have a decent handle on them, considering it's only been a day."

"I don't know." His brow creased. "I have a feeling it's going to get harder. Carson talks about Lee and Kate as if they're still alive."

"I'm sorry. I don't know what's normal."

"Me either. I'm meeting with the elementary school counselor tomorrow. I'm hoping she can give me some guidance." Grant stared at her in silence for a minute. Grief turned raw in his eyes, and she felt the pressure of empathy and respect build in her chest. Not many people could handle the situation he'd been thrust into without preparation. He didn't flinch from the pain, but Ellie leaned away from his piercing gaze—and from the intimacy that passed between them.

"So how can I help? I'm not much of a cook. Nan has charge of our kitchen."

"I wanted to ask you a few questions about the law firm," he said without breaking eye contact.

"I can't tell you anything confidential." Unless, of course, it meant getting her hands on that file.

"Understood." A baby wail pierced the walls. Grant turned his head to listen, but Faith's cries faded. "Your boss asked me to look for some files. I found some papers, but I'm not sure if they belong to the firm. Can you be more specific? Which file was Roger upset about?"

The fact that Lee had agreed to represent the Hamiltons wasn't public knowledge. Even acknowledging client representation could be a breach of confidentiality. Plus, it would be easier to snag the Hamilton file if it were just one among a stack of meaningless clients. If Grant knew the file was significant, he might not give it up.

"Why don't you let me look through the files you found?" Ellie offered. "I can return the firm's property for you, and save you the trip."

Grant tilted his head, his attention sharpening. "Why don't you tell me what I'm looking for?"

"I can't." Ellie shook her head. Lee had taken that file home. It must be here somewhere.

Grant crowded her until their knees touched. The points of body contact, two scant square inches, seemed to be the only parts of her body with feeling. Under her jeans, her skin warmed. Her gaze dropped. His thighs were as thick as her waist. His elbows rested on his legs, his clasped hands falling between his knees. Her heartbeat quickened, her instincts torn between running away at top speed and crawling onto his lap. The second option expanded until her legs were wrapped around his waist. An empty, almost desperate, ache started deep in her belly. It wasn't as if she hadn't dated in the last decade. She'd had a couple of beaus. There'd even been sex, occasionally. Rarely. OK, about as often as a legitimate bigfoot sighting. She'd never had a long-term adult relationship. What would it be like to have a man she could count on? Grant was dependable.

Time to dial her imagination back a notch. Lust she could handle, but those deeper yearnings were downright dangerous.

She lifted her gaze to his face. The intensity of his focus reminded her that, as gentle and caring as he was with his brother's children, he was also a hardened officer, a natural leader who'd seen multiple tours of duty in war zones. She suspected he was looking right through her facade. It would be so much easier to let him take care of her. So much for being a modern, independent woman. Biology was a bitch.

"My brother was murdered," he said in a flat voice.

Ellie slid backward an inch to break the contact between their bodies. "I know. But I can't breach client privilege. I'm sorry. The best I can do is to offer to return the files for you."

"I'll give them to you as soon as I'm done with them."

Ellie's spine snapped straight like a metal measuring tape. Fear rocketed through her. He was going to hold out. "They belong to the firm. Those files are confidential. You've no right to keep them."

"Hypothetically, if I found any files, they're in my brother's house, which makes them his property until I decide otherwise."

"You can't do that." Sweat pooled at the base of her spine. "Those files are stamped property of Peyton, Peyton, and Griffin."

"I guess I won't see any stamps until I have time to look closer."

"Roger can file a legal petition."

Grant shrugged. "Probably, but that'll take some time, and he has to prove I have the files first."

"You just told me you have them."

"Did I?" he asked.

Anger and terror flashed warm in Ellie's chest. "This isn't a game."

"No, it isn't." His voice sharpened. "My brother and his wife were murdered. Someone broke into the house today and searched it. I'm wondering if one of his cases caused Lee and Kate's deaths. Was he working on anything sensitive?"

Alarmed, Ellie stopped him with a raised hand. "Wait. Back up. Someone broke into the house?"

"Yes." His lips thinned as he pressed them together.

"Were the police here?"

He nodded. "Detective McNamara said it isn't unusual to have a robbery attempt after a death."

"That's horrible, but it doesn't surprise me. I drove off several possible burglars. But that was at night. To break in in broad daylight seems bold." And desperate.

"I don't think it was a burglar. The house was thoroughly searched, and nothing was taken. Not my tablet or Kate's pearls, among other things."

"Then why do you think they broke in?" She tried to sound as if she had no idea. "What do they want?"

"I'm not sure." He leaned back. His fingertips scraped on his jaw. His attention was still locked on her face, and skepticism clouded the clear blue of his eyes, as if he suspected she was lying. "But I wonder about that case file your boss was so anxious to get back. Is there something in that file worth committing robbery and murder and now burglary?"

"I didn't read Lee's case notes, so I wouldn't be able to help you." That, at least, was the truth.

"All I want is the names of any sensitive cases or clients." His gaze dropped to her hands.

She was picking at her thumbnail. Ellie interlaced her fingers and clenched them in her lap. "I already told you I can't give you that information."

"Look, Ellie. You can trust me. I'm not out to cause any trouble. I assure you I deal with classified information on a daily basis. I have high-level security clearance with the military."

"In that case, you should understand why I can't discuss cases with you. You wouldn't tell me government secrets just because I seemed trustworthy."

"It's hardly comparable." His face hardened. He wasn't going to give up the file. "OK. If that's the way you want to play it. I'll find out another way."

Just as Ellie would have to find another way to search this house. Though the police and an intruder had already searched it.

She stood. Their knees bumped, but she didn't fall back, even as his much, much larger body loomed over her.

"I don't understand why you're being so difficult," he said.

So much for playing it cool. She would make a terrible spy.

"My job might not seem like much to you, but I've had too many lean years to risk losing a steady paycheck and medical benefits. I have a daughter and grandmother to look after. I'm glad to help you in any way that doesn't compromise my position." She clamped her lips together to keep them from trembling, but they both knew she was lying. It didn't matter. Her daughter and grandmother were too vulnerable. Her family's lives depended on her doing exactly as instructed.

Grant frowned down at her. The anger in his expression made her regret their conflict on more than a professional level. Maybe it was for the best. But she liked him. Really liked him. He was kind and brave and solid. If it weren't for the situation driving them apart, she'd be tempted to break her *no casual sex* rule. Just thinking the word *sex* with Grant this close brought images to mind. Hot images. Scorching images.

Images that had no part in her life, especially in its current state of crisis.

Warm, she tugged at the neck of her sweatshirt. Nan was right, as usual. Ellie had been celibate too long. Maybe if she found that file and no one got hurt, she and Grant could just . . .

There was no way he'd be interested in her after she acted like such an uptight bitch.

"Are you going to tell your boss I have Lee's files?" he asked.

No way. If those files were somewhere in the house, she wanted them to stay right here for her to steal.

"If he asks, I'm going to say I didn't see any of Lee's files in the house." She raised her chin. "Which is the truth, though I hate relying on a technicality. I trust that if you should come across some of the firm's files, you won't keep them from me too long. Can you live with that?"

"I don't have much of a choice." His mouth tightened and guilt threatened to break her resolve. "I will get that information."

"I don't doubt it."

The baby's cries penetrated the office door.

"I should probably get back to my renovations." She leaned to the side and gave the door beyond his big body a pointed look. Maybe he'd run to the baby, and she'd have a few seconds to linger in Lee's office.

He opened the door and stepped back to allow her to exit first. Damn.

"Do you do all the work yourself?" he asked.

"As much as I can. There are some jobs that require more than one person. I have a couple of small contractors I use when I run across something I can't handle." Though tonight, she'd like nothing better than to take out her frustrations with a sledgehammer.

"I bet there isn't much you can't handle." The corner of his mouth tilted in a wry almost-smile.

"You'd be surprised." Ellie's mind went to the night before, the gun in her back, and the threat to her family.

The baby's cries drew Grant down the hall. Ellie let him pass. As she walked out, she made notes of all the places the file could be hidden. It was a long list. A frighteningly long list. The old Victorian house had lots of nooks and crannies. Were there five or six bedrooms? How would she ever get full access to the house?

"Don't hesitate to call if you need a sitter," she offered as she followed him.

"Julia and your grandmother already made that clear," he called over his shoulder.

Ahead of her, his broad shoulders filled the narrow hall, and she was tempted to drag him back into the office and tell him all about last night. But she couldn't risk it.

She was being watched.

Chapter Thirteen

Fully dressed under the duvet, Julia waited. The house had been quiet for an hour. Her mom hadn't even worked on the house the last two nights. She seemed anxious and exhausted in a way that sent guilt washing over Julia. They were all still sad about what happened to the Barretts.

Now that Mrs. Barrett was gone, Julia wasn't even sure she still wanted to be part of the figure skating team. It was fun, but Julia had no illusions about her skills. She was novice material, which was fine. School took up so much time, she didn't need one more serious activity. Mrs. Barrett had made the lessons and occasional competition fun. But the club hadn't decided which coach was going to take over her students. Some of the instructors were downright scary-intense.

She suppressed her guilt with a hot dose of anger. She'd asked about going to a concert the following weekend, and Mom had refused. So the band was total screamo and their last live concert video showed some pretty wild fan behavior. They'd put out the fire in the mosh pit, and no one had gotten seriously hurt. But Mom didn't want to hear any of that. She'd never change. If Julia had to hear her lecture one more time . . . *It isn't you I don't trust. It's everyone else. You're only fifteen.* She'd heard those words so often, they echoed in her brain. Well, tonight was going to be different. Julia was going out with Taylor. She was going to have fun like all her friends.

The Barretts' deaths were totally random. A senseless and bizarre event that illustrated life wasn't something to be wasted. Julia wasn't going to sit at home until she went to college. Who knew what could happen tomorrow? She was going to live a little.

Her phone vibrated. She read the text from Taylor: outside.

But first she had to get out of the house without waking her mother or grandmother. Nan's hearing wasn't great, and Mom was a sound sleeper. But Julia wouldn't take a deep breath until she was in Taylor's car driving far away from her house.

Later, she'd have to sneak back inside. No. She wasn't going to ruin her night by worrying. Live in the moment, Taylor said. He'd been sneaking out of his parents' house for years.

Julia peeled back the comforter and slipped out of bed. She tucked pillows under the blanket and shaped them as much like a person as possible. Standing back, she checked the effect and tugged the comforter a little higher. She propped her hands on her hips and surveyed her work. Good enough for a cursory inspection in the dark. Time to go. Nerves and excitement flapped together. She pressed a hand to her stomach, willing it to chill out. She'd been waiting all year to be alone with Taylor. Tonight it was going to happen.

Carrying her boots and purse, she tiptoed down the hallway. Stepping over the creaky step, she crept downstairs and lifted her jacket from the coat tree in the foyer.

She turned the deadbolt slowly to minimize the click as she opened the door. Stepping outside, she pulled the door closed with equal care. The house behind her sat silent and dark as she slid her arms into her jacket, zipped it to her chin, and stepped into her boots.

Where was Taylor? Still within an arm's reach of her front door, she scanned the street and spotted his old Camry parked at the curb halfway down the block. The windshield reflected the black night sky. She edged closer. Her foot hit the first step.

Something crunched in the half-frozen snow. The hair on the back of her neck tickled. Ridiculous. Only she would sneak out to meet a boy and then get scared when he showed up. Hunching against the cold, she walked down the driveway and into the shadow of a tree. The umbrella of branches overhead blocked the overcast sky.

"Psst."

Julia froze and whispered into the darkness. "Taylor?"

He should go. He'd been sitting down the street from the Barretts' house all fucking evening, looking for any opportunity to get back in. But no one was coming out tonight. In fact, more people seemed to be gathering in there, and that damned dog was back. If he was getting back into that house, he'd have to take the stupid dog out.

Movement caught his attention at the front of the neighbor's house. He dropped his hand.

Interesting. Good thing he hadn't left.

Donnie ducked below the dashboard of the stolen sedan and watched the girl step off her porch. He couldn't risk using his van after yesterday's shit-acular break-in.

Parked a block away, he couldn't see her features. He reached for the binoculars on the passenger seat and held them to his face. Still hard to be 100 percent certain in the dark, but that looked like the girl who'd been walking home from the school bus stop while he'd been breaking into the Barretts' house.

She hadn't seen his face. Once he'd spotted her, he'd kept his head inside the van, and she'd been totally focused on her texting.

In the narrow field of his binoculars, she took another step. Her head swiveled back and forth, as if she was looking up and down the street for someone.

Sneaking out? Bad girl.

She was a nice little piece, and he had a thing for bad girls. They needed to be punished. If she ventured a little closer, maybe Donnie would take her for a little ride. One-way, of course. He hadn't had anything that young and innocent since before he went to prison.

The fact that his new girlfriend actually liked the pain and humiliation he dished out took some of the excitement out of their sessions. So did her age. Bitch was at least thirty. But this little thing was fresh and would be terrified. Picturing her screams stifled in her throat by a ball gag, he touched his groin. She'd also be an excellent bargaining piece. Donnie bet her mom would do anything for him if he had her daughter.

Donnie licked his lips. The brunette started down the sidewalk toward him.

Yes.

Finally, he was going to have some luck go his way. Patience. She had to come closer. So close he could grab her without risking her getting away. The last thing he needed was one more loose kid who could identify him. He reached for the door handle.

Almost.

Come here, baby. I have something for you.

Grant lapped the downstairs, passing through the kitchen and family room for the hundredth time that night. Baby legs kicked restlessly as he shifted Faith to his other shoulder. She lifted her head and complained until Grant bounced on his toes and rubbed her back. He'd tried to put her in the swing earlier, but she was having none of that. Maybe he'd try again in an hour. Until then, he continued his forced nightly march.

On the bright side, he couldn't have nightmares while he was awake.

With a jingle of dog tags, AnnaBelle jumped to her feet and trotted to the front window. The fur on the back of her neck rose as she inhaled for a woof.

Grant caught her collar. He did *not* want Carson up, too. "Shh."

He tracked the dog's line of sight. A dark figure stood in the shadow of a tree on the front lawn. Anger bristled in Grant's chest. He hurried up to Hannah's room. He knocked softly and opened the door.

Hannah lifted her head. "What's wrong?"

"Someone's out front." He held the baby toward her. "Take Faith."

Hannah swung her legs off the bed. In flannel pajama pants and a Syracuse University sweatshirt, she looked like a college student. "Got her. Do you want me to call the police?"

"Not yet." Grant headed for the door. "Could be anyone." Plus, whoever was out there wouldn't stand and wait while the cops pulled into the driveway. Grant didn't want him to get away.

Hannah followed him downstairs into the foyer, jiggling the baby in her arms as Grant stepped into his boots. He stopped at the front door to peer out the sidelight. The shadow was still there, unmoving, waiting. Grant went to the kitchen and slipped out the back door. He gave his eyes a minute to adjust to the lack of light, though the snowy ground brightened the landscape. Hiding behind the tree trunk, the tall, thin figure looked male from his posture and size. His dark clothes stood out in stark relief against the dirty snow. Beyond him, another figure, smaller and more slender, walked in the opposite direction on the sidewalk.

"Psst," the figure whispered.

He was definitely not walking a dog or doing anything else innocent.

Grant stepped into the yard. Snowpack crunched underfoot. Sneaking up on the watcher would be impossible. He sprinted in a crouch. The guy whirled to face him. Under a black knit hat, his shocked eyes widened. He threw a panicked hook punch. Grant ducked under the wild arc, caught him in a tackle, and took him down to the ground. Grant landed on top. Levering a knee under his body, he flipped the guy onto his belly, locked an arm behind his back, and patted him down.

"Are you armed?" Turning pockets inside out, Grant discovered a wallet and keys. No weapons. No drugs.

"No, man," the guy panted. "What the fuck? Who are you?"

"I'll ask the questions," Grant said. He applied weight to the knee on the guy's back. "What are you doing out here in the middle of the night?"

"Nothing," the guy in the snow whined. "Ow. That hurts, man."

Grant levered his arm higher. "Don't lie to me."

"OK, OK. Stop." The guy's voice rose in nervous pain. "I'm here for Julia. We're supposed to go out."

Ah, shit. Grant had interrupted a late-night rendezvous. "At midnight?"

Silence answered his question.

Grant had just been sucked into a situation that would be awkward with a capital *A*. After he'd refused to give her Lee's files earlier, the last thing he needed was more conflict with Ellie. "What's your name?"

"Taylor."

Grant didn't need the rest explained. Julia was sneaking out to meet this boy. Footsteps scraped on pavement. Julia stood on the sidewalk. The porch light spilled onto the snow in the front yard, highlighting the horror and humiliation on her face.

"Get up." Grant stood, pulling the young man to his feet but keeping his arm behind his back. He frog-marched him across Ellie's lawn.

"You can't." In the yellow light, Julia's eyes begged.

"I'm sorry, Julia." Grant released Taylor and knocked on the door. "I don't have any options here."

"She's going to kill me." The girl shrank back into the corner.

"I doubt that," Grant said, but he wasn't looking forward to delivering this bit of news to a woman who owned a shotgun.

Barely fifteen seconds passed before Ellie opened the door. She took in the scene in one sweep of her gaze. Her eyes went from worried to pissed in the span of one blink. She stepped back and gestured to the interior of the house. "Let's do this inside."

Yeah. There was nothing warm and fuzzy about Ellie tonight.

Taylor hesitated. His feet turned as if he was going to bolt, but Grant caught him by the collar. "No, you don't."

He guided Taylor to follow Ellie into the kitchen.

In pajama bottoms and an oversize T-shirt, she paced the kitchen. Anger pressed the blood from her lips. Her hair was tousled, her eyes shadowed with stress and fatigue that seemed too ingrained to be caused entirely by one night's activities. As much as Grant wanted to know what was keeping Ellie awake, first they had to deal with the disaster in front of them. One clusterfuck at a time.

Ellie stopped and faced her daughter. "Would you like to explain why you were outside with this boy at midnight?"

"We were going out," Julia mumbled.

"So he didn't kidnap you from your bed?" Ellie asked in a wry tone.

Julia shook her head.

Still holding Taylor's wallet, Grant opened it. The bright kitchen light revealed Taylor's young age. Picking up a pen and a grocery store receipt on the kitchen table, Grant copied the boy's name and address from the driver's license.

"Do you want to keep him?" he asked Ellie.

Ellie looked over the license. "So you're Taylor. You're over eighteen. Did you know Julia isn't sixteen yet? I could call the police."

"You can't!" Red splotches colored Julia's pale cheeks. "It was all my idea."

Sweat beaded on the boy's forehead. He shoved shaking hands into his front pockets.

"Do you really think this is a police matter?" Grant almost kicked himself for asking when Ellie turned angry-mother eyes on him. Why was he getting involved? Because the kid was terrified and really, what had he done? If a pretty young girl agrees to sneak out, the average teenage boy isn't going to put much thought into his actions.

With one hand on the small of her back, Ellie exhaled with force and rubbed an eyebrow. "No. Not really."

Grant handed the identification back to the boy. He glanced at Julia, who retreated into the far corner of the kitchen. She crossed her arms over her chest and glared at the floor. Pissy teenage attitude mixed with I-am-in-big-trouble on her face.

Grant escorted Taylor to the door before Ellie changed her mind. "Here's a piece of advice. Don't do this again. It's stupid."

"Yes, sir. Thank you, sir."

"Don't make me regret this." Grant set him free.

"No, sir." The kid bolted through the opening, half running toward a car parked a few houses up the street. Grant went back into the kitchen.

"I can't believe you were sneaking out." Astonishment filled Ellie's tone.

"You never let me do anything." Julia's response exploded with long-built resentment. "None of my friends take the bus. They all get rides. I'm the only sophomore not allowed to date."

"You can date boys your own age. Taylor is too old for you. Do you know how dangerous it is to go out in the middle of the night without anyone knowing where you'll be or what time you'll be home?" Ellie's voice cracked. "If something happened to you, I wouldn't even know where to look."

"Taylor is the only boy I like. If you just took the time to get to know him, I wouldn't have to sneak out at night," Julia retorted.

Sensing the conversation was just getting started, Grant cleared his throat. "I'm going to leave."

"Thank you, Grant," Ellie said.

"You're welcome. I'll let myself out." Grant left the house, feeling old and crappy. He remembered what it was like to get into trouble, though he hadn't experienced much teenage wildness, not with his father disabled. But this wasn't Grant's first disciplinary action. As an officer, he had plenty of young recruits who couldn't resist the occasional lure of stupidity. But none of them were a fifteen-year-old girl making a sad, you-ruined-my-whole-life face at him.

But Ellie was exactly right. Julia had to understand the risk she was going to take that night. The thought of her out there, alone, with a boy Ellie didn't know, going who knew where, gave Grant a cramp in the center of his gut. Considering everything that was going on in the neighborhood, he didn't blame Ellie for keeping her daughter close. And, after spending these past few days with full-time care of Carson and Faith, Grant could imagine far too clearly the soul-clenching terror a parent felt when a child went missing—and the despair when she didn't come home.

As he crossed the lawn, snowflakes drifted from the clouded sky. Heat enveloped him as he went into the house. Carson's and Hannah's voices, along with Faith's cries, poured down the hall. Everyone was up. Again. Grant shook his head. These kids never slept. A few white flakes fell from his hair onto the doormat. He toed off his wet shoes.

Chaos. Total chaos. Life in Afghanistan was less insane.

He trudged toward the kitchen. It was going to be a long night.

Family responsibilities and Julia's behavior brought his return to the military to mind. How was he going to make sure the kids were all right when he returned to Afghanistan?

Chapter Fourteen

Lindsay
December

I push the brown bag with my lunch in it away. I'm not hungry. Fear is a great appetite suppressant. I'm tired of this.

I stare down at my open notebook, but I'm only pretending to work on my calc problems. I used to love school. In California, I got straight As*. Now I can barely think.*

Maybe they're right. I am ugly. I am not worth the air I breathe. They say so every day, enough that I think it must be true.

I have no one to talk to. I've made zero friends since we moved here. Everyone is afraid of becoming the next target. I don't blame them. I'm not worth it.

My phone buzzes. I don't want to look at it. Technically, I'm not supposed to use my phone at school, but what can they do to me? Expel me, please. A phone number comes up on the display. I don't recognize it. I shouldn't open it. I know it's from them*. But I can't help myself. It's almost like I want the punishment.*

I look down at the screen: You should die.

My eyes fill. A tear slides down my cheek. I wipe it away with the back of my hand. I shouldn't cry in front of them. They get off on it. But I really don't care anymore.

I don't care about anything.

They aren't even in this lunch period, but they have minions that follow their orders. At this very minute, someone is probably taking a video of me crying.

My phone vibrates again. This time it says Drinking bleach should do it.

I power the phone down. I'll check for any messages from Jose later. I can't handle any more right now.

I just want to crawl in a hole and die. It would be a lot easier to do what they want. I can't win. I can't go on like this. I don't want *to go on like this.*

The bell rings. I pack up my stuff and join the flow of bodies toward the exit. Near the door, I toss my lunch in the garbage. A hand shoves me in the middle of my back, and I fall forward toward the trash can. I catch my balance at the last second, but my books flop into the can. Half-chewed fries and ketchup splatter over everything.

I reach down to pull my books out of the mess. Tears pour freely down my cheeks now. I don't even bother to wipe them away. My stomach flip-flops as I shake a glob of macaroni and cheese off my notebook. A second later, a teacher is beside me, helping. But she is too late—as always.

I am tempted to leave. My house is only a mile away if I cut through the woods. My parents don't think it's safe for a young girl to walk alone, as if I'm safe anywhere.

The rest of the day is quiet, though I can't focus on my classes. I keep looking over my shoulder, waiting for the next strike. By the time I get home, I'm a mess. Forget homework. Needing a mindless distraction, I opt for TV. I settle on the couch and slip a disc of CSI into the DVD player.

Later that night, my mom asks, "Why are you so quiet lately?"

So I finally tell her about Regan and Autumn.

"Stand up to them," she says.

I don't think she gets it. I just shake my head. Words will not form. My throat feels like it's packed with cotton balls.

"I'll call the school," she says.

"No," I say. "That'll just make it worse."

I know without a single doubt that getting Regan and Autumn in trouble is a very bad idea. They are hostile now, when their only motivation for tormenting me is amusement. I can't imagine being the subject of their revenge.

Chapter Fifteen

"I can't believe it." In the crowded home office, Grant bumped elbows with Mac, sitting on an ottoman they'd dragged in from the living room. Grant had the schoolhouse chair, and Hannah sat at the desk. In front of her, Lee and Kate's records were organized into neat piles on the blotter. Hannah twisted sideways to face her brothers.

On the corner of the desk was the box of legal files Grant had brought in from the car. Lee had handled a variety of cases. The files that had been in Lee's office were boring, mundane legal issues: he was representing a local businessman in a DWI, drafting wills for a married couple, and drawing up a partnership agreement for a trio of doctors. Grant had scanned every page. There wasn't even a hint of controversy.

"Lee was broke," Hannah said.

"Are you sure?" Grant leaned toward the office door, left open a few inches so he could hear the kids, who were taking a miraculous and simultaneous morning nap. No one had slept much last night. "That doesn't sound possible."

Hannah skimmed through a pile of papers. "I've double-checked all their financial records. Lee and Kate were beyond broke. Their debt was crushing them."

"How can that happen?" Mac shook his shaggy hair out of his face. "I know Kate didn't make much money, but Lee was an attorney."

"Lee was a good lawyer, but he made terrible financial decisions." Hannah lifted a bank statement. "Lee's law school debt totaled six figures. He deferred payments for years, and he hasn't paid much of the principal off. I know law practices have been hit hard by the economy, but his salary was a lot lower than I expected. He wasn't willing to move to chase a higher-paying job." She thumbed to another page. "They couldn't afford this house or the BMW."

"Why do you make so much money?" Mac asked Hannah.

"I speak three languages. I work eighty-hour weeks for a large private firm, and I'm willing to live in hotels. Small-town firms can't pay hefty salaries." Hannah dropped the paper on the blotter. "I didn't borrow as much money as Lee either. I had scholarships and a work-study program. Basically, I've had no personal life for the last ten years."

Grant knew all about having no life outside of work. "Why would he keep borrowing if he was already underwater?"

"You know Lee, the perennial optimist." Hannah rubbed her neck. "Remember when we were kids. Lee was always the one to say things would work out."

"So what will happen to the house now?" Grant asked. "I'd hate for the kids to be forced from their familiar surroundings."

"Lee's student loans go away with a death certificate. We're lucky there. They don't always. Actually, both Lee and Kate had decent life insurance. It should be enough to bring everything current, with a bit left over. If they hadn't died, they would have lost the house in six months." Hannah set the paper down.

"Did they have any money in the bank?" Grant couldn't believe Lee was broke. What the hell was going on with his brother?

"No." Hannah shook her head. Her short, straight hair fell back into its precise cut. "Their savings ran dry months ago. They used every dime for the down payment on this house." She paused, sucking a deep breath in through her nose.

"What is it?" Grant asked.

"I don't know how to say this. I feel guilty for even thinking it." Hannah stared at the desktop. "In the last few weeks, Lee's account shows two inexplicable cash deposits of nine thousand, five hundred dollars each, just small enough to avoid federal reporting requirements."

Shock silenced them.

"There has to be an explanation." Grant's mind scrambled. "Could he have closed an account somewhere?"

"I'm still looking." Hannah's eyes reflected Grant's disbelief. "But so far, the money seems to come from nowhere."

"Where could Lee have gotten almost twenty grand?" Mac asked.

They stared at each other for a minute.

"Keep digging. There must be some logical explanation." Rejecting the possibility that Lee could have done anything amiss, Grant rubbed his forehead. "But if their life insurance should cover their outstanding debts, then whoever takes the kids can stay in the house."

"I think so. Unless more liabilities turn up, or we find their will and it makes other provisions." Hannah gathered the papers on the desk. "But if it comes down to it, I have some cash put aside. They won't have to leave this house if we decide they should stay."

"Same here." Except for the money he sent to the nursing home, most of Grant's pay went into the bank. He didn't have a family to support and had few housing expenses. His savings account was healthy. If Lee had told him he was so broke, Grant would have helped out.

Maybe if Grant had called more, he'd have known his brother was in financial trouble.

"Where could they have stored their legal documents?" Grant scanned the room. Its small size limited possible locations, but the rest of the house . . .

She shook her head. "I've been through his entire desk and computer files. If they had a will, it's not here."

"Maybe they didn't have a will." Mac rubbed an ink mark on the tan leather ottoman next to his thigh. "They didn't count on dying this young."

"True, but Lee was a planner." Hannah slid the papers into a folder. "Even in debt, he provided life insurance for his family. The will must be here somewhere." She opened a second file, and they all drew a collective, silent breath. "Now we need to talk about funeral arrangements. I thought we'd use Stokes Funeral Home on First Street. It's the one we used for Mom." Her voice cracked. She paused to press her knuckles against her mouth.

Grief filled Grant's chest like concrete.

Mac slid the ottoman forward and pulled her into a hug. "Why don't you let me take care of the funeral arrangements? I'll go down there today, talk to the director, and we can reconvene here tonight. That way, when . . ." Mac paused as if he couldn't get the words out. "When the medical examiner releases the bodies, we'll be ready."

"Are you sure?" Grant was used to handling the tough decisions. Of course, he was also accustomed to his orders being followed, and that only applied in the military. His family did not recognize him as a superior officer. The only one who listened to him was Carson. Faith screamed in his face for eight hours a night. Mac's lifelong modus operandi was to agree, then do whatever he wanted. Hannah would argue until the season changed. And he didn't even want to think about his discussion with Ellie next door. *She* clearly wasn't following any orders.

"Yeah." Mac exhaled hard, then nodded. "Hannah has the legal and financial stuff under control. You've got the kids handled. Let me contribute something."

"It's all right with me," Grant agreed. "Hannah?"

She nodded. "Thanks, Mac."

"We need to coordinate errands so one of us is here with the kids. I asked Julia from next door to babysit for a couple of hours this afternoon to help out. But considering everything that's happened, I'd still feel more comfortable if one of us is in the house."

"Agreed." Hannah frowned. "What about Dad?"

"I don't know. He didn't remember me when I visited him," Grant said. "I didn't see any point in telling him about Lee and Kate."

"How do you think he'd feel if he misses the funeral?" Hannah's voice caught.

Was their father's illness one of the reasons she stayed away from Scarlet Falls? She'd been chasing his attention all her life. As a teen, Hannah was the best marksman of the four of them. But the Colonel had still been focused on his boys. His slight hadn't been intentional. He didn't know what to do with a girl. Intentional or not, Hannah had felt his disinterest. She probably would have gone into the service after college if their father hadn't been so outspoken in his disapproval of women in the military.

"If he doesn't remember Grant, he won't remember the rest of us," Mac said.

Grant turned. "Why do you say that?"

Mac lifted a palm. "You were always his favorite. For the last few years before the dementia took over, all he ever talked about was you becoming a general. Lee was never aggressive enough for the Colonel. Hannah was, but the old man didn't see it." Mac rubbed his sister's shoulder. "Sorry, Sis. He totally missed the boat on that one. You're the toughest of all of us."

Hannah's lip twisted into a weak smile. Grant knew that, on the outside, Hannah was tough as nails, but inside? Not so much.

"What about you?" Grant asked. "Mr. Outdoorsman."

"Nah." Mac waved a hand. "By the time I was old enough for him to take any interest in me, he already had you in the military academy. I skated under the radar. Could you imagine if he knew I spent my time living in a tent, studying families of otters? At least Lee and Hannah are lawyers. I'm a biologist who can't keep his own fish alive."

"That is pretty sad." Grant laughed, then sobered.

"There's an option for Carson, though," Mac said. "Boarding school—"

"No." Grant interrupted him. "I hated that place."

"Really?" Hannah lifted her head. "I was so jealous I couldn't go."

"Yes," Grant admitted. "Well, maybe I didn't hate the place as much as being away from all of you. I was only twelve. And there were no girls."

"You never said anything." Hannah straightened the already perfect piles of papers on the desk.

"How could I?" Grant sighed. "Dad was so proud. I would have broken his heart. But that brings me to my next item for discussion." Grant paused and listened at the door for a second. No sounds from upstairs. He lowered his voice. "What are we going to do about the kids?"

"Is it really just the three of us?" Mac asked. "Doesn't Kate have any family?"

"Not that I know of—"

"She does." Hannah reached for the bottom desk drawer. "I found an old address book with Kate's handwriting." She lifted out a small black book and opened it. "*Mom* is penciled under M. There's a phone number."

Mac leaned forward. "That's a Boston exchange. That book looks old."

"Probably is." Hannah flipped through pages. "I found it stuck behind the drawer. Shall I call the number?"

The baby's cries echoed in the hallway.

"The master calls." Grant stood up. "I vote yes. The number might not even work, but I think Kate's parents have a right to know about her death."

Faith cried louder. Grant turned and hurried to the kitchen. The TV was on in the adjoining family room. Before Hannah had summoned him to the office, he'd been watching the news. As he prepared the formula, he read the weather report scrolling across the bottom of the screen. Shaking the bottle, he turned to leave the kitchen.

"Stay tuned for the noon report as the parents of Lindsay Hamilton speak out on the murder of their attorney, Lee Barrett."

"Oh my God." Mac's voice came from behind Grant.

He turned. In the doorway, Mac stared at the screen. Upstairs Faith jacked up the volume. The girl had lungs.

"Can you record that?" Grant pointed to the TV. "And then turn it off. I don't want Carson to hear it if he comes downstairs."

"I'm on it." Mac moved toward the digital cable box.

Grant grabbed the bottle he'd already prepared and climbed the steps to the nursery. Could the Hamilton case file be the one Lee's boss was seeking? He'd have to find out later. If the report made the noon news, it would be on the Internet somewhere. He'd either watch the recording when Carson was asleep or he'd web surf until he found it. The news network would probably have the clip on their website feed.

Faith was on her belly holding her head and chest off the crib mattress.

"I guess you know how to roll over." Grant picked her up and settled in the rocking chair to feed her. He grabbed the book he'd found on Kate's nightstand, *What to Expect in the First Year*, and looked for the page where he'd stopped reading earlier. "OK, Faith, where were we? *By your baby's fourth month, you both should be enjoying a full night's sleep.* Faith, have you read any of this book?"

Footsteps at the doorway interrupted him. Hannah walked into the nursery.

"Do you want to feed her?" Grant asked.

"She looks comfortable with you." Hannah perched on the edge of the toy box. "So I called that number. Kate's mother answered. She and Kate's father live outside of Boston. She said they haven't spoken to Kate in almost ten years. She didn't say why. They're driving down."

"Get any vibes from the call?"

"Icy ones."

Coming from Hannah the corporate attorney, who could negotiate billion-dollar contracts in three languages without breaking a sweat, that said a lot.

"So if she hasn't seen Kate in a decade, she doesn't know the kids." Second thoughts weighed on Grant. "I hope we haven't let a panther out of the bag."

"Me too," Hannah said. "Mac left for the funeral home. That's all right with you?"

"Definitely. I have enough on my plate. I have to run to the ice rink where Kate worked. I won't be long. You're on kid duty."

Staring at the baby, Hannah took a deep breath. "I hope I can do this half as well as you."

Grant traded places with Hannah. "Sit." He handed the baby to his sister. "Burp her halfway through."

"But—"

"You'll be fine. In the daytime, she's a happy baby." He ducked out to check the room across the hall. Carson had flung off the covers and sprawled sideways across his twin mattress. Grant pulled the door closed and went back to the nursery. "Carson's still asleep. Keep an ear out for him. He'll want a snack when he wakes up."

Downstairs, Grant donned a coat and boots. AnnaBelle whined at the back door. "All right, you can come outside with me." AnnaBelle bounded out into the snow. Grant found a shovel in the garage. He cleared a path from the garage to the back door. Shovel in hand, he headed for the front of the house. Barking drew his attention to Ellie's house.

"Good dog." A small figure huddled on the front steps leading to the porch. AnnaBelle crowded close.

Grant crossed the lawn. "Nan?"

"Grant." Nan exhaled in relief. Dressed in jeans, a sweater, and sheepskin boots, Ellie's grandmother shivered on a patch of ice. She clutched one arm to her chest. Her teeth chattered. "I'm so glad to see you."

"What happened?" He dropped to one knee beside her.

"I came out to get a package on the porch, and I slipped down the steps. I twisted my ankle and landed on my wrist."

"How long have you been out here?" He looked her over.

"I don't know. Maybe half an hour."

Given her age and absence of body fat, that was too long. "Is it just your ankle and wrist?"

"My pride took a nice knock, too." Nan winced. "I didn't hurt anything vital. I tried to crawl back into the house, but I couldn't get up the steps."

Grant eyed the three cement steps she'd fallen down. No doubt she had bruises she wasn't feeling yet. "Let me get you inside and we'll get a look at that ankle. Ready?" Grant scooped the tiny old woman off the icy concrete.

"Oh, my." She gripped his shoulder as he carried her into the house.

AnnaBelle pranced beside him past the gutted living room. Grant walked back to the kitchen and set Nan down on a chair. He sat in the chair opposite and put a hand on the back of her boot. "This is probably going to hurt." She didn't make a sound as he eased it off her foot, then peeled down her wool sock, but her ashen face tightened. Her ankle was swollen to an angry purple. "I think I'd better take you to the ER."

"Oh, maybe we could try icing it for a while" Her voice shook as she shivered again.

He gave her foot a doubtful glance. "I'm afraid it could be broken." Hypothermia was also a concern. "You should call Ellie."

"I hate to bother her while she's at work."

"She's going to want to know."

"Oh, all right. Would you hand me my cell?" She pointed to the end table, and he passed her the phone. "I hope she doesn't get in trouble."

"I'm sure Ellie's boss will make an exception in an emergency." While Grant was in there, he snatched a blanket off the back of the sofa. He wrapped it around her shoulders. Her color was graying. She was clearly in much more pain than she would admit. He didn't want to wait any longer. "Tell her to meet us at the hospital."

Chapter Sixteen

Ellie finished reviewing her flash drive. There was no sign that anyone in the office, including Frank, was hiding any information about the Hamilton case. Where could she look next? Grant had been less than cooperative. She put her palm to the fatigue ache in the center of her forehead. She hadn't slept since Julia had tried to sneak off the night before. She'd never be able to close her eyes again.

Her top drawer vibrated. She opened it and checked her cell phone in case it was Nan or the school. A message alert displayed, but she didn't recognize the number. Ellie opened the text, discreetly leaving the phone in her drawer. Normally, she wouldn't violate the no-personal-calls rule, but there was nothing normal about this week. A photo appeared on the screen.

She gasped.

Though the image was dim, Ellie recognized the picture of her house. Grant, Taylor, and Julia stood on the front lawn, their images grainy but recognizable in the dark. Grant held Taylor by the arm. Under the photo was a caption: Have you found the file?

Helpless tears prickled the corners of Ellie's eyes. Hoodie Man had been at the house last night when Julia was outside, vulnerable.

If Grant hadn't been there, Hoodie Man could have gotten her daughter. She typed need more time and hit the Send button.

What was she going to do? Would more time even help? She had no idea where to look.

Her phone buzzed with a return message: time is running out.

The piles of work on her desk blurred. Ellie had to get inside Lee's house. Though Grant's words had been ambiguous, she knew he had some of the firm's files. Hoodie Man wasn't going to wait.

She shuffled the expense reports on her desk, but her mind wasn't on her work. Her phone buzzed from her drawer. Alarm coursed through her. What else did Hoodie Man want?

Nan's cell phone number appeared on the display. Ellie's already thudding heart went into overdrive. No. They couldn't have hurt Nan. She stabbed her keypad three times with a shaking finger before successfully hitting the Answer key. "Nan?"

"Don't get upset. I'm all right."

Fear washed cold through Ellie's veins. "What happened?"

"It's not a big deal." But her grandmother's voice sounded weak. "I just slipped on the steps. I didn't want to call, but Grant made me."

"Let me talk to him." Ellie heard Grant's voice in the background, then the sound of the phone being passed.

"Ellie?"

"What happened, Grant?" she asked.

"She fell in the driveway, and her ankle is pretty swollen. Wrist, too." Concern deepened his voice.

"I'll be home in twenty minutes." Ellie opened her bottom drawer and pulled out her purse.

"I'm going to take her to the ER," Grant said. "Why don't you meet us there?"

If he didn't want Nan to wait twenty minutes, then her injuries must be more serious than a twisted ankle.

"All right." Ellie ended the call. Purse in hand, she knocked on Roger's door.

"Yes," he called.

She opened the door. "I'm sorry to interrupt." Actually she'd totally forgotten he was in a meeting with the accountant.

Roger's expression went from annoyed to worried as he met her gaze. "What's wrong?"

"My grandmother fell." Ellie's voice shook as she said the words out loud. "I don't know how badly she's hurt, but she's on her way to the emergency room. I have to leave."

"Of course. Are you all right to drive?" he asked.

"Yes, thank you." Ellie gripped the doorknob.

"Go. Take the rest of the day. Let me know how she is."

"Thank you." Ellie found her car and drove to the hospital. The fifteen-minute drive felt like hours. Dread filled her belly. Was this a warning? A taste of what could happen if she didn't do as she was told?

She parked her car in the hospital emergency room parking lot. The shakes spread through her entire body by the time she locked her car and hurried across the asphalt. Her shoes slipped on a patch of slush. Her feet went out from under her, and she went down with a splash. Pain radiated down her leg. She rubbed at her hip. She'd forgotten to change into her boots. Heels were not made for walking on snow and ice.

Nan is fine. Ellie had talked to her grandmother. So why was she freaking out? Because it could have been much, much worse. She got to her feet and brushed ice crystals off her wool coat. The hem of her skirt was soaked through and streaked with brown old-snow filth.

The ER doors slid open. She wiped her feet on a thick black floor mat. Skirting a yellow Caution Wet Floor sign, she stopped to scan the waiting room. A dozen people huddled on chairs, filling out forms on clipboards. She spotted Grant on the other side of the room.

He stood as she walked over. His face was grim. "They just took her back."

"What's wrong? It's more serious than she said, right?" She tugged off her gloves. Fear pooled in her belly. Nan was fit for her age. She'd stayed active in the church and community since retiring, but there was no denying that she was getting older.

"Take a deep breath and calm down. She's tough." Grant's tone was firm.

"She's seventy-five, but she refuses to act it." Ellie unbuttoned her coat. "She said she was staying home today."

"She was just bringing in a package," Grant said. "Some snowmelt dripped off the roof and froze on the porch. Your gutters probably need to be cleaned."

Ellie spun toward the check-in counter. "She should have stayed in the house."

He caught her by the arm. "Sit down and relax for a minute." His tone sharpened into a command.

The order irritated Ellie's already-frayed nerves. Her gaze dropped to his hand. "Excuse me?"

Grant loosened his grip. Sighing, he moved in front of her, blocking her path, and took her other arm, this time gently. "If she sees you like this, it'll upset her."

"You're right. I'm sorry." Ellie's eyes filled with tears. She pressed her palms to her closed lids and took a deep breath. "She could have really been hurt."

"But she's not." His gaze zeroed in on her grime-streaked skirt. "Are you all right?"

"Fine." She hated the weak tremor in her voice.

Grant guided her into a chair. "Take a minute and pull yourself together. Initially, I was worried about hypothermia. She'd been out in the cold for a while. But she seemed to warm up on the way over here."

Ellie lowered her hands and opened her eyes. He was crouched in front of her. Concern deepened the blue of his gaze as he studied her.

"I'm sorry." She sniffed.

"No apologies necessary."

"Yes, there is. You found Nan and brought her to the hospital. I should be thanking you for taking care of her, not giving you a hard time." Ellie exhaled, letting some of the tension inside of her out with her breath. He was still focused on her. God, he was perfect. He took a screaming baby in stride. Her acting like a crazy woman didn't even scare him off. "If you hadn't been there—" Anxiety stoked fresh. She put her hand to her brow.

He caught her hand and held it. His warm fingers wrapped around her freezing digits. "Stop. I *was* there."

Just for a minute, Ellie stopped fighting her feelings. She let him hold her hand and accepted the strength he offered. This man had it to spare. The heat flowing from his body to hers felt good—too good, and Ellie reminded herself that Grant was only here for another three weeks. Then he was off to Afghanistan for several months. And he was stationed in Texas when he was stateside. Even if she wanted to, she couldn't allow herself to rely on him. Someone was watching her, someone who might still be around long after Grant was gone. For this moment, having him to lean on was a relief, but it had to end here.

"Thank you." She tugged her hand free. "I'm all right now."

Grant stood and stepped back, giving her room. "Would you like me to stay?"

"No. We've taken enough of your day. This will likely take a while." She climbed to her feet.

His gaze searched hers. "If you're sure." He pulled out his cell. "What's your number?"

Ellie rattled off the digits, and he entered them into his phone. A second later, her own phone vibrated in her pocket.

"Now you have my cell phone number. Call me if you need anything. I mean that. I'll be around."

"Thank you again." Watching him walk away, she tamped down the regret in her heart and went in search of her grandmother. A nurse directed her to a small exam room cubicle. Nan reclined on a narrow gurney. Pillows elevated her left foot and hand. Dual ice packs were poised over her injuries, and blankets were tucked around the rest of her body. Pain tightened the skin of her face, but otherwise, she looked all right.

Relief flooded Ellie. Her head felt too light, the muscles of her legs weak. She covered her reaction by setting her purse on a folding chair by the bed and removing her coat.

She leaned over to kiss Nan's cheek. "How does it feel?"

"Pff. It's not that bad. I told Grant I could wait until you got home from work, but he insisted."

Thank goodness. "Well, I'm glad."

"I hope you didn't get in trouble at work. I hated to bother you."

"I have paid time off that I rarely use," Ellie said.

Nan shifted her position and winced. "You should start your own business anyway. You design the best bathrooms and kitchens."

"Maybe someday," Ellie said, because she knew better than to say no outright. Nan loved a good debate, especially one that involved what Ellie should and shouldn't do with the rest of her life. "First I have to get Julia through college."

Time dragged on as they waited for the doctor and Nan pointed out more reasons that Ellie should go back to school. Eventually, the doctor proclaimed her wrist merely sprained, but her ankle was broken. She encased it in a metal-and-neoprene boot and released Nan with a prescription for pain medication and instructions not to put weight on her foot for a week. An hour later, Ellie drove her grandmother home.

"Oh, there's Grant," Nan pointed out the windshield. "He cleared and salted the porch."

Parking in the driveway, Ellie looked next door. Grant leaned on a shovel. Carson was on his back in the snow, flailing his arms and legs snow-angel style. If she'd thought Lee's brother was handsome before, that gazillion-watt smile he flashed his nephew took him to a whole new level of sexy.

How was she going to resist him for the next three weeks? Even more important, how could she resist asking him for help? But how could she ask? She scanned the street. Just because she didn't see anyone watching didn't mean they weren't there.

He rested the shovel against the house and started toward the car. AnnaBelle raced to him and spat a tennis ball at his feet. Grant scooped it off the ground and tossed it far into the backyard without missing a stride. The dog whirled and shot off in pursuit.

Grant opened Nan's door for her. "Let me help you."

Nan, who usually protested anyone's help with anything, took his hand without complaint. She turned and eased her feet out of the vehicle. Grant half lifted her out of the car.

Ellie got the crutches out of the backseat and brought them around. "She's not supposed to put any weight on that foot."

Grant frowned at the crutches. "Those are going to be tough with a sprained wrist. How about I just pick you up again?"

Again?

"Oh, all right," Nan said. *Oh. My. God.* She was simpering.

"Carson, come on over here for a minute." Grant gently scooped Nan off her feet. "This is easier."

Nan wrapped her arms around his shoulders. "Yes, it is." She looked back at Ellie and winked.

With a mental groan, Ellie carried the crutches into the house behind them. Grant set Nan on the sofa in the family room. "Do you need anything else?"

"No, this is wonderful. Thank you so much." Nan beamed at him.

"I have to go." He smiled back. "Call me if you need anything. You have my number, right?"

"I do." Nan nodded.

Yeah, and Ellie had Nan's number, too.

"I have to run out, but Hannah is at the house." Grant turned toward the hall.

Ellie walked him to the door. "Thank you again. For everything."

Carson waited on the porch, his nose smashed against the glass pane.

"Call me if you need me. I'll only be gone an hour or so." Grant leaned closer and lowered his voice. His eyes went serious. "When you get a chance, we need to talk."

Ellie nodded. "All right. I'll come over after Julia gets home from school."

Grant went outside, picking up his nephew and flinging him over one shoulder.

Ellie closed the door to the sound of Carson giggling.

"That is quite a man." Nan took off her coat and handed it to Ellie.

"Mm." Ellie made a noncommittal sound. "Let me get you an ice pack."

"So when are you going to talk to him?"

"What, do you have supersonic hearing or something?" Ellie filled a ziplock baggie with ice and set it on her grandmother's foot.

"Honey, when a man that handsome talks, I listen." Nan adjusted a pillow behind her back.

"And let him carry you around?"

"Damned straight."

"You're incorrigible." Ellie's quick laugh died off. Normally, Nan's infatuation with the handsome neighbor would be amusing, but the reality of Ellie's situation wouldn't fade.

Nan sucked in a sharp breath. "I hate to send you out again, but would you please get my prescription filled? This is really starting to hurt."

"Of course. I should have dropped it off on the way home. Do you want something to eat?" Ellie checked the time. Two thirty. "We missed lunch."

"I'm not hungry."

"OK. Will you be all right here by yourself?"

Nan held up her cell phone. "I'll be fine. Julia will be home soon anyway."

What did Grant need to discuss? Maybe he'd found Lee's files.

She went out onto the front porch, rock salt crunching under her shoes. A shipping box sat on the cement. That must have been what Nan had been retrieving when she fell. Ellie brought the package inside and set it on the hall table. She slit the packing tape with scissors. An odd, raw smell rose from the opening. Ellie lifted the cardboard flaps. Inside, in a plastic bag half filled with ice, sat a red and bloody heart. A knife pierced the organ. Pinned to a board beneath the gruesome package was the enlarged, grainy photo of Julia, Taylor, and Grant that Hoodie Man had sent her earlier. Her daughter's face was smeared with blood. Bold text printed on computer paper read: JUST SO YOU KNOW I'M SERIOUS.

Chapter Seventeen

Grant parked the minivan in front of the ice rink between another van and an SUV. He dropped the keys and fished under the driver's seat. Ugh. He pulled out an empty juice box, a granola bar wrapper, and enough crumbs to feed a flock of pigeons before finding the keys. He crossed the parking lot, his boots scraping on the salt-dusted asphalt.

The interior was rough, the decor leaning heavily on concrete. The main office was on the left. A middle-aged woman sat at a desk behind the waist-high counter that separated the waiting area from her workspace.

Grant placed both palms on the laminate countertop. "I'm Major Grant Barrett. I'm here to collect Kate Barrett's things."

Tucking her reading glasses into the V neck of her sweater, she approached the partition. "I'm so sorry, Major."

Grant nodded. People meant to be respectful, but their constant expressions of condolences slammed his loss home dozens of times a day.

"Could I see some identification, please?" she asked.

Grant produced his military ID. She squinted at it for a minute and then handed it back.

"Coach Victor should be next to the rink." She pointed to an open door.

"Thank you." Grant exited the office. He followed a hall and emerged in a cavernous open space. A waist-high dented red wall, topped by a Plexiglas shield, surrounded the rink. Parents huddled on bleachers. Some bent over phones. Others focused with painful intent on the oval rink beyond, where figures twirled on skates. Blades scraped on ice.

Two men stood at the opening to the rink, pointing and murmuring at the skaters. A group of teenage boys in pads and black skates burst out of another door labeled Locker Rooms. Hockey sticks clacked as the boys jostled each other.

"Hey, watch where you're going, asshole," one yelled.

"Fuck you."

Two boys dropped their sticks, tugged off their mitts, and lunged at each other. One kid tackled the other. They went down hard, nearly knocking into a little girl in a miniature skating outfit and tiny white skates.

One of the men sprang forward, caught the child under the arms, and lifted her out of the way. Grant grabbed the teen on top by the back of the collar and lifted him off his combatant. "Knock it off!"

Fighter number two scrambled to his feet. The boy started forward, but the man grabbed his arm. The boy's face was heated, his hair mussed, his eyes glowing with resentment. He broke the man's hold and swung at his combatant. Still holding the first kid, Grant stepped between them and caught the sloppy fist in one hand.

He leaned in close and glared down at the angry teen. Their faces were barely an inch apart. "You do *not* want to do that."

The boy opened his mouth and closed it as Grant stared him down. The kid swallowed as he registered the seriousness in Grant's eyes. The teen backed off, but the hatred burning in his eyes didn't dim a watt.

"Thank you." An athletic man dressed in a black parka and jeans pointed at the two boys. "Save the aggression for the game. Both of you, go wait for your ice time in the penalty box. Coach Zack will be along in a few minutes."

One protested, "But—"

"I said go." The coach's voice dropped an octave as he herded the boys off. Sulking, the two fighters picked up their pads and sticks and dragged ass toward a bench box surrounded by head-high Plexiglas.

One of the men offered a hand. "I'm Corey Swann, and this is Josh Winslow." He gestured to his companion.

Grant shook it. "Major Grant Barrett. Thanks for the help."

Josh lowered his voice. "The arena has a hockey program for delinquent teens. It's an effort to keep them out of jail and channel their energy in a positive direction. But if you ask me, it's a big mistake. Some of these kids are just plain trouble."

Grant glanced over at the boys sitting in the glass-walled box. Mac had been like that, all anger and confusion. He'd been in juvie too, arrested for possession after falling into a gang. Grant was gone. Mom was sick. Dad was a mess. Looking back, Grant wondered if dementia was beginning to take hold back then and no one recognized the symptoms. Lee had been the one who'd coped with Mac's drug and delinquency problems, and Mom's deathbed talk had snapped her youngest out of it. A program like this might have helped his brother. "Who knows what those boys have had to deal with in their lives."

Corey's eyes turned somber. "We're all sorry about Kate."

Reminded of Kate's death, Grant's chest deflated.

"And thanks for the help," Corey said. "These boys can be a handful."

"Is your son on the team?"

"No." Corey nodded toward the rink. A pretty blond teenager executed a spinning jump on the ice. Corey beamed. "That's my daughter, Regan. She's on the junior figure skating team with Josh's daughter, the one in black. The hockey team has the next slot of ice time."

"The girls look very talented." Even with an ex-skater for a sister-in-law, Grant knew next to nothing about figure skating. He should have paid attention. He should have known Kate better.

Josh stood taller. "They are. The team went to the sectional championships last fall. Next year, they'll make nationals, right, Victor?"

Josh gestured toward the coach in the black parka, who had deposited the offenders in the penalty box and was walking back to them. "Victor coaches our daughters."

Joining them, Victor offered a hand. He was a head shorter than Grant, maybe fifty years old or so, with a fit body and salt-and-pepper hair cut as short and sharp as his black eyes. "Victor Church."

"Major Grant Barrett."

"That was impressive, Major." Victor smiled, the expression sharkish on his angular Slavic features. "Do you play hockey?"

Grant smiled. "Not since I was a kid."

Victor shook his head. "Too bad. We could use another coach who can handle those boys." He paused, sadness dimming his eyes. "I assume you're here for Kate's things?"

"Yes." Grant glanced back at the girls twirling on the ice. The blond, Corey's daughter Regan, reminded him of Kate. She'd been twenty and still skating competitively when he'd met her. He'd been on leave and had gone with Lee to Los Angeles to watch her skate in her one and only national competition. He imagined her gliding on the ice, her pale blue costume and golden hair giving her a princess air. He'd known then that Lee was a goner. His brother hadn't been able to take his eyes off her. Grant still couldn't believe she was gone, that someone had fired a bullet into her head. A quick vision of the insurgent's face exploding in a red mist flashed into Grant's mind. His pulse quickened, and anger simmered in his chest. He blinked the image away and, breathing deliberately, turned back to the coach. He couldn't let his nightmares intrude on his day.

Victor gave him a tight-lipped nod. "Please accept my condolences. Let's go to the office." He turned toward Corey and Josh. "You're both staying for the meeting, right?"

"We'll be there," Corey said. He and Josh walked back to the rink.

Grant followed Victor away from the ice and down a corridor. They passed the locker rooms and entered a small, dusty office. A brawny bald man scanned a grid on a clipboard. He looked up as they entered.

"Major Barrett, this is Zack Stuart, the hockey coach." Victor gestured between them, then gave Zack a brief rundown of the fight.

Zack shook his head and tucked his clipboard under his arm. "Maybe an hour of power skating drills will drain off some of that hostility."

Grant laughed. "I like to run new recruits long distances with heavy packs to keep them out of trouble."

"Excuse me while I go do my best to wear them out." Zack grabbed a jacket off a peg and left.

"Are you sure you don't want to coach hockey?" Victor asked. "Our coach has his hands full. His assistant coach quit last month to play for a minor league team."

"I'll pass, but thanks," Grant said.

Victor moved behind the desk. "We're all sorry about Kate."

"You worked closely with her?"

"Yes. She was in charge of beginners through preliminary level competitors. I handle the advanced skaters." Church crossed his arms over a lean chest.

"Were you a competitive figure skater too?"

"I was a national champion, but that was a long time ago," Victor said.

Grant scanned the half dozen trophies lined up on a row of shelves behind Victor's head. "Have you been coaching here long?"

"Almost seven years." Victor's gaze followed Grant's. He pointed to a golden trophy. "Kate's had several preliminary skaters place in a local competition last season. She was thrilled. Building a good team takes time. This year will be my year. I have the best skaters I've ever coached." Pride filled his voice. He cleared his throat, as if suddenly realizing, again, that Kate was gone.

Grant understood. He had moments of happiness with Carson and Faith, laughs that burst out of his chest before he remembered he should be sad because Lee and Kate were dead. All positive emotions felt inappropriate and selfish.

A few seconds of awkward silence followed.

Clearing his throat, Victor turned to a shelving unit behind him. He lifted a nearly empty cardboard box and, turning, transferred it to the desk. "Here are Kate's things."

Grant took the box from him. "This is it?"

"That's what was in her desk and locker." Victor shrugged. "I don't keep much here either. A lot of people come and go here at all hours. Things tend to go missing."

"Well, thanks." Grant hefted the box. Like Lee's, Kate's personal effects seemed too light given that she'd worked here for eight years.

"No one's going to forget her," Victor said as if he could read Grant's mind. "The kids are devastated by her death, especially the girls she coached."

"Thank you." Grant turned toward the door, a connection in his mind stopping him. "Do you know anything about the Hamilton case? The girls all skate here, right?" He'd watched the clip on the news. The media had speculated on a connection with Lee and Kate's murder. Lee's public life was short on dirt, and the press had focused on the more controversial bullying story. Grant had spent some time on the computer learning about the case.

"Sure. Everyone here does, but we aren't allowed to discuss it." Victor's friendly demeanor vanished. "There's still a civil case pending. Plus, the whole thing was a nightmare."

"Any time a kid dies it's horrible," Grant said. "Did you coach Lindsay?"

Victor nodded. His gaze dropped to the desktop. "I'll just say one thing. She was a nice kid."

"You coach the two accused girls too?"

"Yes, which is why I can't say anything." Victor's sigh was full of regret and maybe a touch of anger.

Grant waited, sensing something was coming.

Victor's eyes rose to meet Grant's. "You just met their fathers."

"Really?"

The bullying case had been summed up, but the accused girls hadn't been mentioned by name because they were minors. Grant didn't know why the news came as a shock. The arena had been named. He'd known the girls involved skated here. But Corey and Josh seemed too normal to have children who would torment another girl into taking her life. Maybe the police hadn't found any evidence because there wasn't any. Maybe the case was blown out of proportion.

But given the murder and break-in, it seemed unlikely.

"I've said too much." Victor rounded the desk and escorted him to the hall. "Good luck, Major."

Grant held out a hand. "Thanks for getting Kate's things together for me."

Exiting the office, Grant headed for the main room. He passed the rink. Corey's daughter had come off the ice and was talking to her father. Beyond them stood Josh and his daughter. Grant saw them all with fresh eyes. The teens looked more spoiled and arrogant than pretty now, and Grant didn't know what to think of their fathers. The hockey team surged onto the ice and flowed into a warm-up skate, blocking Grant's view. Uneasy, both with the foursome and his own reaction, he turned away. According to the police, the case was unsubstantiated by solid evidence. He shouldn't judge, but deep breathing didn't dispel his growing need to break something. Like those young hockey players, he needed a hard run to burn off his tension.

A hand on his elbow jolted him. He whirled, a hand raised on instinct.

"Oh." An attractive brunette woman about his age pressed a palm to the center of her chest.

With a throbbing yet relieved heart, Grant forced his mouth into a smile and lowered his fist. "I'm sorry. You startled me."

"I didn't mean to." She smiled back. "It's just that you look familiar. Did you go to Scarlet Falls High School?"

"No. Sorry." Grant edged toward the exit, but she fell into step beside him. Their footsteps echoed on the concrete. Guilt slowed his steps. Blowing the friendly woman off would be rude. He sighed. "I went to the military academy, but my three siblings went here. Maybe you know Hannah or Mac."

"Could be. Is Hannah tall and blond like you?"

"She is."

They reached the front door.

The woman dipped her chin and glanced at him through her lashes. Was she flirting with him? "I think she graduated a year behind me. Tell her Lisa Shayne said hello."

"I will." Grant ducked out. Cool air hit his face.

First pretty Ellie Ross piqued his interest. Now a cute skating mom flirted with him. If he wasn't headed back to Afghanistan, he'd have some interesting options in Scarlet Falls. But he was going back. His whole career—his whole life—was based on being an army officer. He didn't know what else he'd do. Now that he thought about it, he couldn't remember making an active decision to join the army. He'd been raised to be a soldier.

The civilian suburban life wasn't so bad, though, full of kids, parents, friendly people not actively trying to blow him up. Maybe if he lived like this for a year or so, he wouldn't reflexively react to a stranger's touch with violence.

He'd nearly struck that woman.

His realization settled into his lungs, choking him like Afghan dust. There was no getting around it. After this deployment, he needed some downtime from combat.

Shifting the box into one arm, he dug his keys from his jacket pocket. A vehicle pulled into the space next to him. Ellie Ross was behind the wheel. He dumped the box in the cargo bay and walked around to her car door just as she swung her legs out of the vehicle. She was still in her work clothes. Her coat was open and her skirt rode up a few inches, treating him to an inch of thigh. The skating mom a few moments ago might have been cute, but she didn't make Grant's chest expand the way it did when Ellie was nearby.

"Grant." Ellie stood, tugging her skirt down with a surprised frown. Leaning back into her van, she lifted a box from the passenger seat. "What are you doing here?"

"I had to pick up Kate's things. You?"

She avoided eye contact, and her face was pale. "I'm supposed to be at a parent meeting, but I'm going to have to just drop off these programs for the spring carnival and run." She closed the van door and shoved a piece of long, dark hair behind her ear. Her hands and voice were shaky. "Now that Kate won't be coaching her, I'm not sure Julia will even stay with the club."

She'd been nervous at the hospital, but she should have calmed down now that she knew her grandmother was fine. She almost seemed *more* upset.

"Are you all right?"

"Fine." Still avoiding his gaze, she faked a smile and glanced at her watch. "I have to hurry. I dropped off Nan's prescription at the pharmacy. It'll be ready in twenty minutes. I don't want to leave her for long."

"How's the ankle?"

"Painful." She sidestepped toward the arena.

"Call me if you need anything."

"Thank you." Ellie turned away. "Bye, Grant."

"Bye, Ellie."

Returning to the minivan, Grant watched Ellie hurry across the pavement and disappear inside the building. He couldn't shake the feeling that Ellie Ross was hiding something.

And he had every intention of uncovering her secret.

Chapter Eighteen

Ellie glanced over her shoulder. Grant was folding his big body into the minivan. Once again, she was tempted to tell him everything. He radiated capability. But this morning's text and the package on her doorstep reinforced Hoodie Man's assertion that she was being watched. She scanned the salt-dusted parking lot. Her neck tingled, and her stomach clenched. Hoodie Man could be anywhere. He could be staring at her through a windshield right now.

Once her initial panic had passed, she'd realized the heart he'd sent her was far too large to be human. Still nasty, though. She'd hidden the box with its bloody contents in the chest freezer in her garage until trash day. Seeing the bloody organ pinned to her daughter's picture made his point clear. Hoodie Man wasn't screwing around. She swallowed her fear and pushed through the door into the building, then walked back to the meeting space. Even away from the ice, cold seeped from the concrete floor into the soles of her shoes. She hadn't taken the time to change since leaving work. Normally, she'd wear thick boots and a heavy sweater to the arena. She walked past the rink, the temperature dropping with each step.

Voices drew her into the long, narrow all-purpose room. Two dozen adults, a mix of coaches and parents, packed the small area.

She only recognized a few faces. Two rectangular laminate tables were set up end to end to form an impromptu conference table. Plastic chairs surrounded it.

Victor Church greeted her. "Hello, Ellie."

"Hi." Ellie set the programs on the table. She glanced at the clock above the door. "I can't stay long. I'm sorry. My grandmother is ill."

"No problem. We can get started now, and it will only take a few minutes." Victor went to the front of the room and raised a hand. "Hello everyone. I want to thank you for coming in for this emergency meeting. I know many of you have jobs and need to get back to work. There are also a number of parent volunteers who couldn't make this meeting, so I would appreciate if you could spread the word."

Ellie moved to the side of the room and put her back against the wall. The chairs around the table were all occupied.

"As you all know the spring exhibition and carnival is scheduled for next week," Victor continued. "Coach Barrett ran this event, and we're all sorry about her death. But we think the carnival should go on as scheduled. We can't get our deposits back from the vendors. If we cancel, we'll lose a large amount of money."

People murmured. Parents already paid steep fees for instructors and ice time. Figure skating and hockey were expensive sports, especially at the more competitive levels. The skating club depended on a few large events in the spring and summer to raise money for fall/winter competition season.

Ellie scanned the faces seated at the table. She recognized the tan face and blond-streaked hair of Corey Swann. His surfer looks didn't blend in with any crowd. Corey's IT company heavily sponsored the club. Josh Winslow sat next to Corey. Every time she saw Corey, Josh, or their daughters, her stomach curled up. They went about their business as if nothing happened. They should all be deeply affected by Lindsay's suicide.

At the front of the room, Victor was talking about the event timetable. Ellie kept one ear tuned on his speech as he reviewed the carnival planning agenda for the next week.

She couldn't blame parents for supporting their children. The Hamiltons' position was easy to understand. But if someone accused Julia of tormenting another student, Ellie would stand up for her daughter too, especially if there was little concrete evidence and if Julia said she was innocent. Ellie couldn't imagine Julia being deliberately unkind. But then, she hadn't expected her daughter to sneak out in the middle of the night either. She still couldn't believe that had happened.

Perhaps Corey Swann felt that way about his daughter. Julia's foray had taught Ellie that, as a parent, it was often hard to accept that your child lied or made a bad decision. Even teenagers without prior disciplinary issues made mistakes.

Thinking about her daughter's deception still sent fear skittering through her belly and made her wonder how any parent could know what was really going on inside a teenager's mind.

Victor picked up a program from the box Ellie had brought. "The event agenda is in the program, and we'll be adding a moment of silence at the event opening for Kate. We don't want to focus on her death, but the kids expressed that they wanted to honor her in some way." His voice grew clipped as he listed a few last-minute details that required attention. Parents raised hands to volunteer, and Victor assigned tasks.

Ellie pressed a knuckle to the corner of her eye. She wished they'd just cancel the event. It was Kate's project. It seemed wrong to continue without her, but Victor was right about the financial risk. The club couldn't afford to take the loss.

"Does anyone else have any questions or concerns?" Victor asked. Heads shook. "All right then. If you have any questions this week or next, please feel free to e-mail or call me."

Chairs scraped as people stood and moved toward the door. Shuffling toward the front of the room, Ellie said a quiet hello to the other parent volunteers.

An elbow brushed her ribs. She turned and looked up at Corey Swann.

"Excuse me," she said pointedly.

Standing far too close, he glared down at her. "Do you work for Peyton, Peyton, and Griffith?"

Ellie took a step back and reestablished her personal space. "Yes."

"I can't talk to you." He frowned, lines etched in his tan face.

Not knowing what else to say, she went with, "All right."

Her gaze dropped to his black sweatshirt. The logo on the chest read Computer Solutions, Inc. His brown eyes glittered with anger. He pressed closer and lowered his voice. "Your firm is involved in the lawsuit."

"Not a problem." Ellie raised a hand to his chest and firmly pushed him six inches away. "*I'm* not the one who bumped into *you*."

He leaned away. Regret washed the anger from his face. "You're right. I was totally out of line. I'm sorry."

Ellie nodded.

"Hey, Corey." Giving Ellie a polite smile, Josh Winslow tugged on Corey's arm. "Come on. Let's get out of here."

Corey let his friend pull him to the back of the group.

How did Corey even know where she worked? This morning's news report had identified Lee and given the firm's name, but Ellie certainly wasn't mentioned. One of the other parents could have mentioned her job, she supposed. Julia had only been skating since they'd become neighbors with Lee and Kate. Some of the kids had been skating at the arena their whole lives, moving up from team to team as their skills advanced. Ellie didn't have time or desire to work her way into the gossip chain. Discomfort stirred in her as she realized she'd likely been the subject of a few of those hushed conversations.

She had been the object of public disapproval as a pregnant high school dropout, but she was no longer an insecure teenager. She felt bad for Corey, but that didn't excuse his behavior.

Maybe bullying ran in the family.

Grant let Ellie into the house. She stopped to give the dog a scratch behind the ears. She'd changed clothes since he'd seen her at the arena a short while ago. The worn jeans and sweater hugged her curves just as well as the suit she'd been wearing earlier.

"Ellie!" Carson ran toward her and flung his arms around her waist. "Is Julia home?"

Ellie stooped to give him a return hug. AnnaBelle butted her head between them, and Ellie wobbled.

Grant steadied her with a hand on her shoulder and took the dog's collar with his free hand. "AnnaBelle, no knocking visitors over."

"It's all right." She put a hand on the floor and regained her balance. She ruffled Carson's blond locks and smiled at him. "I'm used to the warm welcome. Yes, Julia is home. She's taking care of Nan."

"Is Nan's foot all better?" Carson asked.

"I'm afraid that's going to take a while. I'll bet she could use some cheering up." Ellie stood. "You want to go over and say hi?"

Carson's nod was eager and quick.

"Go put on shoes and a jacket."

Carson ran toward the back of the house, his socks sliding in the hall.

Ellie glanced at Grant. "I'm sorry. I should have asked if it was all right with you. He's over at my house so frequently, I didn't think."

"It's fine. I'm sure he could use a change of scenery," Grant said. "As long as you don't think he'll be in the way."

Ellie shook her head. "Nan is already bored. He'll entertain her for a while."

Carson raced back. His jacket hung open and his snow boots were on the wrong feet. Ellie and Grant went out onto the porch to watch him race across the front yards to Ellie's front door. Julia let him in.

"Where's Faith?" Ellie asked.

"In the kitchen with my sister."

"Good," Ellie agreed, but her eyes turned wary. "When you called, you said you had something for me."

Grant suddenly wished she'd give him half the warmth she'd shown his nephew. "Let's go into the office so we can talk in private."

He'd decided to come clean with her. None of the files he'd found were the sensitive Hamilton case. There was no point in hanging on to them. Maybe if he gave them to Ellie, she'd start to trust him.

He closed the door behind them. Ellie turned and backed away from him. Her thighs hit the seat of the old chair, and she eased back into it as if exhausted.

Grant turned the desk chair to face her and sat. He pointed to a box on the desk. "You can take those files to your boss."

Ellie's eyes brightened. She lurched to her feet. Her boot caught on the chair leg, and she toppled forward.

"Whoa. Easy." Grant sprang forward and caught her by the shoulders just before her forehead hit the edge of the desk.

She scrambled to get her feet underneath her body. Her face flushed.

"There's no rush. Those files aren't going anywhere." Satisfied she had regained her balance, he released her arms. "I already made one trip to the ER today. Let's not make it two."

Her face paled. "I'm sorry. I'm not usually this clumsy."

What the hell was wrong with her? He understood why she'd been upset at the hospital, but there was no reason for Ellie to still be a mess. Her grandmother was fine.

She lifted her chin and straightened her sweater. She lifted the files from the box and thumbed through the tabs. Disappointment sagged her shoulders and for a brief moment, Grant thought she was going to cry.

Then it hit him. He knew exactly what she was looking for.

"It's not there," he said.

"What isn't here?" she asked, her voice wary.

"The Hamilton file."

The look she shot him was defensive and desperate. She didn't deny that's what she was seeking. "Do you have it?"

"No." He shook his head.

She dropped the files back into the box. "How did you find out about it?"

"I saw a news broadcast this afternoon. In an interview, Mr. and Mrs. Hamilton claimed that Lee was their attorney and that he'd found new evidence in their daughter's case right before he was killed." He'd spent some hours reading every article on the case he could find online about the suicide.

"I didn't see any news this afternoon. We were stuck in that ER cubicle for hours. Did the Hamiltons say what kind of evidence?"

"They said they didn't know."

Ellie dropped into the chair. Her face was still pale, her focus inward.

"Tell me what's going on, Ellie."

"Nothing." She brought her hands to her face and pressed her fingertips to her forehead.

"I know something is wrong." Grant moved closer. He reached out and took one of her hands in his. He pressed his palms around her cold fingers. "Maybe I can help."

Her eyes lifted to meet his. For a moment, turmoil and helplessness looked back at him. Then she pulled her hand free and clenched it tight enough to whiten her knuckles. "I'll take these files back to the firm tomorrow."

"Ellie, tell me what's wrong. Tell me what you know about this case." He reached for her hand again. "You can trust me."

But Ellie jerked her fist back to her body. "It has nothing to do with trust."

"I want to help you."

"I know, but you can't." Her voice sharpened. She picked up the box of files, took three steps to the door, and opened it. "I'm going to run these files to the office. I'll tell Julia to walk Carson home."

"Thank you." But Grant was talking to empty air. Ellie was gone. He heard the front door open and shut.

He went back to the kitchen. Hannah was shaking a bottle of formula while Faith fussed on her hip. Though she still acted tentative, his sister's skill with the baby surprised him.

"I have to go to Carson's school." The only time the teacher, principal, and counselor had all been available today was after school hours. "He's over at Ellie's house. Julia will bring him home when he's ready. You OK here for a while? I shouldn't be that long. The grammar school is only a mile away."

"We're fine." Grabbing a dish towel, she moved to the family room and settled on the couch to feed the baby. "Could you hand me the remote before you go? I want to catch the market reports."

"Market reports?"

Hannah shrugged. "I have to do something."

Grant was tired of waiting, too. The police had made little headway on the murder case. The future of the children was undecided. The funeral was on hold until Lee's and Kate's bodies were released. Grant had only been in town a few days, but it seemed like much more time had passed.

Driving to the school, Grant pondered Ellie and her changeable attitude. He would keep working on her. Something was very wrong with Ellie Ross. He hadn't known her long, but the woman he'd interacted with today seemed totally different from the smiling woman he'd met at a barbecue and the level-headed woman who'd kept her grandmother from shooting him Monday night. Today's Ellie was terrified.

Something happened to change her entire personality in the last few days, and Grant's gut instincts suspected Ellie's 180 was connected to Kate and Lee's murder.

Chapter Nineteen

Donnie slouched in the front seat, peered over the dashboard, and watched the hot teenage neighbor and the little boy go into the Barrett house. He'd done his research, and the details of Friday night's shooting had been reported to death. He'd learned all about the Barrett family. He pegged the big man who left thirty minutes ago as Major Grant Barrett, Lee's brother. He was military and therefore the one person Donnie would prefer to avoid. The blond woman he'd seen through the window was probably Lee's sister. She didn't worry Donnie. A female lawyer wouldn't be any more of a threat than her dead brother had been. One bullet had put him down. He hadn't even attempted to fight back.

If Donnie was going to get that boy, now was the time. But how to get in? A security system had been installed since he broke into the house last. If it weren't for the damned dog, he might be able to get past a few door and window contacts without anyone noticing him.

He rubbed his freezing hands together. He'd parked his vehicle in a shadow. The absence of the sun's rays kept the vehicle cold. His toes and ass were numb.

The front door opened. The teenager pushed a stroller out onto the stoop. The little boy followed her. Could Donnie get more lucky?

No.

This was perfect. But he'd have no choice but to take the teen, too. His new motto was no witnesses. A six-year-old shouldn't be that hard to grab, but the two of them at once would be hard to manage. The thought of having that young girl all to himself for a couple of hours felt nearly as important as getting rid of the boy.

Kids were loud, so he needed to do this fast. The neighborhood seemed empty now, but at four o'clock, the window of opportunity was closing. He knew from his earlier stakeouts that homeowners would start returning from work soon.

If he grabbed the boy, would the teenager fight for him? She'd be torn because the baby was there, too. She might choose to protect the baby and run for help. Too many variables.

Whatever. Donnie would have to improvise.

He straightened his knit hat and brushed the wrinkles from his jeans. Too bad he didn't have a tie or jacket to make him look legitimate. Hood up or down? Definitely down. In this neighborhood, guys didn't wear hoods. He flipped down the visor and checked the concealer he'd used on the teardrop tattoo. It was heavy-duty, made for scars, the girl at the store had said. The blue ink bled through. Lying bitch. It was less noticeable, though. Hopefully, no one would see it until he got close.

He zipped his jacket to his chin, got out of the van, and headed toward the children.

Julia lowered her side of the seesaw to the ground, lifting Carson into the air. A red knit cap pulled low on his forehead shadowed the little boy's eyes, and cold colored his cheeks red. He wiped a hand under his nose, but a little snot on a mitten was worth the first smile she'd seen on his face all week.

Had it been almost a week since Mr. and Mrs. Barrett died? No, not quite. It had only been six days but seemed longer.

She glanced over at the baby stroller, parked next to the seesaw. Tucked under a thick pile of blankets, Faith slept. She'd just finished a bottle when Julia had brought Carson home and volunteered to take both kids outside.

Thin patches of snow still dotted the playground. Where the ground cover had melted, the grass was wet and squishy underfoot. Major Barrett didn't seem the kind of man that would mind some mud on the floor. Besides, Carson desperately needed the fresh air. Julia, too. She was grounded for a to-be-determined length of time. Sitting in the house had been making all three of them depressed.

After Julia's stunt with Taylor, this was as close to the outside world as she was going to get for a long time. Mom was really mad. Not yelling mad, but quiet mad, which was way worse. Now she was freaking out about Nan's broken foot, too. She'd probably be angry that Nan had suggested Julia take the kids to the playground.

With a woof, AnnaBelle raced to Julia. She spit a tennis ball next to her, then danced backward, barking. Julia hurled the ball across the park. The dog streaked off after it.

"I wish I could throw that far," Carson said, climbing off the seesaw. He jogged over to the slide and started climbing.

Julia checked the baby again. She slid off her glove and reached under the blanket to make sure Faith's body was warm. The space under the fleece blanket felt toasty.

A sharp bark drew her attention. AnnaBelle was racing across the muddy ground toward her. She slid to a stop.

"Where's the ball, AnnaBelle?"

But the dog wasn't looking at her. Her ears were pricked toward the street. A white van was parked at the curb. She'd seen that vehicle before, but when? Julia's neck prickled.

To keep the small kids away from the street, the playground was separated from the sidewalk by a basketball court and rectangular patch of grass. The space between the van and the kids didn't feel like nearly enough distance.

Instinctively, she glanced around for Carson. He was scampering off the bottom of the slide.

"Carson," she called.

He ran over, bits of mud flying from under his snow boots and splattering his waterproof pants. His eyes were bright as he chewed on the end of his mitten. "What?"

Julia put a hand on the stroller handle. The van's door opened, and a man got out. He looked familiar, but she couldn't place him.

"It's him again." Carson backed up a step. His eyes filled with apprehension.

"Have you seen him before?"

Carson nodded. "He knocked on the door the night Mommy and Daddy left, remember?" The little boy's expression darkened, the happiness of playing in the mud wiped out as he remembered his new reality.

But movement pulled Julia's gaze back to the man. He was walking toward them. She searched her memory but came up with nothing except a weird, creepy sensation that made her want to get away.

"Let's go home." She pushed the stroller in the opposite direction.

"Hey," the man called. "I need to talk to you."

Julia walked faster. So did he. The stroller wheels slogged in the mud. Julia leaned into her task. Carson tried to help, clutching the handle with both mittens and pushing hard.

"I'm a reporter. I just want to ask you a few questions." He increased his speed.

There was no way they'd get away with the stroller bogging down in the muck. Julia reached into the stroller and picked up the baby. "Run, Carson. I don't think he's a reporter."

One glance at Carson told her he didn't believe the man was with the press either. Carson darted for his house.

Clutching the baby to her chest, Julia broke into a run. There were no cars in any of the driveways between them and the house. No one was home from work yet.

At her side, Carson's boots splashed in the mud. The little boy's short legs couldn't cover much ground, and Julia couldn't go any faster carrying Faith. The man was gaining on them. AnnaBelle ran between them, barking. Julia's lungs burned. She slipped in the mud and nearly went down.

"Hurry," Carson cried. He grabbed her sleeve and pulled. Julia straightened out her legs, but she'd lost precious time. The man was closer. She could hear his ragged breathing as he sprinted toward her.

A whimper slid from her lips. Her shoes hit the pavement. A few seconds later, she heard his boots scrape asphalt. No! Barely thirty feet separated them.

What could she do?

He was going to catch them. They didn't stand a chance of escape. Maybe if she slowed him down, Carson and Faith could get away. She couldn't fight him off carrying the baby, and Carson had no chance against a full-grown man. AnnaBelle barked, but Julia doubted the retriever would attack.

"Carson." Still running, she shoved the baby toward Carson. "Can you carry her?"

He nodded, stopping to take his sister before waddling toward the house with his heavy burden.

"Get help!" Julia moved between the man and the children. Facing the threat, she backed toward the house, praying that assistance came before the man hurt her. Her body shook. He ran closer. She trembled as her gaze locked on his face and registered his fury.

Chapter Twenty

With her mind occupied with estate paperwork, Hannah flipped through financial statements at her brother's desk. She reached for a paper clip. Lee kept them in a small, misshapen bowl at the edge of the blotter. *To Daddy from Carson* was carved into the cavity in sloppy, lopsided letters. The vessel was roughly formed, obviously by childish hands, and cracked, but Lee had displayed it proudly. Hannah surveyed the office. Where had he gotten the money? She couldn't think he'd been involved in anything shady. Not Lee. But why had he indebted his family to buy this monstrosity of a house and lease a BMW? He'd never been concerned with prestige or image in the past. Had ambition finally snagged Lee the way it tugged at Hannah and Grant?

How could Lee be gone?

A sob slipped past her lips, and from there her control broke. She covered her face with her hands and fought the tears, but it was no use. Her breakdown had been building since she found out about her brother's death. There was no holding it back now.

She reached for a tissue and blew her nose. Thankfully, Grant was out of the house, and Julia had taken the kids to the playground. Hannah would hate to be another source of sadness for Carson. The prospect of outdoor play had put him in a happy mood. A glance at the clock on the computer told her Grant could be back any time. She blotted her eyes. She needed to get it together. He needed her help, not one more person to cry all over him.

Most days it took all her effort to smile instead of swear. What happened to Lee was wrong on a base level. He was the good guy, kind and considerate. The one who'd visited Dad in the nursing home while the rest of the Barrett clan chased their dreams all over the globe. As far as Hannah traveled, she'd always known Lee was here. He had things covered. He was home base. She could return at any time and things would seem unchanged.

But that was all over. Lee was dead.

Pain welled up inside her chest, creating pressure that restricted her breaths. Since her mother died, it was fear of this feeling, this helplessness, this sense of all being lost that made her a loner. The fewer people she loved, the lower her risk of experiencing this overwhelming sadness again.

A frantic scream snapped her attention to the front window. She jumped up and crossed the tiny room. Fear gripped her belly like fingertips on a ledge at the sight through the glass. Beyond Lee's driveway, Julia and Carson were running toward the house. A man chased them, gaining ground.

Hannah ran for the door. Her socks slid on the hardwood as she bolted down the hall and yanked open the front door. In the street ahead, Julia handed the baby to Carson. The girl put herself between the younger children and the threat. The dog stood at Julia's side, barking. Hannah leaped over the front steps.

Hell, no. He was not getting that girl.

Hannah burst forward, sprinting down the driveway toward the children.

The man whirled, taking off in the opposite direction. Hannah passed the children and chased him, anger fueling her long legs. Mud soaked through her socks. She cranked up her speed.

He cut across the park toward a white van. Hannah turned onto the grass just as he leaped into the vehicle and took off with the squeal of tires on pavement.

She stopped, shaded her eyes, and squinted at the license plate, but it was covered with mud.

Damn it.

She noted the make and model of the vehicle. Winded, Hannah wheezed back to the house. She needed to get back in shape. Julia and the kids huddled on Ellie Ross's front porch. In front of them, Julia's grandmother sat on the step. Nan's booted, broken foot was extended on the concrete. A shotgun lay across her lap. With her left wrist in a brace, she gripped the gun with one hand, using her knee to hold up the barrel.

Hannah stopped on the walkway that curved to the steps. "Is everyone all right?"

Though fear shone in her eyes, Julia nodded over the baby's head on her shoulder. Carson lunged off the step and threw his arms around Hannah's waist. She hesitated, her hands hovering above his shoulders for a minute, before folding him into an awkward hug. The kind of love Carson offered terrified her with its strength and wholeheartedness. Was she capable of returning that much affection? What if she messed up?

Grant pulled into the driveway and jumped out of the minivan. "What happened?"

"Julia took us to the park. A man chased us." In a single breath, Carson abandoned Hannah for Grant's strong embrace.

Hannah was simultaneously disappointed and relieved.

"I'm calling the police." Hannah turned toward the house, away from Grant and Carson and the baby clinging to Julia, away from the responsibility, the dependency.

"Already did that," said Nan.

"Did you call Ellie?" Grant asked.

Nan shook her head. "No. She's on her way home from dropping off some files at the office. I didn't want her driving upset."

Hannah eyed the shotgun across the older woman's knees. She approved of the old lady's spunk, but doubted Nan could even fire the gun if necessary.

"You bet I can fire it," Nan said.

Hannah paused.

"Honey, I didn't need to read your mind to know what you were thinking." Nan held a hand out. "Would you be a dear and help me up?"

"You aren't supposed to put any weight on that foot." Grant set Carson down.

"It was an emergency." Nan shrugged, but pain lined her face. She unloaded the gun, putting the shells into the pocket of her cardigan.

Grant scooped her off the step and turned toward his brother's house. "Let's all stick together. It'll be easier when the police show up. Julia, could you get your grandmother's crutches?"

Julia handed Faith to Hannah. She folded the baby close, trying to ignore how much she liked the scent of baby powder. Hannah had only been here a couple of days, and these kids were already burrowing into her heart. She was clearly not meant to be in charge of children. They'd been in her care for an hour, and she'd failed them. Grant couldn't run one errand without Hannah putting the children in danger.

Clutching Faith close to her chest, Hannah herded Carson into his house. Grant went back to the adjoining family room and set Nan on the sofa. He stowed her shotgun on top of the refrigerator, out of Carson's reach.

Hannah slid into a kitchen chair. Faith babbled in her ear. The baby wailed for ten hours every night for no reason, but being chased down the street by a strange man thrilled her.

Carson and Julia took chairs at the table, too. Grant crouched down in front of them. "You're both all right?"

They nodded.

He removed Carson's coat and boots and put them by the back door. Julia removed her outer garments as well. She shivered and sat next to her grandmother. Nan wrapped an arm around the girl's shoulders.

"Somebody needs a change." Grant took Faith out of the room.

Hannah looked down at her feet. Her formerly gray socks were black and soaked through. Her feet tingled, almost numb with cold. Mud spattered her jeans.

AnnaBelle announced the cop's arrival with a bark and a wag.

Detective McNamara. The cop's expression was shuttered, as usual. He'd kept his cool when she'd practically cross-examined him the other day, too. Didn't anything tweak this guy? His gaze swept over the children at the table. Was that a spark of anger in his eyes? Maybe he did have emotions.

"Who's bleeding?" McNamara pointed at the mud-streaked hall behind him. Barefoot prints were smeared with wet red smudges.

Hannah glanced down at her feet. She was the only one not wearing shoes.

"That must be me." She peeled off her socks. A cut on her heel dripped with blood. "I must have stepped on something sharp. It's not bad. I don't think it needs stitches. Doesn't even hurt."

"Yet." McNamara crouched next to her and lifted her foot for inspection. His hands were unexpectedly callused. "That needs to be cleaned. Come on."

"I can do it myself." She pushed to her feet.

"The bottom of your foot?" He didn't roll his eyes, but she could tell he wanted to, which was a relief. Most of the time, the cop acted like a robot. He put his arm under her elbow.

With his help, she hobbled to the powder room. "I think there's a first aid kit under the sink."

"Got it." He made quick work of cleaning the cut and covering it with a Band-Aid. "Is that all right?"

"It's fine," she said, although her foot was beginning to throb. "I'm just glad no one else was hurt."

McNamara got to his feet. "You were lucky. Those kids could've been hurt."

"You don't have to tell me that."

The cop frowned down at her. "There's no point beating yourself up. No one had any idea the kids were in danger."

Hannah would never be able to close her eyes without seeing that man chasing them down. Her lungs contracted, and pressure built behind her ribs. "Regardless, I should have gone to the park with them."

"When you learn how to predict the future, let me know. That ability would certainly make my job easier."

Not sure how to take his statement, she studied his face.

"That was a joke," he sighed. "Look. The kids are all right. Take a minute to breathe and appreciate that. Sometimes, you have to balance being worried with being grateful."

Hannah breathed. The weight on her chest eased, but the relief was minimal. "Why would anyone go after the kids?"

"I don't know, and that's what's most terrifying." He took a small notebook and pen from his pocket. "I'd better take your statement first. What did he look like? Tell me everything."

For a few seconds, Hannah wanted to let all her fears and insecurities spill out. But he was only asking about the incident, not volunteering to be her therapist. Besides, who had *that* much time? Her gaze raked over his lean, hard physique. No. The cop didn't look like any shrink Hannah had ever seen.

"I didn't get a good look at him. He took off as soon as he saw me."

She steadied herself and relayed the event in a logical and linear manner. But in the back of her mind, all she could see was that man chasing down the children.

"One more question for you." The cop pointed his pen at her. "Your brother had two large cash deposits hit his account a couple weeks ago, both just small enough to avoid federal reporting requirements. Do you know of any assets he could have sold, accounts he could have closed?"

"No." As much as Hannah didn't want to face the possibility that Lee could have been involved in something illegal, she had no explanation for the sudden appearance of nearly twenty thousand dollars.

Grant changed Faith's diaper. She alternated between sticking her toes in her mouth and babbling. The baby talk made his chest ache. She could have been hurt this afternoon. Carson and Julia, too.

He zipped up her one-piece footed coveralls. With her feet secured, she chewed on her fist. Drool ran out the side of her mouth. Grant wiped her chin with his sleeve, which should have been gross but didn't bother him.

Why would anyone chase the kids? What did that guy want? Did he kill Lee and Kate?

He leaned over and pressed his forehead to Faith's. She grabbed his hair with both fists and let loose with a high-pitched, excited shriek. He wouldn't be able to take it if anything happened to these kids. They'd already had their parents stolen from them. Kate should be here for every baby squeal. Carson should have his father to comfort him after a nightmare.

Grant's gut twisted. Anger burned a path through his chest.

Gently prying her fingers loose, he picked her up and held her close. In an active mood, she squirmed and batted her chubby fists on his shoulder. Her feet moved as if she was running in place.

The police were making zero progress investigating the murders within the boundaries of the law. Enough was enough. Lee and Kate's deaths had to be connected to the bullying and suicide of Lindsay Hamilton. Ellie knew something about that case, and Grant needed to make her talk to him. He also needed to find out where Lee had gotten that twenty thousand dollars, even if discovering the truth was painful. Scarlet Falls was festering with secrets, and Grant was going to drag them all out into the light.

Grant made two vows. No one would hurt these children, and he would find the person who killed his brother and make the guilty party pay.

Chapter Twenty-One

Ellie turned her car into her neighborhood. A police car passed her, lights on, and her pulse scrambled. She pressed the gas pedal harder. *No! It can't be.*

The police couldn't be going to her house.

Nausea flooded her belly as she drove down her street. A police car sat at the curb next to the park. Two more were parked at Lee and Kate's house. Relief, and then guilt, surged through Ellie. She shouldn't be grateful the police were needed at her neighbor's house instead of her own. Her gaze was drawn to the policeman taking photographs at the playground.

What had happened?

Ellie parked in her driveway, got out of her car, and slammed the door. With one eye on the Barrett house, she ran up to her front porch and went inside. An empty hush greeted her.

"Nan," she called out in the foyer. Silence answered her. "Julia!"

Ellie hurried back to the kitchen and family room, but the rooms were empty. Nan wasn't there. She'd made sure her grandmother was settled on the sofa before she'd left to deliver the files Grant had found to the firm. Ellie jogged upstairs and checked the three bedrooms anyway. No Nan. No Julia.

She raced outside and across the front yards. In the Barretts' driveway, a uniformed officer stood next to his open cruiser and talked into his radio. On the front porch, she pressed the doorbell.

Another officer opened the door.

"I'm Ellie Ross. I live next door. What happened?"

"This way, ma'am." He stood back and gestured for her to enter the house.

Ellie walked into the foyer, dread gathering behind her sternum. She looked up as Grant carried Faith down the stairs.

"Ellie." He moved toward her. "Everyone is fine."

"What happened?" she repeated. "Are Nan and Julia here?"

"Yes, and they're all right." His words were reassuring, but his eyes went flat.

Still, knowing that her family was OK made her light-headed with relief. Ellie reached for the wall.

"Whoa." One-handing the baby, Grant caught her elbow. He steered her into Lee's office. "Sit down. I'll be right back. Keep your head down and breathe slowly."

In the desk chair, she rested her elbows on her knees and let her forehead drop into her palms. The room pitched beneath her. Her vision went fuzzy. Closing her eyes, she concentrated on sucking air in and out of her lungs. The increased oxygen didn't help.

They are all right. They are all right. Do not throw up.

Her inability to find the file hadn't gotten her grandmother or her daughter killed.

Yet.

She heard the office door close. A hand splayed between her shoulder blades. Grant. The warmth and weight of his touch anchored her to the present.

Everyone was all right.

"Are you OK?" he asked.

Ellie lifted her head and nodded. The room tilted, then stilled.

"What happened?" she asked again, this time without the hysteria in her voice.

"Julia took the kids to the playground down the street for some air."

"I told her to stay with Nan."

"Nan is the one who sent her over. Your grandmother thought some fresh air would cheer them all up."

"If I wanted her cheered up, I wouldn't have grounded her." Ellie swallowed her anger, but her hands clenched into tight fists.

"While the kids were at the park, a man approached them. Julia didn't like the looks of him. She grabbed the kids and ran home yelling. Hannah chased the guy off. No one was hurt. I brought your grandmother over here just in case. I didn't want her alone." He paused, his gaze seeking hers as she stared at her fists. "They're OK, Ellie. Your daughter reacted in exactly the right way. She listened to her instincts and saved them all."

Ellie raised her chin. Her eyes locked with his. Her gut was screaming at her to trust him. He had taken care of her family while she wasn't there. But could she count on him to keep quiet?

Thoughts spinning, she let her head fall into her hands. Her palms pressed against her temples as if trying to contain the terrible images rolling through her mind.

"Ellie!"

Hands shook her shoulders. She opened her eyes.

"Tell me what's wrong." Grant crouched in front of her. Concern filled the blue of his eyes.

She shook her head. How could she trust him? She'd just met him. He was a military officer. He followed orders and rules. He'd tell the police, and her family would suffer the consequences.

"Ellie, what is going on with you?"

Her eyes began to burn as fear overwhelmed her. Before she could react, Grant folded his arms around her. He didn't say anything, just held her against his chest. She resisted for a few seconds, then gave in. His arms surrounded her with solid comfort. She buried her face in his shirt and stopped trying to hold back. Tears stormed her, part relief that her family was unharmed, part terror that next time they might not escape.

The outburst passed in a few seconds. She became gradually aware of Grant's hand stroking her back. The touch was more than comforting.

She lifted her head from his chest. "I'm sorry." Grabbing a tissue from a box on the desk, she blotted her eyes. "I'm not usually such a mess."

Get your act together.

"Talk to me, Ellie."

"I can't."

"Why not?"

Unable to stay hidden, helplessness—and words—tumbled from Ellie's mouth. "Because my family might die if I tell you."

"What?"

"I've said too much." She stood on shaky legs. "I'll get Julia and Nan and go."

"Julia and Nan are waiting to talk to the police. They can't leave yet, and damn it, I want to know what the hell you're talking about. Carson and Faith were in danger this afternoon, too. If you know something, you have to tell me. I won't let anything happen to them."

Ellie pressed a knuckle to her lips. No matter what she did, her family could be hurt. She was following orders, and Hoodie Man came after the kids anyway. And even if she gave him the file, she had no guarantees he'd leave them alone. She couldn't win.

"Please, Ellie." Grant put a hand on her arm. "I can help."

"You have to promise not to tell the police."

"I don't know if I can do that."

"Then I can't tell you." Ellie pulled away from him.

Grant stepped around her, blocking her path to the door. "All right. I'll give you twenty-four hours."

"Forty-eight."

"Thirty-six," he countered.

"Done." Relief flooded Ellie. She wasn't alone.

"But why not tell McNamara? He seems competent."

"The man in the hoodie said if I told anyone, he'd kill my family." Words spilled from her mouth. She told him everything that had happened from being taken at gunpoint from the firm parking lot to finding the heart and threatening note on her porch. "He said he's watching me."

"Do you have any idea who he is?"

"No." She wrapped her arms around her waist.

Grant rubbed the back of his neck. "But I don't understand. Why would he chase Carson and Julia? What could they possibly have to do with the Hamilton case?"

"I assume he did it to scare me."

"And you still don't want to tell the police?"

"No. They haven't made much progress finding Lee and Kate's murderer. The only physical description I can provide is average-size guy, probably not elderly. That's not much to go on. If I tell them and they can't find him, how long do you think they'll be able to protect my family? Their resources are limited. You'll be gone in a few weeks. My family will be alone—and vulnerable."

A knock sounded on the office door, and they both went quiet. Grant opened the door. Detective McNamara stood in the hall. "I have Hannah's statement. I'm going to question the kids. I'd like to take them down to the police station to do it. The county police artist is on her way to see if she can get a sketch. If we can come up with some suspects, I'd also like to show them mug shots. Is that all right with you?"

Ellie's breath locked up. Would Grant give her away?

"Of course. We're coming." Grant's hand settled under Ellie's elbow in silent support. He steered her out into the hall, and they followed the policeman back to the kitchen.

Relief weakened the muscles in Ellie's legs. Grant had kept her secret. But that was no guarantee that her family would be safe.

Chapter Twenty-Two

In the kitchen, Grant pulled Hannah aside. In the background, the baby cooed from a playpen parked next to Nan. "There are cops here, but when they leave, set the alarm."

"I called Mac and left a message for him." She lowered her voice. "He has Dad's weapons collection. I asked him to bring it here."

"He didn't answer his phone?" Irritation and anxiety sparred in his chest. Damn Mac. How hard was it to keep his phone on?

Hannah shook her head and lowered her voice. "He keeps the firearms box in his attic. If he doesn't call, we could drive out to the cabin and help ourselves."

Grant nodded. He would love to have his M-4, but a machine gun was hard to conceal around the house, not to mention the difficulty of tucking it into his waistband.

"I wish I'd had my Glock this afternoon," she said.

"Don't blame yourself, Hannah." Grant gave his sister a quick hug. "None of us expected this. I still don't understand it, but from now on, we're on guard. No chances."

"Right."

"You'll look after Faith and Ellie's grandmother?"

"I will." Hannah's mouth tightened, the ferocity of her expression sharpened by her lean face and edgy haircut. "I won't let you down again."

"You didn't let anyone down, Hannah. You saved those kids."

Her sideways glance was full of self-reproach.

"You'd scare the crap out of me." But Grant's attempt to lighten her mood only gleaned him a scant, tight-lipped smile.

He herded Ellie, Julia, and Carson into the minivan. He glanced at his nephew in the rearview mirror. Carson seemed to be holding up all right, but the boy hadn't needed any more trauma. His eyes were too serious for a six-year-old. "Do you need to talk about what happened, Carson?"

The boy shook his head. "I'm not allowed."

"Detective McNamara asked us not to discuss it until we'd given him our statement," Julia explained.

"I listened," Carson said.

"You certainly did. Good job, buddy." Grant adjusted the mirror and studied Julia. The teen's face displayed more anxiety than Carson's. She had a better grasp of the danger they'd been in that afternoon. But neither kid had cracked under the pressure. They'd held it together like soldiers. From what Hannah had told him, Julia had behaved like a hero.

"OK. Well, we can talk about it afterward." Grant backed out of the driveway and headed toward town. A glance at Ellie's face showed her gaze fixed on the passenger window. Her revelation had rocked him.

His mind conjured up images of a man holding her at gunpoint and threatening her family and Ellie spending the next two days searching for the file.

Abducting Ellie was one more reason for Grant to extract payback. He'd given her a hard time agreeing to keep her predicament from the police, but the truth was, Grant wouldn't mind finding his brother's killer before the cops. Plus, Ellie made fair points about the lack of progress on the murder case and her inability to provide a description of her extortionist. Grant wanted the killer punished before he went back to Afghanistan. It wouldn't be fair to force her to expose her secret and risk her family's safety when he might have to leave her with the threat still viable.

Ellie and her family had worked their way into his heart over the past few days. In a perfect world, he'd tuck them under his wing along with his family. But nothing was perfect.

He parked at the police station and escorted them inside. Ellie and Julia took chairs in the waiting area. Carson walked in a circle, touching everything. His little hands ran over plastic chair backs and desk edges, as if he needed to ground himself physically in the police station to hold it together. Grant took a seat and offered the boy a knee, but Carson shook his head and kept moving.

While they waited for McNamara to get organized, Grant checked his messages. Mac hadn't responded to his text. He would feel a lot better about Faith, Nan, and Hannah being alone if his sister had her handgun. Her hand-to-hand self-defense might be rusty after years as a corporate attorney, but she'd been a natural marksman at birth. Shooting came as easily to her as studying to Lee and sense of direction to Mac. Grant swore his youngest brother could find his way out of Siberia with a stick and a roll of duct tape. If only Mac were as reliable as he was directionally gifted. In the meantime, at least Hannah had Nan's shotgun.

"We're ready for Carson." McNamara gestured toward an open door.

Grant put his hand on his nephew's shoulder and guided him inside a small conference room. Five chairs surrounded an oval table.

McNamara stopped at the door. He motioned toward a slender young woman with long red hair and glasses seated at the table.

"Kailee is a police artist for the county. She's going to work with Carson while I take Julia's statement. Then we'll switch."

"Good plan." Grant settled in a chair, trying to look comfortable and hoping his attitude rubbed off on Carson.

"Hi, Carson. I'm Kailee." Kailee smiled. On her lap she held a sketch pad and pencil.

"Hi, Kailee." Carson crawled into Grant's lap.

Grant hugged him close. No matter what happened, he wanted the boy to feel safe while he was reliving a scary incident.

McNamara crouched in front of Carson. "Kailee is really good at drawing people. Do you think you can describe the man you saw this afternoon?"

Carson turned his head to give Grant a questioning look.

Grant tightened his grip. "It's OK."

The boy pressed closer to Grant's chest and nodded. "Yes." His voice was small.

"OK, then. I'll be back in a little while." McNamara closed the door on his way out.

"Carson, tell me about the man's face," Kailee said.

"He's always crying."

Kailee tilted her head. "That's interesting. How do you know?"

"He has a teardrop on his face." Carson pointed to his own cheekbone, just below his eye socket. "Right here. It's blue."

Kailee's pencil moved on her paper. "Like this?" She turned the paper to face Carson. She'd drawn the outline of a face with a tear where Carson indicated.

His head bobbed.

"Does he have any other pictures on his body?" she asked.

"He has a lucky charm on his arm."

"A lucky charm?" Kailee's pencil hovered above the page.

Carson's missing drawings flashed in Grant's head. "A shamrock?"

The boy smiled. "Uh-huh."

"Show me where it is," Kailee prompted.

Carson pointed to the inside of his wrist. "Here."

Grant pictured the park and Carson and Julia being chased down the street. The tattoos seemed small. How did the boy get a clear picture? "How did you see the pictures? Weren't you running away?"

"Today I was running." Carson gave him a solemn nod. "But not last time I saw him."

Grant's heart missed a beat. "Last time?"

"He came to our house."

"When?" Grant asked.

Carson's eyes teared. He wiped under his nose with the back of his hand. "A little while after Mommy and Daddy left." He sniffed and his little body shook with a single and silent bone-deep sob.

Grant hugged his nephew tighter and met the artist's shocked eyes. The murderer had been to the house the night he'd killed Lee and Kate. If he'd missed them at the house, how did he know where they were going?

And he'd gone after Carson. The obvious reason why sent a blast of cold through Grant. His nephew could identify the killer.

"Carson, tell me exactly how you saw the man up close," Kailee said.

"Julia babysits when Mommy and Daddy go someplace. She brought me macaroni and cheese. Nan made it for me special 'cause she knows I like it." He took a breath. "Faith was crying, like always. I was watching TV. I'm not allowed to do that much, but Julia said it was OK." Carson laid his cheek against Grant's chest. "AnnaBelle barked, so I knew someone was outside. But I didn't open the door 'cause there wasn't a grown-up home." He went quiet.

"If you didn't open the door, how did you see the man?" Kailee prompted.

But Grant knew before the child answered. He pictured the

chair in the foyer, Carson dragging it in front of the door and climbing on it.

Carson shrugged, his skinny shoulder moving in an abrupt up-and-down motion. "I looked out the peephole."

Kailee continued her gentle questions, sketching while Carson talked. An hour later, Detective McNamara interviewed Carson while the artist went to work with Julia. The cop was brief, just asking the little boy to tell him what happened. Afterward, Ellie and Julia joined them in the now crowded conference room. Julia slid into the remaining chair. Ellie stood behind her daughter. With both kids' input, Kailee had a rough sketch of the suspect.

Julia also confirmed the dog had been barking the night Lee and Kate were killed. "I was busy with the baby, though. I didn't see anyone at the door."

Kailee handed her sketch to Detective McNamara, who said, "Why don't you take the kids and get them something from the vending machine in the break room?"

Carson gave Grant a questioning look.

"It's fine. You're safe here." Grant pulled out his wallet and took out a few ones. He handed the bills to Carson. "Get whatever you want. I'll be right here waiting for you."

Carson took the money and followed Kailee and Julia down the hall to an open door.

McNamara studied the drawing. "Those tattoos suggest prison to me. The shamrock is a sign of the Aryan Brotherhood. We'll enter this description in the National Crime Information Center and see if we get a match. We could get lucky. We'll also get this picture out to the media. Someone might recognize him."

Grant folded his arms across his chest and glanced at Ellie. "I don't want Julia's or Carson's name on the news."

With a grim nod, Ellie eased into the chair her daughter had vacated.

"Agreed," McNamara said. "But attempted child abductions are big stories. I would expect the media to be all over this. There's really no way to keep them out completely, but they won't be able to name Carson or Julia because they're minors. You're lucky the press isn't already here. We can't stop them, so we might as well use them."

"I saw on the news that my brother had agreed to represent the parents of Lindsay Hamilton in a civil trial. Do you think that could have anything to do with all of this?" Grant gestured to the kids in the break room.

McNamara scratched his head. "Honestly, we don't know."

"During the interview, the Hamiltons said Lee had discovered something about their daughter's case."

"We have no new evidence in the case," McNamara said. "We never had enough to charge anyone. Bullying is harassment. Bullying someone until they commit suicide isn't exactly murder. Bullying cases get a lot of national media coverage, but it's damned hard to prosecute kids criminally. Sometimes a civil case is easier to win. Look at the O. J. Simpson trials. He was acquitted of murder, but found liable in the wrongful death suit."

"So what kind of evidence would Lee need to win a civil suit?"

"That's hard to say," McNamara evaded. "We can't ask your brother, and we don't know what he had in mind. Do you?" The police would clearly like to have Lee's file, too.

"No." Sweeping a frustrated hand over his head, Grant glanced down the empty hall. Through the open door of the break room, he saw the little boy kneeling on a cafeteria chair at a round table. The artist handed him an open bottle of water and a bag of pretzels. Bluish semicircles of exhaustion hung under Carson's eyes. His childish innocence and vulnerability sent Grant's protective instincts rushing through him. "I'd better get Carson out of here before he's spotted."

"Give me a few minutes." McNamara took the drawing and the verbal description with him to his office down the hall. "Let me make sure I have everything I need from him."

"I can't believe this is all happening," Ellie said. "You know what this means, right? This guy is after the kids because they can identify him. They're the only witnesses."

She was right, and while the police were investigating the break-in and the attack on the kids, they didn't know this guy had also threatened Ellie. Grant was tempted to come clean with McNamara, but he'd promised. And really, what could the cops do? They didn't have the file. They had no idea who was behind all this, and all they had was the perpetrator's description from the kids.

Their best bet was to keep looking for Lee's notes and wait to see if the cops came up with any possible suspects from the composite drawing and kids' descriptions. All Grant needed was a name to go on the offensive.

Chapter Twenty-Three

As soon as the kids and the cop were out of sight, Ellie's legs collapsed. She couldn't believe this was happening. She'd overprotected Julia since her birth, and she still hadn't managed to keep her daughter safe.

Grant eased into the chair next to her. His face looked as tired as she felt. He covered her hand with his. As much as she didn't want a relationship with him, at this point there was no denying that they were in this together. Although he likely wanted to tell Detective McNamara everything, Grant had kept his promise. He hadn't told the police about her abduction.

"What are we going to do?" she said, staring down at their joined hands.

"I don't know." Grant scratched his jaw. Beard bristle scraped. The blond scruff gave him a new, dangerous edge.

She lowered her voice. "Thank you for sticking with me." She didn't know if the police had listening devices in the room, but she wasn't taking any chances.

"I keep my word." He squeezed her fingers. "Though we might want to rethink that decision as time goes by."

She nodded. If they hadn't found the file in another day or so, she'd have to tell the police everything. She couldn't risk Hoodie Man showing up and finding her empty-handed. Maybe the kids could be placed in protective custody or something. She almost laughed out loud. As if a town the size of Scarlet Falls would have anything like protective custody, and she doubted Hoodie Man was a mafia kingpin worthy of FBI attention. Though Lindsay's suicide had made the national evening news, it was a one-day event. The case was forgotten in the wake of other tragedies in the month that had passed since her death. The Hamilton case was a local disaster.

"I think you, Julia, and Nan should temporarily move in with us." Grant stroked the back of her hand with his thumb. "I had a security system installed, and Hannah and I will be armed. Mac too, if I can talk him into staying for a few days. Plus, the dog barks if anyone even gets close to the house."

As much as Ellie treasured her privacy, Grant offered her family protection she couldn't provide alone. "OK."

"That was fast." He raised his brows, obviously surprised by her quick agreement.

"Safety in numbers and all that." She wasn't going to tell him that she felt more secure simply being with him. "I'm not sure how Julia will react."

"What about your grandmother?" Grant asked.

"Oh, Nan will be fine with moving in with you." More than fine, Ellie suspected.

"OK, then. I'll text Hannah and let her know." Grant picked up his phone. "There are extra bedrooms, but I'm not sure about sheets and pillows."

"I have plenty at my house. We'll work out the details."

"Either Hannah or I will drive Julia and you to school and work tomorrow."

"I'm calling in sick." She had weeks of accumulated personal time. Roger would have to get along without her until this mess was over. "The file isn't at the office. I looked everywhere. I even went through Frank's computer files and saw nothing related to the case. I plan to spend tonight and tomorrow searching your brother's house."

"Good plan." He nodded. "And you can tell me what you know about the case."

"I'll tell you everything," she said.

"Everything about what?" Detective McNamara walked in.

Ellie exhaled. Grant made her forget they were sitting in the police station. "My daughter's father." The lie slipped out on impulse, and Ellie regretted it the moment the words left her lips. Now Grant was sure to ask her about Julia's dad, a subject that embarrassed her fifteen years later. Nan was right. She needed to put her old news behind her. She'd already trusted Grant with her family. Her backstory hardly compared.

The cop's gaze dropped to their hands on the table. Did he believe her? "I'm going to post a patrol car on your street overnight. I'm not sure how long I can do that, but the chief has approved it for tonight. We'll address it again tomorrow. You had a security system installed?" he asked Grant.

"Yes." Grant nodded. "It's basic, but it covers all the doors and windows."

"Better than nothing." McNamara paced the tiny room. "We put out a BOLO, that's a *be on the lookout* bulletin, for this guy. We're pulling possible suspects from our records. I'll come by as soon as I can to ask the kids to look at some mug shots."

"All right."

McNamara turned to Ellie. "Do *you* have a security system?"

"No," she said.

Grant stood, pulling her to her feet beside him. "Ellie and her family are going to stay with us. We'll keep them safe." His voice held no doubt.

But Ellie was uncertain enough for both of them. She felt safer with Grant, but he was temporary. What would she do if the situation wasn't resolved when his leave was over?

"What do either of you know about the Hamilton case?" McNamara asked.

Grant shrugged. "Just what I saw in the interview on TV."

"They said your brother was their lawyer." McNamara watched Grant's face.

"I know." Grant gave nothing away. "But you'd have to ask the law firm to confirm that. There were some files in Lee's office, but none were labeled Hamilton."

"Where are those files now?" the cop asked.

"They were returned to the firm," he said.

"How about you, Ms. Ross? You work for the firm." The cop shifted his focus to Ellie. She wished she could be half as calm and collected as Grant.

Ellie nodded. "But I'm contractually bound by a confidentiality clause. I can't discuss client business without permission from my boss or a subpoena. I'm sorry."

"I understand." But the tension in the cop's shoulders suggested he didn't like it one bit. "I'm hoping to have one of those soon." He searched her face for a reaction.

But really, she didn't know much about the case that hadn't made the news or been school gossip. Lee had just taken them on as clients. She lifted a palm. "Honestly, Lee didn't share his notes. I doubt I can give you any new information about the case."

Except that everyone wanted the file, and at least one man was willing to hurt her family to get it.

"Any progress on Lee's murder?" Grant asked.

McNamara gave him a quick head shake. "I'll drop by later with those mug shots."

So that Julia and Carson could help identify a killer.

Chapter Twenty-Four

The wallpaper in the dining room was covered in faded hummingbirds in flight. They hovered on the walls as if they could swoop down and steal a slice of pepperoni. Eating in the big, formal space was like being trapped inside Alfred Hitchcock's classic horror film, *The Birds*. But the kitchen table wasn't big enough for the entire group.

Grant closed the pizza box. Carson and Hannah sat across from him. Julia, Ellie, and Nan clustered at the other end of the table. Faith fussed in her car seat in the corner. Mac hadn't responded. Damn it. When Grant finally got a hold of his youngest brother, he was going to teach him to be responsible. How the hell would Mac be able to take care of these two kids if he couldn't even remember to keep his cell phone charged and handy? At least he'd dropped the guns off with Hannah this afternoon before going AWOL again. Mac had also left Grant a special present, Dad's best knife, a KA-BAR he'd carried when he was a young Ranger.

Hannah claimed her favorite weapon, a Glock with the stopping power of an elephant. Grant stuck to the Beretta that matched his service issue. The security system was armed. At the moment, AnnaBelle's vigilance was focused on the slice of pizza dangling from Carson's fingers, but later, Grant was sure the dog would be on watch. An SFPD cruiser sat in the driveway. They were as safe as they were going to be for the night, but tomorrow, who knew?

Cleanup consisted of one run to the garbage can by the back door.

"Can you walk Faith for a while?" Grant asked his sister. "Ellie and I are going to search this house from top to bottom."

"All right." Hannah sighed and scooped the baby out of her car seat. "You know what? I saw a baby bath tub upstairs. I'm going to make an attempt to get my girlfriend here cleaned up because she's beginning to smell ripe. Maybe a bath will distract her."

"Or she'll scream through it," Grant said.

Hannah lifted a *whatever* hand. "She's going to cry anyway, so it's not like I have anything to lose."

Carson scooted out of his chair and tugged on Hannah's T-shirt. "Can I take a bath too?"

"Of course." Hannah smiled.

"I'll help." Julia pushed her chair back. "Come on, Nan. Let's get you to the sofa."

"Thanks." Hannah carried the baby out of the room on her hip. His sister seemed to have softened over the past couple of days, as if she'd lost her icy, tough veneer when she'd shed the suit and put on her jeans.

Julia helped her grandmother hobble out of the room.

Grant watched Carson head off happily with Julia, the dog at their heels. "I'll admit it's nice to have some help with the kids."

"Has it been rough?" Ellie asked.

"Carson's pretty easy. I just hope I'm not messing him up for life."

"He seems to have bonded with you," she said.

"Yeah." Which was part of the problem. Grant only had three more weeks stateside. Mac was proving to be too unreliable to handle the kids. But Hannah . . . she acted almost domestic tonight. Almost. But with every day that passed, she behaved more like his little sister and less like a hotshot corporate attorney.

"Where do you want to start?" Ellie pushed the chairs under the table.

"I already searched the office." Grant headed for the stairs. "The master bedroom is the next most likely place to keep important documents."

He stepped aside and let Ellie go up first, enjoying the view of her hips swaying in front of him.

"Agreed." Ellie stopped in front of Lee and Kate's bedroom. Grant had straightened the downstairs, but the master bedroom was still in disarray from the break-in. Clothing was scattered, and articles hung from gaping drawers.

Grant hesitated at the threshold. "Would you mind putting away Kate's things?" Searching through his sister-in-law's intimates would feel like an invasion of her privacy.

"Of course." She nodded grimly and pulled out the top drawer of Kate's nightstand.

"We're looking for places easily overlooked." Grant pushed aside the clothes in the closet and felt along the walls. Nothing. The shoe boxes on the top shelf held only shoes. Containers stored off-season clothes. Grant left the closet. He walked around the room, lifting prints off the walls and checking behind them. He inspected the floor for any sign a board had been pried loose. "Do you know if they had a safe?"

Ellie shone a flashlight behind the headboard. "No." Her voice was strained with sadness.

"Why don't you tell me about the Hamilton case while we search?" He had read articles on the case, but he wanted Ellie's perspective.

"Lindsay Hamilton was a junior at Scarlet Falls High. She moved here from California and joined the skating team. Within a couple of weeks of starting, she was targeted for torment. This bully faction was allegedly led by two girls, Regan Swann and Autumn Winslow. Both girls are stars of the team, top of the high school class, et cetera. According to Lindsay's parents, these girls harassed Lindsay until she hanged herself in the woods behind her house."

"If the girls were guilty, why isn't there enough evidence to charge them?" he asked. "Are you sure the accusations aren't groundless?"

"I've heard too much bullying in general at the rink to dismiss the allegations. Ice-skating is a cutthroat sport. You wouldn't believe some of the things that go on." Ellie climbed to her feet and brushed her hands on her jeans. "I suspect Regan and Autumn were smarter than most and didn't leave a trail. Regan's dad is some kind of computer specialist. If anyone would know how to wipe an electronic trail, it would be him. But Lee must have discovered something that convinced him he could win a civil suit. He was a little bit of a sap for a lawyer, but he wouldn't take a case if he didn't think he had a chance of winning. His caseload was already large. He didn't have the time to throw away, and I doubt he'd want to get Mr. and Mrs. Hamilton's hopes up for no reason either."

"No, he always sounded stressed when I talked to him." Which hadn't been for a long time.

"Oh, I almost forgot." She straightened. "There's money missing from the firm. Roger's dad, the Grand Poobah of the firm, gave him a thorough verbal lashing the other day. A series of fraudulent checks were cashed in the past couple of weeks."

"How much was missing?" Grant's gut sank.

"About twenty thousand dollars."

"Lee had some unusual cash deposits."

"You don't think . . . ?" Ellie's voice broke. "Not Lee. He would never steal anything."

"I don't know. I'm beginning to think I didn't know my brother as well as I thought." He hesitated before opening Lee's armoire. He was determined to separate his emotions from his task, but rifling through Lee's socks gave him an ache in his chest. He pulled a T-shirt from the bottom drawer. His fingers clenched in the fabric as he shook it out to see the word ARMY emblazoned in olive-green letters across the chest. Grant had given it to his brother twelve years ago when he left for his first deployment. Under the shirt was a familiar walnut box. He lifted the lid. Inside was the purple heart Grant had been given when he'd been shot in Iraq. He'd asked Lee to hold on to it for him for safekeeping. Underneath were their father's medals.

No matter how much Grant traveled, he'd always known his brother was here, holding down the fort at home, taking care of Dad, and providing Grant with a sense of home even though he hadn't lived in Scarlet Falls in more than a decade. He massaged a tight spot in the center of his chest with one hand. *Damn it, Lee. What happened?*

He snapped the lid—and his memories of Lee—shut.

"It's not in here." He needed to get out of this room. "Let's go look somewhere else."

Ellie looked up at him, her expression puzzled. Tears shone in the corners of her eyes as she met his gaze. Without speaking, she crossed the room, took his hand, and tugged him into the hall. The sounds of water splashing, muted conversation, and the baby's babbling echoed from the bathroom. She led him through the door at the end of the hall and up the stairs to the open attic. Dust motes danced in the light of three bare bulbs suspended from the rafters.

"I doubt Lee would have hidden the file up here," Grant said.

"Shh." Ellie wrapped her arms around his waist and hugged him.

Shocked, he pulled back, but she tightened her hold. Grant, ignoring the warning signals from his conscience, returned the embrace. He rested his forehead on her hair and accepted the comfort she offered. His heart stirred in an uncomfortable and dangerous spiral. He liked this. Too much. This was the sort of thing his married friends missed while they were deployed: human contact, shared emotions. For a second, he thought maybe it was worth missing. But no, that would be selfish. This wasn't just about him. It wouldn't be fair to Ellie to start something he couldn't finish. He moved every year or so, and if he really wanted to be a general, he didn't need emotional ties tempting him to turn down assignments that could further his career. It was much easier to remain emotionally detached, because until this week, that's what he'd been. He thought he'd had a relationship with his brother, but it was all an illusion. He'd barely known Lee. Grant had spent most of his adult life alone and aloof, avoiding personal connections and complications.

But damn. He couldn't seem to let go of the soft woman in his arms.

She sighed, and her body relaxed. She shifted, leaning back. "I'm sorry."

"For what?"

Her warm brown eyes filled with empathy. "That this all happened to you. You haven't had time to grieve."

A small shudder passed through him, followed by a wave of need he couldn't explain or deny, except that his soul was an empty shell. He pressed his lips to hers and let the taste of her fill the void inside him. Instead of resisting, she clutched his shirt and let him in. What started out tender and innocent shifted. Desire warmed him and pooled low in his groin. A hungry groan eased out of her throat.

He wrapped a hand around the back of her neck, tilting her head and angling her mouth for a deeper invasion. She wound her arms around his neck. His free hand slid around her body and splayed at the base of her spine. He urged her hips closer. There. Right there.

"Grant." She moved her mouth an inch away from his.

"Mm." There was nothing more he'd like to do than strip Ellie naked and make love to her. And even though he knew there was no way that was going to happen at this moment—he didn't have a condom, there were too many children and other family members in the house, and they were in the middle of searching for a key piece of evidence—he wasn't ready to let her go yet. Holding her, kissing her, thinking about making love to her, eased his loneliness. She gave him hope.

She squirmed. "We can't . . ."

"I know," he whispered against her cheek. "Just give me another minute. Please."

He wanted an hour or ten. Hell, since he was fantasizing, he might as well wish for a whole day of Ellie without distractions.

But that was not to be.

Reluctantly, he pressed a kiss to her temple and eased away from her body. "Thank you."

Her mouth tilted in a sad smile.

"Were you close to Lee and Kate?" he asked, getting back to business.

"I worked with Lee for years, but since I moved next door, Kate became a good friend. We had a lot in common. They were new to the neighborhood, too. They'd just moved into this house a few months before me."

"I don't know much about Kate." Grant sighed. "I spent two weeks of my leave with them each year, but I feel like I didn't know her as well as I should have."

"You can hardly help being sent to Afghanistan."

But he could have visited more when he was stateside. He'd been so focused on his career that he'd neglected his family.

"Kate was quiet." Ellie turned away from him and walked to a small octagonal window. "She and Lee were proud of you."

He shoved his thumbs into the front pockets of his jeans. "I still wish I'd been here more."

She nodded in understanding. "I'm sorry you can't change that, but being here for Carson and Faith is what's important now."

And that was only temporary.

"I guess. I really don't know where else to look." He scanned the attic. A row of storage containers was lined up under the eave. "We'll check these boxes, then start on the guest rooms."

The boxes were full of clothes Carson had outgrown. Had they been saving them for a future little boy? Grant closed the lid before the sadness enveloped him. There was no point speculating. He moved containers and lifted insulation but found no secret hiding places.

They moved downstairs to the guest rooms and did the same checking of floorboards and spaces behind and under heavy furniture. They had no more luck on the first floor.

Two hours later, Ellie emerged from the laundry room. "Did you find anything?"

"Nothing." Grant righted the sofa. They'd torn apart every cabinet and closet in the house. All that was left was the detached garage, and he doubted the file was under the lawn mower or in Lee's workbench.

She brushed a cobweb from her hair. "What next?"

"I don't know. I'm out of ideas."

Her eyes went round. "What am I going to do if I can't find the file?"

Grant stood and crossed the room. He took her by the arms. "You're not alone."

"He's going to hurt my family." Her horrified whisper rent his soul in two.

"I won't let him." But what would happen if he had to leave and the threat hadn't been eliminated? "We have to figure out what Lee discovered the hard way. Lindsay Hamilton skated at the same rink as Julia. Do you know her parents?"

Ellie dropped onto the sofa. "No. I've never met them. Lindsay was older. Plus, Julia isn't a serious skater. She only goes to her lesson and one team practice a week. Once in a while, Kate would talk her into practicing in a free skate, but Julia hated it. The advanced skaters are aggressive on the ice."

"Aggressive?" Sitting next to her, he thought of the combative hockey players.

"They act like they own the rink. They'd skate in her path or spin close enough to make her uncomfortable." Ellie rubbed her hands together, pushing at the skin until it reddened. "Julia likes skating, but it's a hobby, not a passion. She certainly doesn't love it enough to put up with the hassle."

"Do you know Regan and Autumn's parents?"

"I know who they are, but I've only spoken to them a couple of times."

Grant reached over and put his hand on Ellie's to still them. He wanted to fix everything for her. Frustration stirred in his chest, along with the desire to pull her onto his lap. "So maybe those skaters really are bullies?"

"The only thing I know for sure is that they hog the ice." Her eyes met his, and the fear in them stirred his anger. "I feel so helpless. What do I do?"

"Do you have the Hamiltons' phone number?"

"I do. I had to change one of Lee's appointments with them. Let me sign in to my e-mail account." She pulled her hands out from under his grip. He missed holding the contact immediately.

They went into the office. She sat down in front of Hannah's laptop on the desk. "Here it is."

Leaning over her shoulder, Grant inhaled the flowery scent of her hair and resisted the urge to wrap his arms around her. "Call them and see if they'd be willing to meet with us."

"OK." Ellie dialed the number. A minute later, she covered the receiver with a hand. "Voice mail." She left a message and hung up.

"Do you think they'll call back?"

She thought for a moment, then nodded. "Yes. Mr. and Mrs. Hamilton have shown no signs of giving up on their daughter's case. They're going to assume I'm calling them as a firm representative. Roger has been avoiding them since Lee died."

"Why?"

"He doesn't want to deal with it, and without whatever evidence Lee discovered, the case won't go anywhere."

Grant scratched his chin. Beard scruff rasped under his fingers. "Who has the biggest stake in this case?"

"Regan and Autumn." Ellie brushed hair off her face. "Regan's dad, Corey, is a computer guy, which explains how his daughter would know to buy and use burner phones."

"I'd think most kids would be able to figure that out with a basic Google search. But Lindsay's phone was wiped out with a cell phone virus. That seems like more specific knowledge. Do you think Corey would have helped his daughter eliminate her cybertrail?"

"I'd hope not." Ellie frowned. "He's kind of an ass, but helping his daughter torment another teen seems extreme. But I suppose it's possible."

"What does Josh Winslow do for a living?"

"He used to be an administrator for the juvenile justice system. But he stepped down. The media coverage of the bullying case was brutal."

"I thought the media isn't allowed to name minors?"

Ellie sighed. "This is suburbia. Everyone knows who they are."

"So everyone believed Lindsay?"

"No, but there was speculation that the girls were getting special consideration because Josh was a civil employee."

"Is that wrong or right?" he asked. "His daughter wasn't charged with anything. I don't know whether to feel bad for him or not."

"I know what you mean. I thought I had a good handle on Julia, but considering she sneaked out in the middle of the night, obviously I was wrong. I don't know what to think of Josh. At least his wife is a surgeon, so financially, they're going to be all right."

Ellie had given him a lot to mull over: information on the case and a smoking hot kiss that rocked him to his soul. He hoped the Hamiltons would be able to shed more light on the case. He was on his own with the kiss and his needy soul.

The doorbell rang. Barking erupted in the hallway.

Grant walked to the window. "It's the police."

Chapter Twenty-Five

AnnaBelle went ballistic, barking and circling in the foyer of the Barretts' house. Ellie followed Grant to the door. He opened it. "Please come in."

Detective McNamara wiped his feet on the doormat and stepped inside. Hannah joined them. She quieted the dog with a hand on the retriever's head.

"We have some pictures to show the kids." McNamara lifted an eight-by-ten envelope in his hand.

The cop zeroed in on their handguns. "Do you have permits for those?"

Hannah crossed her arms, her eyes hardening. "Yes. Do you need to see them?"

"Not right now." McNamara gave her a tight head shake. He obviously didn't approve. "Can you shoot it?"

"Yes." Her mouth pursed. Mutual irritation passed between them.

Grant cleared his throat. "What can we do for you, Detective?"

McNamara shook the envelope. "As I said before, I have some pictures we'd like to show to Julia and Carson. Are they still awake?"

"I think so. I'll get them." Ellie jogged up the stairs. Julia's voice carried from the open doorway of Carson's bedroom. Ellie peered in. Julia and Carson snuggled on the bed in their pajamas, relaxed. A copy of a Henry and Mudge chapter book lay open between them. Julia read a page, then tilted the book toward Carson. The words were slower, but he read well.

Sadness filled Ellie as she interrupted the peaceful scene. "Would you two come downstairs for a minute? Detective McNamara wants you to look at some pictures."

Carson's eyes went from relaxed to scared in a blink. Julia frowned and gave his shoulder a squeeze. She took him by the hand and led him down the hall.

Downstairs, the cop and Grant were sitting at the kitchen table. Mac, who'd finally returned Grant's call and agreed to move in for a few days, walked by with a fussing Faith on one shoulder. On the other side of the kitchen, Hannah leaned backward against the cabinets. A coffee mug steamed in her hand. No relaxing for Grant's sister. She caffeinated 24/7.

McNamara rubbed his face with both hands. Bags under his eyes attested to the hours he must be putting into the case.

"Can I get you some coffee?" Hannah offered.

"Please," the detective said.

Hannah poured a mug. The detective waved off cream and sugar. He drank while Carson and Julia shuffled into the room.

"Hi, kids. Do you think you're up to looking at a few photos for me?" McNamara opened the envelope. "We'll do this one at a time, OK? Julia, would you wait in the hall?"

She nodded.

Carson pulled his hand out of Julia's and hurried to Grant to climb on his lap. Grant folded his arms around the child and brushed blond bangs off his forehead. Ellie took her daughter's hand and led her to the hallway. It had been a long time since Julia had allowed her mother to hold her hand, but tonight, she curled her fingers and hung on.

"Now that I've recovered from the sheer terror, I want to tell you how proud I am of the way you handled the situation today," Ellie said.

"Proud enough to lift my sentence?" Julia's attempt at humor told Ellie her daughter was all right.

"Not a chance." She squeezed her daughter's fingers.

"It was worth a try." Julia shrugged.

"But maybe I haven't given you enough credit."

They heard papers shuffling, then Carson's small voice. "This is him."

"All right," McNamara said. "Julia, your turn."

Grant stood with Carson in his arms and walked out of the room. Ellie and Julia took their places at the table. McNamara spread six head shots across the table. The photos were all of young, rough-looking Caucasian men in their early twenties. None had tattoos.

Julia scanned the photos. Her eyes moving back and forth. She pointed to the third picture. "I think this is him."

"Think?" the cop asked.

Julia's face scrunched. "The closest he got to me was about thirty feet, and it was only for a few seconds before he ran away. I wasn't even close enough to see the tattoos Carson was talking about. And I was pretty scared."

Ellie wrapped an arm around her daughter's shoulders. She was simultaneously proud and terrified that Julia had defended the children at her own risk.

McNamara called Grant and Carson back into the room. Carson was perched in Grant's arms. His little blond head tilted to rest against his uncle's broad shoulder.

"Can the kids go?" Grant asked.

"Yes." McNamara nodded. "Thanks, both of you."

Julia took Carson from Grant. Ellie's stomach clenched. No doubt both kids would have nightmares tonight. At least she and Julia were sharing a room. Ellie would be there if Julia needed her.

"Well?" Grant eased into a chair.

"The kids both identified Donnie Ehrlich. Julia was hesitant, but Carson seemed sure. Donnie is a local. Twenty-one years old. He did eighteen months for ID theft and has an earlier assault charge he weaseled out of with community service. He's been out for three months."

"ID theft and assault? That's a big stretch to murder and kidnapping," Ellie said. "Does he have a juvenile record?"

"That would be sealed." But McNamara's pointed expression made her suspect Donnie had been in trouble in his younger years.

"The man in the picture doesn't have the tattoos," Ellie pointed out.

McNamara gathered the pictures and lined them up with a tap on the tabletop. He slid the neat pile back into the envelope. "The teardrop and the shamrock are tats he picked up during his incarceration. These mug shots are from his original arrest. We're going to pick up Donnie and ask him some questions. I'll call you in the morning to let you know if we have him."

"Thanks." Grant showed the cop out. After he left, Grant steered Ellie back to the office and closed the door. He perched on the edge of the desk. "Did the guy in the picture look familiar at all? Could it be the man who abducted you?"

Standing in front of him, she lifted a palm to the ceiling. "I can't say. I didn't see his face, but the body structure is about right."

"What about his voice?" He scraped a hand across his unshaven jaw. "Would you recognize it if you heard him speak?"

She thought about the encounter in her car. "He whispered the whole time, so I doubt it."

"What about an accent?"

"I didn't hear an accent." She put a hand on her head, where a mental clip of her abduction played in an endless loop. "What now?"

"We try to get some sleep." Grant let out a short laugh. Exhaustion lined his face as he rubbed his temple. "As if that's a possibility with Faith around."

"There are four adults in this house tonight perfectly capable of walking that baby. I vote that you go to bed. You look like you haven't slept since you came home." Ellie put a hand on his forearm.

He didn't deny her assumption. His head tilted. "She's rough. Are you sure you want to take her on?"

Ellie lifted a shoulder. "She's just a baby."

"Was Julia a tough infant?"

"Not really, but I was only eighteen. I had no idea what I was doing. I had Nan, thank God, but she had to get up for work. She was still teaching then."

"What happened to Julia's father? You mentioned him earlier, so now I'm curious."

She regretted her previous slip. "I got pregnant senior year in high school. My boyfriend wasn't ready to be a father."

"What about your parents?"

And now for the topic even more uncomfortable than teenage pregnancy. But what the hell? She was tired of pretending her disastrous high school years didn't exist. Maybe Nan was right. It was time to make peace with her past. "They wanted me to give her up for adoption. When I refused, they kicked me out. I'm so glad I had Nan."

Ellie didn't like to think about what would have happened if she'd been younger and didn't have a grandmother willing to tell off her own son. Ellie's and Julia's lives could have turned out much worse.

"What about Julia's father? Is he alive?"

"I have no idea. I haven't heard from him since she was a baby."

"Really?" Grant sounded incredulous.

She shrugged. "He didn't want any part of being a father. He voted with my parents for putting the baby up for adoption. When I wouldn't do it, he said it was my problem. He went to college in Northern California, as far as he could get from me and still be in the continental United States."

"You could have sued him for child support."

Ellie gave her head an angry shake. "I didn't want anything from him. For all I know, he could be dead or in prison or be married with two point five kids by now. It's been a long time." Unexpected bitterness welled in Ellie's throat. She'd thought she was over his callous abandonment. "I wasn't about to beg him for anything."

"I can't imagine knowing I had a child and not caring what happened to her." Grief flashed in his eyes. Was he thinking of how much his brother would miss raising Carson and Faith? "How did you even end up with a guy like that?"

"I was a teenager and full of rebellion." She stared at his strong forearm under her palm. "And he was hot."

Grant laughed. "I thought guys were the only ones who thought like that."

"If they were, girls wouldn't get pregnant in high school."

"Good point."

But it suddenly occurred to Ellie that, while she encouraged Julia to be independent and educated, maybe she'd been too strict in other areas. Sure, Taylor was older, but Ellie hadn't taken the time to get to know him before forbidding Julia to date him. Her daughter had a good head on her shoulders. This afternoon, she'd exhibited intelligence and courage. Ellie needed to allow her to make some of her own decisions. Within reason.

Ellie dropped into the chair.

Grant's hand fell away. "Kate was estranged from her parents, too."

"I know. It was one of the things we had in common."

Grant heaved his frame off the desktop, pivoted, and paced toward the door. "Hannah called Kate's parents. They're coming here this week sometime."

Ellie lifted her head. "I'm not sure that was a good idea."

"But their daughter died. Don't they have a right to know?" He stopped, his face creased with indecision.

"Maybe," she conceded. "But Kate had no contact with them. Did you know they hadn't spoken to her since she married Lee?"

Grant stopped, whirling to face her. "What? Why?"

"They have serious money. Kate said her mother was a Daughter of the American Revolution." Ellie looked away. "They told her Lee was a gold digger."

"That's ridiculous." His jaw clenched. "My father was a colonel in the army. He gave up his life for his country. It doesn't get any more worthy than that. We didn't have a lot of money, but we were far from destitute."

Ellie held a hand up. "I agree with you, and so did Kate. She wanted nothing to do with them."

"Why are families full of so much conflict?" Grant massaged his forehead as if it ached. "Now I wish I didn't have to invite anyone to the funeral. It's going to be stressful enough without all the drama."

"What are you planning?"

"I'm not sure. We can't plan anything until the medical examiner gives the OK, but Mac is supposedly handling the preliminaries. I don't even know how many people will come."

Ellie did some quick mental math. "Between Lee's firm and clients and the families from the skating club, you'll have a hundred at minimum. I'd plan on more. They were both popular in the community."

"I really wanted to keep it small for Carson's sake."

"Will you bring him?"

"The school counselor said I should let him make the decision, but I'm not leaving him at home, not after that guy tried to grab him. If he doesn't want to go, I'll stay home. Or maybe we won't have one."

"People will expect a service of some kind."

"I don't really care what other people expect." Grant resumed his pacing, his movement fueled by agitation. "Carson is all that matters. If he wants to go, a small, private service would be best for him."

Ellie frowned. "You're right, of course."

"But?"

Muffled crying sounded through the door.

"No buts. Now, go to bed. I'll handle Faith for a few hours. If I get tired, I'll wake someone to relieve me. Earlier you said I didn't have to handle the situation alone. Neither do you." She took two steps and reached up to cup his jaw. The impulsive and sudden desire to touch him surprised her, but his willingness to shoulder everyone's burdens made her want to lighten his load. "I know you aren't staying in Scarlet Falls, but for now, we're in this together."

"We shouldn't indulge ourselves. Whatever happens between us can't be long-term. I'm career military, Ellie. An infantry officer. Wherever the army is fighting, that's where I'm sent. The base in Afghanistan was bombed a dozen times. Snipers and suicide bombers are a constant threat. Even though I see less actual combat now that I'm a major, there's still no guarantee I'm coming home alive or in one piece."

"There are never any guarantees in life. Look at what happened to Lee and Kate."

"I know. But we both know that the fact that Lee is dead instead of me is backward." He paused and looked away for a few seconds. "Until he was disabled, I saw very little of my dad. It wasn't just the military. It was his ambition that kept him from us. I don't want to leave anyone behind because I'm too focused on my career." He leaned down and gave her a gentle kiss on the mouth. Lifting his head, his gaze locked with hers. "But I can't resist."

Neither could she. His honesty and desire to do the right thing touched her.

Ellie placed her hand in the center of his chest. Under her palm, his heart beat steadily beneath muscles as hard as iron. "My eyes are wide-open. I don't have any expectations that our relationship is permanent."

"I don't want to hurt you."

"I know, and I appreciate that."

He kissed her again, his lips lingering on her mouth for one wistful breath. "Good night, Ellie."

"Good night." She watched him walk away. But even though she knew he'd be leaving in a few weeks, it was going to hurt to say good-bye.

Chapter Twenty-Six

Ellie finished loading the breakfast dishes into the dishwasher and drank a third cup of coffee. Walking the baby half the night had fuzzed her brain. Not that she could have slept anyway. Last night's conversation—and kissing—with Grant had boosted her adrenaline for hours. The near-giddy excitement his simple kiss stirred in her belly was more appropriate for a teenager. Actually, she couldn't remember ever reacting to a man in this way. She could easily imagine sharing years of memories with him, and frankly, she felt a little cheated that those years weren't a possibility.

Grant was in the office reviewing paperwork with Mac. Hannah was upstairs with the kids. Nan snored on the sofa. The pain pills made her tired.

Her cell phone vibrated in her pocket. She glanced at the display. The number was familiar. Not Hoodie Man. She answered the call. "Hello."

"What are you up to?"

Now she recognized the number. "Frank?"

"Yes. What the fuck is going on, Ellie?" Why was Frank Menendez calling her cell from his?

"I don't know what you mean."

"I know you copied my hard drive." Frank's voice dropped. "And I saw you searching desks."

Damn it. Frank's computer skills were more advanced than she'd thought.

"And now you're taking a day off? You never take days off." Anxiety reverberated through Frank's voice.

"My grandmother needs me," she said.

He paused. "Why aren't you in work today?"

"You know what, Frank? That isn't any of your business." Ellie wondered why he was so upset over her personal day. He barely let her do any work for him.

"Did you know there was money missing from the firm?" he whispered.

"Yes."

Frank was quiet for a few seconds, no doubt digesting the fact that she knew more than he did. "You'd better not screw with me, Ellie."

The line went dead.

What. The. Hell?

Seated at the desk in the office, Grant pointed to the screen of Mac's laptop. "Is that him?"

Mac pulled the old chair closer and leaned over Grant's arm. "That's what the caption says."

An online search had yielded a mug shot of Donnie Ehrlich attached to a short news article from the day of his arrest a few years ago. Detective McNamara hadn't left a copy of the photo, so they'd conducted their own search. Donnie had been arrested multiple times, though he'd only been convicted once as an adult.

"He's only a couple of years younger than you. Do you recognize him?"

"No," Mac said. "But those prison tats make me glad I got out of the gang before I ended up in jail." He shook his hair off his face in a dramatic movement. "I'm way too pretty for prison."

"Your stint on the dark side is nothing to joke about." Grant flicked a paper clip at him. "Neither was rehab."

Mac caught it. His expression turned somber. "I owe my transformation to Lee. He never gave up on me. I bet he's the one who put Mom up to making her final request that I straighten my ass out."

"He knew you'd do it for her," Grant said quietly. How typical of Lee to keep trying until he found a way to turn Mac around. That dogged determination had made him a good lawyer. Had it also contributed to his death?

"Yeah. I was a real asshole at the time, but not enough of an asshole to deny Mom her dying wish."

Grant studied his brother. Mac had been fifteen when Grant went into the army. Lee had been in school and dealing with Dad's declining health. When Mom got sick too, Mac had rebelled. Lee had been split in too many different directions. A man could only be in so many places at once. Maybe if Grant had been around, he could have kept Mac out of trouble.

Grant would be carrying a convoy of regrets back to Afghanistan.

"Any idea where we might find Donnie?"

Mac scratched his chin. "I can ask around. I know a guy who might be able to help." He pressed Print. The printer on the credenza chugged, squealed, and spat out a copy of the photo.

"You aren't going to visit someone from your old gang?"

"It's our best shot." Mac frowned.

"Isn't it dangerous?"

He shook his head. "Nah. I'll be fine."

"How do you still know this person is still in your old gang?" Grant couldn't stop his voice from turning parental. "You haven't seen him, have you?"

"I've run into him a couple of times over the years." Indignation filled Mac's tone. "You don't think I'd go back to that life, do you?"

"I'd hope not."

Mac laughed. "Grant, I camp with otters for a living. That's quite a distance from working for a drug dealer."

Grant winced. "I'm sorry. I should trust you."

"We haven't seen each other much in the years since you left." Mac shrugged.

"I know, and I'm sorry about that, too."

"You've been fighting a war. So I'll give you a pass." His brother snatched the picture from the printer output tray.

But guilt nagged Grant. He could've been around more. He didn't have to take every assignment and move he'd been offered. He'd let his desire to advance in rank take precedence over his family's needs. He'd left Lee to deal with their father's dementia and Mac's foray into crime, once a year swooping in for two weeks like some BFD. When in reality, Lee had been the big fucking deal, quietly getting unpleasant shit done on a daily basis. But it seemed Lee had also fallen prey to the Barrett family weakness: blind ambition.

Mac put a hand on his shoulder. "Really, Grant. It all turned out all right. If you hadn't done the military thing, Dad would have pressured me or Lee into it. Let's face it, neither one of us was army material. Lee was too sensitive, and I was too lazy. You did us a favor by living the old man's dream so we didn't have to."

Mac had a point. Lee could never have shot a man in the face, not even to protect a fellow soldier. It wasn't a fault, just a fact. Lee had believed in people's inherent goodness. No man went to war and came back the same person. Grant would have nightmares for the rest of his life, but combat would have destroyed Lee.

Mac folded the picture in half. "Enough of this touchy-feely crap. I have to go. It'll be easiest to find Freddie early in the day."

"I'm going with you."

"I don't know if that's a good idea." Mac scanned Grant from head to toe. "You don't blend in with that crowd. They're an ugly bunch."

"No worries. I've seen plenty of ugly."

"Yeah. I guess you have." Mac shrugged. "I know you're used to giving the orders, but you'll have to follow my lead this time out."

"OK." As if anyone in the family followed Grant's orders anyway. He closed the Internet browser. His Beretta was as heavy on his hip as his current control issues weighed on his mind. Weapons and instability were a bad combination, but the cops hadn't been able to find Donnie Ehrlich. Grant couldn't go back to Afghanistan with his brother's killer on the loose, still a threat to his family. Donnie needed to be stopped. Carson deserved to sleep without nightmares.

Mac tucked the folded picture into his pocket, then ran upstairs for his wallet. Grant ducked into the kitchen. The scent of fresh coffee teased his nostrils. Ellie sipped from a mug as she folded a load of baby laundry.

"You don't have to do that," he said.

"I need to keep busy." She folded the last tiny sock and set the basket aside. The sight of her brightened the darkness inside him. He wanted to scoop her up and take them both to bed. Pathetically, he actually wanted to *sleep* with her. For some reason, he couldn't get the thought out of his head that his nightmares would be easier to take with her at his side. He had no doubt making love to Ellie would be amazing, but his attraction to her ran deeper than sex. It was a completely foreign feeling for him.

"Coffee?" she asked.

"No, but thanks."

Nan snored on the couch. Hannah came down the stairs and went directly for the coffee pot. She set the baby monitor on the counter.

"Where are the kids?" Grant asked.

"They both fell asleep." Hannah dumped milk into her coffee and downed half the mug. "I feel like I've been run over by the minivan." She'd taken the third baby-walking shift. "Didn't Carson get any sleep last night? He looks beat."

"He crawled in with me about midnight." Grant hadn't minded. The boy had interrupted a nasty nightmare.

"So you didn't get to sleep all night?" Sympathy creased Ellie's face.

"It's all right," Grant said. "I've gone without sleep before."

"But it isn't ideal," Ellie said.

"Mac and I are running to the store," Grant lied. "Need anything?"

Hannah squinted at him in suspicion.

"Milk and bread." Ellie refilled her mug. "And coffee."

"Milk, bread, coffee. Got it." Grant headed for the door. Hannah was right on his tail.

"Where are you really going?" she whispered.

"Just taking a drive."

"Not buying it." Hannah crossed her arms. "You're going after Donnie."

Grant didn't answer.

"I should go with you," she said. "I'm a better shot than Mac."

"You're a better shot than me too, which is why I want you here to protect them." Grant nodded toward the back of the house, where the family was gathered. "One of us has to be with them all the time."

Her mouth twisted into a frown. "I don't like it."

"I know." He kissed her on the cheek. "And that's why I love you."

Her brow creased. Their family wasn't big on emotional pronouncements or public—or private—displays of affection, but maybe being so tight-assed was a mistake. He wished he'd told Lee at least once that he loved him. Now it was too late.

He put a hand on his sister's shoulder. "I trust you to take care of them."

Her head bobbed in a tight nod.

"We'll be back soon." Grant grabbed his jacket from the closet.

His sister's eyes softened with the affection she couldn't vocalize. "You'd better be."

"We will." When this was all over, the Barretts were going to start spending time together whenever possible.

Mac jogged down the stairs into the foyer. "Ready."

"Let's do this." Grant opened the door. He scanned the street before leading the way to his rented sedan. The neighborhood looked quiet.

Mac jerked a thumb toward his SUV. "Would you rather take my truck?"

"No. I don't want anyone to recognize it or us unless it's necessary." Grant slid behind the wheel. "Besides, I paid for the damned rental insurance."

"All right then." Mac got into the passenger seat.

"Where are we going?"

"Let's try the rail yard first. That's where Freddie's been hanging lately." Mac checked the clip on his 9mm and returned the weapon to his shoulder holster.

They were both quiet while Grant drove across town. He stopped in front of a closed gate marked with *Private Property*, *No Admittance*, and other threatening signs. No one paid any attention. The abandoned rail yard had been hosting illegal activities for decades: underage keggers, teenage sex, drug deals, and more. They got out of the car.

Mac pulled a set of wire cutters out of his pocket. "In case I can't find the entrance, we can make our own."

Grant eyed the six-foot chain link barrier topped with three rows of twisted wire. "Make sure the fence isn't hot."

His brother rolled his eyes. "Like this is my first break-in."

"I'm not going to respond to that."

"The electricity on this fence hasn't been live in years." Mac led the way down the fence line. Behind a patch of scraggly bushes, he found a crudely snipped hole in the wire. He tossed the cutters at the fence. No flash or sizzle. The power was off. "See?"

They slipped through, the knee-high weeds brushing the legs of Grant's jeans. Soggy spots squished underfoot, and mud sucked at their boots. They walked between the tracks, rows of cast-aside freight cars forming a tunnel. His skin itched. He could feel eyes on them. Grant crouched to look under the cars. Their blind flank spooked him. Ahead, a thin plume of smoke curled into the overcast sky. They moved past the serviceable cars into the realm of the abandoned. Weeds grew waist-high through the corroded, unused tracks.

"Wait a minute." Grant climbed a ladder on the back of one of the cars. From the roof, he scanned the back of the rail yard. He didn't see anyone, but he couldn't shake the feeling that they were being watched. He returned to the ground. "You sure we should just walk in like this? I'd feel better if we had Hannah and a sniper rifle covering us."

"It'll be OK." Mac kept walking. "This is Freddie's realm. He owes me. I guarantee someone's been watching us since we went through the fence. If Freddie wanted to kill us, we'd already be dead."

"That is not a comforting thought." Adrenaline warmed Grant's body, and nerves jittered up his spine. What if they were ambushed? What if this Freddie guy Mac claimed owed him one decided to cancel his debt with a bullet? Sweat soaked Grant's back. He unzipped his jacket to let the heat out, and to give him better access to his weapon.

Mac stopped, slapping his arm. "You should have left the gun in the car."

"No way." Grant followed his brother over a set of tracks. "This isn't the first time I've met with people of questionable loyalty. I'll be fine." Meetings with Afghan tribal leaders had been dicey. Allegiances were hard to predict and could shift as quickly as a dust storm. But Grant wasn't feeling like his usual disciplined self.

"We will be significantly outnumbered. Drawing your weapon might get us both killed."

Discarded cars lined up like vertebrae. A dog barked and a chain rattled. Two men leaned out of the rusted door of a black car. Next to the opening, smoke and flames swirled out of a barrel. One of the men wore motorcycle boots and a leather jacket. The other was decked out in cargo pants and a black zip-up. Their accommodations suited the homeless, but the men appeared fit and well-fed rather than indigent.

"Do you know them?" Grant asked quietly.

Mac shook his head. "No."

The two men jumped down, their shoulders squared, backs straight, and postures aggressive.

Leather Man hung back and let his buddy take the lead. From under a black knit cap pulled low on his brow, the leader eyed Grant and Mac with suspicion. The men moved apart, covering Grant and Mac from both sides.

"You want something?" the leader asked, his tone suggesting they should say they were lost, then get the fuck out of there before they got hurt.

"Maybe," Mac said. "Is Freddie around?"

Grant let Mac take point on the conversation. He stepped away from his brother to cut off the flanking maneuver and keep a collapsed freight car at his back. No one was sneaking up on them.

The leader leaned forward and tilted his head. "You know Freddie?"

"I do." Mac kept his gaze on the leader. "Tell him Mac is here to see him."

Interest glimmered. Grant scanned their surroundings. The hairs on his neck waved in a batshit frenzy. He could feel the weight of other eyes on him. They shouldn't be out in the open while the enemy had cover. His hand twitched, but pulling his weapon was the wrong move. He had no idea how many armed men were watching. Damn it. He shouldn't have let his brother talk him into this. They were in the middle of nowhere. Two shots and a shovel, and no one would ever find their bodies.

The leader turned and went back to the freight car. Two minutes later, he reemerged. The man following him was at least six foot six with a heavily muscled body that had to weigh three hundred pounds, none of them fat. A mix of blond and gray hair fell from a receding hairline to his shoulders. His bushy mustache and scraggly beard matched.

He strode toward Mac without hesitation. Mac's eyes clouded with anxiety for the first time. Grant's lungs locked down. He curled his hand into a fist to remind himself not to go for his weapon.

"Mac!" The giant enveloped him in a bear hug. With one hand still on Mac's shoulder, Freddie's gaze shifted to Grant and darkened. "Who the fuck is that?"

"My brother," Mac said, relief softening his features.

"Brother, huh? I've met your brother. This isn't him." Freddie jerked a thumb in Grant's direction. "He looks like a cop."

"You met Lee. This is my other brother." Mac shook his head. "Grant's military. Been in Iraq and Afghanistan."

Freddie nodded, his suspicion morphing into something else. Respect? "Man, thanks for your service."

And that was the absolute last thing Grant expected to hear. "Uh, you're welcome."

"Let's go somewhere more private." Freddie looped an arm around Mac's shoulders and steered him past the barrel fire to the rail car. They hoisted themselves inside. The interior had been fitted out with discarded upholstered furniture. A makeshift table held ziplock bags of pot and white powder. Two guys with assault rifles lounged behind the tables. A third man, nearly as large as Freddie, counted bags and stuffed them into a duffel bag. His blond hair was cut in a razor-sharp style that could have graced the cover of *Esquire.* Instead of the leather look favored by the rest of Freddie's men, this man wore European casual: dark jeans and a white shirt open at the neck. Though they were dressed as complete opposites, this man had to be related to Freddie. His son, Grant bet.

He looked up as they entered. A smile split his face. "Mac!"

"Rafe, how the hell are you?" Mac gave Rafe a shoulder-slapping, one-armed man hug.

Grant looked away. He had no idea Mac had been involved with a drug dealer of this scale. Freddie had said he'd met Lee. Looked like Lee had kept the truth from Grant.

Mac dropped into a chair, far too comfortable for Grant's comfort.

Freddie frowned from Grant to the drug display. "You sure he's not a cop?"

"Positive," Mac said.

"Dad, it's Mac," Rafe protested. "He wouldn't bring a cop here."

Grant leaned on the wall, tried to look casual, and lied. "I could care less about your business dealings."

"Then why are you here?" Freddie crossed massive arms over his chest. "I'd like to think you just came for a visit, but you look like you're on a mission."

"You're right." Mac leaned forward and rested his forearms on his thighs. "We're looking for a guy."

Freddie nodded. "What'd he do?"

Mac pulled the folded computer paper out of his pocket and handed it to Freddie. "He killed our brother Lee, the one you met when he helped me and Rafe out of that . . . predicament years back."

Freddie unfolded the paper and frowned. He stroked his beard.

"Do you know him?" Mac asked.

"He looks familiar." Freddie's gray eyes remained impassive. He passed the paper to Rafe, who scanned the paper without exhibiting any tells.

"Can I keep this?" Freddie asked as Rafe handed the picture back.

"Yes," Mac said.

Freddie refolded the paper. "I'll get word to you tomorrow. Where are you staying?"

"Lee's house." Mac placed his palms on his thighs. "I appreciate your help."

Freddie rested a hand on Mac's shoulder, the gesture filled with fatherly affection. "Man, I owe you. You know that."

"Actually, I owe him," Rafe corrected. "It was my life he saved."

Freddie's eyes misted as he glanced at his son. He swallowed and turned back to Mac. "I will have something for you tomorrow. But we have one other piece of business to discuss."

Grant tensed.

"Your dead brother owes me twenty grand," Freddie said. "Money lending isn't normally a business I engage in, but I did it as a favor because of how he helped Rafe out that time."

"I assume the debt is transferrable," Grant said. On the bright side, if Lee had borrowed the money from Freddie, he hadn't stolen it. Lee must have been desperate to go to Freddie for money. Why hadn't he called Grant or Hannah? Had he been too embarrassed?

Or didn't he feel comfortable asking his family for money? Either way, they'd failed him.

"This is business." Freddie shrugged. "But since you're practically family, I'll waive the interest if you can pay the debt by the end of the week."

"If we can't?" Grant asked.

Freddie's eyes darkened. "Penalties for nonpayment are steep."

"Don't worry. We're good for it." Mac slapped Freddie on the shoulder. "Thanks for your help."

Rafe escorted them back through the freight car gauntlet. When they reached the fence, he offered Grant a hand.

Grant shook it. Yes, he'd been appalled at the drugs in the train. Freddie and Son Inc. were probably dealing guns, too. Drugs and arms went together like macaroni and cheese. And now they had to come up with twenty thousand dollars in the next week. But if it meant finding Donnie Ehrlich, Grant would willingly make a pact with Satan.

Chapter Twenty-Seven

"I hate waiting." Ellie paced the tiny office.

Grant closed the laptop. "You need to *do* something."

But mostly what they were doing was waiting. Waiting for the Hamiltons to return Ellie's call. Waiting for tomorrow morning, when Mac's friend promised them information. And waiting for her thirty-six-hour agreement with Grant to run out. "I would have gone with you this morning if I'd known where you were headed."

"I know. That's why I didn't tell you. Mac's friend doesn't trust strangers. It could have been dangerous."

Ellie stopped and faced him. "Please don't lie to me again."

"I won't."

But her trust was as thin and delicate as an eggshell. It wouldn't take much to crack it. A betrayal from Grant would hurt. He was the first man to inspire faith from her since Julia's father left.

"I can't even run the vacuum." Hands clasped behind her back, she pivoted and strode in the other direction. "We can't make any noise."

Faith snoozed in her baby seat in the family room. As they'd all learned the hard way, as backward as it seemed, being overtired or overstimulated aggravated the baby's colic.

"I'm used to a full hour of PT every morning. Being cooped up is driving me nuts, too. The only exercise I've gotten lately is baby-walking." Grant stood and stretched. "What do you normally do for exercise?"

Ellie watched his muscles ripple and flex under his snug T-shirt, her bundled nerves imagining a highly inappropriate outlet for her excess energy. "Renovations."

"Construction as exercise?" Grant laughed.

"It would be great to accomplish *something*." The case infused her with a sense of futility and helplessness. "I'm used to being busy. I can't handle downtime."

He smiled. "I doubt there are many things you can't handle."

At the moment, there was only one thing she wanted to handle.

Where did *that* come from?

Ellie coughed. She should get out of this small space, where his big, hard body was never more than a few feet away. He clearly hadn't meant his compliment to be dirty, but her undersexed and overactive mind was on a roll. But sex was never simple, and with Grant, she knew intimacy would be even more complicated. She simply felt too much for him.

"I should go set the table or something." Her mind was still focused on *handling* him, but she opened the door and headed for the kitchen. She'd already put the mac-and-cheese casserole together that morning, and there was a cold ham in the fridge waiting for dinnertime. Maybe two kids and her grandmother would be ice water for her libido.

"Wait. We have a little time before dinner." He crossed to the window and peered through the blinds. "Do you really want to go work on your house?"

"Yes. That's normally what I do when I'm not at work."

"Come on." He took her hand and tugged her out of the office. "There's a cop parked in the driveway. We'll let him know we'll be next door for a while."

They stopped in the kitchen. Hannah typed on her laptop at the table.

"Ellie needs to go to her house for a little while. I'm going with her. Can you manage things here?" Grant asked in a hushed voice.

Hannah glanced into the adjoining family room. Nan watched TV from the couch, her booted foot elevated on a pillow. Also within view, Faith snoozed in her baby seat. Mac, Julia, and Carson were upstairs playing a board game in Carson's room.

"Shouldn't be a problem," Hannah whispered.

"Thanks," Grant said. "The alarm will be on. Call me if you need anything."

With her hand still held tightly in his, they walked out the front door. Grant pressed the fob to reset the security system. He stopped to tell the cop in the driveway then pulled Ellie toward her house. Inside he checked every room before they settled in the living room.

"What are you working on?"

Ellie stood in the center of the room and surveyed her progress. "I was filling holes in the wallboard and sanding the trim, but that's nearly done."

"What's next, painting?"

"No, I'll probably wait until the kitchen is done and paint everything at the same time." Through the archway that led to the dining room, she eyed the sledgehammer leaning against the wall.

"What do you want to do next then?"

She walked into the dining room. Her hand closed around the handle of the sledgehammer. She returned to the kitchen. "I have hated this room since the day we bought this house."

Surveying the giant yellow flowers, Grant winced. "It is a little dated."

"Dated?" She snorted. "This was hideous when it was chosen."

"What's the plan for the kitchen then?"

Still holding the hammer, she went to a drawer and pulled out a folder. "Here are the plans."

Grant looked over her shoulder. His body pressed into hers. "That wall needs to come down, but this is a nice design. Who drew these up?"

"I did."

"I'm impressed." His compliment warmed her.

"This is the fourth house I've done." Energy suddenly filled Ellie's muscles. She fished two pairs of safety goggles out of her toolbox. Leaning the hammer on her thigh, she settled a pair of goggles on her face and tossed the other set to Grant.

Grinning, he put his on.

She walked to the wall that divided the kitchen and dining room, raised the hammer over her shoulder, and swung it like a baseball bat. The heavy steel head sank into the wallboard, splintering a stud. Bits of drywall scattered. Gray dust poofed. She slammed the wall again, satisfaction surging through her body. She'd felt so helpless about the danger to her family, so angry at the man who had been threatening her, that it was invigorating to finally have something to take it all out on. After a moment, she handed the sledgehammer to Grant. "Want to take a shot?"

"You bet. Is this a load-bearing wall?"

"No."

His swings did considerably more damage than hers. But then, there was a lot of power behind his body. They took turns with the demolition. She enjoyed watching the play of his muscles almost as much as she appreciated the help with a job she usually tackled alone. Working with Grant made a difficult task enjoyable. An hour later, the wall lay in rubble at their feet.

"That felt great." She set the hammer down and pulled off her goggles. "It would have taken me all day to do that myself." Although one wall was only a tiny part of the kitchen demolition, the tearing down felt symbolic. The traumatic events of the past week had forced Ellie to prioritize her life—and commit to some positive changes.

"Glad to help. In fact, I enjoyed it." Grant removed his goggles and handed them to her. Except for the rings around his eyes, his face was coated with dust. Sweat dampened the chest of his T-shirt. "It's almost dark, so we'll have to wait until tomorrow to haul this rubble out of the house."

Ellie shrugged. "Actually, I have to arrange for a Dumpster."

Grant laughed. "Did we get ahead of your schedule?"

"Yes, we jumped the gun, but that's all right. I need to learn to roll with changes anyway." The number of ways that statement applied to her life couldn't be counted, but first on the list was Julia. Her daughter was growing up. When this was all over, Ellie had to let her.

Within reason.

She shouldn't automatically assume her daughter would make the same mistakes she had at her age. Her sneaking out fiasco aside, she'd been an exemplary daughter.

Ellie could think of another thing that should make the top of her list. Walking close to Grant, she twined her arms around his neck. His eyes widened in surprise, then darkened when her intent sank in. "And it really felt good to let loose."

"No argument here." He leaned down and kissed her. His mouth slanted, his tongue sliding into her mouth for a tentative sweep.

Adrenaline buzzed through her veins as Ellie answered him. The kiss went wild. Grant broke the contact and slid his mouth down the side of her neck, tasting a path from her jaw to her collarbone. She tilted her head back to give him better access. A wave of desire heated her blood. A deep moan started in her boots, reverberated through her bones, and escaped her lips.

"I'm filthy," she protested.

"Me too," Grant gasped. "Don't care."

"We shouldn't do this." With an answering groan, he slid his hands under her shirt. His rough palms scraped up her rib cage.

But it wasn't enough.

"Definitely not." She pushed him away and ripped her shirt over her head, flinging it over her shoulder. Her bra followed. Cool air rushed across hot skin. Her nipples budded as if he'd touched them. She'd been holding back on her impulses her entire life. Baring her body to him was liberating.

She wanted him, and she was going to have him, even it was just for a couple of weeks or days or hours. Grant made her feel alive. And life was too uncertain not to grab a moment of happiness when it was right in front of her.

He pressed a hand to his chest. "Jesus, Ellie. There's only so much a man can resist."

"I don't want you to resist." She went to him and grabbed the hem of his shirt. Yanking it off, she threw it across the room. He'd been impressive in a snug T-shirt, but without the shirt, his physique was stunning. Her eyes sought every delicious inch of him from the chiseled planes of his wide chest to his rippled abdominal muscles. His jeans rode low on his hips. Ellie tracked the sparse line of blond hair that started at his navel and pointed south.

Grant's gaze followed his shirt as it hit the floor next to hers. His Adam's apple bobbed as he swallowed hard. He took a step back, his attention returning to her face, and raised his hands in surrender. "You know I'm not staying in town. I have to go back. This isn't a good idea."

"I know." But Ellie cupped her own breast and raised a playful eyebrow at him. She brushed a thumb across her nipple and reveled as Grant's mouth dropped open. She'd never been a bad girl, not even in high school. She'd simply made one mistake. But now she felt positively wicked.

It felt wonderful. Freeing. Exhilarating.

"Ellie." Grant took another step back.

She stalked him. Stopping just short of touching him, she grabbed the front of his pants and pulled him closer. The skin-on-skin contact pumped more heat, more desire, through her veins. Their chests pressed together, the rough hair on his pectorals abrading her nipples. "I want you. I *need* you. Right here. Right now."

Between their bodies, she wiggled her hand, stroking his lower abdomen inside the waistband of his jeans. A fingertip brushed the head of his erection.

He jumped. "Jesus."

"Mm." She tongued his nipple as she flicked open the top button of his jeans and carefully lowered the zipper. Her hand slid inside his pants and cupped him. "God, you're hot."

"I'm on fucking fire." Jumping on board, Grant's hands dove for her jeans. He had them down around her hips in two seconds. One big hand delved inside, a finger stroking the wet flesh beneath.

Pleasure weakened Ellie's knees. She sagged against him. Releasing his erection, she shoved his jeans lower. She needed him inside her. "Do you have a condom? If not I have one upstairs." A small package leftover from a promising series of dates that had ended in disappointment before she'd had a chance to use them.

Grant pushed her pants down around her knees and yanked one leg of her jeans over a boot. "Wallet. Back pocket."

Obviously, if he was carrying around a condom, he hadn't been that determined to stay out of Ellie's bed. Unless he needed them frequently . . . no, she wasn't going there. His personal life was his business. This was just going to be one pleasant moment seized in a week of misery.

"Here." She opened the package with her teeth and sheathed him.

He was scanning the room, his expression almost desperate. Debris covered the floor. The makeshift worktable wasn't strong enough. Guiding her backward, he shuffled a few feet to the opposite wall. One big hand caressed her rump, then slid between her legs. Pleasure surged through her as he stroked. Her hips flexed as he circled. She groaned. A finger entered her, then two.

The pressure, the stretching, it wasn't enough. Greedily, she pressed into his touch, her legs separating to make room for him. "Need. More."

Hands clutching the backs of her thighs, he lifted her and entered her with one steady, wet slide. The fit of their bodies was perfect, combining to make one whole being.

"Yes." This was what she needed. Him. She clutched his shoulders. "Grant."

The heat of his skin fused with hers. His mouth was on the side of her neck, his lips near her ear. He retreated and surged into her again. Her body responded with an electric wave of pleasure that started in her center and spread outward through her limbs.

"Ellie."

She cupped his neck, and her mouth sought his. The slide of their tongues mimicked their lovemaking. Their pace increased. The grip of his hands on her thighs tightened. His fingers dug into her flesh, holding on. Her back slammed against the wall as he pumped into her. Tension built, her back arching to take every inch of him. Nearly desperate for release, she rocked her hips faster.

"Easy." He wrapped a hand around the front of her pelvis. His thumb circled slowly until he touched a nerve that sent pleasure bursting through her. Finally. She clamped around him. His body responded with a final surge and a groan that sounded as if it were ripped from the soles of his boots. Which he was still wearing, she noted.

Giddiness rose through her chest and burst from her lips as laughter.

Grant lifted his head and frowned. "That's not the response I was shooting for."

Still giggling, she kissed him and looked down. His pants were around his knees. Her jeans and panties dangled from one of her ankles. They were both still wearing their boots.

He sighed. "Yeah. This is not normally how I like to make my first big impression."

"Don't worry." She cupped his jaw and kissed him again. "You made quite an impression."

"Still, if we do that again, I'm going to want some more room to maneuver." He stopped. "But maybe that's not a good idea. I just hope we both don't end up regretting this."

She put a finger to his mouth. "I have no regrets."

But pain gathered inside her. If they'd met under different circumstances, who knew what could have blossomed between them. In less than a week, Grant had gently worked his way inside her heart. He was a special man. A man she could let share her life.

Lord, she was being ridiculous. They'd just met. Maybe this *feeling* was dependent on the security Grant provided for her family. It wasn't as if Ellie had any real experience with successful relationships.

It hardly mattered. A career soldier would never be satisfied with domestic bliss. She'd have to be satisfied with a little tenderness, some terrific sex, and a bittersweet memory. She couldn't get too used to having him around. He'd be gone soon, and once again, she'd be alone.

Chapter Twenty-Eight

Lindsay
January

I limp into the locker room. My knee stings from an epic fail of a double axel. Stopping in the U-shaped alcove that houses my locker, I pause. The hairs on the back of my neck wiggle. I can feel someone's attention on my back. A shudder rides my spine and cramps my belly, as if I'm a vampire's next victim in a horror movie. With one hand on my combination lock, I turn around. On the other side of the locker room, Regan and Autumn stand in front of Regan's open locker. Excitement churns in their eyes. They might not be bloodsuckers, but they are sucking the will to live from my soul.

Too much melodrama, I know. I need to lay off the comics.

Mom did it. Last week, she complained to the school and Victor. She said the principal promised to talk to Regan and Autumn. Victor won't say a word, though. He tries to look out for me, but let's face it. They *have the power, not him. His career is already shaky. Everyone says this club is his last chance. What is a skating coach supposed to do if no one will pay him to coach skating?*

Anyway . . .

They. Are. Pissed. Every day since has been the worst yet.

Yesterday, I stuck my finger down my throat and threw up so I could stay home, but my mom didn't buy the fake sick act today.

"You can't let them win," she says.

She is clueless. I am the only possible loser here. Regan and Autumn and their Shrew Crew have been at me for six solid weeks. I am their mission. Making me miserable is their purpose in life.

My dad called the phone company. They blocked the number. Texts started coming in from a different number a couple of days later. The cell phone company said the numbers are burner phones, disposable and untraceable. I told my parents these kids are smart, but they didn't believe me. Plus, Regan's dad is a computer guy.

Dad says he's going to the police next. He wanted to take my phone away, but it's my only link to Jose. Dad made me close all my social media accounts because nasty messages started showing up on those last week. They've cut me off from everything.

Mom is taking me to see a psychiatrist after school tomorrow. Because I am not enough of a freak, now I have to see a shrink, too. I had one in California, but I only saw him for my ADHD meds. This is different. This time, they think I'm a head case.

Despite my parents' best intentions, I am all alone.

I spin the numbers into place. The weight, the intensity of the girls' focus practically burns. What are they planning? Sweat breaks out under my arms, and it isn't from my skating practice.

Those girls hate me. I've been in Scarlet Falls more than two months. I keep waiting for them to tire of taunting me. Doesn't devising ways to make me miserable take up a large chunk of time? The junior skate team made sectionals this year, and they've been practicing before and after school every day. Don't they get tired? Regan and Autumn have National Honor Society and student council meetings to attend. Straight-ironing their highlights must consume at least thirty minutes a day. Their hair is perfect.

Instinct tells me not to turn my back to them, but Mom will be here soon. The last thing I want is for her to come looking for me. Then she'll have time to talk to Victor. My life is humiliating enough without every single person in it constantly discussing my public shame.

I open my locker and jump backward. Inside, a Barbie swings from a string tied around her neck. Her hair is black, and someone has glued a pink stripe on one side to match the streak in mine. Her fingernails are even painted black. A note glued to her chest reads, "Do everyone a favor and die."

I close the locker and pull out my clothes. I pretend not to have seen anything, but I can feel the girls' glee burning my back. I change quickly, an embarrassing act on the best of days. I'm too skinny. Seventeen years old and no boobs yet. Since I moved here, my acne has flared up too, as if my own skin is collaborating with the enemy to make me yet uglier.

In my black T-shirt and army cargos, I put a foot on the bench and lace up my combat boots. Most of the other girls have left now. I look over my shoulder. Regan and Autumn are gone. Did I disappoint them by not freaking out? I hope so. Though I'm not sure if my ignoring them will make them get bored and move on to someone else, or if they will only see my attitude as a challenge and try harder.

It could go either way. It probably all depends on whether another possible victim gets their attention. But for now, we all know I'm their bitch.

I toss the doll into my gym bag. I don't want to see it there again tomorrow, and it's the first piece of actual physical evidence of their torment. On the way out of the locker room, a hand to my spine sends me sprawling forward. Pain slams through my bruised knee as it hits the concrete. My duffel bag slides down the aisle. I drop my purse. The contents scatter on the concrete. Why do the tampons always go the farthest?

I scramble to scoop my stuff back into my purse. Where is my duffel bag? I spot it near the door. The zipper is open. I look inside. The doll is gone. As if it never existed. My evidence just went poof.

Chapter Twenty-Nine

Grant slowed the rental car and surveyed the rows of crumbling buildings. Two rows of ten attached units faced each other across a hundred feet of blacktop. Clumps of frozen slush dotted the parking/delivery area. Despite the recent snowfall, weeds sprouted through cracks in the asphalt. Snow spread in random patches on the surrounding fields. Brick walls had fared better than the roofs. Most units sported broken windows and doors.

"This is the address?" Grant lowered his window a few inches and listened. On a flagpole at the entrance to the complex, a tattered American flag whipped in the wind. The sight of the torn and faded Stars and Stripes stirred his anger.

Mac checked the piece of lined paper in his hand. "That's what it says."

A ten-year-old boy in a scout uniform had knocked on the front door early that morning. He'd sold Mac a candy bar and passed him the note with his change. The note read: *Last known address, D's BFF, Earl.*

"How did Freddie know where to find Donnie?" Grant asked.

Mac gave him a casual shrug. Grant was tense enough for both of them. The recent snow had blown across the open fields and drifted against the buildings. Even with recent warm temps, a few inches remained on the concrete walkways. Zeroing in on footprints in the slush, he pointed toward a unit in the center of the row. The roof and windows seemed intact. "Looks like he's squatting in that one."

The remaining snow appeared undisturbed. Grant saw no other signs of occupation, but he circled the entire complex to be sure. A POS sedan was parked behind the unit he'd targeted.

He parked the car and pulled his Beretta. He checked the inverted knife strapped to his boot. Secure. They got out of the car.

Grant ran to the building and crouched beneath the window. Mac took position on the other side. Peering over the sill, Grant scanned the interior. The unit was narrow. The rear of the space was an open room. A few doors suggested offices and restrooms toward the front. A kerosene heater glowed a few feet away from a mattress on the floor. A man slept under a pile of blankets. The space had been fitted out with a few tattered lawn chairs, a card table, and a camp stove. Canned goods were lined up on the table next to a stack of red Solo cups. Plastic grocery bags and trash littered the concrete floor. A few items of clothing were piled on the floor next to a backpack.

Mac slid a tool from his pocket, knelt at the back door, and worked the lock, while Grant watched the inhabitant. A faint click signaled the movement of tumblers. Mac grinned, and Grant wondered what other skills his brother hadn't lost in the years since his reformation.

Grant shooed his brother away from the door. Rolling his eyes, Mac moved his arms in a grand be-my-guest gesture. The door swung open without sound. Bonus. Grant crossed the space and whipped the blanket off the sleeping man, a skinny guy in his mid-twenties. Pointing his Beretta at the guy's face, Grant put a finger to his lips. Skinny Guy's eyes bugged.

Letting Mac cover Skinny Guy, Grant checked the remaining rooms.

"You're alone?" he asked.

"Yeah." Skinny Guy's head bobbed.

"Are you Earl?"

Earl nodded again. He licked dry lips.

Grant patted down Earl's hoodie and jeans with gloved hands, tossing a switchblade and a 9mm aside. He found another small knife tucked in his boot. The jacket on the floor next to the mattress was empty.

Grant nodded at the gun and knives. "Three weapons. No ID. Earl, you are either really paranoid or up to some serious shit."

"What do you want?" Earl shivered. The kerosene heater wasn't large enough for the size of the room, though it did make the room habitable.

Satisfied that Earl was unarmed, Grant stood. "Tell me about your pal, Donnie."

"I haven't seen Donnie lately." Earl's gaze shifted.

Liar.

"Aw, Earl. I don't like to be lied to." Grant's gaze flickered to the empty mattress.

"OK." Earl's voice quivered. "Donnie crashed here for a couple of weeks after he got out of prison. But then he took off. I haven't seen him in weeks."

"Who's he been hanging with?"

"I don't know," Earl lied with a quick jerk of his shoulders.

Grant pressed forward. Earl scooted back, eyes widening. A single drop of sweat dripped down his forehead, and Grant caught a pungent whiff of fear. Good. This little piece of shit was lying to him while his pal Donnie stalked Grant's family. Earl's buddy had shot Lee and Kate in cold blood. An image of Lee's face exploding into a red mist closed off Grant's throat for a second. Fury rose in his chest, dimming the sound of his conscience. Everything inside him went as cold and hard as the concrete under his boots.

"You haven't been to war, have you, Earl?" He scanned the man's cowering frame.

Earl cringed, his head shaking.

"No, you don't look like the soldier type. You look like a fucking coward." Grant crouched. He pulled his inverted KA-BAR from the sheath strapped to the inside of his left calf. The seven-inch blade gleamed in the light pouring through the back window.

"Holy shit." Earl scooted backward.

"The Taliban uses a knife just like this one to behead prisoners, except my blade is nice and sharp. They prefer a dull knife. The longer it takes, the more the victim screams. That all makes for a great episode of *Terrorism Today*." Grant grabbed the shrinking man by the throat and dragged him off the mattress onto the cement. "You need a stable surface to do a proper job of it."

A tear leaked out of the coward's eyes, and he began to wheeze. "Oh, God. Don't. Please."

He squirmed. Grant pressed a knee to his sternum, pinning him in place like the insect he was. Earl's arms and legs flailed. Grant leaned on his knee. Satisfaction welled as Earl sucked wind.

Grabbing a handful of hair, Grant turned Earl's head and held the knife to the side of his neck. "If I start on the side, you'll bleed out faster." He shifted the knife's position to Earl's windpipe. "A slice to the windpipe and you drown in your own blood. Takes a little longer to die that way. Or there's always the back of the neck. Supposedly, that's the least painful. Severs the spinal cord and paralyzes you. I've seen it done different ways. They all looked like pretty painful ways to go. Do you want me to do this slow or fast? How do you want to die?"

Earl gasped.

"Your pal Donnie killed our brother and his wife." Grant let the blade kiss the man's skin, not enough to cut him, just enough so he could feel the cold steel against his neck. Grant eased off Earl's chest and let him gulp air for a few seconds. "You're going to tell me where I can find him, or denying it will be the last thing you do."

"I can't. He'll kill me if I talk." Earl's breaths huffed in and out of his mouth like he'd just cleared the base obstacle course in record time. As if he could get over the first wall.

"I'll kill you if you don't. Right here. Right now." Grant shifted his weight forward again.

"OK. Stop," Earl blurted out. "Donnie is staying with some broad he picked up. She lives in Happy Valley Trailer Park."

"What's her name?"

"Tammy. I don't know her last name or the house number. I only been there once, but she has pigs all over the place. Pig statues outside. A pig flag next to the door. Fucking pigs everywhere. You can't miss it."

"Is that the truth?" Grant's hands shook. Scumbags like the man under his blade were ruining the country he risked his life to defend. Killing this coward would be another service to his country.

"Grant!" Mac grabbed his shoulder. "Snap out of it. You can't kill him."

Grant let his brother pull him off. Earl crab-walked twice, stopping when his hands met the mattress. Cringing, he drew his knees up and curled inward.

Grant stood. Adrenaline poured through his bloodstream. He sheathed his knife with fingers that trembled with anger, not fear. The only thing about this encounter that alarmed Grant was the ease and surety with which he'd applied his knife.

"If I find out you lied to me, there won't be a corner of this earth where you can hide." Grant pointed. "And you're not going to talk to Donnie either."

Earl shook his head. "No. I won't talk to Donnie."

"If I find out you warned him, I will find you. Then I will castrate you, behead you, and drop you in the Hudson. In that order."

Grant gathered Earl's weapons and pocketed them. "I suggest you disappear. You don't want to see Donnie right now."

"No, I don't." Earl scrambled to his feet and shoved food and clothes into his backpack.

Two minutes later, Grant and Mac were in the rental sedan.

His brother watched him with a wary expression. "I thought for a couple of minutes, you were going to kill him."

Grant turned toward Scarlet Falls. "Relax. It was all an act." Mac had never seen him in full combat mode. But Grant knew it wasn't an act. He could still feel the rage simmering just below the surface of his skin, ready, willing, and able to take an unarmed man's life in pure anger. Earl wasn't the man who'd killed Lee and Kate.

Grant had nearly lost control. That couldn't happen again, but it seemed like the more time he spent with his family, especially Carson and Faith, the angrier he became over Lee and Kate's deaths. And the closer he came to snapping. Grant had seen it happen. Once a man crossed that line, retreat was not an option. The damage could never be undone.

"Now what?" Mac asked.

"Now we check out the trailer park." But a stop at the trailer park would put him behind schedule. They'd be late getting back to the house. Grant consulted the map in his smartphone for directions. "It's only a couple of miles from here."

"Maybe we should just tell the cops where Donnie is?" Mac said.

"Two problems with that scenario. We'd have to tell them how we got the information, and we don't even know if Earl was right. I don't think he was lying, but we can't be sure until we check out the trailer."

"I don't think Earl was lying." Frowning, his brother studied him.

Grant glanced sideways. "What?"

"I'm worried about you."

"I'm fine."

"You're not fine." Mac's voice grew bitter. "Just like I'm not fine. Hannah and the kids aren't *fine* either. You know why?"

Grant assumed the question was rhetorical and kept his mouth shut.

"Because Lee and Kate were murdered, that's why." Mac crossed his arms over his chest. "We lost our brother. Two kids have been orphaned. No one could possibly be fine under these circumstances."

Grant sighed. "Then what I meant was that I was as good as can be expected, considering."

"Bullshit. We might not have spent a lot of time together lately, but I know something is going on with you."

Grant drove in silence for a few minutes. Mac radiated anger from the passenger seat.

"Right before I got word about Lee, something happened over there." Grant kept his eyes front, but he could feel the weight of Mac's gaze. He gave him a quick rundown of the ambush. "I did the math. With the time difference, I could have shot that guy in the face at the exact same time Lee and Kate were being murdered." He stopped short of telling Mac that every time he closed his eyes, he saw Lee's face explode. The parallel universe bullshit was freaky enough.

"I can see how that might fuck with your head." Mac's hand scratched three days of beard scruff. "Talk to me, Grant. But if you can't talk to me, find someone who can help. The military has psychiatrists, right?"

"I'll be all right. I just didn't get any time to decompress after the ambush. It's easier to deal with this stuff then and there."

"You've had issues before?" Mac sounded surprised.

Grant struggled for the words to describe how senseless killing, cruelty, and horror left their imprint on man. He settled on, "nobody goes into combat and comes out the same."

Mac leaned back into his seat, his face thoughtful. "I'm sorry. I always thought you loved what you did."

"No one could love combat." Grant thought of all the good men he'd seen maimed and killed, all the flag-draped coffins he'd saluted, the crying widows and shock-faced children.

"Then why do you do it?"

"Duty. The country needs soldiers. I'd been groomed my whole life to serve. To protect American citizens and their way of life."

"People like Lee and Kate," Mac added.

"Ironic, isn't it? I was protecting them thousands of miles away from where they were being murdered."

"Whoa." Mac raised his hands. "Even those Mr. Clean shoulders of yours can't bear guilt over this. Or at least not any more than me and Hannah. None of us were paying attention. None of us knew anything about what was really going on in Lee's life. If any of us failed him, we all did. Don't think for a second that me and Hannah aren't feeling plenty guilty, too."

"I have no intention of failing him again." Grant drove the rest of the way without speaking. Mac's revelation about their shared guilt shouldn't have come as a shock. Of course they felt remorse and regret. None of them knew Lee's life was in shambles. Were the three of them so wrapped up in their own lives, so disinterested in Lee, that he felt like he couldn't share his troubles? The answer was an obvious and resounding yes.

Ambition would be the Barretts' downfall.

The trailer park occupied a field in the middle of fucking nowhere. Forest surrounded an open space the size of two side-by-side football fields. Dirt roads bisected a grid of small, square lots. Grant turned at the ingress, where white script on a faded green sign proclaimed they were entering Happy Valley Trailer Park.

He drove up and down multiple rows, the muddy road grating and squishing under the tires.

The sedan lurched over a deep rut. Mac grabbed the chicken strap hanging above the door. "We should have brought my truck."

"I didn't anticipate going off-road."

"Over there." Mac pointed through the windshield. "I see a pig."

"Son of a bitch." Grant kept driving past a white trailer outfitted to look like a miniature farmhouse. Black shutters flanked the windows. A two-foot picket fence surrounded a patch of weedy lawn adorned with decorative pig silhouettes. The pig flag waved from its bracket next to the door.

"No car out front." Mac scratched his chin. "How do we sneak up? There's no cover."

"No." Grant spotted an empty space two spots down the lane and parked the sedan. "Sneaking doesn't appear to be an option. Any ideas?"

"Yeah. Let's talk to the neighbors. I suddenly feel interested in this empty lot." Mac reached for the door handle. "Try not to scare the piss out of anybody."

"I'll do my best." Grant rolled his eyes. "Unless we find Donnie. Then all bets are off."

"Fair enough." Mac opened his door and got out. "I'll do the talking." He pointedly scanned Grant from boots to jacket. "No one would believe you were interested in a trailer park."

Grant looked down at his clothes. "What's wrong with my clothes?"

"Nothing. You're just too . . . ironed." Mac's attire leaned toward scraggly. His hiking boots were scuffed from use, and the holes in his jeans weren't a fashion statement, but a lack of interest in shopping or his appearance.

Mac walked past a dinged pickup truck to the trailer between the empty lot and the pig house. The unit was neat but basic. He knocked on the door.

A thin, middle-aged man in a flannel shirt, jeans, and tan work boots answered. His Bee Gees beard was neatly trimmed but made him look like he stepped out of the 1970s. "Yeah?"

Mac backed down the step, giving the guy some space. He jerked a thumb over his shoulder. "I'm interested in the lot. Can I ask you a couple of questions?"

"Sure." Tugging a Mets cap over a salt-and-pepper shag cut, he locked his door and walked down the steps to join them on the square cement landing. "I'm leaving for work. I only got a couple minutes."

"I'm Mac." He held out a hand.

The Mets fan shook it. "Bob."

Mac crossed his arms over his chest. "How is this place?"

"It's OK." Bob shrugged. "Folks mostly mind their own business. Some people have been here forever, but there's a fair amount of turnover."

"Is it quiet at night? I get up early for work."

"I hear you. I hate first shift." Bob huffed. "Broad next door and her boyfriend are into some weird shit. They go at it till late some nights. Pain in the ass. Some nights I got to put on fucking headphones. Forget leaving the windows open."

"Have they been here long?"

"She has, but he's pretty new. I'm hoping he moves on. She goes through boyfriends like napkins. Seems like a lazy piece of shit to me. Probably an ex-con. Mean-looking dude." Bob touched his face just below his eye. "Got one of those blue ink tats right here."

"Huh." Mac made a noncommittal sound of interest.

"Three kinds of people live in a place like this." Bob held up a hand and ticked them off on his fingers. "Broke seniors, hardworking people trying to scrape by, and scumbags. The boyfriend is a scumbag, freeloading on a lonely woman." Pure disgust colored his voice.

"Maybe I'll knock on the door and see for myself."

Bob glanced over at the pig-adorned trailer. "She ain't home. Must be at work. She runs a register at the Walmart on the highway."

"Hmm. I really need my sleep." Mac scraped a toe on the concrete. "Maybe I should come back at night and listen for myself."

"Probably." Bob nodded. "Hey, I gotta get to work. Can't afford to get docked."

"Thanks for the info, man."

"Anytime." Bob got into his truck and drove away.

"Well, what do you think?"

Grant scanned the area. There was no one outside. "Can you work your magic on the lock?"

"Sure. Kind of ballsy in daylight though."

"I'm feeling kind of ballsy."

"OK." Mac followed him to the trailer, raised his hand, and pretended to knock. Grant crowded him, using his body to block Mac's hands from view. Two seconds later, Mac cracked the door. Grant nudged his brother out of the way and took point. His Beretta was in his hand as he crossed the threshold. He inhaled. Something smelled off. Raw.

Dead.

Mac sniffed and handed him a pair of latex gloves. "Not good."

"Do you just carry those around?"

His brother shrugged. "Thought we might need them. I like to be prepared."

"I feel like we need hazmat suits."

The door opened into the living area. Nothing interesting in sight. Grant moved through the empty kitchen. A door led to the single bedroom. Grant gestured toward the assortment of BDSM toys scattered on the bed: handcuffs, whips, a spiked collar, something that looked like one of the dog's Kong toys with straps on it. "Is that a ball gag?"

"You are asking the *wrong* person."

Five minutes later, Grant pulled a manila envelope out of the bottom of a drawer. He opened and tilted it. A picture of Lee and Kate fell into his other hand. They were walking out of their house. Lee's arm curled around Kate's waist as he spoke in her ear. Her head was tilted toward him. The address was written on the bottom of the photo. "Shit."

Grant turned the picture over. Notes were scrawled across the back. Locations of both of their employers, license plate numbers, e-mail addresses, and their daily schedules. The login information for their online calendars was scrawled in the middle of the page. That explained how he knew where to find them. Grant's gut went sour as he focused on the last note: $5,000.

"Look what I found." Mac said across the room.

Grant used his cell phone to snap a picture of the photo and the notes on the back.

Mac was holding a pricy laptop. "What the hell is a lowlife scrounging off a cashier doing with a machine like this?"

"Probably stole it. McNamara said Donnie had done time for ID theft."

Mac returned the computer to the closet and crossed the floor. He sucked air when he looked at the photo. "Someone paid this guy to kill them."

Instead of the hot rage Grant expected, ice flowed through his body. In front of him was evidence that Donnie Ehrlich had been hired to murder Lee and Kate. Grant didn't want to call the cops. He wanted to lie in wait for this guy, then ambush and kill him after he beat a confession from his lips. Grant wanted Donnie's blood, and the blood of the person who'd hired him, on his hands. But he wouldn't do it. He'd do the right thing. As a soldier he'd sworn to protect his country, and that included all the laws that comprised her. Going vigilante wasn't defending democracy.

But his hands—and his determination—were shaky as he returned the photo to its hiding place.

"Now what?"

"Only one place left to look." Grant opened the door to the bathroom. His stomach curled at the sight—and smell. The body lay on its side in the bathtub. She was nude, wrapped cocoon-style in a sheet of plastic, the seams thoroughly duct taped. Ice was piled around the shrouded body. Empty plastic bags marked ICE, the kind sold in liquor stores, littered the floor. Her features were blurred by multiple layers of plastic, but Grant could make out a slender shape, long dark hair, and one, wide-open blue eye. Another layer of anger tested his tenuous control.

Mac looked over his shoulder. "I assume that's the cashier."

"Seems likely."

"Now we call the police."

Grant's gaze swept over the clutter of hair spray bottles and body lotion, the personal items the cashier would never use again. He glanced back at the body. What a fucking waste. "Yeah. It's time."

They slipped out of the trailer and returned to the car. Grant drove to the end of the street and pulled out his cell phone.

"Are you calling the cop?"

"Yes."

Mac shook his head. "Might be best to deliver this tip anonymously."

"Good point." Grant circled to the front of the park, where the office squatted next to a gravel parking area. A pay phone hung on the exterior along the side of the building.

"Let's see if this works." Grant parked behind the office. He dug some loose change out of the ashtray. The phone was live. McNamara didn't answer the call, and Grant left an anonymous message, though the cop might recognize his voice. He wiped his prints off the phone and went back to the car.

"Are we going to sit here and wait?"

"No." It took all of Grant's willpower to turn the car toward the exit and drive out of the trailer park. The urge to confront his brother's killer seethed under Grant's skin like bits of shrapnel, but deep down, he was afraid he'd lose control, that he'd kill Donnie before he found out who'd hired him. "I don't want to tip off Donnie."

"He'd definitely bolt if he saw us."

"Hopefully, the cops will pick up Donnie, and he'll tell them who paid him. His stuff was still in the trailer. I assume he was coming back." But under all the civilized pretense, Grant's heart and soul were screaming for revenge, and instinct told him that Donnie would cave faster to him than to the police. When put in just the right place, there was no better motivator than a sharp blade.

His fingers tightened on the wheel. "I hope we're doing the right thing."

"We are," Mac said. "I've operated outside the law. It's not a good place to be."

"No. I imagine not."

Mac pointed at him. "You know Lee wouldn't want us to take risks. We can't take care of the kids if we're dead or in prison. Plus, if you go all apeshit and kill this guy, how will we find out who hired him?"

It seemed as if Mac was reading his mind.

"I know, but I don't like it." At a stop sign, Grant texted Ellie to let her know they were headed home. He could do this, but sitting back and waiting wouldn't be easy. He'd only be able to hold back for a short time. If the police couldn't find Donnie, Grant would go hunting.

Chapter Thirty

The hall bathroom of the Barretts' house needed a serious renovation. Ellie attempted to duplicate an intricate braid in her daughter's hair, but her mind was redesigning the space.

Could the cast-iron claw-foot tub be restored? The answer depended on how deep the rust had eroded into the finish, but it was a lovely, elegant fixture. The clunky vanity had to go. A pair of pedestal sinks would fit the house far better.

Julia sat in front of her in a desk chair they'd dragged in from the guest room. On an iPad propped on the vanity, a girl demonstrated the hairstyle Julia wanted for her skating routine at the winter carnival.

"If I don't make practice tonight, I can't perform in the show. Coach Victor said so."

"I know." Ellie folded one piece of hair over another and pulled the strands tight. "I'll do my best to get you there. Major Barrett said he'd take us later as long as he gets home in time."

"I like him, even if he did get me and Taylor in trouble."

"Major Barrett did not get you in trouble. You got you in trouble." Ellie missed a step with her hairdo and had to backtrack. She unwound two sections, rewound the video, and did it again. Better.

Disheveled hair was a no-no on the ice. "What you did was dangerous. What did you expect him to do?"

"I don't know." Julia lifted her shoulders.

"Hold still." Ellie wove and tucked hair, but panic was inching up her esophagus as she thought of Julia sneaking out of the house while Donnie Ehrlich was after her.

"You're mad."

"I'm not mad." Ellie fastened the end of the braid with an elastic band and bobby pinned it into place. "I'm scared. It's my job to protect you. I can't do that if you sneak out in the middle of the night. What if that man was watching and waiting for you?"

"I didn't know about him," Julia protested.

"No. You had no idea who was out there, but now you do. Close your eyes." Ellie gave Julia's hair a good blast of hair spray. She picked up a hand mirror and showed Julia the back of her head. The braid was twisted around and woven into a bun. "What do you think?"

Julia smiled. "It's pretty. I hope it holds up during practice."

"That's why we're giving it a dry run." Ellie set the mirror down and stopped the video. "Look, I know I've been strict with you. When this is all over, I'll take the time to get to know Taylor."

"You'll let me go out with him?"

"I'm not making any promises. Maybe we'll start with him coming to our house. He will need to be driving a safe vehicle. I'm sure I'll have other conditions when I have a chance to really think things through, but yes. Your sixteenth birthday is coming up. I think it's time."

"How many conditions?"

"I'll try to be reasonable and balance my sanity with your safety. But you have to promise you'll never try to sneak out again."

"Deal." Julia stood up and hugged her. Ellie closed her eyes and enjoyed the embrace. With every year that passed in her daughter's life, hugs became scarcer.

"Now go run around and see how that braid holds up."

"I promised Carson a game of Candy Land."

"Thank you for helping out with the kids," Ellie said. "I know Major Barrett appreciates you pitching in."

"I like Carson."

"He likes you, too."

Julia bounced out into the hallway. How she could be that happy when the man who'd chased her was still on the loose, Ellie had no idea. She tidied up the bathroom, then went to the room she and Julia were sharing. Carson's and Julia's voices floated down the hall, childish, innocent, sweet. Who could want to hurt either one of them? A text came in on her phone. Grant was on his way. She ignored the pleasure that knowledge gave her. This was not his home or hers. He would be leaving again in a few weeks, and he didn't know when he could come back.

Images of their brief and intense lovemaking seared her mind. She'd been near desperate to have him, to connect with him as a physical expression of the feelings she wasn't ready to acknowledge. But whether she was ready to admit it or not, the possibility of love hovered around her heart.

Her phone vibrated in her hand. A call, not a text. The number on the screen belonged to Mr. and Mrs. Hamilton. She closed the bedroom door for privacy and stabbed the green Answer button. "Hello."

"Is this Ellie Ross?" a woman's voice asked.

"Yes."

"This is Aubrey Hamilton."

"Mrs. Hamilton. Thank you for returning my call."

"Frankly, I'm disappointed it took your firm this long to contact us." Mrs. Hamilton's tone carried her annoyance.

"About that." Guilt nagged Ellie. Hoping the woman wouldn't hang up, she said, "this call isn't exactly about firm business."

"Excuse me? I don't understand. We've been waiting for a call back from Mr. Peyton. That's not what you're calling about?"

"No. I'm sorry. But I need to speak with you. Can we meet? I'd rather explain in person."

"All right," Mrs. Hamilton said. "I think it would be better to do this in private. Do you want to come to me or shall I come to you?"

Ellie did not want anyone to come to the house. "Are the media still outside your house?"

"No. Our daughter's case is no longer exciting news. The press gave up their vigilance when the police declared there wasn't enough evidence to file charges." Mrs. Hamilton sounded bitter. "They jumped on that interview, but only because bullying is such a hot-button topic."

Ellie checked the clock. "There'll be a tall man with me. Say in about an hour?"

"All right." Mrs. Hamilton provided her address. "My husband and I will be here."

"See you then." Ellie sent Grant a text, letting him know about the meeting. Distracted, she paced the foyer until the dog ran to the front door. Not wanting barking to wake the baby, Ellie led the dog back to Hannah. The baby was sleeping in her seat in the corner.

"Thanks," mouthed Hannah.

Ellie ran out to the car as Mac went into the house. One look at Grant's face told her something was wrong. She closed the car door. "What happened?"

"Mac and I found where Donnie's been staying." His knuckles were white on the steering wheel.

"How did you find him when the police don't know where he is?"

Grant's answer was too slow, as if he were carefully choosing his words. "Mac knows people on the other side of the law."

"Really?" She wouldn't have guessed the shaggy biologist had a dark past.

"Unfortunately, he went through a rebellious stage in his youth."

"We all have some bad decisions behind us. What's important is that he came through it." As she spoke the words, Ellie realized how much they applied to her as well as Mac. Nan was right. It was time she forgave herself for one stupid mistake in high school.

"I know, but it wasn't easy to see the evidence of how far Mac really fell. I was away. I had no idea." He frowned. "I think that bothers me more than what actually happened. I left Lee to handle everything back home. I never considered the amount of responsibility he shouldered."

"Did he ever say anything to you?"

"No."

"You were at war, Grant. He probably thought you had enough on your plate."

"Did you know they were having financial difficulties?" he asked.

"Neither of them said anything outright, but I knew Kate was sweating the mortgage and the BMW lease payments. They couldn't afford to fix the house up the way I was working on mine. But then, my house is smaller, the price was lower, and I had a substantial down payment from the last house I flipped."

"I don't understand why they bought a house they couldn't afford. Sure, their previous place was small. Two kids would have been a tight fit, but wouldn't that be better than being in debt?"

Ellie squeezed his hand. "Lee wanted that partnership. He'd put seven years into that firm, and the senior Mr. Peyton, Roger's father, told Lee if he wanted to be a partner, he'd better look the part."

"That makes no sense."

"Old Mr. Peyton is superficial. He wouldn't give the partnership to anyone who didn't look successful," Ellie said. "But I'm not sure why Lee took the case, considering the partnership was so pivotal for his career. Before Peyton hired Frank, Lee didn't really have any competition. He thought the partnership was a sure thing. But with Frank vying for the same position, taking the Hamilton case was a risky decision."

"So Lee worked his ass off, and Peyton screwed him by hiring a competitor."

"Unfortunately, that sums it up. He probably thought he'd get more out of Lee if he kept him on edge."

"Maybe Lee thought taking the case was the right thing to do. He had this optimistic streak. He always thought things would work out. Usually, he was right, but this time I guess he wasn't." Grant was quiet for the next few minutes.

"There's something you're not telling me," she said.

He nodded. "Are you sure you want to know?"

"Yes." Apprehension bubbled into her chest, but she didn't want to be sheltered from any truth that could affect her family's safety.

"Looks like Donnie killed his girlfriend. He put her on ice in her trailer bathtub."

She recoiled. "I don't know why I'm shocked. He already killed Lee and Kate." But another murder drove home the danger to her family. "Did you call the police?"

"I did. Don't worry. I used a pay phone and didn't leave my name." Grant's posture was stiff. He steered the car with one hand. The other rested on his thigh, clenching and loosening repeatedly. He was acting stoic, but finding that woman's body had disturbed him.

"I wasn't worried." She reached over and grabbed his hand. He curled his fingers tightly around hers, and a small amount of tension eased from his muscles.

Ellie directed him through a few turns. The Hamiltons lived in a development of big houses on large lots. A meadow and forest edged the rear of the property.

"Lindsay hanged herself in those woods behind the house, right?" Grant steered the car up a long driveway.

"Yes." Ellie placed a hand on the tension building in her stomach. The thought of living so close to the place where a child took her own life sent a wave of nausea into her throat. "How can they live here?"

He parked in front of the porch steps. "Maybe they don't want to let go."

Mrs. Hamilton let them in. Thin to the point of gaunt, she wore wrinkled silk slacks and a light sweater that bagged on her frame as if she'd lost the weight recently and hadn't bothered to buy new clothes. Her face and lips were colorless. A half inch from her part, a stark line of gray bisected her bobbed hair. The house was as elegant and unkempt as its mistress. Dust coated the expensive furniture, and dirt marred the red oak floors.

Ellie introduced Grant.

Mrs. Hamilton showed them into a study at the rear of the house.

A man sat on the sofa, his gaze fixed vaguely on the view of the woods through a set of French doors. He didn't wait for an introduction. "I go out there every day and sit under that tree. You probably think that's sick."

"No, sir. Everything about this situation is wrong. I imagine you can't take it in." Grant took the wing chair diagonal to Mr. Hamilton. "I'm Lee's brother, Major Grant Barrett."

"Your brother was a good man." Mr. Hamilton returned his gaze to the glass. "He wanted to help us."

Ellie sensed a connection of grief between the two men and let Grant take the lead. She settled in a chair across from Grant. Mrs. Hamilton sat on the sofa but not immediately next to her husband. She left the middle section empty. The distance between them seemed larger than a couch cushion.

Grant leaned forward and rested his forearms on his thighs. His jacket stretched until Ellie could see the weapon at his hip. He carried it so naturally, she'd nearly forgotten about it. "Did he give any indication of how he was going to do that?"

"No. We were so pleased he'd agreed to take our case. No one else seemed to care, but he did. I'm sorry he died." Mr. Hamilton turned back to the woods, his gaze clouded with pain. "Do you really think his murder could be related to my daughter's case?"

"We're not sure," Grant said in a raw voice. "But I'm sure you understand why I have to find out."

"I do." Mr. Hamilton shuddered. He took off his glasses and cleaned them with the hem of his sweater. "The first time she asked to quit the skating team, we should have known. She loved skating. That would have been the last thing she willingly gave up. We should have pulled her out of that school. We should have taken her back to San Francisco. She was so unhappy here. It broke my heart." His voice cracked.

"I didn't want her to let those bullies win. I was afraid if she gave up and ran away, it would damage her forever," Mrs. Hamilton said quietly.

"No worries about that now, right?" Her husband's voice cut like a blade. "She didn't care about any of that. She just wanted to get away from a bunch of nasty, spoiled bitches getting a real charge out of making her miserable."

His wife turned away from him without comment. Mrs. Hamilton drew her legs onto the sofa and curled them under her. "Everyone else in town, including the police, was more focused on Lindsay's emotional problems. We kept telling them she didn't have any emotional problems until we moved here, but it didn't seem to matter."

"I don't understand. That seems simple to me," Grant said.

"She'd been treated by a psychiatrist and was taking medication for ADHD in California. So even though her emotional issues were new, she had a past history of being treated by a psychiatrist. Then her new doctor here prescribed an antidepressant. We didn't tell anyone. She asked us not to." Mrs. Hamilton sighed. "She seemed to be feeling a little better."

Mr. Hamilton stirred. The set of his mouth disagreed with his wife. "I didn't want her to take them. One of the warnings on the label said that the drug could cause an increase in suicidal thoughts. How the hell can they make an antidepressant that causes suicidal thoughts? The doctor gave us a list of signs to watch for. It seems we missed them."

Mrs. Hamilton shifted. "That's the real reason no one will take the case. They said we held back critical information that could have changed the way the school and the arena management dealt with the situation." Mrs. Hamilton interlaced her fingers and clenched her hands until her nails turned white. "And that the medication, along with our misreading Lindsay's moods, could have been determining factors in her suicide. They also suggested she had an undiagnosed mental illness before moving here."

Actually, the arguments sounded reasonable to Ellie, but she didn't say it. The Hamiltons were suffocating in guilt and blame. They didn't want to believe they were partially responsible for their daughter's death. *That* she could understand.

"You don't think that's possible?" Grant asked gently.

Mrs. Hamilton twisted her hands. "She always *seemed* happy before we moved."

"She was happy," her husband snapped. "We should have moved back, but you made her feel inadequate for wanting to give in to those bullies."

Mrs. Hamilton recoiled as if he'd slapped her.

Her husband rose. "I'm sorry." He bolted through the French doors, crossed the back porch, and descended the wooden steps to the ground. He strode into the meadow toward the woods. His anger left an electric-like charge in the room.

Mrs. Hamilton watched him go with a dead eye. Then she turned to Grant. "Your brother seemed particularly interested in copies of the threatening text messages Lindsay received, but I don't know why. The messages came from a burner phone, and the police couldn't prove who sent the calls. The phone never turned up. I've no doubt it was destroyed. Lindsay had received photos and video as well, but her phone was wiped out with a cell phone virus attached to one of the messages. Even the police experts weren't able to recover them. I didn't even know there was such a thing as a cell phone virus." Mrs. Hamilton paused and picked at her fingernails. "We were supposed to meet with your brother again the Monday following his death."

Grant's torso tilted forward. "Do you have copies of the texts?" When Mrs. Hamilton nodded, he asked. "Would you mind letting me read them? I promise to bring them back."

"I guess it doesn't matter now. It's not an open case. I'll make you a copy." Mrs. Hamilton rose and left the room. She returned in a few minutes with a sheaf of papers in her hand. "I don't know why you're doing this, but thank you. Since your brother died, we haven't been able to find another lawyer who will take the case." She paused. "That's not entirely true. We've actually had dozens of attorneys calling and knocking on the door, but none have been of the same caliber as Lee. We didn't want to damage our case by hiring someone disreputable. We wanted to be taken seriously."

"I won't share these with anyone, and if I discover anything, I'll let you know." Grant stood. "Thank you for your time."

Mrs. Hamilton showed them to the door, and they returned to the car.

"What do you think?" Ellie fastened her seat belt.

"They blame each other and themselves. He wanted to move back. She didn't want to give up. So he feels guilty for not fighting for his daughter, and she feels guilty for her decisions."

"It's a toxic environment. I wonder how their marriage fared before Lindsay's death."

"Who knows?" Grant turned the car around. "Having your child commit suicide could break anyone, but then again, the fact that they couldn't really come to an agreement over their daughter's predicament tells me they likely had problems before it happened."

Ellie's purse buzzed. She fished her phone out of the side pocket. Her nerves quivered. "I don't know that number."

"Is it the same number he used to threaten you before?"

"No." Ellie pressed the message bubble.

"He's probably using a burner phone once and destroying it. That's what I would do."

She read the message aloud. "I didn't tell you to talk to the Hamiltons."

Grant's gaze swept their surroundings. "I don't see how anyone could know we were here."

Ellie glanced behind them. "Unless he was watching the Hamilton's house from the woods."

"How would he know to do that?" At the end of the driveway, Grant stopped the car and got out.

"What?" Ellie followed him.

"How did he know where we were?" Grant circled the vehicle. "Do you have a flashlight in the glove box?"

"Yes." Ellie got it for him.

She rubbed her biceps against the breeze as he circled her car, running his hands under the bumper and fenders. He dropped to the ground and shone the light across the vehicle's undercarriage.

"Damn it." He pulled off a two-inch black box that had been duct-taped to the undercarriage of her minivan.

"What is it?"

"Looks like a GPS tracker."

"Oh my God." Ellie's jaw dropped. She put a hand over her mouth. "He can track my movements with that?"

"Yes."

"Will he know you took it off the car?"

"No, as long as it's still transmitting, he'll just assume your van is where the unit is located." Grant got to his feet. "I know I promised I wouldn't tell McNamara, but I think we should call him."

"He said he'd hurt my family if I did that." Fear gathered in Ellie's throat.

Grant held up the device. "But we're no closer to delivering that file."

Tears burned at the corners of Ellie's eyes. What should she do? Grant was right. His thirty-six-hour promise had expired, but he was asking, not forcing her to change her mind. She couldn't deliver what Hoodie Man wanted. But going against his instructions and involving the police felt dangerous.

"Look, I can't stand sitting back and letting this all play out without taking action. How about we go back to Lee's, we'll read through these texts, and we'll make a plan?"

Ellie's phone buzzed again. "He sent another message."

Get that file by tomorrow or your family is dead.

Chapter Thirty-One

Grant looked up from the page of text messages on the desk. "These are really nasty."

"They are." Sitting across from him, Ellie had her own stack of papers attached to a clipboard. "What kind of kid tells another to kill herself?"

"I don't know, but it doesn't matter how nasty the messages were if no one can prove who sent them."

Ellie rubbed the back of her neck. "I don't know what to do. He's going to message me tomorrow. We don't have the file."

"We have two options. We could call the police. Or we could make our own file. He has no way of knowing it isn't the real file."

"I never thought of that." Ellie shifted backward, her skeleton straightening as the small hope he'd just presented gave her strength.

"I'm still thinking, but I think I can do even better than that." A couple of ideas were rolling around in his head. The thought of taking this campaign on the offense sent a bolt of energy through him. His desire to personally take care of Lee's killer was the real reason he hadn't insisted Ellie call the police. "Have you found any clues in those texts?"

"No." Ellie set the clipboard on the desk, stood, and stretched. "I have to run home for some clothes, and Julia needs clothes for skating practice tonight."

Grant went hard as his mind played a reel of their last visit to her house. They shouldn't do that again. Ellie didn't deserve to be hurt, but the solace he found with her was difficult to resist.

"I'm coming with you." Grant stood and picked up the baby monitor on the desk. "I'll let Hannah know."

"I'll tell Julia and Nan and see if there's anything else either of them needs from our house." Ellie left the office and headed upstairs, where Julia was finishing her homework before skating practice. Worn out from another night of little sleep and an outdoor play session with Grant and the dog, Carson was out cold.

Hannah was in the kitchen working on her laptop. Grant poked his head through the doorway. Piles of papers were spread out on the table in front of her. The baby was sleeping in the corner.

"Maybe the kids are actually vampires who don't like daylight," he said.

Hannah sighed. "That would explain a lot."

"Work or estate stuff?" he asked.

She lifted her head. "Yes."

"Where's Mac?"

"He went upstairs. Said he'd get some sleep now and take the first baby-walking-night-watchman shift."

"Good." Grant nodded toward the baby. Her screaming fits had been spaced further apart the last two nights. He prayed the colic was easing. "Want to risk putting her in her crib upstairs?"

"Hell, no." Hannah grimaced. "Haven't you heard? Never wake a sleeping baby."

"I'm running next door with Ellie for a few minutes. She needs some things." He set the baby monitor on the corner of the desk.

Since the baby wouldn't sleep in her crib at night, Grant had put the baby monitor base in Carson's room. The house was so big, he couldn't hear the boy from downstairs. "Can you listen for Carson?"

Hannah nodded. "Sure."

"Text me if either of them wakes up."

"All right." She bent her head over her papers again.

Stepping in front of Ellie, Grant scanned the outside through front and back windows before turning off the alarm and opening the front door. Locking the door behind him, he reset the security system with the fob on his keychain.

At Ellie's house, Grant went in first, Beretta in hand. A quick trip through the house verified they were alone. He ended the tour in the upstairs hall.

"It's clear." He holstered his weapon.

Ellie went into her bedroom. Grant followed, leaning on the wall while she set a small tote bag on a chest at the foot of the bed. She left the room for a few minutes and came back with an armload of clothes.

His phone buzzed. He read the display, hoping it wasn't Hannah. He really needed an hour off. At a swipe of his finger, a message from Mac displayed on the screen: Medical examiner released the bodies.

His mind resisted the news.

"Is everything all right?" Her eyes searched his.

He put the phone down. "Yes."

"OK. I'm just about done here." Her brows furrowed. She didn't believe him, but he didn't have the energy to explain. Exhaustion weighted his body, and he eyed the bed. Late nights with nightmares and crying children were taking their toll. "Would you mind if I closed my eyes for a combat nap?"

Ellie looked up from her packing, a folded sweater in her hands. "Not at all. Do you want me to leave the room?"

Grant stretched out on the bed. "Actually, would you mind lying here with me?"

"Not at all." She eased onto the bed next to him.

He rolled over, put an arm over her body, and buried his nose in her hair. She smelled like flowers. "Wake me in thirty minutes."

With years of practice, he slipped into a combat nap in seconds.

"Grant?" Ellie's whisper pulled him back. "It's been an hour, but you can sleep more if you like."

He opened his eyes. "You were supposed to wake me in thirty minutes."

"You were out cold." Her face was inches from his. Her hand rested on his shoulder. Contentedness washed over him. The moment felt almost painfully ordinary in the quiet bedroom. That was the most restful chunk of sleep he'd gotten since he came home. He could get used to seeing her when he woke.

He reached up and touched a lock of hair that fell over her shoulder. He twirled it around his finger. Every moment since he'd received the call about Lee had been filled with worry, grief, and fear. He didn't want to let this peaceful moment end. Just for a few minutes, he could pretend that waking to a beautiful woman was his normal. What would it be like to have moments like these all the time? Instances of intimacy that were earth-shatteringly common.

"Do you want to sleep more? You're up most of the night."

Sleep? That was not anything close to what he wanted to do right at this moment. He dropped her hair and curled his hand around the back of her neck, tugging her down to lean across his chest. Suspicion and desire darkened her eyes. Both emotions sent Grant's blood rushing south. He lifted his head and touched his lips to hers. The soft moan that slipped from her throat pulled his hips off the bed. Her mouth opened. He slipped his tongue into her heat, wishing for more. Ellie could heal him. But it was selfish to ask for her help. Whatever transpired between them couldn't be permanent.

But he tugged her across his chest. Wrapping his arms around her, he deepened the kiss. His tongue stroked hers. She answered, opening her mouth for more. He delved deeper, want and need building until they blotted out the pain he'd been carrying for more than a week. All he wanted was Ellie. He wanted to steep himself in her until nothing else existed, and he wanted it badly enough to ignore the limits of their relationship. Just for now. One afternoon. That's all he was asking.

He slipped a hand under her sweater to caress the smooth skin of her waist. Her soft groan spurred him to move higher until he cupped her breast through the cotton of her bra. Her fingers clenched in his T-shirt, and the scrape of her nails against his skin made his erection pound. His hips lifted off the bed, seeking her body. She sat up, peeled her sweater over her head, and tossed it on the floor.

"Are you sure?"

Instead of answering, she flicked the front closure of her bra and freed her breasts. Small and round, they were in perfect proportion to her slim body. Grant cupped one in the palm of his hand. His thumb flicked over the nipple. Ellie arched back, the pleasure on her face transforming her wholesome looks into an erotic dream.

Needing more direct contact, he levered his torso up on the bed and whipped off his shirt. He slid his jeans off his legs, reached into his pocket for his wallet, and took out a condom.

Ellie stood and stripped. When she rejoined him on the bed, he rolled until she was beneath him. Skin on skin, heat on heat. This was what his body demanded. Her hand slid down his abs until she stroked his erection. Anxious to get started, it pulsed in her palm.

He gripped her wrist. "Let's slow this down a little."

"Says the man who isn't used to having kids around." Ellie reached down and cupped his balls. His hips surged toward her.

"Our time is limited. I can guarantee you'll be summoned just when things are getting good."

The truth in her statement rang in his heart. "Things are already pretty good, but indulge me, just for a few minutes." He wanted, needed to savor her so he could remember these moments in the lonely hours when he returned to Afghanistan.

He slid down her body. The salty, sweet tang of her skin drove all thoughts save her from his mind. Moving down her belly, he licked and tasted. The pitch of her moans guided him to her sweet spot. Her body arced. Her hands reached for his head. A primitive and shameless groan made his erection throb. Her fingers tightened on his scalp. He wanted this moment to last for as long as possible, but she was right. Their time was limited.

With a heavy feeling that almost felt like regret, he opened the condom and sheathed himself. He moved up the bed. One hand slid between her legs, testing.

"Grant." Ellie wrapped her legs around his waist. Her whisper was breathless and urgent in his ear. "Now. Please. I'm more than ready for you."

He nudged inside her, intending to be gentle. But pleasure flooded him, and his body surged into her without input from his brain. She bowed backward.

"I'm sorry."

"Why did you stop?" She arched, her heels digging into his ass, pulling him even deeper.

"I thought I'd hurt you." He panted, his muscles shaking with the effort of holding still.

"Obviously not." Her hips moved beneath him. "Now stop thinking. That's an order."

"Yes, ma'am." He pulled back and surged forward again. Her body tightened around him as if it couldn't get enough.

Her eyes widened. Her pupils dilated. "Grant." His name was a moan from her lips. "More."

Levering his torso on his hands, he swung his hips forward. Her body bent backward. Her nails dug into his shoulders. His body, his need, took over, increasing the speed and urgency of his motions. She kept pace, her hips thrusting to meet him, their bodies locked into a natural rhythm.

Ellie's limbs tensed. Her eyes closed, and a guttural sound emanated from her lips. She clamped around him, and he let go. Pleasure shot through his spine as he surged into her one final time. Ellie wrapped her body around him, riding out the pulsing wave of their joint pleasure.

Grant's arms gave out, and he collapsed on top of her. She eased her legs from around his waist. He planted a kiss on the corner of her mouth. "Thank you."

"I think I should be thanking you." Her words were light, but her eyes were worried. "Next time you say you need room to maneuver, I'll be more than happy to comply."

Knowing there likely wouldn't be a next time turned the moment bittersweet, but Grant refused to let go of this small happiness. She'd just given him a gift. Soul-cleansing freedom from the grief that had been strangling his heart for days. Ellie's warm body was better than any therapy, but their afternoon was fleeting. As she'd said before, their time was limited. "I remember the first time I saw you."

"The barbecue."

"Yes. You were wearing a yellow sundress. Your legs were tan. I couldn't take my eyes off of you. If I hadn't been shipping out . . ."

Ellie cupped his jaw. Her eyes were moist. She pulled his head down and kissed him tenderly on the lips. Grant's heart swelled until it threatened to burst from his chest. It was too much, too fast, and the timing was all wrong. But he could be happy with nothing more than Ellie in his life.

"I'll be right back." He eased off her body and went into the bathroom. He'd dispose of the condom quickly and return to her bed. But when he walked back into the bedroom, ready to flop down on the mattress and enjoy her naked body, she was sitting up. His cell phone was in her hand.

"You have a message." She held the phone out to him.

Remembering the previous text, his grief and anxiety returned in an instant flood, almost as if their lovemaking had never occurred.

The message was from Hannah. The baby and Carson were both awake, and Hannah was needed on a conference call.

Disappointment flushed through Grant. No time for postsex intimacies. Those few minutes—way too few—with Ellie had energized him. They'd shown him what could be, and because of that, it could never happen again. He wouldn't want to leave her when the time came. And he didn't want to get used to something he was going to give up.

"Do you have everything you need?" Grant reached for his socks. "That was Hannah. We need to get back."

"All right." She pointed to his calf. "What's that?"

"Shrapnel." Grant brushed his hand over the patch of gray bumps below a burn scar on his lower leg, where tiny bits of metal had been embedded since his first tour in Iraq.

"They just left it in there?"

"Doctor said they'd do more damage trying to dig it out than leaving it alone. It's been in there for years." He shrugged. "I know it's ugly, but it doesn't hurt."

She reached for his shoulder and turned him away from her. He felt her finger lightly trace the puckered pink scar on his back. "And this?"

"Bullet. Also Iraq."

He turned back to her and took her hands. "Now you see why I didn't want you to get attached to me."

Instead of answering, she leaned closer and pressed a soft kiss to his lips.

"We'd better go." Moving away from him, she dressed.

With a fresh wound in his heart, Grant did the same. He stuffed his feet into his boots and picked up her bag of clothes. Ellie locked up as they left the house. He scanned the street, looking for any signs of surveillance. Was Hoodie Man, as Ellie called him, watching right now? He hadn't relied on GPS technology alone. The picture he'd sent to Ellie clearly showed he'd also been doing personal surveillance. But tonight, Grant didn't see or feel any eyes on him. A few cars were parked along the street. No signs of occupation, but he made a note to do another check later. He'd had enough waiting for the police to do things legally. Grant's leave was ticking away. He needed this situation settled and his family and Ellie's safe before he returned to the army.

He'd been formulating a plan. Tomorrow, he was putting it into action. They went out onto the porch. A silver Mercedes sedan was parked out front.

"Who is that?" Ellie asked.

"Boston plates. Must be Kate's parents." Grant hustled across the front yard. "I hope calling them wasn't a big mistake."

Chapter Thirty-Two

Ellie followed Grant into the house. An older couple stood in the foyer. Hannah was taking coats and hanging them in the closet.

"These are Kate's parents, Bill and Stella Sheridan." Hannah introduced Grant and Ellie. "Let's go back to the kitchen. I just made coffee."

Bill was tall, with a thick head of silver hair, blue eyes, and a slight stoop. His thin wife had a gray bob cut precisely to swing at her chin, pointy and angular as her face. They were well-dressed in slacks and sweaters.

Stella frowned at the peeling wallpaper in the hall. In the kitchen, Hannah set out mugs and coffee on the table. The baby stirred, making a fussy sound. The Sheridans crossed the floor and stopped in front of Faith's baby seat.

"That's your granddaughter, Faith." Grant squatted and released the harness. He lifted the baby and turned her to face the Sheridans.

Stella reached a tentative hand and touched Faith's chubby thigh. "Babies should take naps in their cribs."

"She's colicky," Grant said.

Stella shook her head. "Babies need routine, Major. Put her in her crib and leave her be. She'll cry for a while, but she'll soon learn to be independent. If you coddle her, she'll never learn that the world doesn't revolve around her. I understand there's an older child as well?"

"Yes. Carson is six. He's taking a nap." Hannah measured formula.

"I imagine this has been an awful week for him." Stella lowered her hand from Faith's leg. Was Kate's mother nervous? She'd never seen her grandchildren. How many regrets was Mrs. Sheridan battling behind her gray eyes?

"He's having a rough time." Grant's brow creased. Hannah handed him a bottle, and he settled at the table with Faith in the crook of his arm. The Sheridans sat across from him. Ellie contemplated backing out of the room and giving the family privacy, but the grief in Grant's eyes pulled her to him. Ellie took the chair next to him, pressing her leg against his. He shot her a grateful look.

Bill ignored the coffee Hannah set in front of him. "When is the funeral being planned?"

Grant shifted the baby to his shoulder and burped her. "We haven't made plans yet. The medical examiner just released their bodies a couple of hours ago."

Remembering Grant's tight hold on her as he slept in her bed, Ellie's heart clenched. He hadn't told her. Didn't he trust her? He'd lied to her yesterday about where he was going with Mac. Was he holding anything else back?

"What about the children? What plans have been made for them?"

Grant cleared his throat. "We haven't made any decisions yet."

"What are the options?" Stella interlaced her fingers and leaned her forearms on the table. "Are either of you married?" Her gaze shifted between Hannah and Grant.

"No," Grant admitted. "Why didn't you speak to Kate over the years?"

"Kate made her decision. She rejected us." Stella's cheeks flushed. "We all made mistakes. Now we've no opportunity to rectify them. Something I will regret until the day I die." She placed her palms on the table. "Major, it seems to me that the best option for those children is for us to raise them. We have sufficient income to ensure they get the best care and private education. We know an excellent child psychologist, and we've already made inquiries to find a qualified nanny. They won't want for anything."

Except affection, thought Ellie, but she kept her mouth shut. This wasn't any of her business. The Sheridans didn't appear mean, just standoffish. But Carson craved physical contact. Ellie couldn't imagine either of the Sheridans cuddling with him after a nightmare.

"I think you should meet Carson before we discuss any long term plans." Grant said.

Stella nodded. She didn't have to wait long. Carson appeared, sleepy and rumpled, in the kitchen doorway. Grant passed the baby to Hannah, and Carson climbed onto Grant's lap.

"Carson, these are your grandparents," Grant said.

"Hello, Carson. It's nice to meet you." Stella reached out and touched his arm. "You look like your mommy when she was little."

Carson curled a hand around his lips and leaned close to Grant's ear. "I don't know her."

Grant patted him on the back. "It's OK."

Bill cleared his throat. His eyes were misty. "You can call us Grandma and Grandpa if you like."

Carson turned his face into Grant's chest and wound his arms around his uncle's neck.

Stella pulled a tissue from her pocket and blotted her eyes. "Why don't we come back tomorrow, after he's had some time to adjust to the idea?"

"I think that's a good idea." Grant stood, with Carson still in his arms.

Ellie put a hand on the ache in her chest. How would it feel to be estranged from a child for more than a decade and have her die violently before you could make amends?

"Remember our offer," Stella said.

"As I said before, we haven't made any decisions yet." Grant rose, patting Faith on the back. They escorted the Sheridans to the foyer. Hannah fetched their coats.

"Children need stability." Bill held his wife's coat. "Please keep that in mind."

Stella paused in the doorway. "We're staying at a bed-and-breakfast." She handed Grant a card. "I've written my cell phone number on the back. Please call if you decide on a funeral date."

Grant closed the door after them. Mac came down the steps. "Who's hungry?"

"Me." Carson lifted his head from Grant's shoulder. He set the boy down, and Carson followed Mac down the hall into the kitchen.

Hannah rested her cheek on Faith's head. "Not the most demonstrative pair of grandparents."

"Our family is hardly perfect. We've barely seen each other in the past few years."

"I don't know." Hannah shook her head. "Carson didn't seem too keen on her, and she didn't ask to hold the baby."

"She's had a shock. I imagine she always thought there'd be time to reconcile with Kate. And now there isn't." Grant sighed. "Maybe it's just as well they weren't too pushy. I'm not sure he's ready. He doesn't ask about the future. He can barely get through today." Was Grant talking about Carson or himself? "He'll warm up to them."

Hannah stopped and stared at him. "You can't be thinking of letting those people raise the kids? Or maybe I should say, letting their hired help raise the kids."

Ellie agreed with Hannah, but this was the Barretts' decision, not hers, though her heart broke for Carson. The little boy was attached to Grant. Ellie could relate. She didn't want to think about Grant leaving.

"I don't know," Grant said. "Are you prepared to quit your job? I'll be in Afghanistan for at least another month, and it wouldn't surprise me if my deployment gets extended. It usually does. I could end up overseas until fall. Mac is headed for South America. What else are we going to do?"

Ellie washed out the baby's bottle and put it in the dishwasher. Grant leaned back against the counter next to her. He hadn't shaved today. The blond scruff on his jaw made her think of their lovemaking. She'd never experienced anything that intense—or sweet. Her face heated. She tugged her turtleneck higher, making sure the faint beard burn on her neck was covered.

She turned and leaned toward him, then stopped midmotion. She'd been leaning in to give him a comforting kiss. That sort of intimate domesticity could never happen between them, but shock filled her at how much she wanted it. Grant was so unlike any other man she'd dated. Strong, reliable, honest. If she allowed herself, she could easily imagine weekends of blissful, boring, ordinariness. Grant looking sexily rumpled. Kissing her with the wicked promise in his eyes that he'd do a lot more at the first opportunity. The family innocent and ignorant of his intent.

Well, not Nan. She didn't miss much.

Ellie's phone vibrated once. An incoming text. A second buzz in her front pocket reverberated in her hipbone. She felt the blood drain from her head as she pulled out her cell.

Afraid to look at the display until she was in private, she ducked out of the room with a quick, "excuse me."

Out of the corner of her eye, she saw Grant following her as she went into the office.

He closed the door. "Same number as yesterday?"

"No. It's a new one."

"What does it say?" he prompted.

She read the message. "Do you have the file?"

"Type yes."

"What?"

"I'm done screwing around with this guy." Grant's eyes chilled to ice blue. "Today, we're making him a file."

A sense of the inevitable filled her. Grant was right. This had to end. Her hands were steady as she typed Yes into the phone and hit Send.

They stared at each other as nearly five minutes passed.

"I think your answer surprised him," Grant said. "Which is good."

The return message came in and Ellie read it. "Eight o'clock tonight. Same parking lot as before. Come alone or everyone dies."

Turning into the parking lot of St. Vincent's Thrift Shop, Grant adjusted the wig and slid down in the driver's seat of Ellie's minivan. He drove past a brick bungalow on his left and into an asphalt rectangle approximately thirty by sixty. A light fastened to the back of the building cast a puddle of light onto the pavement. Beyond the reach of the single light, darkness waited. The shop was a few blocks from the commercial district, with the closest residence a half mile down the road.

Plenty of privacy.

With all senses on high alert, Grant drove to the rear of the lot and parked in the darkest corner. He scanned the surroundings but saw no sign of company. A flip of a switch killed the headlights. The van's interior dome light had been disabled back at the house. Ellie's phone sat on the console next to the GPS tracking device. Hoodie Man knew the van was here.

Where are you, Donnie?

If Grant had been running an operation like this, he would have arrived early and secured the area. Hoodie Man wasn't here yet, so he was likely an amateur. Adrenaline flowed hot and fast through Grant's veins. Tonight he'd face his brother's killer and find out who'd hired him to kill Lee. Then Grant and his family could begin to heal. He lowered the window to listen to the night. A vehicle engine approached. Tires grated on salt and sand left on the blacktop after the ice had melted.

A sedan pulled into the lot behind the minivan. So far, so good. The driver got out. In the van's mirrors, Grant watched the black-clad, hooded figure give the lot a cursory scan before approaching the vehicle. The sedan's headlights glinted on the metal of a gun. Without speaking, Grant stuck the fake file out the open window. He held it vertically and used it to block his face from view.

The hooded man stepped forward until he was next to the driver's side door. He snatched the file, his excitement getting the best of him. Grant's hand closed on the door handle. He jerked it back and pushed. The door slammed into the man and knocked him off his feet. The gun and file flew out of his hands. They slid across the asphalt, blank sheets of paper scattering in the wind. Grant launched his body out of the vehicle. Fueled by fury, he landed on top.

Out of his peripheral vision, he glimpsed Mac running out of the adjacent field. Grant had dropped him off well before the meeting to provide cover.

Straddling his opponent's chest, Grant yanked back the hood and ripped off the bandana. He raised his hand—and froze.

It wasn't Donnie. Corey Swann stared up at Grant.

"*You* killed my brother." Grant's fingers curled into a fist. He wanted his knife. "I should just slit your throat right here."

"Killed your brother?" Corey wheezed as Grant sat on his sternum. "What are you talking about? I didn't kill anybody."

Damn it. Corey must have hired Donnie to kill Lee but hadn't trusted the hit man to recover the file. "You hired someone to kill him. Same thing."

Corey coughed.

Grant pulled his dad's KA-BAR from its sheath on his calf and pressed the blade to Corey's throat. "I know about the GPS. I know you threatened to kill Ellie's family. I saw the texts you sent, using a burner phone just like your daughter used to torment Lindsay Hamilton."

Corey drew a ragged breath. Reluctantly, Grant shifted his weight slightly to let him draw a breath.

"Yes," Corey gasped. "I threatened to kill them, but I didn't hurt anyone. I just wanted that file."

"Why?" Grant asked, vaguely aware of Mac coming to stand next to him. "What's in the file?"

"I don't know!" Corey cried. "But your brother found something to implicate my daughter. I had to find out what it was and destroy it."

"You don't even know what it is?" Shock flowed through Grant. This man had hurt people to prevent his daughter from being accused of the crime she committed.

"No, but whatever it is, no one can find out about it." Corey's eyes watered, the moisture shining in the headlights, fear etched in his expression. "All I did was threaten Ellie Ross. That's it. I was afraid Lee Barrett found enough evidence to convince the police to file charges against my daughter. I couldn't risk that. Even a civil suit would destroy her future. I won't let her life be ruined for one mistake."

"One mistake? She drove a girl to commit suicide."

"She didn't kill anyone. That girl had mental problems. No one could have predicted she'd hang herself because of a little teasing."

"A little teasing? I read the texts she sent to Lindsay," Grant said. "Your daughter was brutally and intentionally cruel. She taunted that poor girl mercilessly."

"Regan had no idea the girl was medicated. I'm sure she wouldn't have teased her if she did." But Corey's eyes weren't convinced. He was making excuses and he knew it.

"You don't even care, do you?"

"I need to protect my child."

"What about teaching her to be a decent human being? What about forcing her to live with the consequences of her actions? Do you not care what kind of person you've borne and raised?"

Corey's gaze went flat. Clearly, that ship was halfway to the Caymans.

Mac tapped Grant on the shoulder. "You can't kill him."

"I can hurt him." Grant's blade was poised directly over Corey's carotid artery, but he could easily move it to a less fatal location.

"Grant, let's call the cops," Mac said. "We need to find Donnie."

Donnie. Shit. Donnie could be anywhere.

Grant grabbed Corey by the hair and pressed his knife to his throat. "I can take your whole fucking head off from this angle. So where is he, Corey? Where's Donnie?"

Corey's face twisted with resentment. "I don't know what you're talking about."

"You *can't* kill him." Mac pulled out his phone and punched numbers.

But Grant wanted to. Listening to his brother summon the police, red hazed Grant's vision. Rage muddied his thoughts. This man had threatened to kill Ellie's family, and now he was holding back information. As soon as the cops got here, Corey would shut up and call a lawyer.

"Grant!" Mac yanked on his shoulder. "You can't kill him."

That caught Grant's attention. He straightened, removing the knife from Corey's throat. Corey's head fell onto the ground, and his body shook with self-pitying sobs. Grant stood and sheathed his knife.

"What now?" Mac asked. "The cops will be here any minute."

"We tie him to something, and we split up. Do you want the house or the skating rink?" Grant looked behind him. Corey's sedan was still running. "I'll take his car. Hopefully the cops will be able to get him to talk."

Sand grated on blacktop. Grant whirled toward the sound as Corey launched his body at his legs. Grant sprawled, his legs shooting back, his weight coming down on the back of Corey's shoulders. Corey hit the pavement face-first and went still.

"So much for questioning him," Mac said. "Now how are we going to find out where Donnie is?"

Grant poked Corey with his boot. No response. "Hey, I didn't expect the idiot to try and tackle me. I didn't even hit him. Fool fell down and knocked himself out."

"Doesn't matter how it happened." Mac lifted his palms. "An unconscious man can't tell us anything."

"Shit." Grant sheathed his knife and swept both hands through his hair. What now? He nodded toward the vehicle. "I have some zip ties in the van."

"Here." Mac handed the plastic fasteners over Grant's shoulder.

He bound Corey's wrists behind his back. He dragged the man by his feet to the building and zip-tied him to the natural gas pipe running from the meter into the ground. "I'll call McNamara from the car, explain everything, and get him to send men to the house and the rink."

Mac was running for the minivan. "Where do you want me?"

"I don't know." Grant ran for the sedan. "Donnie was after Carson and Julia. I have to make sure they're safe. Ellie is at the rink with Julia."

But which one would Donnie go after?

The ice rink was a very public place. When Grant had dropped off Ellie and Julia, dozens of parents had crowded the bleachers and lobby. The house was the easier target, and Carson, who'd gotten a clearer view of Donnie, was the better witness. Chances were, Donnie would be going after the boy. Also, the rink was all the way across town. Mac might not even get there before the police.

"I'll take the house. You head for the rink." Grant drove off. He called the cop. Though supremely pissed off, McNamara promised to send units to both the rink and house ASAP. Grant shoved the gas pedal to the floor. He'd get there first. He'd call Hannah and Ellie and put them both on alert. His instinct told him the ambush on Corey had gone all wrong. Punching numbers on his phone, he ran through a stop sign, the case whirling in his mind. Grant had missed an important piece of information. Now all he could do was hope his failure wouldn't cost the people he loved their lives.

Chapter Thirty-Three

Donnie parked his van down the street from the Barrett house. He'd had it with these people. He was tired of being jerked around. That applied to his client as well. He'd killed two people for that loser. Sure, he'd enjoyed the act, but he still deserved to be compensated for his effort and risk. Motherfucking coward was too chicken to do his own dirty work. Well, he was going to pay up. Donnie was a killer. Nobody was going to fuck with him.

His mind wandered back to the night he'd strangled his girlfriend. Her death was an accident, but what a rush! Donnie still got chills thinking about his submissive's final session. That night was going to be hard to beat. He was going to have to find a new place to crash. Even on ice, she'd been getting ripe enough for the neighbors to smell. It was far too risky to go back to her trailer. But first, he needed to get this job behind him.

He opened the back of the van and pulled out a backpack. Mentally, he tacked an extra 10 percent on to his invoice. His aggravation and effort didn't come cheap. Shrugging into the backpack, Donnie took out the gas cans and headed down the street. If he couldn't find that motherfucking one piece of evidence, he'd destroy it. It had to be in that house somewhere. If the house was incinerated, the evidence would be history, and the little fucker who'd IDed him would be gone, too. Donnie was never going back to prison.

Enough was enough. He was through with this shit. In the next ten minutes, the whole cluster would be behind him.

He'd find his client, demand his payment, and be on a fucking beach in fucking Florida by fucking next weekend.

The big house loomed against the clear, black sky. The place was ugly as sin anyway. Donnie was doing everyone a favor by burning it to the ground. He walked across the front lawn, massive snow-melt leaving the grass squishy underfoot. At the corner of the porch, he picked up the first can and started pouring. The sharp scent of gasoline punched through the night air. He splashed can number two across the clapboards along the side of the house. Kneeling on the soggy ground, he opened the backpack and pulled out handfuls of roman candles, bottle rockets, and a round box called a cake, some combination of pyrotechnics that could be lighted all at once. Whatever. Donnie didn't need a carefully calculated explosion. He just needed a nice, raging fire. The time for finesse had passed. This old tinderbox of a house ought to burn hot. He'd rid himself of the evidence and his witnesses in one big whoosh of fire.

Excitement zinged through his blood as he piled the fireworks on the porch, stepped back, and lit the closest fuse.

Sitting cross-legged on the family room area rug, Hannah ended the call with her brother. Goose bumps rose on her arms as she thought of Lee and Kate's killer coming after the children. Next to her, Faith wriggled on a blanket. Hannah had been flipping her onto her belly for rollover practice and some hopefully tiring exercise. Faith rolled onto her back and squealed with joy. Nan was knitting on the sofa, her booted foot elevated on the ottoman. Kneeling at the coffee table next to the older woman, Carson colored a picture. The dog snoozed, her head resting on Carson's leg.

The quiet, peaceful scene stirred fear in Hannah's belly. Everyone in that room depended on her to keep them safe. The enormity of the responsibility outweighed any deal she'd negotiated.

Hannah picked up the babbling baby and set her on her hip. Though she curled toward Hannah's body for support, Faith held her own head and upper body weight. Hannah went into the laundry room and checked the alarm panel. The green light flashed, letting her know the system was up and running with no issues. She carried Faith to the living room. Standing to one side, she peered through the window but saw no movement outside. They moved from room to room. Hannah didn't see any signs of trouble or company through any of the windows, but her spine tingled and her belly cramped. Something was happening. She could feel danger approaching.

Or had Grant's warning call fired up her paranoia?

The dog rushed past. A low growl emanated from her throat. Hannah followed her to the window.

Movement at the corner of the house caught her attention. A shadow stretched across the grass. Someone was outside. She moved closer to the glass. At the edge of the porch, a glow flared brightly and then dimmed, briefly illuminating a man's figure. Next to Hannah, AnnaBelle barked.

Oh. Shit.

Fire.

Hannah hugged the baby close. Dialing 911 on her cell phone, she inhaled her panic and rushed down the hall. The house was set up as a fort, with everything aimed at keeping the inhabitants secure. Getting them all out quickly hadn't been included in the plan. Thank God they were all in the same room. The dog raced from window to window.

"I need everyone to go out the back door right now." She spied the detached garage through the kitchen window. She snagged the keys from a bowl on the kitchen counter on her way past. "We're all going to the garage and getting in the minivan."

Nan's eyes caught Hannah's. Alarm registered. "Let's hurry, Carson."

With one hand, Hannah grabbed the crutches in the corner and handed them to Nan.

A whistle and boom sounded from the front of the house. Carson screamed and covered his ears with both hands. Faith wailed.

"Don't wait for me. Get the kids out of here." Nan took the crutches and gave Hannah a push. "Go!"

Hannah swallowed her indecision. With her sprained wrist, the older woman could barely hobble across the room on crutches. The children had to come first. Hating every step, she ran for the back door.

"AnnaBelle!" Carson cried as Hannah pushed him over the threshold. Fire crackled behind them, and Hannah could hear the dog still barking from the living room. She whistled. Leaving the door open, she ran for the garage. Carson turned back toward the house, calling for Nan and the dog in a pitiful, frightened scream. Hannah dragged him toward the garage.

"No!" he screamed. "We can't leave them."

"I'll go back in a minute." Hannah released him to open the garage door. She pushed him into the garage and helped him get into the minivan. With the baby still in her arms, she climbed into the driver's seat and backed the van out of the garage. When the vehicle was clear of the building, she drove it across the grass and parked it behind Ellie's house, where she hoped the fire couldn't reach. Then Hannah climbed into the back and set Faith in her car seat. "Can you buckle her in, Carson?"

He nodded, his face wet with tears.

"Do you know how to lock the van doors?"

He nodded again. Hannah put the keys on the front seat. "Lock the door behind me, and don't open it unless it's safe."

"OK."

"I'll be right back." She jumped out of the vehicle. The locks clicked behind her.

Praying that the car was far enough from the house, Hannah raced for the back steps. Flames shot from the front of the house, and smoke poured from the open door. She pulled the neck of her sweatshirt over her nose and ran inside. The front of the house popped, whistled, and boomed. Fire crackled.

"Nan!" Hannah coughed as she ran into a cloud of black smoke. In the corner of her eye, she caught movement. Outside, a man ran across the backyard. He was heading for the van—and the children.

Chapter Thirty-Four

Grant turned into the development on two wheels. Tires squealed as the car lurched around the corner.

He called Ellie and told her what had happened. She and Julia were fine. In a crowded ice rink, they should be safe enough, and Mac would be with them any minute. He hung up and dialed Hannah; her phone rang four times and switched to voice mail.

Damn it. He pounded the steering wheel.

Grant turned down the street. The thin wail of sirens announced emergency vehicles were on the way, but the sight of flames pouring from the front of Lee's house sent Grant's heart catapulting into his throat. No!

He slammed the car to a stop in the middle of the street. Leaving the door open and the engine running, he raced toward the door. But the porch was completely engulfed in flames. Grant ran around the building to the back lawn. Sweeping his eyes across the scene, he took in the sight of his sister disappearing into the smoky house and a man running toward Ellie's backyard, where the minivan was parked. Through the side van window, he could see Carson's face pressed to the glass.

Grant hesitated for a second. Heart breaking, he veered toward the children. His body slid into combat mode as he overtook the running man. Grant tackled him in the grass, landing on top of him. The man flipped onto his back. His hood fell away.

Donnie Ehrlich.

Fury fueled Grant's first punch. His fist connected with Donnie's face with a crack of bone. Blood spurted. Grant hit him again. And again. Making the sonofabitch pay for what he'd done to his family.

Then a loud boom behind him snapped him out of his rage.

Hannah!

Ellie glanced at the crowd around her. Twenty parents had been on the bleachers ten minutes ago, but the majority of the kids had already rehearsed their routines and left. Still, she was hardly alone. At the entrance to the ice, the remaining few kids and coaches queued up, watching their teammates perform and waiting their turns. Julia's name was read over the loudspeaker. She was next on the ice.

The nerves playing Ellie's skin had nothing to do with her daughter's rehearsal performance. All she could think about was Grant's phone call. She couldn't believe Corey Swann had been her extortionist. She scanned the crowd again. Grant had said Donnie Ehrlich was still on the loose, but she didn't see anyone in the arena who didn't belong.

The skating club was running the evening exactly as the carnival would occur next week. Julia's lower-ranked team had to wait until the end of the show. The beginning of the carnival was always the most crowded. The advanced team would perform first and get to enjoy the rest of the evening. By the time the younger kids performed, the bleachers would be mostly empty. But that was to be expected.

The advanced skaters were the most serious. They practiced hours every day, coming in before school and again in the afternoon. Their dedication deserved to be rewarded. Their prima donna attitudes still grated on Ellie, and after the bullying episode with Lindsay Hamilton, she would never look at those girls the same way again. She'd read those horrible texts, and while the police had no way of proving that Regan and Autumn had sent them, everyone knew they had.

"Do you think Autumn's choreography is original enough?" a man's voice asked.

Ellie followed the sound. Rinkside, Joshua Winslow was talking to Coach Victor. The coach crossed his arms over his body. "Don't worry. Autumn is going to nationals. We have all summer to perfect her routine."

"Maybe we need to hire a new choreographer." Josh frowned. "I thought her moves looked stale."

"Her routine is fine," Victor argued.

"Autumn isn't happy with it, and it's her career. If she wants a new choreographer, we'll hire one." Josh's hand flew up in the air in an angry Kermit flail. He stalked away from Victor. The coach rubbed a frustrated hand down his face. Ellie turned away. Parent tantrums were hardly new.

Anger and shock welled in her throat as she thought about Corey. He'd threatened to hurt Ellie's family just to get his hands on whatever evidence Lee had found. Had Corey arranged to have Lee and Kate killed as well, all to protect his daughter from the consequences of her actions?

The first notes of Julia's music floated over the PA system, and Ellie turned her attention to her daughter, waving as Julia skated to center ice and positioned herself. She glided through her moves with the grace expected of her ability and level. Ellie held her breath as Julia poised for a single axel, the hardest move in her routine. She hadn't practiced much this week, and Kate's death had obviously dampened her enthusiasm for the sport. She leaped and twirled, landing with only a slight bobble.

Ellie exhaled.

Julia finished her routine with a spin and the biggest smile she'd worn since Kate and Lee had been killed. Maybe everything was going to be all right. Corey was in custody. Surely, the police would find Donnie soon. Ellie went to the rink exit and waited for Julia to step off the ice.

"Nice work!" She wrapped an arm around her daughter's shoulders.

Julia paused, her eyes searching the bench next to the exit. "Do you have my blade guards?"

"No."

"Someone must have taken them," Julia frowned.

"We'll get a new pair tomorrow."

"Beautiful routine, Julia." Victor walked by. "I'm keeping my eye on you."

"I even landed the axel." Julia grinned at Ellie, then sobered. "It's a shame Mrs. Barrett isn't here. Do you think she can see me?"

"I don't know. Maybe." Ellie sighed.

"It would be nice to think she was still watching over me." Julia clomped across the cement.

"It would." Ellie followed her to the locker room. Usually she waited outside, but not tonight. She wasn't leaving Julia alone for a second until Donnie was caught. They walked through the doorway into a cinder block hallway that led to the locker rooms.

Josh Winslow followed them into the corridor. He caught Ellie by the arm. Her pulse spiked. Julia disappeared inside.

Ellie jerked her arm away. "I don't have time for this."

"Your daughter looked good on the ice tonight, but remember she's not advanced team material." Josh leaned close enough that she could smell alcohol on his breath. "You know that, right?"

"What the hell is the matter with you?" Ellie pushed at his chest. "Back off."

He sneered. "Just so you don't think that little priss of yours is any competition for my daughter."

Oh, my God. Could Josh be involved too? He and Corey were tight. Fear pulsed through her as she took in the animosity shining from his eyes.

"They are kids. It's ice-skating. Get some perspective."

"Now that Kate's gone, Julia won't get any more preferential treatment."

"What are you talking about?" Ellie tugged at her arm, but Josh tightened his grip on her bicep. "Julia likes skating, but it's a fun hobby for her. That's it. She's several levels below Autumn. What is your problem?"

"Just as long as we're clear that she's never going to be competition for Autumn."

"You have issues. Now let go of me." Ellie pushed against his windpipe with her fingertips.

He gagged and staggered backward.

Ellie stepped back and looked down the empty corridor. The insulated door between the locker room hallway and the rink was closed.

One hand clutched his throat. Josh moved closer, backing Ellie against the wall. "You bitch."

Grant looked down at Donnie. His face was a bloody pulp. His eyes were closed, his breathing ragged and wet. How many times had

Grant hit him? The thug probably wasn't getting up anytime soon, which was good because Grant didn't have time to restrain him.

He levered his body up and off Donnie. Racing for the house, Grant followed the barking through the thick black smoke. He dropped to the floor and belly-crawled under the worst of it. Hannah was in front of him, on her knees, trying to drag Nan toward the back door. Unwilling to leave without her humans, AnnaBelle barked beside them.

"Go. I got her." Grant pointed toward the exit in case his sister couldn't hear him over the roar of the fire.

Hannah lunged for the dog, grabbed her collar, and stumbled toward the exit. Grant picked up Nan and followed them out.

They lurched for the next yard. Sirens wailed in the street. Red lights swirled and flashed.

McNamara ran toward them between the houses.

Grant laid Nan down on the grass. Her bloodshot eyes opened, and she coughed. Relieved that she was awake, Grant stood. A paramedic dropped to his knees beside her, an oxygen mask already in his hand. Grant backed away and almost tripped over Donnie's still form. He glanced down. The killer's face was hamburger.

A soot-streaked Hannah was helping Carson out of the van. Sobbing, the boy ran to Grant, who picked him up, turning his face away from the beaten man on the ground. Oh God. Had Carson seen Grant beat Donnie?

McNamara put his hands on his hips. His gaze swept over the ragged bunch, paused on Hannah for a heartbeat, then settled on Grant, as if he'd just identified the guilty party. Hannah had the baby out of the car and was holding her close. Red-faced, Faith hiccuped into her shoulder.

"Is that Donnie?" McNamara asked.

"Yes." Grant met the cop's frustrated gaze. With a nod to the now quiet, but still trembling child, Grant made it clear he wasn't answering any more questions until Carson was out of earshot.

McNamara seemed to get it. He waved a uniformed cop and a paramedic toward the prone man, then turned back to Grant. "Are Ellie and her daughter still at the rink?"

"They should be." Grant shifted Carson in his arms and patted his back pocket. Damn. Where was his phone? He must have dropped it. "Mac should be there with them by now. Did you send a patrol car?"

"I did. The officer should be there."

"I'll call Ellie and make sure she's all right." Grant coughed hard and forced a shout out of his raw throat. "Hannah, do you have a phone?"

His sister checked her pockets and shook her head. "I must have dropped it in the house." She gasped.

Her coughing drew the attention of another paramedic, who sat her on the car bumper and slid a mask over her face. When he tried to take the baby, Hannah bumped his hand away and hugged her tighter.

Carson leaned away from Grant's chest. He wiped his running nose with his forearm. "I have a phone, Uncle Grant." He held out a cell phone.

Grant took it. "Where did you get this, Carson?"

"It slid out from under the seat in the van." The little boy lifted a skinny shoulder.

"Is that your mom's phone?" McNamara asked.

Carson shook his head. "She has the *I* one."

This was no iPhone. It was a burner phone, with camera and video capabilities. Grant passed it to McNamara. The cop used the hem of his jacket to accept it. He turned it on.

While he scrolled through the phone Carson had found, McNamara handed Grant a cell. "Use this to call Ellie."

The cop stepped away.

Grant dialed Ellie's mobile number. The phone rang. And rang. And rang. Panic slid through his veins.

"She's not answering." Grant dialed his brother.

Mac picked up on the first ring. "I've been trying to call you. I just got here a few minutes ago. There's a cop here with me. We haven't found Ellie yet."

McNamara's hand settled on Grant's forearm. "Hey, Carson, could you go make sure your Aunt Hannah is OK?"

"Keep looking," Grant told his brother. "I'll call you back in a minute." Reluctantly, he set the boy down. Even the weight of the small body in his arms wasn't enough to convince him that everyone had emerged from the fire relatively unscathed. Hannah and Nan were both alert and talking to the paramedics. Donnie was handcuffed and being loaded onto a stretcher. Disaster had been averted. But Grant's instincts stirred uneasily in his chest. Until he saw Ellie and Julia, safe and well, he wouldn't relax.

McNamara held the phone between them and hit Play. Everything inside of Grant went cold as he watched the video.

Chapter Thirty-Five

Lindsay
February

Every day is the same, a complete misery. The pills I'm taking now numb me out a little, but not enough. They make me tired, too. I'm sleeping better, but I haven't finished my homework in weeks. In fact, I could sleep all day long and wish I didn't have to wake up at all.

I. Just. Don't. Care.

The waiting room walls are thin. I listen as the psychiatrist and my mom talk about me switching schools. Maybe going to some private academy not far away or homeschooling even.

The doctor nudges my mom in this direction. "You have to think about what is best for Lindsay."

But Mom has this "never give up" attitude ingrained in her soul. It's how she finished college in three years, got grants for graduate school, and taught herself to speak Spanish.

For a smart lady, she is fucking clueless.

"Aren't I teaching her to be a quitter?" she asks. "Aren't I enabling these other kids if I pull her out of school? Most people get teased or harassed at some point in our lives. What kind of life lesson am I teaching Lindsay if we surrender? If I let her quit the skating team, the other kids win. Lindsay loses. She needs to learn to stand up for herself."

I block the rest of the conversation out. I'm a big disappointment to Mom. I can hear it in her voice. She wishes I was stronger, more like her.

Well, I'm not.

I feel like I've been sent into battle empty-handed. I have no options. No friends to support me. No weapons to fight back. Really, what can I do? They're smarter than me. All of them. I am worthless.

I want to give up. Surrender. Just don't make me go back to Scarlet Falls High. This morning, I flat-out told Mom I'm not going back to the skating rink. She can't make me. The arena has become my Guantánamo Bay. I'm surprised Regan and Autumn haven't tried waterboarding me in the locker room.

I don't want to go back to school either. Talking with the shrink always makes me feel raw, exposed, as if my clothes have been peeled away and left me naked. But back we go. Mom signs me in just after noon. From the looks on the teachers' faces when I walk in, they think I'm a whiner. Regan and Autumn have them all snowed. They are top students with disciplinary records as perfect as everything else. There's no proof they're behind any of the bullying. Actually, except for the texts of anonymous origin, there's no proof any of it even happened. It's all my word against theirs.

Dad is just pissed. He's been down to the school six times, and he's argued with the director of the arena. Each time, he comes home more frustrated. He's not a confrontational guy, though. So when he and Mom fight about the situation, which is all the time, she wins. Last night, though, I heard him say, "I'll give you until spring break. If things don't improve, she's out of there."

"Hamiltons are not quitters," was her response.

I get through the day without incident. This doesn't happen very often, but have no fear. My locker is jammed. By the time I hunt down the custodian to help me get it open, I've missed the bus. I have a choice: wait an hour for the late bus or walk home through the woods. At the most, the trek will take fifteen minutes, and the last thing I want to do is stay at school for another hour. This place is my prison. I just want to go home, but I'm not calling Mom or Dad. Besides, Mom's job is the closest, and it would take her a half hour just to get here. She'd taken the morning off for the appointment with the psychiatrist.

My favorite hours are the ones between school and when my parents get home, before the questions about my day begin.

"What happened today?"

"Did you write it down?"

I'm supposed to keep a log of all the bullying, but I only put about half the incidents in the notebook. Writing it down is like living it all over again. Once is enough, you know?

I don't want to lose my alone hours today. I shut my locker and sling my backpack over my shoulder. The winter air slaps my face as I head out the door. On the bright side, I avoided a nasty bus ride with lots of staring. Shivering, I cross the parking lot. The track team passes me, decked out in winter running tights and hats. And then I am alone.

I like being alone.

Once I cross the street and enter the woods, the trees protect me from the wind. This isn't so bad. Maybe I should stop taking the bus home. Mom leaves first in the morning, and Dad has been driving me in on the sly. So walking home would completely eliminate the torturous bus ride.

Cheered, I speed up my pace. There's a snowstorm forecast for next week, but today, the ground is clear, frozen like rock under my feet. A bird shoots out of the underbrush, startling me. I take a deep breath of pine-scented air and watch a rabbit dart across the trail. This is nice. For the first time since I started school here, I relax. I always considered myself a city girl, but maybe I could learn to be a nature lover. But my peace is short-lived.

They are waiting for me in a clearing. Regan, Autumn, and four other kids. Two of them are boys who want to get laid. They'll do whatever the girls ask in exchange for blow jobs. Regan is famous in the junior class for giving head. I don't understand how the teachers and administration can be so duped. I'd roll my eyes if I wasn't so terrified.

I know instantly that me missing the bus was no accident. I walk right into an ambush.

I'm almost home. I can see the bright spot ahead where the trail opens to the meadow behind my house. If I ran, I could be on my porch in five minutes.

My heart sprints, mimicking the way my feet want to run away. But my combat boots are frozen to the ground. The muscles of my legs feel weak. Sweat rolls down my back and soaks my waistband.

"Hey, look who it is," Regan sneers.

I make my feet move, backing up to try and get away from them. Over their heads, I can see freedom. My escape is right there. I can see in her eyes she has something special planned. This is not like in school or at the arena. No security cameras in the woods. No adult within shouting distance. There's no limit to what they can do to me out here.

As the possibilities roll through my head, I turn and break into a run. I get maybe three steps before one of the boys has me by the arm. He drags me back to the small clearing.

Liquid drips down my face. Tears or sweat. I can't tell which, not even when it runs salty into my mouth. My body is shaking so hard, my molars chatter.

They surround me.

Regan leans in. "Are you scared?"

"She should be." Autumn is grinning.

I rip my gaze off her face and look around.

They have a rope and a long log turned on its end. The rope is draped over a tree limb overhead. My brain goes blank as I realize the end is fashioned into a noose. Numbness washes over me.

The boys have my arms. I struggle, but they are much stronger than me. The only thing fighting does is hurt my shoulders. But I can barely feel my arms pulling in their sockets. Adrenaline sends my pulse skittering. Light-headed, I pant for air.

"Smile for the video." Autumn steps in front of me. She holds a cell phone in front of her, steadying it with two hands, recording the event for posterity.

"I told you we'd be happy to help you commit suicide. The world will be a better place without ugly you in it." Regan tosses the noose over my head.

Someone ties my hands behind my back. I'm lifted by my arms onto the upturned log. The leather soles of my boots find little purchase on its unsteady top. The rope is tightened until there's no slack.

"Stand up, stupid." Regan slaps my ass.

I straighten my legs and stand. Then I kick at her, my sudden motion breaking the boys' holds. But I miss. My balance goes haywire. The log teeters. My vision goes red around the edges. My throat narrows until it feels like I'm breathing through a milk straw.

"Grab her."

My boot connects with a head.

"Ow."

I can't stop kicking my feet. It's like they aren't connected to my body. Panic whirls in my head. My lungs burn. The rope isn't tight enough to cut off my air, but I can hardly breathe. My bladder gives out. Warm wetness floods my legs, soaking my jeans with hot liquid.

"She pissed herself." Autumn laughs. "Oh my God. This is even better than we expected." I can see her in my peripheral vision. I watch, almost detached from my jerking and spasming body, as she circles around to film the incident from all angles.

My body goes into full flight mode. I have no control over it. I am twisting and kicking and pulling away from the boys' attempts to get ahold of my legs. The log wobbles more.

"Hold still, stupid," Regan yells, grabbing my legs. "Or you really will *die."*

My knee catches her under the chin. I hear her teeth clap together. She falls back with a loud grunt.

"Cut her down," one of the boys yells.

"You said it was only a joke," the other boy chimes in. "You said we wouldn't really hurt her."

"We won't. OK. OK. Get her down." Autumn giggles, but her voice rises with apprehension. "I have enough footage."

Regan moves toward me, a knife in her hand.

But my feet slip. The log tips over, something cracks, and I fall into darkness.

Chapter Thirty-Six

Grant's stomach turned as he watched Lindsay Hamilton's feet sway. The video shifted to the dirt.

"Oh, my God. She's dead!" someone shrieked.

"What should we do, Regan?" a voice asked. "We need to get out of here. We need an alibi."

"Shut up. No one will suspect anything other than a real suicide." She paused, as if considering her options. "We'll call Victor. He'll come get us and cover for us." This voice was calm. Other than a slight tremor, the only emotion seeping through her tone was irritation.

"He won't cover for us."

"Unless he wants to go to prison, he certainly will."

The phone screen went black.

"The coach is at the rink with Ellie and Julia." Grant's gaze swept across Nan and Hannah and Carson. "I have to go get them."

From under her oxygen mask, Nan waved, her eyes wide and frightened. Hannah shifted the baby to one side and wrapped an arm around Carson.

"I suppose I'd have to arrest you to get you to stay here." McNamara sighed.

"Yeah. That's about right." Grant turned toward the street, where he'd left Corey Swann's sedan running. The car was blocked in by emergency vehicles.

"Then you might as well come with me." McNamara jogged toward his car. Grant followed him into the unmarked police cruiser. Swirling lights reflected off something in the tree on Ellie's front lawn. Grant ran over. A small surveillance camera was mounted on a low branch.

"What is it?" McNamara yelled.

Grant sprinted back to the police car and jumped into the passenger seat. "A wireless video camera. I think I just figured out how Corey kept watch on Ellie's house."

The cop pulled away from the scene.

Grant dialed Mac again and told him about Victor. McNamara used his radio to call the dispatcher and call for backup from the county sheriff's office.

They headed for the rink, Grant praying that Mac found Ellie and Julia in time.

The cop turned on his vehicle lights but not the siren. "We don't know what happened. Victor has no reason to hurt Ellie or Julia."

But Grant did know what happened. Those girls accidentally killed Lindsay Hamilton, and their coach had covered up their crime.

Ellie tried to slide out from between Josh and the wall, but he blocked her exit with a knee. Julia would be out any minute, and Ellie didn't want her daughter anywhere near Josh.

She pushed against his chest, but he sneered down at her, clearly enjoying his physical superiority. Ellie glanced down. Her knee and his groin were perfectly aligned. She tensed, drawing her leg back to gain force. She had one shot at a solid blow to incapacitate him. If she missed, she'd just make him angrier.

The door to the rink opened.

"Hold it, Josh." Victor's voice boomed down the concrete corridor.

Thank God. Ellie nearly sagged with relief. Victor stalked across the cement. With a furious glare, Josh backed away.

The coach positioned himself between Josh and Ellie. "Go on home, Josh. You can't talk to the lady like that."

Josh scowled, but he backed off. "Remember what I said." He walked down the hall and disappeared through the heavy door into the arena. The metal door shut with a loud clack.

Julia came out of the locker room in jeans and a sweatshirt. She hefted the long strap on her duffel bag higher on her shoulder. Her ice skates dangled from her hand. She handed them to Ellie. "I broke a lace."

Ellie took the skates and turned to Victor. "Thank you."

"You're welcome." But his gray eyes were flat. Angry with Josh, no doubt.

The door to the rink opened again. Mac burst through. "Ellie!"

A police officer entered the hallway behind him.

Shock bloomed in Victor's eyes. He reached into his pocket and drew out a gun. He pointed it at Ellie. "Come with me."

Ellie had no time to think about why Victor was pointing a gun at her—or why the hell he even had a gun here at the rink with him. She needed to get her daughter away from the threat.

"Julia, run!" Ellie shouted. She threw her body into the coach, making sure she was between the gun and her daughter.

But Victor was an athlete. His body was solid muscle. He didn't budge as Ellie's weight slammed into him. He wrapped his hand in her ponytail and dragged her backward, using her body as a shield, but relief coursed through Ellie as Julia got away. Sobbing, the teen ran toward Mac.

"Drop it." The cop pointed his weapon at Victor.

Mac pushed Julia behind him. His eyes sought and held Ellie's gaze. Anger sharpened his features.

Victor pressed the gun to Ellie's temple. The muzzle dug into her skin. "I'll kill her if you follow me."

He pulled her down the hallway and through the emergency exit door that led to the employee parking area behind the arena. The door closed with a heavy click. "Hurry." He yanked her hair, throwing her off balance.

She stumbled, trying to keep up. "Why are you doing this?"

"I'm not going to prison for those little brats." Victor headed for a black SUV parked twenty feet away. "I made one mistake. One. I let that little whore Regan seduce me, and I've been paying for it ever since. Stupid bitch wanted to keep the phone and video. She wanted to be able to watch it over and over. But I took it. If she wanted me to cover for her, she had to do it my way."

"I don't understand."

But Victor ignored her and continued his manic, frustrated rant. "It's all Kate's fault, really. She heard me arguing with Regan and stole the phone. She said she was going to give it to the police. I reminded her of our past indiscretion. I told her I'd tell her husband she'd been in my bed if she turned the phone in. We fought for weeks. She was wavering, but I knew in the end she'd do the right thing, just like she broke off our affair to save her marriage."

What phone? Shock numbed Ellie's scalp. Victor slept with Regan *and* had an affair with Kate. Wait! That meant . . . "You had Kate and Lee killed. Why?"

Victor was lost in his own head. He shoved her toward his vehicle. "Get in."

Light flashed as police cars poured into the parking lot. They blocked both exits. Cops angled vehicles and got out, drawing their weapons and pointing them at Victor and Ellie. Victor put his back against his SUV and pulled Ellie to his chest. "Don't come any closer. I will kill her."

"Mac says Julia is safe, but Victor has Ellie. He took her out the back door." Grant ended the call.

The cop swung the car around the outside of the arena. Three patrol vehicles turned into the parking lot behind them.

"There!" Grant pointed across the parking lot. Victor dragged Ellie across the pavement by the hair. Fury and fear fused in Grant's chest.

McNamara reached for the radio, called dispatch, and requested a sniper and hostage negotiator from the county. He angled the car and opened his door. His weapon was in his hand.

"Sniper won't get here in time." Grant joined the cop behind the engine block. They crouched, watching Victor and Ellie over the hood of the car. "He's not waiting around to chat."

If Grant could just get to Ellie without Victor shooting her, he'd kill the skating coach with his bare hands. He wanted to do it with a ferocity that should have alarmed him.

The patrol officer next to them took an AR-15 out of his trunk. He hunkered down behind his engine block and aimed at Victor over the hood of the car.

"Is he a good shot?" Grant asked.

McNamara glanced sideways. "Yes. If we can get a little space between them, and it seems as if he's going to pull the trigger, Officer Tate can take him out."

"Let her go, Victor," the cop yelled. "You can't get away."

"We're getting in the car and driving away." He tugged Ellie toward the driver's side door. The gun muzzle was pressed to her forehead. Ellie's eyes were white-rimmed with fear as they met

Grant's. The thirty feet of pavement that separated them could've been a mile. The urge to kill surged through him. He wanted Victor's throat under his hands.

"You'll never get out of the parking lot," McNamara retorted.

Grant's heart thudded in his chest as he watched, unable to help. The rifleman shifted his position. Ellie's head was too close to Victor's. In Grant's mind, he pictured Ellie's face exploding into a red mist. The insurgent's ruined face. Lee. Images crowded Grant's brain, a nauseating slideshow of blood and death. How many people had he watched die? How many men had he seen maimed? Blown to pieces. Bleeding out onto the sand.

Victor moved sideways, his hand searching along the side of the vehicle for the door handle. His gaze shifted. The gun moved a few inches from Ellie's temple. She moved quickly, swinging the ice skates in her hands over her shoulder and hitting Victor in the face. The gun went off, the blast echoing in the damp air. Blood spurted. Ellie fell to the ground. Grant's heart stopped. He was on his feet and rounding the cop car as Officer Tate fired. Victor's body jerked and fell sideways.

Grant and the cops raced across the asphalt. Ellie! Blood soaked her pale blue sweater. Grant skidded to his knees beside her, his hands on her head, seeking the damage. He had to stop the bleeding. She couldn't be dead. She couldn't.

"Grant." She wriggled in his grip. "I'm all right."

His fingers delved through her hair. Her hand came up and covered his, stopping his frantic examination of her scalp. "I'm OK. It's Victor's blood, not mine."

Unable to comprehend her words, Grant turned. Victor was on his back. The cop's bullet had caught him in the shoulder. They'd handcuffed him. One officer was applying pressure to the shoulder wound while another tried to stop the bleeding from a huge gash on his head. Ellie's blow with the ice skate had split his forehead open. His skull gleamed white through the blood. Once Victor was restrained, an EMT took over.

Ellie's tug on his arm broke his stare. "Please, let's get away from him."

"Of course." He scooped her off the ground.

"I can walk," she said.

"I know, but I want to hold you right now." He wished he never had to let her go.

She leaned her head on his chest. "That works for me."

He carried her to the grass twenty feet away and set her down. A second EMT knelt beside her.

"I'm fine," she said.

Grant took her hand. He needed constant physical contact to convince himself she really was all right.

"Let me make sure." The EMT cleaned her face with water and gauze. "That's the best I can do. I don't even see a scratch. You're sure nothing hurts?"

"Positive. Thank you."

The EMT walked away.

McNamara approached. He stood in front of them, both hands propped on his hips. "You're not hurt?"

"No," Ellie said. "But I don't understand what happened."

Grant squeezed her hand. She might be physically uninjured, but the events of the last week would leave a psychological scar. "Lindsay Hamilton didn't commit suicide. Regan and Autumn killed her by accident in a prank that went horribly wrong. For some reason, Victor helped them cover up their crime."

"Oh, no." Ellie pressed a hand to the base of her throat. "Victor said Regan seduced him."

"So she threatened to tell unless he covered for her." Grant glanced at the cop. "What's the age for statutory rape in New York State?"

The cop sighed. "He's older than twenty-one, so sixteen. Third-degree rape is a class E felony. He could have gotten four years in prison."

The rear door of the building opened. Mac came out. Julia peered around his body. He scanned the situation before allowing her to run out from behind him. Sobbing, she ran to Ellie and threw her arms around her mother. Even as Ellie comforted her daughter, Grant kept hold of her hand. After the horrors he'd endured over the past week, he'd finally gotten lucky.

Chapter Thirty-Seven

Grant crept into the bedroom of the Residence Inn. Carson and Hannah shared a double bed. His sister was on her side, snoring, one arm draped over the boy. Grant tugged the covers over Carson's shoulders. Moving to the portable crib, he reached down and placed a hand on Faith's back. Well past her witching hours, she slept soundly. The rise and fall of her body under his palm tightened his chest. He could have lost all three of them in that fire.

With a deep breath, he left the room and softly closed the door. He walked past the second bedroom, where Julia and Nan slept, and into the kitchenette. The sight of Ellie making coffee stirred more emotions inside him, gratitude, affection—and desire. Always desire, it seemed.

Stepping up behind her, he wrapped his arms around her body. "I should have gotten another room. Then you could be sleeping, too."

"It's dawn, and I'm too keyed up to be still." She leaned back, resting her head against his chest. "The couch opens if you want to lie down."

Her hair was still wet from her shower, but Grant could still see it splattered with Victor's blood. He'd never get that sight out of his head.

"I'm fine." He rested his chin on her head. "McNamara will be here soon. He texted me a few minutes ago." The street had still been blocked by emergency vehicles. After they'd finished answering questions at the police station, the cops had dropped them all off at the motel. A uniform had brought Grant's phone from the rental sedan and some clothes from Ellie's house. The convenience store across the street from the motel had supplied them with enough staples to get through the night.

A soft knock sounded on the door. Reluctantly, he released her and let Detective McNamara in.

"Thanks." The cop accepted a cup of coffee and sat at the small oak table. Ellie and Grant joined him.

"Do I need to wake my lawyer?" Grant asked.

"Please don't." McNamara sighed. "I'm only here to give you an update, not arrest you."

Last night at the police station, Hannah had neatly cut off an obstruction of justice charge.

The cop downed half his mug. "Here's how it shakes out. Regan and Autumn were pissed that Victor was giving this new girl attention. They decided to torment her. But it backfired. Victor felt bad and started looking out for Lindsay. Regan and Autumn got madder and meaner. They planned that stunt in the woods knowing Lindsay was close to quitting the skating club. They thought they'd pushed her over the edge. As you saw," McNamara nodded at Grant, "it went as wrong as it could, and Lindsay died."

With the replay of the video playing in his head, Grant reached for Ellie's hand. She anchored him.

"Regan and Autumn went to Victor. Regan had plenty of leverage on him. In case there's any question about Lindsay killing herself, he gives the kids an alibi. He also took Regan's burner phone. She wanted to keep the video, but Victor knew that was a bad idea. He also knew that deleting the video wasn't enough. It could still be recovered, so he takes the cell as a condition of his cooperation, planning on destroying it after he finishes at the rink for the night. But it went missing. The only other person in the rink that night was Kate.

"Victor and Kate had had an affair about a year and a half ago, so their working relationship was already strained, but she started treating him very oddly. They argued. Kate overheard his conversation with the girls. She took the phone from his jacket in the office. Victor threatened to tell Lee about their affair if Kate didn't give the phone back. But in the end, he knew she'd do the right thing. So he hired Donnie to kill Kate and recover the phone."

Disbelief floored Grant. "So the target was Kate, not Lee."

"That's insane." Ellie turned her hand over and squeezed his fingers.

"How does an ice-skating coach find a contract killer?" Grant asked.

"Donnie played hockey under the scholarship program for troubled kids," McNamara answered. "And Victor was Donnie's first client. As far as we know, Donnie never killed anyone before he was incarcerated. Most of his early crimes were Internet-based. In fact, he knew how to find Lee and Kate by hacking into Kate's online calendar app. But after he was assaulted in prison, the Aryan Brotherhood helped him kill his attacker, who was a member of a rival gang. Donnie developed a taste for violence. His girlfriend's death was caused by autoerotic asphyxiation. They were both into BDSM. That last night Donnie was with her, he got carried away."

Grant intertwined his fingers with Ellie's.

"The fireman ran across some other things we've been looking for in the house." McNamara pulled an envelope out of his briefcase. "Your brother's will. There's nothing in it that pertains to the case."

"Where did you find it?" Grant touched the envelope.

"Your brother was using the old dumbwaiter as a hidey-hole. He'd boarded up the opening, but the shaft is brick, and the contents survived the fire," McNamara said. "The Hamilton file was in there as well."

"So what did Lee know?" Grant asked. "Though I guess it doesn't matter, since he wasn't the target."

"Something we all missed." McNamara tapped the edge of the table. "Lindsay had received harassing pictures on her phone, but her phone had been wiped by a virus. Lindsay had a friend back in California that she texted extensively with. His name is Jose. Lee called him and found out that Lindsay had forwarded one of the photos to him before her phone was wiped out. It was a particularly nasty picture of a doll made to look like Lindsay and hanging by a string. Here's where Regan and Autumn screwed up. The picture was geotagged."

"Geotagged?"

"The location where the picture was taken is embedded in the picture. This particular picture was taken at Regan's house," the cop said. "So Lee really did find something to tie one of those girls to Lindsay's harassment."

"And Corey Swann?" Ellie asked.

The cop nodded. "Not saying a word, but he was in possession of the burner phone he used to text his threats to you. The camera mounted in front of Ellie's house was wireless and motion sensitive. He used your own wireless network to send himself footage. Seriously, 'Julia1' isn't a very secure password. He could watch the house live or view the captured feed at his leisure. Possession of the burner phone is enough to charge him with extortion. I'm sure we're going to find all sorts of evidence in our investigation."

The cop got up. "Call me if you have any other questions. I'll let you two digest all this and get some rest."

Ellie locked the door behind McNamara. Still sitting at the table, Grant tapped on the envelope.

"Are you going to open that?" she asked.

"No. I should wait for Mac and Hannah." He stood and stretched. "That couch is looking pretty good. How about we stretch out and close our eyes until everyone wakes up?"

He tugged her to the sofa and pulled her down next to him. Wrapping an arm around her shoulders, he leaned back and closed his eyes. McNamara's information was almost too much to absorb. Kate had an affair? She'd been the target of a killer because she'd withheld information from the police. She'd sat on that phone for weeks, afraid of losing her husband when he found out about her infidelity.

Ellie put her hand in the center of his chest, right over his heart. "Are you all right?"

"I just need a little time to take it all in."

Faith cried from the bedroom.

"I'll get her." Ellie stood.

He stopped her with a hand on her arm. "No, I got it."

Maybe the last thing he needed was time to think.

Chapter Thirty-Eight

"Excuse me." Grant stopped at the nursing station on his way to his father's room. Only one day had passed since the fire. Ellie, Julia, and Nan had returned to their home. Hannah and the kids were still in the motel. Lee's house wasn't salvageable.

A nurse in pink scrubs looked up at him over her reading glasses. She blew short, gray-blond bangs out of her eyes. "Yes, sir?"

"I'm Colonel Barrett's son." Grant hesitated. "I was here last week, and the visit didn't go well. He got agitated when I said I was his son. He doesn't recognize me."

Her mouth twisted in a sad smile. "That happens a lot. He didn't know your brother most of the time either, if it makes you feel any better."

"Really?" Grant pulled back in surprise.

"Yes. Your brother just went with whatever the Colonel called him."

"I don't understand."

"If the Colonel thought your brother was Private First Class Andersen, your brother answered to that." She swept her glasses off her face. "Mr. Barrett just wanted the Colonel to have a calm day. He found reading to him worked better than trying to have a conversation. The Colonel gets agitated when he can't get the words out right. He knows he can't remember things, and it frustrates him. Dementia also makes emotions hard to control." Empathy shone from her eyes. "Try calling him Colonel instead of Dad, and use your first name. I know it hurts that he doesn't remember you, but it isn't his fault. Dad implies you have a relationship, and he'll instantly feel stressed trying to make the connection. Some days you might be surprised, and he might know you, but that's not going to happen often." She paused. "You can't fix this."

Grant accepted her statement as the truth, finally.

"His overall health has deteriorated significantly in the last year." She reached out and touched his forearm. "I'm sorry. Do you want me to have the doctor call you?"

"Yes, please." Grant gave her his cell numbers. "You should change the emergency contact numbers anyway." He gave her Mac's and Hannah's cell numbers as well.

She entered the information into the computer system.

Grant digested her advice on the way down the hall. His father was awake, staring blankly at a mute TV screen hanging from the opposite wall. Cloudy eyes blinked at Grant. "Who are you?"

"Hello, Colonel. I'm Grant." He took a deep breath and waited.

"What are you doing here?"

Grant spied the book on the tray. "I'm here to read to you."

His father nodded, still wary, but seemingly satisfied with the response.

Grant walked closer and eased into the seat next to the bed. He picked up the book and started reading aloud. His father settled back and closed his eyes. Calm. Lee had been right. It didn't matter if Dad knew their names. Maybe a lot of things didn't matter.

Two chapters later, after the Colonel fell into a deep sleep, Grant knew exactly what he needed to do. No, not just what he *needed* to do, what he *wanted* to do.

He drove back to the motel with a sense of purpose.

The silver Mercedes was parked in front of the unit. Inside, Kate's parents sat at the dining room table with Hannah. Carson sat on her lap. Faith bounced in a baby seat on the floor.

"Uncle Grant." Carson hurled his body across the room.

Grant scooped him off the floor. The boy was shaking. "What's wrong, buddy?"

"They said they're going to take us," he sniffed.

Grant scanned the faces at the table.

Stella Sheridan stood, brushing the wrinkles from her gray slacks. "We thought, since the children currently have no home, we could just take them with us now. It would save everyone time. The sooner they get settled in their new home, the better."

"I don't think so." Grant hugged Carson closer. Tiny fingers fisted in his sweatshirt.

Stella crossed her arms. "The more you let them get attached to you, the harder it will be when you leave, Major."

"That would be true, if I was leaving." Grant shifted Carson to his hip. The boy smelled like grass and sweat, as if Hannah had taken him outside to run around.

Hannah's head snapped up. "What are you saying?"

"I requested a hardship discharge." Grant's heart felt lighter than it had since he'd gotten the news of Lee's death. "Just got off the phone with my CO."

Stella's frown sagged, deepening the lines around her mouth. "Still, you're a bachelor. What do you know about raising two children?"

"I'll figure it out as I go along," Grant said.

"We'll see what our attorney has to say about that." Stella lifted her chin. Her eyes went bright and cold.

The baby fussed, and Hannah picked her up. "Actually, I reviewed the will this morning. Lee and Kate named Grant as the kids' guardian, so you really don't have any legal standing."

Stella turned and scooped her coat off the chair. Staring at the floor, she wiped a tear from her face with the pad of her thumb. "Will you still let us see them?"

"Of course," Grant said. "You're welcome to visit whenever you like."

Bill got up with a disappointed sigh and held his wife's coat. "If you change your mind, you know how to reach us at the inn."

They each gave Carson a quick hug. Stella kissed Faith on the head before leaving.

"You're not going to let them take us, are you?" Carson rested his head against Grant's shoulder.

"No way, buddy." Grant rubbed his back. "You're going to stay with me. Is that OK?"

Carson nodded and curled his arms around Grant's neck.

"Are you really staying?" Hannah asked.

"I am. I'm not sure whether it was Lee's death or too many tours of combat that changed me, but I have no desire to go back to the military."

"What are you going to do?"

"After I pay Freddie his twenty thousand?"

"I already requested the funds from my bank. I assume he wants cash."

"Good assumption." Grant smiled at his sister. "We can split the bill."

"Nah. I got this one." Hannah shook her head. "Do you have any plans after the payoff?"

"I don't know. I have a lot of options." And as soon as he got written verification from Lieutenant Colonel Tucker that his discharge was in process, he wanted to talk with Ellie about some of those options. Grant's grief was still tender, but for the first time since he'd received news of his brother's death, he didn't feel hopeless.

Lieutenant Colonel Tucker's words were still ringing in his head. *Grant, you've given your country thirteen years of your life. This operation is winding down over here. Go. Have a life. Enjoy a little of what you've been protecting all these years. You've served with honor, but you're needed elsewhere now.*

Two days later

Ellie shoved her goggles onto her forehead and lifted the kitchen cabinet she'd just ripped off the wall. She half dragged, half carried it out the front door, past the flower bed and tiny shoots of daffodils poking out of the soil, past the greening lawn, to the curb. The air still held a sharp bite, but spring was finally coming. There would still be some cold, nasty days, but new life was on its way.

"Can I help you with that?" Grant pulled into the driveway.

Her heart thumped as he got out of the minivan. She couldn't believe how much she'd missed him in the last two days. It would hurt when he had to leave for good. "How are the kids?"

"Quarters at Mac's place are tight." Grant walked closer. He picked up the cabinet and tossed it into the Dumpster effortlessly. "But Hannah goes back to work after the funeral on Wednesday, and Mac is leaving for South America in a couple of weeks. The three of us will fit there just fine for a while, and AnnaBelle loves the woods. She's brought me enough sticks to build a tree house."

"The funeral will be small?"

"Just family and closer friends. You'll come?" Grief shone raw in his eyes.

Her heart ached for him. He hadn't had a chance to mourn his loss. "Of course."

"What will happen to the house?" She nodded at the burned-out shell of Lee and Kate's home.

"It's not salvageable."

He hadn't shaved, and her fingers itched to touch the sexy rasp of his beard. She restrained herself. The moments they'd shared had been stolen. There would be no more of them. "That's a shame."

"It is, but this way the kids will get to start fresh. Once the lot is cleared, I'll put it up for sale. There are too many dark memories here for Carson."

She'd miss the children, too. Ellie swallowed the grief in her throat to get her next question out. "When do you leave?"

"I don't." Grant stopped in front of her. He leaned down and pressed a kiss to her lips.

Shock kept her from kissing him back. "What?"

"I'm not going back. I'm leaving the military."

"I don't understand. I thought the army was your life."

Grant brushed his fingers over her cheek. A tiny piece of wall-board floated to the ground. "Mac said something to me the other day that made me think. I've been living my father's dream, not mine. I don't want to be away. I want to watch Carson and Faith grow up. I want to be there for them the way Lee was always there for the family. I want to make sure my father is taken care of the best that I can." He took Ellie's hand. "I want to get to know you better. I'm not sure what is developing between us, but I don't want to walk away from it. I've left good things behind in the past. I'm done with that."

Ellie couldn't believe what she was hearing. He was staying. Her heart fluttered with possibility. "Do you have to give up your career? Can't you try to get stationed in New York? Or go to reserve status?"

"I could, but I don't want to. If I stay in the military, even as a reservist, there's always that chance I'll be called up." He took both her hands in his. "IEDs. Suicide bombers. Snipers. The risks are always there, even if I see far less combat now than I did when I was a lieutenant or a captain. Carson and Faith already lost both their parents. I can't control the future, but I can do my best to stay alive for them. They deserve stability."

"What will you do?"

"I don't know. I haven't made any decisions. I have some savings. I've been banking most of my pay for years. There's the life insurance. I really enjoyed demolishing your kitchen. I'd like to help you renovate it. Gutting rooms and building something new sounds appealing right now."

Joy swelled in Ellie's chest. Her eyes filled with tears. "I was all ready to say good-bye."

Grant wiped a drop from her cheek with a thumb. "So it's OK with you that I'm staying?"

His words finally sank in. He wasn't going to Afghanistan or Texas or anywhere else. Ellie flung her arms around his neck.

"I'll take that as a yes." He kissed her. "Tell me there's still something to demolish in there."

"No worries." She laughed. "It takes me a long time when I have to do it all myself. It'll be a lot easier with some muscle."

"That's me. The muscle." Grant flexed an impressive bicep. "The next two days will be hard. I don't know how Carson will do at the funeral. He says he wants to go, but who knows how he'll react? Kate's parents are upset with me for not letting them have the kids and for scaling this funeral back to the bare minimum."

"What can I do to help?"

"Put me to work?" He turned her and guided her back toward her front door. "I could use some sledgehammer therapy."

Remembering the last time they'd worked in her kitchen together, warmth rushed into Ellie's cheeks. She wrapped an arm around his waist and leaned into him, savoring the solid and real feel of his body against hers. "You can demolish my kitchen any day."

Chapter Thirty-Nine

Four months later

"What do you think?" Grant wrapped an arm around Ellie's shoulders. "You're the expert."

Side by side, they squinted through the setting sun at the old farmhouse. July heat waned as the sun dipped below the trees. It was traditionally designed, with two stories and a wraparound porch that called for a swing.

Behind them, the real estate agent had stepped away to stand patiently by his car and let them talk. Again.

"It has good bones." Ellie flipped through a home inspector's report. "Structurally sound. No lead paint, termites, or radon."

"Five bedrooms and a mother-in-law suite would give us plenty of room to spread out." Grant nudged Ellie's arm. This was their sixth trip to view the house.

"And the kitchen is enormous." Ellie could already see the kids doing homework while Nan cooked.

Carson and AnnaBelle raced past. Mud encased the dog's paws and the boy's sneakers.

"What do you think, Carson?" Grant yelled.

The boy slid to a stop in a patch of dandelions and threw a stick for the dog. "There's a creek out back! We almost caught a frog."

The creek was barely six inches deep. If Grant listened, he could hear the faint tumble of water over rocks.

"Carson's a yes." Ellie laughed. "You realize the entire house needs to be gutted? And we'll never be able to keep either one of them out of the mud."

"I do." With lots of babysitting help from Julia and Nan, after her ankle healed, Grant had done the majority of the kitchen renovation in Ellie's old house and loved every minute of hard labor. Working with his hands became his therapy, and in the same way that Faith's crawling had eliminated her nighttime screaming, daily physical exertion improved his sleep. Though he suspected sleeping with Ellie would work even better. Another reason he wanted to buy this house. Plus, Mac was due back from South America soon. The cabin was cramped enough with just Grant and the kids.

"Nan? Julia? You two want to vote?" Ellie called.

Julia carried Faith on her hip. The baby squirmed. Now crawling, she wanted no part of being carried. Grant held out his arms, and Julia handed her over. He pretended to drop her, and she squealed in delight.

"I love it." Nan crossed her arms and scanned the yard. "You could put a gazebo right there. It would make a lovely spot for a wedding."

"Nan," Ellie sighed.

Her grandmother feigned innocence. "Just saying."

Grant tucked Faith under his arm, football style, and kissed Ellie on the lips. "I like the idea."

They'd talked about getting married. They weren't rushing things, but buying the house together was a step in the right direction. They already spent as much time as possible together. For now, Grant would be satisfied having her in his bed at night.

"Did I tell you what happened at work today?" Ellie asked. "Roger fired Frank."

"Really?" Grant wasn't surprised. Frank was slime.

"He'd gotten himself into some debt in his quest for partnership and decided some fraudulent checks were his only way out." She shook her head. "If he could have held on another month or two, he would have gotten the partnership."

"Some people never get enough." But Grant had plenty. Faith complained and pumped her fists in the air. "OK. We have to make a decision. The boss is getting impatient." No doubt she wanted to stick every one of those dandelions in her mouth. "What's it going to be?"

"Please." Julia pressed her palms together.

"Let's do it," Nan encouraged.

"It's a big project," Ellie warned. She scanned their faces. "All right. We'll buy it."

Grant passed Faith back to Julia and wrapped his arms around Ellie. He planted a kiss on her mouth. "I love you."

"I love you too, Ellie." Carson hugged their thighs.

Ellie ruffled Carson's hair and kissed Grant back. "I love you both."

Grant leaned away and shouted to the real estate agent, "We'll take it. How soon can we close?"

The latest chapter in his life had started out in the worst possible way, but Grant had finally found the life he wanted. He wasn't going to waste one more second.

Acknowledgments

Publishing a book is a group project. As usual, thanks go to my fabulous agent, Jill Marsal, for her indispensable help with this book and her guidance with almost every aspect of my career. Additional thanks to developmental editor Shannon Godwin, and to the entire team at Montlake Publishing, especially editor JoVon Sotak.

Shout out to my morning sprint buddies Kendra Elliot, KM Fawcett, Rayna Vause, and Chris Redding. The daily cyberflogging helped me power through the tough spots on this book. Special thanks to Rayna for techie help, to KA Mitchell for plot ideas, and to Kendra, whose offhand comment about the sharpness of skate blades put the big finale scene in my head.

A final thank you goes to Michael Parnell for his help with military terms.

About the Author

© Marti Corn Photography, 2014

Melinda Leigh abandoned her career in banking to raise her kids and never looked back. She started writing as a hobby and became addicted to creating characters and stories. Since then, she has won numerous writing awards for her paranormal romance and romantic-suspense fiction.

Her debut novel, *She Can Run*, was a number one bestseller in Kindle Romantic Suspense, a 2011 Best Book Finalist (*The Romance Reviews*), and a nominee for the 2012 International Thriller Award for Best First Book. *Midnight Exposure* was a 2013 Daphne du Maurier Award finalist. When she isn't writing, Melinda is an avid martial artist: she holds a second-degree black belt in Kenpo karate and teaches women's self-defense. She lives in a messy house with her husband, two teenagers, a couple of dogs, and two rescue cats.

Made in the USA
Monee, IL
06 October 2020

44138694R00196